KT-222-353

THE BLANKET *of the* DARK

JOHN BUCHAN (1875-1940) was born in Perth on 26th August 1875, the eldest son of a minister in the Free Church of Scotland. He spent part of his childhood in Fife, before the family moved to Glasgow in the 1880s. In 1894 he went to Oxford University and began to write, publishing several books and many articles while still a student. After Oxford he had a successful career as a barrister and Member of Parliament, while continuing to write highly acclaimed novels such as *The Thirty-Nine Steps*, *Greenmantle* and *The Three Hostages*. He also wrote widely on other subjects, including biographies of Cromwell and Montrose, and an autobiography *Memory Hold-the-Door*. John Buchan was created Baron Tweedsmuir in 1935 and became Governor-General of Canada the same year. He died in Canada in 1940, soon after completing his last great novel, *Sick Heart River*.

DAVID DANIELL is Professor of English at the University of London. For twenty years he has been director of Shakespeare studies at University College London, and has published much on Shakespeare. He has a further special interest in William Tyndale, editing his Bible translations and completing a major biography. He has published, lectured and broadcast a great deal on John Buchan: his book, *The Interpreter's House*, (1975) remains the only full-length study of Buchan as a writer, and he has edited two collections of his short stories. His new literary biography of Buchan is nearing completion.

THE MARCHES OF WALES

THE COUNTRY OF THE BOOK

GOD SAVE THE SWAN

NORTH EAST SOUTH WEST

VALE OF EVESHAM

COTSWOLD

Scale Miliarium
5   10   15   20

THE BLANKET
of the DARK

JOHN BUCHAN

Introduced by David Daniell

"Where is Bohun? Where is Mowbray? Where is Mortimer?
Nay, which is more and most of all, where is Plantagenet?
They are intombed in the urns and sepulchres of mortality."
Sir Ranulphe Crewe, 1625.

EDINBURGH
B&W PUBLISHING
1994

First published 1931
This edition published 1994
by B&W Publishing, Edinburgh
Introduction © David Daniell 1994
ISBN 1 873631 41 3
All Rights Reserved.
No part of this publication may be reproduced
or transmitted in any form or by any means
without the prior permission of B&W Publishing.

The publisher acknowledges subsidy
from the Scottish Arts Council towards
the publication of this volume.

British Library Cataloguing in Publication Data:
A catalogue record for this book is available
from the British Library.

Cover design by *Rustling Jack & Associates*

Cover illustration:
Detail from *Robert Cheseman* (1533)
by Hans Holbein.
Photograph by kind permission of
Mauritshuis, The Hague.

Printed by Werner Söderström

CONTENTS

Introduction by David Daniell   vii

   I   THE PAINTED FLOOR   1

   II   IN WHICH PETER IS INTRODUCED TO FORTUNE   14

  III   IN WHICH PETER LURKS IN THE SHADOW   37

  IV   IN WHICH PETER GOES DEEPER INTO
         THE GREENWOOD   51

   V   THE PARLIAMENT OF BEGGARS   68

  VI   IN WHICH PETER EMERGES INTO THE LIGHT   83

 VII   HOW A WOULD-BE KING BECAME A FUGITIVE   109

VIII   HOW PETER SAW DEATH IN THE SWAN INN   122

  IX   THE ROAD TO DAMASCUS   136

   X   OF THE CONCLAVE AT LITTLE GREECE   150

  XI   HOW PETER CAME AGAIN TO AVELARD   164

 XII   OF THE VISION IN THE SNOW   179

XIII   THE UNLOOSING OF THE WATERS   195

XIV   HOW PETER STROVE WITH POWERS AND
         PRINCIPALITIES   205

XV   HOW THE SWAN OF BOHUN WENT DOWN   232

XVI   HOW PETER RETURNED TO THE
            GREENWOOD   247

      EPILOGUE   261

INTRODUCTION

David Daniell

John Buchan began work on *The Blanket of the Dark* in 1929, at the age of fifty four. He had by then lived for ten years at Elsfield Manor outside Oxford, on the eastern edge of the large Cotswold territory ('between Cherwell and Severn' as it is spoken of in Chapter II) which is the setting for this, his eighth historical novel.

The same year he wrote a preface to a book prepared by the Council for the Preservation of Rural England, a *Survey of the Thames Valley*, in which he drew memorable sketches of the valley in Roman, Mediaeval, Tudor and Civil War times. The Roman legacy, now hidden under the soil, and the lost life of the great Benedictine foundations— in particular, Oseney Abbey, 'full of the scent and sound of "chinking rivulets"'—stirred his mind. In that year, 1929, he gave the Rede lecture at Cambridge (the name gets into *The Blanket of the Dark*) on one of his growing interests, the 'ifs' of history: what would have happened if. . . . These matters came together in this novel, telling of the discovery by a humble country boy and clerk at Oseney, Peter Pentecost, that he is a Bohun and thus can challenge the Tudor line: he is to lead a rebellion against King Henry VIII.

Buchan was a prodigious explorer on foot, and an earlier novel, *Midwinter* (1923), carried a good deal of the fresh excitement he felt at discovering the ancient Cotswold landscape on his doorstep and knowing it in his bones. But in *The Blanket of the Dark*, published in July 1931, he moved into a world of deeper feeling. An experienced story-teller—this was his twentieth novel, and there had been dozens of short stories from him—John Buchan was now able to draw on strong springs of a darker energy. The wise secret leader in the underworld is named Solomon Darking. 'The dark' is in the title, and the phrase is often repeated: the land, and people, are in the gravest crisis under that 'blanket of the dark'—the phrase is probably original to Shakespeare in Macbeth, act one, scene five. Darkness is everywhere. The events of the novel move towards severe winter. Several unforgettable set-pieces are of fearful death or entombment. Peter Pentecost is orphaned, separate and alone, even in company.

Yet there is a pleasure in the writing which makes reading this novel a rare experience. Rudyard Kipling called it a *tour de force* and was 'rested and delighted' by it, and Rose Macaulay found it 'so enchanting and beautiful that I often read it for my pleasure'. Though Buchan gets his history right (the date can be worked out as 1536—King Henry is married to Jane Seymour, Cromwell is still in power); the calendar is known by saints' days; and there are a dozen or so words to be looked up ('lanner'; 'barry nebuly'; the indoor games that are played in Chapter VI, and so on), this is not really costume drama. Nor are the characters much developed from the inside, though most of them are strongly and feelingly sketched. This novel's strength is something new, for Buchan, and, it may be, in popular fiction.

One of John Buchan's strengths had always been an ability to convey landscape and weather. His first novel, a historical romance, *Sir Quixote of the Moors*, written in 1895 as he began to be an Oxford undergraduate, is a good example. *The Blanket of the Dark* takes this forward into an extraordinary ability to give the reader the feeling, amounting almost to memory, of having been there. Though the plot is strong and significantly shaped, the book can be said to be figures in a landscape, in weather. Almost all of it takes place in a wide, usually secret, and apparently sparsely peopled, countryside. London is barely mentioned: Oxford, after Chapter II, ignored. There are interiors in isolated houses, from the King's audience chamber at Woodstock down to the dreadful hovel where Dickon's parents die. Mostly the reader is out of doors, learning with Peter Pentecost to smell rain coming or know what curlews and whimbrels can tell him about weather. In this novel the ground and the sky go together. The phenomenal snow storm and the portentous thaw, for example, affect the action, but they also comment on human ambition. The snow leads to Peter's exhausted vision of the Queen of Heaven, beautiful and ennobling, but as insubstantial as the goddess uncovered in the Roman mosaic, or as Sabine Beauforest, who twice fails to seduce him. The great thaw brings the melting away of the forces of insurrection, and to Peter's rescue of the King, an action which leads to an underground scene both surreal and existential at once. There, with the King himself at literally the deepest level, Peter finds in himself no desire to reign. The novelistic symbolism of that chamber under Minster Lovell is remarkably handled. Supposed by witchcraft to contain treasure, it holds only a horrifying cadaver: to such has the line of the Bohuns come. But Buchan then repeats the scene (which chimes with the other death-scenes) to bury His Majesty and the Oseney clerk together. As they shiver and sleep and talk, and the crippled king grimaces with pain, the mechanism of the rebellion across the countryside above them fails. Peter recognises for the first time the reality of royal power—and does not want it. Buchan put a boy and a wounded man of near-absolute power in a cave, at the climactic failure of a rebellion, at least once before, in Prester John in 1910. The setting of that strong scene is also beside prodigious water. There, however, the romance of Africa was observed with the sharpest eye, and brightly lit. Here, in *The Blanket of the Dark*, is something dark.

Through the learned craft of his novel-writing, Buchan has hit upon a secret of timelessness. The period itself is felt on the nerves with convincing accuracy, from the imminent dissolution of the Benedictine houses, to what it meant to be an old-fashioned lord on the Welsh borders; from details of food or clothing to what it meant to lack both. Buchan has learned from both Sir Walter Scott and Robert Louis Stevenson. But his trick here is his own. His great 'if' is not what would have happened if the challenge to the Tudor line had in that moment succeeded so much as what might happen if the ignored and hidden life of England were stamped out.

Like Shakespeare, Buchan gives a sense of layer upon layer of life below the surface. Political power is manipulation, and even the alluring Sabine is part of the grand plan for using Peter Pentecost, as he soon discovers. Surrounding and disrupting the scheming of unwitting lords lies England's real power, people hidden in the furze and greenwoods, vanishing into the roadside at the sound of hooves, and given names—'John Naps of Greece'—used by Shakespeare. Like the Africans of *Prester John*, the Spoonbills and Naked Men of *Midwinter*, and the Free Fishers of the novel of that name, they can communicate secretly and at great speed. Like those, only here very much more, they are one with the landscape and weather, and may disappear into both, as Peter does at the end. Buchan elsewhere quotes Burke's comment 'A common soldier, a child, a girl at the door of an inn, have changed the face of fortune, and almost of Nature'. In this novel not only does he want to show history from the point of view of such casual and 'unimportant' figures: hidden in the furze, the Parliament of Beggars in Little Greece discusses issues as real as those the King does in his time under ground. But Buchan also suggests that though the names and events pass, something constant remains, which is the power of the land itself for constant renewal. It is curiously satisfying that Peter ends as he does. His spirits have swung from one state to another, as insight has come: like all Buchan heroes, he suffers with real pain and depression and long sickness.

How he sees himself mirrors how he sees his world, and that can change on the instant, as the glamour of Oseney Abbey does in Chapter III:

> He saw only the crumbling mortar and the warped beams . . . and heard Brother Lapidarius and Brother Johannes disputing shrilly about the Kidlington dues, over their fried onions at supper. . . .

His view of the King, seen first from a tree, then in a swollen river, then in the dark and cold of Minster Lovell, then in comfort and power, changes over and over again. So does, more significantly, the image of Sabine. Such volatility is significant, for both figures have a large element of illusion, established indeed in Peter's first sight of each of them, in private moments of transport, unaware of observation. The beggars, however, do not change. The password always works to bring Peter instant entrance to reality. At the level of the outcasts, the only change is brought by death, and that can be terrible indeed to a sinner like Rustling Jack or to the woman holding the secret of Bohun. These folk live under the blanket of the dark in a different and more elemental sense, but they can melt into the countryside like the snow and the rich monasteries, leaving, in their case, no disaster behind them.

Buchan's craft of giving the reader such a sense of infinite recession into elemental forces would not work were his prose itself not so layered. His King speaks convincingly, even when not on show (it may be recalled that Buchan was a friend of a very different monarch, King George V, and wrote a book about him, *The Kings Grace*: he was no stranger to the intimate conversation of a king). The thieves' cant is lightly touched, and good by the standard of Tudor writers. Sabine speaks like a refined but high-spirited young lady. Various courtiers suggest various levels of flattery and deceit. Tobias is a convincing Oseney canon. The landscape and weather appear with immediate force.

Inside that variety of line, however, lies Buchan's capacity to suggest other worlds. Bible phrases appear: there is work to be done to identify the translation used and already made so commonly known; in 1536, the New Testaments of William Tyndale, and his Pentateuch, had not been long in secret circulation. Peter, like his creator, is an Oxford classical scholar and Platonist, and thinks like one. John Buchan the military historian is not far away in the accounts of the plans for the uprisings. (Buchan wrote twice on Montrose and his exploits, and on Julius, and then Augustus, Caesar, on Scottish and American campaigns, and, supremely and at extraordinary length, on the whole of the War of 1914-18, as it happened.) The English Reformation seen from Oxford, mentioning the new Biblical scholarship of Erasmus and Colet and the dismissal of Peter Lombard's older *Sentences* as the sole way into Scripture, allows another challenge to 'the dark'; the new Gospelling force is allowed much multivalency.

The working out of the plot is leisurely, even slow. This is an advantage. Just as there is no consummated love-romance, only momentary invitation, so there is no climactic battle, only a brief skirmish at a bridge. Buchan is not working towards a swashbuckling, nail-biting climax. The campaign of the uprising is destroyed by a well-meaning but greatly mistaken woman and a lunatic self-styled prophet. All the surface action at the end melts away, as nameless figures emerge at the roadside and absorb the hero back into nonentity.

Yet, like all Buchan's fiction, it is immensely readable and satisfying. It haunts the memory as something experienced. Buchan is skilful at making a central figure, Peter Pentecost, who can carry what happens to him to the reader. Sir Walter Scott in *Waverley* (1814) first gave us a hero who is taken into great historical events and then records rather that moves them. Peter Pentecost's political potential is greater than Waverley's. His responses are both simpler and across a greater range. Like Scott in his fiction,

John Buchan is interested in a 'great refusal', but Buchan's humbler, younger, hero is perhaps better established as restless and sensitive to atmosphere and mood.

The novel is about what is firm and what changes under the seasons, about common humanity under the illusory schemes of ambitious grandees. Something politically momentous set up for a lowly youth did not in the end happen. The king would not be removed by a reluctant Absalom and some plotting Achitophels. The monasteries, suggests Buchan, were ready to fall, in the cycle of national life. The events did not matter very much after all to an aristocratic young woman ready to fall in love if bidden, to a countryman's life in the round of the seasons, to the turf covering the Roman mosaic among the trees at Woodeaton.

TO
DOROTHY GASKELL

THE BLANKET
of the DARK

CHAPTER I

THE PAINTED FLOOR

Peter Pentecost, from his eyrie among the hazels, looked down on the King's highway as it dipped from Stowood through the narrow pass to the Wood Eaton meadows. It was a King's highway beyond question, for it was the main road from London to Worcester and the west for those who did not wish to make Oxford a halting-place; but it was a mere ribbon of rutted turf, with on each side the statutory bowshot of cleared ground between it and the forest fringes. And, as he looked, he saw the seventh magpie.

Peter was country-bred and had country lore in the back of his mind. Also, being a scholar, he respected auspices. So, having no hat to doff, he pulled his forelock. Seven magpies in one day must portend something great.

He had set off that summer morning on an errand for the cellarer of Oseney Abbey to the steward of the King's manor of Beckley, some matter touching supplies for the Abbey kitchen. The sun had risen through lamb's-wool mists, the river was a fleckless sheet of silver, and Peter had consecrated the day to holiday. He had done his errand long before noon, and had spent an hour watching the blue lagoons on Otmoor (there was much water out, for July had begun with rains), with the white geese like foam on the edges. The chantry priest at Horton had given him food—a crust only and a drink of ale, for the priest was bitter poor—and in the afternoon he had wandered in the Stowood glades, where the priory of Studley had right of pannage and the good sisters' droves of swine rooted for earth-nuts. Peter was young, and holiday and high summertide could still intoxicate. He had lain on the spicy turf of the open spaces, his nose deep in thyme and rock-rose; he had made verses in the shadow of the great oaks which had been trees when Domesday Book was written; he had told his dreams aloud to himself at the well under the aspens where the Noke fletchers cut their arrows. The hours had slipped by unnoted, and the twilight was beginning when he reached his favourite haunt, a secret armchair of rock and grass above the highway. He had seen four magpies, so something was on the way.

The first things he saw in the amethyst evening were two more of the pied birds, flapping down the hollow towards Wood Eaton. After them came various figures, for at that hour the road seemed to have woken into life. Travellers appeared on it like an evening hatch of gnats.

First came a couple of friars—Franciscans by their grey habits—who had been exploiting the faithful in the Seven Towns of Otmoor. Their wallets swung emptily, for the moor-men had a poor repute among the religious. They would sleep the night, no doubt, in the Islip tithe-barn. After them appeared one of the Stowood hogwards, with the great cudgel of holly which was the badge of his trade. Peter knew what he was after. In the dusk he would get a rabbit or two for his supper on the edge of the Wood Eaton warren, for the hogwards were noted poachers.

From his view-point he could see half a mile down the road, from the foot of the hill to where it turned a corner and was lost in the oakwoods of the flats. It was like the stage of a Christmas mumming play, and Peter settled himself comfort-ably in his lair, and waited with zest for the entry of the next actors. This time it was a great wool-convoy, coming towards him from the Cherwell. He watched the laden horses strain up the slope, eleven of them, each like a monstrous slug buried in its wool-pack. There were five attendants, four on foot and one riding a slim shaggy grey pony. They might be London bound, or more likely for Newbury, where Jack Winchcombe had his great weaving mill and the workmen wrought all day in sheds high and dim as a minster—so many workmen that their master twenty years back had led his own battalion of spinners, carders and tuckers to Flodden Field. Peter viewed the convoy with no friendly eye. The wool barons were devouring the countryside, and ousting the peasants. He had

2

seen with his own eyes hamlets obliterated by the rising tide of pasture. Up in Cotswold the Grevels and Celys and Midwinters might spend their wealth in setting up proud churches, but God would not be bribed. Let them remember Naboth's vineyard, those oppressors of the poor. Had not the good Sir Thomas More cried out that in England the sheep were eating up the men?

The next arrival was a troop of gipsies, a small furtive troop, three donkeys laden with gear, five men on foot, and two women, each with an infant at breast. In his childhood Peter remembered how these vagabonds had worn gaudy clothes and played openly on fantastic instruments of music; they were shameless priggers and rufflers, but they were welcomed everywhere except by the dwellers in lonely places, for they brought mirth and magic to the countryside. Now they were under the frown of the law, and at the will of any justice could be banished forth of England, for it was believed that among them they harboured Scots and Spaniards, and plotted against the King's peace. This troop were clad like common peasants, and drab and dingy at that, but there was no mistaking their lightfoot gait, and even at that distance Peter could mark their hazel-nut skins and bird-like beaks. They came on the stage stealthily, first reconnoitring the patch of open road, and, when they neared the other corner, sending out a scout to prospect ahead. Peter saw the scout turn his head and give a signal, and in a second the Egyptians, donkeys and all, had taken cover like weasels, and were deep in the wayside scrub.

Presently the cause was apparent. Down the hill trotted an imposing cavalcade, four gentlemen, no less than six servants armed with curtal-axes, and two led baggage-horses. One of the gentlemen was old, and his white hair mingled with the ermine collar of his purple cloak. The others rode cloakless in the warm evening. Two had the look of lawyers, being all in black and white, except for their tawny horsemen's boots, but the fourth was a gay gallant, with a wine-red doublet, a laced shirt, sleeves monstrously puffed and slashed, and on his head a velvet bonnet with a drooping blue feather. Two of the

3

servants carried at their saddle-bows the flat leather boxes which scriveners used. Peter guessed their errand. They were some of the commissioners whom the King was sending far and wide throughout the land to examine into the condition of the religious houses. Their destination might be the Augustinians at Bicester or the Benedictines at Eynsham—the latter he thought, for there were better roads to Bicester from London than this, and these men were doubtless from the capital. They were in a hurry, and passed out of sight at a sharp trot, the led horses shying at the smell of the gipsy donkeys hidden in the covert. In two hours' time they would be supping off Thames trout—for it was a Friday—in the Eynsham fratry.

When the last of the company had jolted round the far corner the stage was empty for a while. The amethyst was going out of the air, and giving place to that lemon afterglow which in a fine summer never leaves the sky till it is ousted by the splendours of dawn. The ribbon of road was beginning to glimmer white, and the high wooded sides of the glen to lose their detail to the eye and become massed shadows. But the play was not yet ended, for up the road towards him came a solitary rider.

Down a gap from the west fell a shaft of lingering sunlight which illumined the traveller. Peter saw a tall man mounted on a weedy roan, which seemed to have come far, for it stumbled at the lift of the hill. His head was covered with an old plumeless bonnet, he had no cloak, his doublet was plain grey, his trunks seemed to be of leather, and between them and his boots were hose of a dingy red. He wore a narrow belt fastened in front with a jewel, and from that belt hung a silver dagger-sheath, while at his side dangled a long sword. But it did not need the weapons to proclaim that this was no servant. The man's whole poise spoke of confidence and pride. His shaven face was weathered like a tinker's, his eyes searched the covert as if looking for opposition, his mouth was puckered to a whistle, and now and then he flung back his head and sniffed the evening odours.

Peter watched and admired with a pain at his heart. Here

4

was one who rode the broad ways of the world and feared nothing; a masterful man who would have his way with life; one who had seen with his own eyes that wonderful earth of which Peter had only read; a fierce soul who would be a deadly enemy, but who might also be a delectable comrade, for there was ease and jollity in his air. Peter sighed at this glimpse of the unattainable.

And then he saw the seventh magpie.

The heats of the day, the constant feasting of the eyes upon blue horizons, had had the effect of wine upon Peter's brain, and this drunkenness had been increased by the spectacle of the masterful traveller. The scholar, whose days were spent among books, felt himself within hail of the pomp of life. He had almost forgotten the heavy thoughts which had burdened him so many days. The hour was growing late, and he was miles from his bed in the Castle precincts, but he had no intention of going home yet awhile. For he was near to a place which was his own discovery, his special sanctuary, and he was minded to visit it before he slept.

And then came the seventh magpie, a chequered zigzag in that dim world. The bird was an invitation to adventure. Peter rose from his eyrie, shook the moss and twigs from his clothes, and scrambled down the slope to the highway. He was clad in a tunic and long summer hose of thin woollen, and his gown, which was the badge of studentship, he carried loose on his arm.

He padded in the sweet-smelling dust of the road for a little way, and then turned to his left to climb the farther side of the hollow. He had forgotten about the Egyptians in the covert. They were still there, and had settled down for the night, for suddenly he saw in a cleft beside him the glow of a little fire on which a pot was bubbling. He was too late to avoid it, his foot slipped, he slid into the cleft, and found a hand at his throat. The hand was relaxed, and the grip changed to his shoulder, while a sma!! covered lantern was flashed in his face.

Shaken and startled, he saw one of the gipsies standing above him, a man with a thin wolfish face and burning eyes.

5

Peter's youth and the sight of the gown on his arm apparently convinced the man that here was no danger. He grunted, and picked up what seemed to be a book which had fallen to the ground.

"You are far from home, clerk," the voice said. "What do you at this hour prowling in Stowood? You are not of the Children of the Moon."

The Egyptians bore an ill name for secret robbery and murder, and Peter's heart had pounded on his side when he felt the clutch at his throat. But this man whom he could only see dimly, a grey ghost flecked with firelight, seemed no marauder. His voice was not the Egyptian whine, and his words were not the Egyptian jargon. In spite of his rags he had a certain air of breeding and authority. The other gipsies were busy with their cooking, and the women were suckling their babes, but this man seemed to be engaged with papers and he had the lantern to light him. Peter realised that the gaze fixed on him was devouring and searching, but not hostile.

"A clerk," said the man. "One of the blind eyes and dumb mouths that have Oxford for their stepmother. I have forgot what Oxford is like. Do you till plough the barren fields of the Trivium and the Quadrivium? Do you yet mumble the leavings of Aristotle? Are your major gods Priscian and Cato and Alexander of Villa Dei? Is the hand that leads you up Parnassus that of old John Leland? *Ut rosa flos florum sic Leland grammaticorum*—it is so long since I heard it I have lost the jingle. Or perhaps you're for the new masters, for I hear that today in Oxford the Trojans are few and the Grecians many?"

"Troy has fallen," said Peter, amazed to hear such speech from a gipsy's tongue.

"And her folk are scattered. They have put Duns and Aquinas in Bocardo. They tell me that the great vellum leaves of the Sentences flap in the wind about the college courts, and that country louts gather them to make flappers to keep the deer within the pales."

"What know you of Oxford and her ways?" the stupefied Peter demanded.

"This much," said the man fiercely, "that her ways are not the paths of truth, and that her fruits, old or new, are but husks to be flung to swine. I tell you, clerk, there is only one new learning, and that is the ancientest. It is here," and he held up his book, "and it is old and yet ever young. For it is the wisdom not of man but of God."

"Show it me," said Peter, but the man put it behind his back.

"Not yet, clerk. England is not yet ripe for it, but the hour draws near."

"Who are you that speak in riddles?"

The man laughed. "Under the blanket of the dark all men are alike and all are nameless. Let me view your countenance that I may know it when I meet it again."

He held up the lantern, and the light also revealed his own face. It was that of a man in early middle life, very lean and haggard, with a long nose broken in the middle, and eyes that seemed to burn in a fever. But the brow was broad and fine, and the mouth was gentle.

"An honest face," he said. "You were no churl's get, young clerk. Now get you hence to your prayers, and leave me to mine."

During this short dialogue the other gipsies had taken no notice of Peter. He felt the thrust of the man's hand, and in a moment he was out of the hollow and the firelight and back in the midnight dusk of the woods.

He ran now, for his head was in a whirl. The magpie was a wise bird, for that night he was indeed seeing portents. He had observed one kind of authority mounted and jingling on the highway, and now he had witnessed another kenneling with the gipsies. The world was strange and very wide. It was time for him to find his sanctuary, where he could adjust these new experiences and think his own thoughts.

The place was his very own, for he had unearthed it after it had been lost for centuries. In a charter in Oseney he had read how the King of Wessex had given to the Bishop of Winchester a piece of land by Cherwell side, which ran from a certain brook "along the green valley by the two little hills and past the Painted Floor," till it reached a certain thorn patch and a certain spring. The words had fired his fancy. Once the Romans had strode over these hills, the ruins of their massive causewayed highroads ran through marsh and forest, they had set their houses with vines and reaped their harvests where now only wild beasts rustled. To one like Peter, most of whose waking thoughts dwelt on Greece and Italy, the notion of such predecessors among his familiar fields seemed to link his wildest dreams to the solid world of fact. That Painted Floor must be found, for it could only be a fragment of Roman work; there was such a floor in the midget church of Widford on Windrush, a mile or two from the home of his childhood. He knew the green valley and the little hills of the charter; they lay east from Wood Eaton, between the demesne of that manor and the ridge of Stowood. The Romans had been there beyond doubt, for not long since a ditcher in that very place had turned up a pot of gold coins with Emperors' heads on them—some were now at Oseney among the Abbey's treasures.

So Peter had spent the dry March days nosing like a fox in the shallow glade which dropped from the high slopes to the Wood Eaton meads. The Painted Floor was not among the run-rigs of beans and oats and barley, nor in the trodden grass of the common pastureland; it must be nearer the hills, among the rough meadows where the brook had its source, or in the patches of oaken scrub which were the advance pickets of the forest. He found it—found it one April day in a coppice of ash and thorn, guided to it by a sudden flatness in ground which nature had clearly made hummocky. It was a floor indeed, carpeted with fine turf and painted only with primroses and windflowers. Peter's nails clawed up the turf and came on tiles, and in an hour he had cleared a yard or two and revealed what even in the dusk of the trees showed brighter colours than earth and stone.

Peter borrowed an axe and a mattock from an Elsfield forester, and, with the tools hidden in his gown, journeyed to the spinney every hour of holiday. In places seeds had found lodgment among the tiles, and had grown to trees, the roots of which split the mosaic. In one part a badger had made his earth and powdered a yard or two into dust. But when Peter had cut down encroaching saplings and had stripped off the layers of turf, there lay revealed a hundred square yards of tessellated pavement. Perhaps since Roman days the place had been used as a sheepfold, for there were signs of a later circumscribing wall, but once beyond doubt it had been the floor of a Roman's dwelling. Peter fetched water from the spring among the bracken, and washed off the dirt of centuries. Bit by bit he unveiled a picture. In the centre, in the midst of an intricate design of grape leaves, sat a figure of some goddess—Ceres perhaps or Proserpina. At each corner were great plaques which presently revealed themselves as the Four Seasons—Spring with Pan's pipes, Summer with a lap of flowers, Autumn lifting aloft a cornucopia, and Winter a fur-clad hunter holding a rabbit. And all between was a delicate maze of convolutions so that the central goddess seemed to float upon clouds. It was simple rustic work, for the greys were the limestone rock, and the yellows and browns a neighbouring sandstone, and the blue slate or glass, and the reds coarse earthenware; but the design had a beauty which to Peter was a revelation. He felt it akin to the grave music with which sundry Roman poets had ravished his soul.

The place was forest land, he knew, and therefore belonged to the King, though it was very near the Wood Eaton clearing and Sir Ralph Bonamy's ground. But it was his own by the oldest and strongest tenure, effective occupation. No one but himself knew of this marvel. He concealed his movements going and coming as if his purpose had been crime. The Wood Eaton churls were not likely to drag their heavy feet to a place where there were neither tasks to be wrought at nor coneys to be snared, and the foresters would neglect a trivial spinney which offered no harbourage to deer. Only Peter had business there. He would lie in the covert in a hot noon, watching the sun make a chequer of green and gold, till he fell asleep, and awoke, startled, to see what for a moment he thought was the shimmer of a woman's gown and to hear the call of an elfin flageolet. But it was only fancy. The Floor was dim with dusk,

9

and the wood was silent but for homing birds.

Tonight he crossed the brackeny meadow and came to the coppice with a sudden wild expectation. The seventh magpie! There had been marvels many that day, but a seventh magpie must portend still more. The spring bubbled noisily among its greenery; he had never heard it so loud. He lay prone and drank a great draught of the icy water, so cold that it sent little pains running behind his eyes. Then he entered the coppice.

It had been his custom to treat it as a sacred place and to enter with reverent feet and head uncovered. Nor did he enter it direct. He would fetch a circuit and come in from the top to his own perch above the Floor, like a seat in one of the tiers of an amphitheatre looking down on the arena. So he climbed the slope to where half a dozen great oaks hung like sentinels above the coppice, and found his way downhill through the scrub of hazels and briers. The moon was already well up in the heavens, and the turf was white as with frost, but inside the wood it was dark till he reached the edge of the Floor. There, since the taller trees fell back from it, light was permitted to enter from the sky.

Peter parted the bushes, found a seat of moss between two boulders, and looked down from the height of perhaps twenty feet upon the moon-silvered stage.

The Floor had a sheen on it, so that the colours were lost in a glimmer of silver. The colours, but not the design. The enthroned Ceres in the heart of it seemed like a reflection of a great statue in a deep clear pool. Bits of the corner plaques could be seen too—the swung rabbit in Winter's hand, half of Autumn's cornucopia, more than half of Summer's lapful of flowers.

The place was very quiet. It had the scent of all woodland places in high summer—mosses, lush foliage, moist earth which has had its odours drawn out by a strong sun. There was also a faint sweetness of cut hay from the distant Wood Eaton fields, and something aromatic and dry, which was the savour of stone and tile and ancient crumbling mortar. There seemed to be no life in the thicket, though a few minutes before the world had rustled with the small noises of insect

10

and bird. At that hour there should have been sleeping doves in the boughs, and hunting owls, and rasping nightjars looking for ewes and she-goats to milk. Or the furtive twist of a stoat, or the pad of a homing badger. But there were none of these things, no sound even of a wandering vapour; only the moonlight, the scents, and the expectant silence.

But surely there was movement, though it was soundless. Peter, entranced with the magic of the place and hour, saw in the steady radiance of the moon shadows slip across the Floor. It almost seemed as if Ceres had lifted her hands from their eternal entwinement. The flowers had shifted in Summer's lap, Spring had fingered her pipe.

Peter crossed himself with a shaking finger and began a prayer. Suddenly company had come out of the night. He realised that he was not alone.

Something was moving on the Painted Floor, something which so blended with the moonlight that its presence could be known only when it obscured the pattern. From where he sat, Peter looked beyond the little amphitheatre to a gap in the encircling coppice, a gap through which could be seen the descending glade and a segment of far hills. The moonlight on the Floor, being framed in trees, was an intenser glow than the paler landscape beyond. Suddenly against this pallor a figure was silhouetted—the figure of a girl.

Peter tried to pray. He tried to say a prayer to the Mother of God which was his favourite invocation in emergencies. It began, *Imperatrix supernorum, Superatrix ifernorum*, but he did not get as far as *superatrix*. For he found that he had not the need to pray. His fear had been only momentary. His heart was beating fast, but not with terror. The sight before him was less an invocation to prayer than an answer to it. Into his own secret sanctuary had come the appropriate goddess.

It was a mortal who danced below him—of that he had instant and complete assurance. The misty back world of Peter's mind, for all his schooling, held a motley of queer folk, nymphs, fays, witch-wives, who had their being on the edge of credence. But this was not of that kind. It was a mortal with blood in her veins. She had flung up her arms, when she

11

showed in the gap, in a very rapture of youth. He had seen her head clear—eyes over which the eyelids drooped, a smiling mouth, a delicate face on a slim neck. Her garments were now drawn tight round her, and now floated wide like the robes of a fleeing nymph on a Greek gem. They seemed to be white, but all of her was white in the moon. Her hair was silvered and frosted, but it might be gold or ebony by day. Slim and blanched, she flitted and spun like a leaf or a blown petal, but every line of her, every movement, spoke of youth and a rich, throbbing, exultant life.

The pattern of her dance seemed to be determined by the pictures under her feet. Sometimes she tripped down the convolutions and whorls till the eyes dazzled. At the corner plaques she fitted her movements to their design—wild in Spring, languorous in Summer, in Autumn a bacchanal, in Winter a tempest. Before they throned Ceres she became a hierophant, and her dance a ritual. Once she sank to the ground, and it seemed that her lips rested on the goddess's face.

Never before had Peter stared at a woman and drunk in the glory of her youth and grace. He had seen very few, and had usually passed them with averted eyes. They were the devil's temptation to the devout, and a notorious disturbance to the studious. But this woman had come into his sanctuary and made free with it as of right. He could not deny that right, and, since the sanctuary was his, the two were irrevocably linked together. They were worshippers at the same secret shrine. He looked at her more calmly now. He saw the pride and nimbleness of motion, the marvellous grace of body, the curves of the cheek as the head was tilted backwards. It was a face stamped indelibly on his memory, though under the drooped eyelids he could not see the eyes.

Afterwards, when he reconstructed the scene, Peter held that he fell into a kind of waking dream, from which he awoke with a start to realise that the dance was ended and the Floor empty. The moon had shifted its position in the sky, and half the Floor was in shadow. There was still no fear in his mind and no regret. The nymph had gone, but she would return.

12

She must return, as he must, to this place which had laid its spell upon both. He felt very drowsy, so he found a bigger patch of moss, made a pillow of his gown, and went to sleep in that warm green dusk which is made for dreams.

But he was too young and too healthily tired to dream. He woke, as was his habit, at sunrise, sniffed the morning, and turned round to sleep for another hour. Then he rose, when the trees were still casting long shadows on the meadow and the Painted Floor was dim with dew, and took the road towards Wood Eaton and its little river. He would not go back to Oxford yet awhile, he decided, but would seek his breakfast at Oseney, which was without the gates. He came to the Cherwell at a narrow place overhung with willows; there he stripped, bundled his clothes inside his gown, and tossed the whole to the farther bank. Then he dived deep into the green waters, and thereafter dried himself by cantering like a colt among the flags and meadowsweet. The bath had sharpened both his energy and his hunger, so that he passed at a trot the Wood Eaton granges and crossed the Campsfield moor, where the shepherds and cowherds were marshalling their charges for the day. Presently he was looking into a valley filled with trees and towers, with, on the right, below a woody hill, the spire of a great church set among glistening streams.

CHAPTER II

IN WHICH PETER IS INTRODUCED TO FORTUNE

Peter did not slacken pace till he descended from the uplands and crossed the highway which joined Oxford and Woodstock, a frequented road, for by it the staplers sent their pack-trains to load their wool in the river barges. There was a great green plain on his right hand, grazed upon by a multitude of geese, and already country folk with baskets of market stuff were on their way to the north gate. He turned down a lane by Gloucester Hall, where he looked over a close of pippins to the Rewley fishponds, and passed the little stone quays at Hythe bridge, where men were unloading sweet-smelling packages from a lumpish green boat. In the huts of Fisher Row strange folk, dingy as waterweeds, were getting ready their cobles and fishing-gear against the next fast-day. Peter crossed the main stream at Bookbinders bridge, and came on a broad paved path which ran to what seemed a second city. Walls, towers, pinnacles rose in a dizzier medley than those of Oxford, which he had seen five minutes before beyond the north gate. In especial one tall campanile soared as the stem of a pine soars from a wilderness of bracken, white and gleaming among the soberer tints of roof and buttress.

Suddenly from it there fell a gush of lovely sound, the morning canticle of the noblest peal of bells in the land. Peter stopped to listen, motionless with delight. In the diamond air of dawn the bells seemed to speak with the tongues of angels, praising God for His world, with the same notes that birds used in the thickets or the winds on the waters. As the peal slowed and ebbed to its close, one bell lingered, more deep and full than the rest, as if its rapture would not be stayed. Peter knew it for Thomas of Oseney, which had no equal in England—as great as Edward of Westminster or Dunstan of Canterbury.

The bells told him the hour. Prime was long past, and now the Chapter was over. There would be no food for four mortal hours unless he could make favour in the kitchen. He hurried through Little Gate and past the almshouses to Great Gate, with its cluster of morning beggars. It was dark under the portals, so dark that the janitor did not at first recognise him, and caught him roughly by the cloak till his face was revealed. Beyond was the wide expanse of Great Court, one half of it in shadow, one half a pool of light. On three sides, north, east and west, lay the cloisters, roofed with Shotover oak, and faced with the carved work of old Elias of Burford. Peter knew every inch of them, for, far more than his cell in St George's College in the Castle, the Oseney cloisters were his home. There on the west side was his schoolroom, where he instructed the novices; there on the north was the scriptorium, where lodged the Abbey's somewhat antiquated library; there on the south, beside the kitchen, was the Abbey's summer parlour, and the slype which led to the graveyard, the gardens and the river. This last was Peter's favourite corner, for in the morning hours it had the bustle of a market-place. On its stone seats sat those who waited on business with the Abbot, and foreign merchants using Oseney as a consulate, and brethren who could snatch a half-hour of leisure. It was a window from which the Abbey looked out into the world.

This morning there was a great peace in all the cloisters. Two old canons were taking the sun, and a half-dozen children stood in a ring repeating what might have been equally a game or a lesson. To Peter's chagrin there was no comfort in the kitchen. The morning meal in the fratry was still hours distant, and the under-kitchener, who was his friend, had gone to the Abbot's lodging, busied about an early collation for the Abbot's guests. To forget his hunger Peter turned into Little Court, whence by way of the infirmary he could reach the back parts of the Abbey.

He found himself presently in a strange place, a place of lanes and closes, cot-houses and barns, from which came the clang of hammers and the buzzing of wheels. It was a burgh of itself, that part of the Abbey precincts which was known as Oseney-town, where dwelt the artificers. Here during the centuries there had grown up a multitude of crafts—tanners who prepared the Cotswold skins; bookbinders who clad in pigskin and vellum the archives of abbey and college; illuminators who decked the written word with gold and vermilion; wax-chandlers who made the lights for the holy places; shoemakers and workers in all kinds of leather and fine metals. Here were the millers who ground the corn from the Abbey farms, and carpenters and smiths and fullers and weavers of wickerwork. From every doorway came the sound of busy folk, and as an undertone the rhythmic beat of mill-wheels and the babble of little chinking rivulets. From this hive of industry there rose, too, a dozen smells, pleasant smells which told of wholesome human life—the bitter reek of the tan-pits, the freshness of new leather, the comfortable odour of ground corn which tormented Peter's emptiness. And everywhere the clean scent of running water.

But Peter did not linger amid the busyness of Oseney-town. A gate between two dovecotes, where homing pigeons made a noisy cloud, led him across a bridge to the Abbey gardens. First came orchards of apples, pears and plums, quinces and apricots, and a close of plainer fruits, filberts, walnuts, almonds, and the cornels from which sweet drinks were made. There were fig-trees on the west walls, and a vineyard whose small grapes were used for a rough wine, but mostly for sweet pasties. Beyond lay the herb-garden, where Brother Placidus was now pottering. He had beds of every herb that healed the body and some which hurt, for he had mandrakes which must be torn up only by a black dog in the dark of the moon. There were flowers, too, in their July glory, admitted shamefacedly, since they were idle and fruitless things, and served only to make nosegays for the children of the craftsmen. Then came more meadows, some already shorn, some heavy with hay, and more dovecotes and orchards. Through all of these meandered runnels, which spouted sometimes over tiny lashers. Last came the fish-ponds, oblongs of dear green water, where in the depths great carp and bream and tench could be seen, motionless but for an occasional flicker of their tails. Beyond them, after a banked walk among willows, lay a shining loop of river, and across the farther meadows the smoke of Hinksey village and the hills of Cumnor, already dim with the haze which promised another day of breathless summer.

Peter crossed the meadow called Nymph's Hay, the fodder from which was reserved for the Abbot's stalls, and entered the little orchard named Columbine, which was all of apple trees. He chose the place because it had an open view, on one side to Cumnor and Wytham, on the other to the soaring tower of Oseney Great Church, with the hump of Oxford Castle and the spire of St Mary the Virgin beyond it. He was hungry and had long to wait before he breakfasted, but that was nothing new to Peter. It was his soul not his belly that troubled him. The high spirits of yesterday, the vigour of that very morning, had gone, and he was in a mood of profound disquiet. He flung himself among the long cool grasses, and sniffed the scent of earth; he lay on his back and watched pigeons and finches crossing the space of blue between the trees; and then he shut his eyes, for his trouble was within, in his heart.

It had been coming on for a long time, this malady of the mind. There were days like yesterday when youth and sunshine and holiday gave him the unthinking happiness of childhood. Sometimes for as much as a week he would be at peace, busy with his books, his small duties at the Abbey, and the pleasant ritual of food and sleep. And then a film seemed to dim his outlook, and all that had been coloured grew drab, and what had seemed a wide horizon narrowed to prison walls.

He raised his head and looked at the lift of the Abbey towers beyond the apple trees. Sometimes he thought the sight the noblest on earth, not to be bettered surely by Rome or Jerusalem. But now he saw it only as a jumble of grey stone, and under that jumble he knew that there were weedy courtyards, and seventeen ageing canons stumbling aimlessly through their days of prayer, and an Abbot on whose brow sat the cares of the world rather than the peace of God, and shrill-voiced impudent novices, and pedlars who made the cloisters like St Giles's Fair—a shell once full of fruit, but empty now but for weevils and a few dry and rotting shreds. A medley of singing rivulets filled the place, freshening the orchards and meadows, sending strong leats to wash away filth, edging the walks, turning mill-wheels, making everywhere pools and founts and cisterns. In a happier hour he had told himself that Oseney was a northern Venice, a queen of waters; now in his distemper it seemed only a mouldering relic among sewers.

He wanted life and power and pride; not in a sinful cause, but for noble purposes—this he told himself hastily to still a doubting conscience. He wanted to tear the heart out of learning, which was to him the mother of power. He wanted to look the world in the face, to cast a spell over men and make them follow him. In all innocency he hungered for pomp and colour, trumpet notes, quick music, the stir of the heart. And he was only a poor scholar of St George's College in the Castle, entitled to little more than lodging and a commons of bread and ale; a pensioner of Oseney under an ancient corrody of the keepers of Wychwood Forest; a teacher of noisy infants and dull hobbledehoys; a fumbler at the doors of knowledge when he should be striding its halls; a clerk in a shabby gown, whom no woman cast a second glance at and proud men thrust from the causeway; a cypher, a nobody, neither lay nor cleric, gentle nor simple, man nor maid. He remembered the face of the traveller on the weary roan whom the night before he had seen ride in the gloaming into Stowood, and at the memory of his mastery Peter turned on his side and groaned.

The queer gipsy man, who spoke like a clerk, had said he was no churl's get. But he had been wrong. Peter's mind flew back to what he remembered of his youth. His only recollection was of the forester's cottage on the edge of Wychwood, looking down upon Windrush. Mother Sweetbread, the forester's wife, was all of a mother he had ever known, and the forester all of a father. He was not their child, but more distant kin—his father, he was told, had been a soldier slain in the wars. His early life had been that of other country children—

long summer days in wood and meadow, and winters snug at the back of the fire. But there had been sudden odd gleams athwart it. He remembered once being hurried into the deeps of Wychwood by Mother Sweetbread, where he lived for several days in a cold cleft by a stream, and somehow that hasty journey was associated in his mind with trampling horses and a tall man with a scar on his brow. Then there was Brother Tobias, who superintended his schooling. Tobias was an Oseney canon, whose face, as long as Peter remembered it, had been wrinkled like a walnut. Tobias had taught him his letters, and arranged for him to attend the Witney school, where he boarded with the parson. Tobias had spoken to him of wonderful things and opened up new worlds and set him on the scholar's path. It was Tobias who had got him an entrance to St George's College, and had been his guide and benefactor when the Wychwood corrody placed him on the Oseney foundation. To Tobias he had gone in every trouble save his present discontent. That he could not carry to him, for Tobias would declare that it was sin. Tobias hoped that he would presently take up the religious life: it was for such a purpose that he had brought him from the Windrush cottage.

Peter had been now three years in Oxford, and in those three years he had strayed far from the Witney school and the precepts of Tobias. He had found the place humming with a strange jargon and fevered with the beginnings of a new life. There was Greek to be had in the new lectures at Corpus Christi College, and Greek was not a fresh subject to be added to the Trivium or Quadrivium, but a kind of magic which altered all the rest of man's knowledge. It made him contemptuous of much that his betters still held venerable, and critical even of the ways of God. But there was more astir in Oxford than Greek. The sons of great men were coming now to college, instead of going like their fathers to a nobleman's household or the King's Court, and they were bringing the wind of politics into its sheltered groves. All was in a flux in Church and State. Great things were happening, greater still were promised; it was hard to keep the mind on study when

19

every post from London set the streets and taverns in a babble.

It was a moment when barriers seemed to be cracking, and there were wild chances for youth. But in such chances Peter had no share. The most that lay before him was the narrow life of the religious, regular monk or secular priest, or a life not less narrow spent in the outer courts of learning as a copier of scripts and a schoolmaster to youth. He was a peasant and a son of peasants, and there was no place for him in the glittering world. Once the Church might have helped him to a pinnacle, as it had helped the great Cardinal of York, now dead. But the Church was crumbling; soon it would be no more than an appanage to the King's palace, and its affairs would be guided by high-handed oppressive folk such as he had watched last night jingling through Stowood.

Again Peter raised his head, and this time his eye was held by the soaring tower of the great church. It was of Taynton stone, and whiter than the fabric; a sudden brightness seemed to fall on it and make it a shaft of alabaster with a light behind it. He saw again Oseney as he had first seen it, a mystic city filled with all the wisdom of God and man. Especially he remembered how the tower had seemed to him to leap into the skies and marry earth and heaven. Something of the old mood returned to him. Sinner that he was, he had the Faith to hold him up, the Faith for whose mysteries he had once hungered and trembled. The world might go withershins, but here was a cornerstone which could not be removed, an anvil which had worn out many hammers. To remember that he was a clerk gave him a second of pride, almost of defiance, for the Church and her clerks had many foes. He was not obscure so long as he was a member of that celestial brotherhood, nor humble when he had a title to the pride of Heaven. He gazed again at the shining tower, and a fount of affection welled in his dry heart. At that moment Thomas, the great bell, boomed the hour for High Mass.

Peter hurried through the orchard closes and over the little bridges and through the purlieus of Oseney town. The place smelt less pleasingly than it had an hour ago, and, with the dazzle of dawn out of his eyes, he could see the squalor of much of it—the dirt and offal in the runnels, a sluttish woman at a door, crumbling styes and byres, a bridge mended with a broken cart-wheel, a scum of grease filming an eddy in a stream. He ran past the infirmary and across Little Court, for Thomas had had a peremptory note in his voice, and he did not slacken pace till he was in the cloisters of Great Court, and joined a little convoy of canons proceeding to the west door of the church. Then suddenly he was in a hollow like the inside of a mountain, a hollow lit with twinkling lights and strange jewelled belts of sun, thick with incense smoke, and tremulous with the first notes of the great organ.

The growing poverty of Oseney had not yet shown itself in its mighty church. Peter, in his seat below the choir, felt himself once again secure from the temptations of life and lapped in an ancient peace. Nothing could stale for him the magic of this hollow land whose light and colour and scents were not those of the world. He followed the service mechanically from long practice, but his thoughts were far away. Oseney kept up the old fashion: no prick-song with its twists and tremors, but the honest plain-song of their fathers. The solemn cadences dwelt in the dim recesses above him like a night-wind among the clouds. They soothed him, and yet quickened the life in him, so that his fancies ranged in a happy medley. On the wall opposite him hung a tapestry of some saint of the Thebaid, with Libyan lions dogging his heels, and an aureoled angel offering him something in a cup. In the background little yellow hills ran out to a blue river, beyond which, very far away, lay a city with spires, and a sea with two ships. The sun coming in through the rose window in the south transept made the phylactery which the angel bore glow like a topaz, and gilded the hermit's bald head, while it turned the ciborium below into shining gold. Slowly Peter's mind passed from a happy vacuity to making tales about the scene depicted in the tapestry, and, as his fancy ranged, the peace which the dim light and the grave harmonies had given him began to shiver like mist and disappear. *Adoramus te Christe*—sang the pure voices of the choristers—*Jesu fili Dei vivi*—but Peter's thoughts were not on God. That tapestry had become

21

a window through which he looked again upon the secular world which tormented him.

At the benediction he made straight for the fratry, for his hunger was now grievous. At the laver in the cloister he bathed his face, and washed hands which were stained with the soil and moss of the orchard. The fratry was on the south side of Great Court, to be reached by a broad stairway, for all the ground floor was occupied by cellars and store-rooms. It was too large by far for the present community, for the officers, canons, novices and clerks attached made only a cluster at one end of the great hall. The dais was empty, since Abbot Burton was entertaining guests in his own lodgings. The precentor gabbled a grace, and the little company began their meal on the viands already on the table, for there were no hot dishes when fast was broken in summer-time. The food was plentiful and good—rye bread in abundance, and for each a commons of the fine white Oxford loaves called "blanchpayn," the Abbey's own ale, the Abbey's own cheese and butter, smoked London herrings, and dishes of fresh lettuces of Brother Placidus's growing. Peter's place was at the lower end, and he ate hungrily, having no ear for the novice, who in a stone pulpit read aloud from St Jerome. The black dog was on his back again. He was a poor clerk in a poor place, disconsidered even by the disconsidered. The homely smell of the food, of the scrubbed floor and woodwork, of the coarse fabric of his neighbours' clothes, filled him with a childish exasperation. He looked at the grey heads around him. Was he to grow old like them in this place of shadows?

A hand was laid on his shoulder as he descended the staircase into the July sunlight, and he found Brother Tobias beside him. Brother Tobias was a little lame, and leaned heavily on his arm while he spoke in his placid cooing way in his ear. Brother Tobias had a very small face, red and rosy and wrinkled like a walnut, and a very long neck, stringy as a hempen rope. From earliest days he had been Peter's guardian, patron, father in God, or whatever title covers the complete oversight of interests in time and eternity. He had blue eyes a little dim from study, for he was Oseney's chief scholar and accounted a learned Thomist as well as a noted Grecian, but those same eyes saw much that others missed, and at moments they could gleam with a secular fire. For Tobias had not always been a churchman; there were tales of a youth spent in camps and courts, for he was come of high stock from Severn side.

His dragging arm led Peter to the slype beside the summer parlour. On the stone seats some of the brethren, who had already eaten, were basking in the sun. Two men in green, clothiers from the Stour, were engaged in argument with the hosteller about certain coverlets supplied to the hostel beds. Brother Placidus, a lean old man with a skin the colour of loam, was upbraiding Brother Josephus, because the latter, who was skilled in the work of illumination, had plucked as a model the leaf of a certain rare plant, which the former alleged to have been thereby destroyed. The leaf in question was now past the use for which Brother Josephus had designed it, having been rolled into a pellet in Brother Placidus's angry hands. A pedlar of wild strawberries had plumped his baskets on the flags and was extolling the merits of fruit picked that morning in the Besselsleigh woods. Two brethren were imperilling their digestions by a theological argument as to whether our Lord, combining a divine and a human nature, was to be described as *conflatus* or *commixtus*. A third joining in, urged that the proper word was *unitus*, or perhaps *geminatus*, and quoted a sentence of St Augustine. A group of younger canons were discussing the guests whom the Abbot was then entertaining. One was Sir Ralph Bonamy of Wood Eaton—he was a familiar figure; but the other, the old man with the small white beard and the quick anxious eyes? Doubtless a confrater, or lay member of the Abbey, come to consult on Oseney business. One claimed to know the face as that of a lord in the west country who was very close to the King's ear. The reeve from the Abbey's lands at Kidlington was engaged with the sub-cellarer on an intricate computation of the number of beeves to be fattened for the Abingdon market. Peter, who could not choose but hear fragments of the tattle, felt an overpowering weariness of soul.

Brother Tobias, stretching his old legs in the sun's warmth, looked curiously at his friend, whose gown had slipped from his shoulders, and who stood before him very comely in his young grace, but with something listless and dejected in his air.

"I missed you at supper last night, son Peter," he said. "Were you in the woods, maybe? You have become more of a forester these days than a clerk. In this summer of God no doubt the woods are the best school. Would that my limbs were less ancient and I could go with you, but where I must jog on a mule you can stride like a hunter. When saw you Mother Sweetbread last?"

"Yesterday seven days."

"She was in health?"

"In the health which her age permits."

"Ay. That good wife grows old like me. Age needs cherishing, and she is all the kin you have. Next week, if the Lord spare me, we will go together upstream and taste the Windrush trout and the Forest strawberries. But before that we must speak together of some difficult matters. You are a man now, with your twenty-first year behind you. It is time to consult about the future."

"That is what I desire," said Peter moodily.

"Let it be this evening before compline." He looked up at the boy's shapeliness, the clean limbs, the narrow loins, the breadth of shoulder, at the face dark with weather, the straight brows, the noble lines of head and jaw, the candid grey-blue eyes at present sullen and puzzled, the crisp brown hair, for Peter had never been tonsured. All this Brother Tobias gazed at, and then he sighed, before he rose to limp back to his studies. He wondered whether such youth would submit readily to the dedication which religion demanded. "I must require of him some special discipline," he thought.

Peter finished his duties in the novices' school by an hour after noon. He visited his attic in St George's College in the Castle. It was very hot, and, since the window opened to the south, the little room was like an oven. He looked at his unslept-in bed, with its mean bedclothes, his shelf of papers weighted by a book or two, the three-legged stool and the rickety table which were all the furniture, and a pair of blue flies buzzing at a broken pane, and the sight did not increase his cheerfulness. Poverty lay like dust over everything. He had meant to give the afternoon to his own studies, to that translation of a book of Plato into Ciceronian Latin, at which, with a fellow of Corpus Christi College, he had been for some months at work. But he found it impossible. On such a day and in such a mood he would go mad in that stuffy cell. He would go to the library of Merton College, where he had permission to read, and look up certain passages in Diogenes Laertius till dinner-time.

It had become a day of blistering heat. The last summer had been a succession of fogs and deluges, so that the hay rotted in the mead and the beans in the field. But this year, though there had been many comforting rains, there had also been weeks of steady heat, when the sun rose in a haze, glared at noontide from a cloudless sky, and set again in amethyst and opal. Peter entered the city by the west gate, and by way of Friars' Street came into St Aldate's opposite the gate of what had once been Cardinal College. It was still unfinished, a barrack of gaunt masonry, noble only in its size, with beyond the raw gables and the poles of the scaffolding the lovely grey spire of St Frideswide's Church. Peter on his way to Merton passed through the new main quadrangle, which was as yet more like a quarry than a dwelling for men. The older work was of hard Burford stone, but much of the finishing, to save time and cost, was in the soft stone of Headington, and the masons who wrought on it filled the air with a fine dust and made the place in the sultry afternoon like a desert in a sandstorm. On the older plinths and buttresses Peter read the great Cardinal's arms, and he wished his soul well wherever it might be. Wolsey had loved grandeur and pomp, and had made all men bow to him. Also he had loved sound learning, and, had his dreams been realised, the Greek of Corpus would have been to the Greek of Cardinal as a cup of water to a flood.

25

Merton Street gave him shade, where the town houses of the gentry of the shire beetled over the narrow pathway. Beyond he saw bare ground up to the city wall; that had once been a populous quarter of the city, but it had been untenanted since the Black Death a hundred years before. The great Cardinal dwelt in his mind, not as a warning against pride, but as an encouragement to the humble. Though tragedy had been the end of him, he had wrested rich prizes from life. Dukes had held the ewer while he washed, and earls had tied the strings of his shoes. His palaces at Hampton and Tittenhanger and the More had been as noble as the King's. He had travelled about with three hundred servants, and he, the flesher's son, had sat as equal at the council-board with the Emperor and the King of France. Peter's fancy fired at the thought, and in a dream he climbed the library steps with long strides and found his accustomed corner.

But the mood did not last. Wolsey had been Wolsey, and he was Peter Pentecost, without a friend save Brother Tobias and the Oseney canons, and with no means to raise himself from his humility. His obscurity was too deep for any good fortune to disinter him. Diogenes Laertius that day was not profitably studied, for Peter sat on the oak settle with his eye on the page and his mind far away. He thought of his happy careless childhood with irritation. Born a peasant in a peasant's hut, not very clear even about his own humble kin, learning had opened windows for him and given him a prospect beyond his station. But learning having made the promise could not give him fulfilment. The Church offered no career. It was crumbling; as Tobias said, the gates of Hell were prevailing against it. A churchman met hard glances nowadays wherever he went; and, worse, he found the doors of power barred to him. There was a new world coming to birth, and it was a world which, instead of exalting Peter Pentecost, must force him deeper down into the mire. Mother Sweetbread was growing old, and she was all the kin he knew. The thought at the moment brought no kindness to his heart, for youth has its hard patches. He felt something which was almost resentment against the woman who had reared him for so

26

narrow a life. Yet in those days he had been happy. His memory of them was of an infinite series of golden hours, green woods and clear waters and gentle faces. Illusion, no doubt, but it was better than the grim reality of today.

And then his thoughts flew to the Painted Floor, and the strange spectacle of the night before. Since his youth could not be recovered, might he not win that clean and gracious world which the classical poets had revealed to him, another and a fairer youth, an eternal springtide of the spirit? But the harsh present was too insistent, nor did he believe that he had the makings of the true scholar. He could not consent to live only with books and dreams, even if that life were free to him. He had revelled in old poets because they had given him a sphere so remote from squalid reality that he could indulge the fancy that within it he was a master and not a slave. He had rejoiced in the Painted Floor, because it was his own, and he was king there by the strongest right of tenure. But did not the secret of both affections lie in the fact that they made him what he could dream, but could never attain to?

He had a momentary thought of breaking all shackles and seeking another course of life. He had been taught the use of arms by the Wychwood foresters. Brother Tobias himself had seen to it that he had some skill of the sword, a rare thing in a clerk. His chest was deep and his limbs were tireless. What of the big unclerkly world beyond Oseney gates and Oxford walls? The notion only crossed his mind to be dismissed. Learning, even a little learning, had spoiled him for beginning life in the ranks among bullies and cut-throats and fellows whose sole possession was their sinews. It had made him fastidious. He hungered, and yet could be dainty about any offered dish. Peter shut his book and dropped his head on his arms. He was feeling the pressure of life which sets a man's nerves twitching and confuses his brain, and which can be mastered only by blinding the eyes and concentrating on a single duty, or—the poet's way—by weaving tumultuous phenomena into the simplicities of art. What were those words of Tobias which he was always using of England?—"The blanket of the dark." The gipsy with the hot eyes in Stowood had said the same. Peter had a sense of a great cloud of darkness encumbering him, a cloak at once black and stifling.

His restlessness drew him from the shadowed library and sent him by way of Merton Lane into the bustle of High Street. It was cooler now, but, since that narrow street ran east and west, the sun's beams fell in a long slant and there was no shade. Peter, filled with his own thoughts, and keeping close to the booths, found himself so jostled that he was shaken into cognisance of the world around him. A cowman, leading a red bull by the nose, was pulled off his legs and had a wordy brawl with a mounted lackey wearing the Harcourt liveries. For a moment the street was cleared, while a veiled lady on a palfrey was escorted by four running footmen and an armed steward. Great folk from Ewelme, thought Peter, for the men had the Suffolk colours. He saw two friars cross the street and disappear within the Wheatsheaf passage, moving furtively and fast. They were from a Dominican house among the south marshes, a foundation long decayed and now trembling to its fall. Dr John London, the Warden of New College, emerged from the Bear inn, wiping his lips and arguing loudly with a pale priest in a cassock. Dr John's red face and vehement eye dominated the pavement, and the citizens doffed their caps to him, while the friars quickened their pace at the sight, for he was deep in Cromwell's confidence and purposed to make himself a scourge for the religious houses under the direction of the masterful chief whip of the Council.

There were plenty of threadbare scholars of Peter's own complexion, and a sprinkling of a different kind of youth—ruddy boys, richly doubleted and booted, and in defiance of statute bearing arms—young sprigs of gentrice and nobility, to whom the life of Oxford was that of a country house. The sight of them made Peter shrink still farther into what shadow he could find. In a press at a corner he thought he caught a glimpse of the lean face and the hot eyes of the gospeller of the night before. And of one face he was certain. Down the causeway, as if he were its squire, strode the tall horseman whom he had seen twenty hours ago ride up the hill into Stowood. He had changed his clothes, for gone were the plumeless bonnet and battered doublet: now he was handsomely dressed in black and silver, with a jewel in his cap, but the same long sword swung at his side. Opposite Haberdashers' Hall, which was on Oseney ground, there was a loud cry to clear the way, and, a hundred yards off, he saw the head of a mounted man bobbing above the throng. It was a post from London, no less than the Vice-Chancellor's own private courier, and, since he had many acquaintances, he was delayed by people plucking at his stirrups and bridle and asking for news. To avoid the crowd Peter stepped into an open door of the Ram inn, and found a seat well back in the dusk.

It was a place which he sometimes frequented, when his weekly three silver pennies permitted the indulgence. A drawer brought him a pot of ale, and when he had taken the edge from his thirst he looked round the room, which was bright in front where its low windows and door admitted the sunlight from the street, but at the back was dusky as a vault. A clerk sat on the settle next him, and he saw without pleasure that it was that Jeremy Wellaby of Corpus with whom he was at work on Plato.

There was a clamour at the door and loud cries on Master Puncheon the vintner to bring forthwith a hogshead of ale to quench the drought of an honest man. The Vice-Chancellor's messenger had halted at the Ram door and was being treated by his friends. Peter could not choose but catch echoes of the babble, as the said friends discussed the news. The Pope's men rising . . . Norfolk way . . . some say the Bishop leads 'em . . . nay, not the Duke of Norfolk, who was the right hand of the King's grace . . . Darcy maybe, and unnamed lords in the north . . . St Albans had fallen to them . . . some said they were stopped at Huntingdon. Nay, nay, Master Giles had been clear that there was no rising as yet, only the fear of one.

The crowd surged on, but, like an ocean billow, it left some flotsam behind it. Several figures had entered the taproom of the Ram. One was already a little drunk, and had the look of a scrivener's jackal, for there were ink stains over his large splay hands. He sat near the door, spilling his ale as he drank over a grimy doublet, and he seasoned his draught with

29

complaints to all within earshot.

"Ay, my masters," he hiccuped, "the King's grace has gotten the Pope at last in his belly. Now that the big black Cardinal crow is dead, the rookeries will be hewn down, and there will be rook pie for every poor soul that seeks it. A better world, says I. No more mortuaries and probates and a right to sin for every lousy clerk. Dr John! Dr John London! More power to your stout arm! They waxed fat and kicked . . . fat, forsooth . . . three dishes at a meal for the plain gentleman and only six for a great lord of parliament, but nine on the board of him that was Cardinal of York. It is the day of recompense, my masters, and blessed be the eyes which shall see it."

The man saw something in the street which plucked him from his bench and sent him staggering into the open.

"It is the day of loose tongues," said a grave man, an Oxford mercer who was dining handsomely off a roast duck and a cup of sack. "The stocks and a dipped ear await that one. Doubtless it would be a pleasant world lacking mortuaries and such-like, but what an honest man saves from the Church he will pay to the King. An Englishman is born to be fleeced by the mighty ones, and what with subsidies and loans and amicable aids he is like to be worse off than before. His money is lost to him whether it goes to Pope or bishop or exchequer clerk. I am a good citizen and a true and loyal King's man, but it is the right of a freeman to have his grumble."

Master Wellaby spoke up.

"You had an England of laymen and clerks, and you are destroying it. What better will it be to have an England of rich and poor? Will there be more peace and happiness, think you?"

A newcomer had ordered a meal, with an observing eye upon the mercer's fare. He was a countryman by his ruddy face and the dust on his square-toed boots and leather breeches, but from his dress he might be reeve or steward or verderer or petty squire.

"Marry, there will always be rich and poor," he said, "since the Scripture orders it, and since the new breed of rich is less gentle than the old, the poor will fare the worse. Are the new men that lord it today the make of the old? I trow not. What is Russell and Audeley and Wriothesley to Mowbray and Bohun and Mortimer, or Seymour to De Vere, or Fitzwilliam to Lovell? You have a new man at the King's elbow, Master Crummle, of whom they speak great things. Nevertheless he is but a gilded scrivener. My own cousin saw him a score of years back a ragged serving-lad at the door of Messer Friskyball's bank in Florence. It sticks in my mind that the new masters will be harsher than the old, since they are but risen servants."

"History confirms you, sir," said Master Wellaby eagerly. "In ancient Rome the freedman was the worst tyrant."

"I know nought of Rome, ancient or new, but much of England, notably that part of it which lies between Cherwell and Severn, and I declare before God that I love the old ways best, as I love best old ale and old pasture. 'Twere better if instead of bare-back fleshers and scriveners the ancient masters bore rule again in the land. Such an one as the mighty Duke of Buckingham."

"Him that suffered in '21?" the mercer inquired.

"The same. His blood was direct from Bohun and King Edward. There was the great lord! He had fourteen thousand marks of rental each year, and he never stirred abroad without four hundred armed men at his back."

"Too proud," said the mercer. "Too proud for a naughty world. Wherefore did he die, good sir? I was only a stripling then and forget the tale."

"Because of an old wives' gossip of treason. Wolsey, whom the devil burn, feared to go to the French wars and leave such a man behind him. It is our foolish fashion to sacrifice some great one before we fight our enemies. 'Twas Pole in '13, and 'twas Buckingham in '21. I uphold that the Duke's death was a crime in God's eyes, and that He hath visited it not only on Wolsey who was the guilty one, but on the King's grace who was an innocent partaker. Witness his lamentable barrenness in the matter of posterity."

There was a hush at the words, as if each auditor feared

his neighbour. But the countryman went on undaunted.

"And now there is nought left of the proud race of Stafford and Bohun, and old England is the poorer place."

After that he spoke no more but gave his mind to a meat pasty. Presently Wellaby rose to leave, and soon Peter was the only occupant of the taproom. It was the hour of the evening meal at Oseney, but Peter had no mind to it. He expended one of his few coins on a little bread and cheese, and sat on as the dusk deepened and the booths put up their shutters and women called their husbands to supper.

He was in a mood of profound dejection, for two things had befallen him that afternoon. He had realised that the life to which he had vowed himself was in danger of becoming no more than a blind alley, and that the huge fabric of the Church was falling about his ears. Also he had been made aware that great events were toward in the State, and he had seen the happy bustle of men with purpose and power, while he himself sat a disconsidered oddment in a corner. The blanket of the dark was very thick about him.

A hand touched him and woke him from his lassitude. It was one of the Abbey servitors from Oseney.

"Make haste, Master Pentecost—'ee be wanted. I've been rakin' Oxford for 'ee this past hour. Brother Tobias bade me bring 'ee post-haste."

Peter followed him into the street, listless and incurious. This was the consultation, no doubt, for which Tobias had trysted him that morning. But what could Tobias do? Peter had not lost the savour of life; the deadly sin of *accidia* was not his; he felt the savour with a desperate keenness, but he despaired of passing from the savour to the taste of it. The crowd in the street was less, since it was the meal hour, but there were travellers on the road, spurring through the city to some Cotswold inn or manor. Also there were many of the new proud breed of collegians, coming from the Beaumont field to the colleges nearest the river, or forsaking their bare commons for a tavern supper. There were merchants of the town, too, taking the air and discussing the last news,

32

comfortable men, with a proper reverence for a lord and a proper contempt for a poor scholar. To everyone he met, even the humblest, he was nothing—a child of country peasants, a dabbler in unwanted learning, a creature of a falling Church. In the bitterness of his soul he clenched his hands till the nails hurt his palms. As he crossed Bookbinders bridge and entered the Abbey he felt like a dog whistled back to its kennel.

So low were his spirits that he did not notice that he was being conducted to the Abbot's palace till his feet were on the threshold. The messenger handed him over to the seneschal, who appeared to be awaiting him. This was an odd spot for his appointment with Tobias, for he had never entered the place before, but he followed his guide dully through the outer hall, and through the dining chamber and up a stairway of Forest marble. He entered a room part panelled and part hung with tapestries, which looked westward over the Botley causeway and the Wytham meadows. It was lit by the summer sunset, and beside the table stood two men.

One was Tobias, whose crab-apple face seemed strangely perturbed. He looked at Peter with hungry eyes as if striving by them to say that which he could not put into words. The other was an old man dressed soberly in black, who wore a rich chain of gold and a jewel on his breast. His face was deeply lined, his mouth was grim, and he had the eye of one used to command. Recollection awoke in Peter at the sight. This was the very man whom he had seen wearing a purple cloak and an ermine collar in the cavalcade of the evening before. He had guessed that he was one of the King's commissioners sent to deal with the religious houses. Eynsham had not been his goal. He must have been Oseney's guest for the night.

Both men rose at his entrance and remained standing, a strange thing for a great one in the presence of a youthful clerk. The elder looked at him steadily, ardently, his eye taking in every detail of the threadbare clothes and lithe form and comely face. Then he sighed, but his sigh was not of disappointment.

"The same arch of the brows," he murmured, "and the

little cleft in the upper lip."

"You are he whom they call Peter Pentecost?" he said. "I have searched long before I found you, my child. They told me that you were an inmate of a religious house in these parts, but which I could not learn. Having found you, I have much to tell you. But first answer my question. Who and what are you and what was your upbringing?" There was no rudeness in the interrogation, but nevertheless it was peremptory, and the speaker's air had that in it which compelled an answer.

"I was reared by one Mistress Sweetbread at Leafield, the wife, and now the widow, of a Wychwood forester."

The old man nodded.

"Your father?"

"Of him I know nothing. I have heard that he was a soldier who fell in the wars oversea."

"Your mother?"

"I never saw her. She was, I think, of near kin to the Sweetbreads, a sister or a sister's child."

The other smiled.

"It was a necessary imposture. There was no safety for such as you except to bury you deep in some rustic place. You remember nothing of the years before you came to Leafield?"

Peter shook his head. A wild hope was beginning to surge in his heart.

"Then it is my privilege to enlighten you. There were some who knew the truth, but it did not become them to speak. This good man for one," and he turned to Tobias.

"I judged it wiser to let the past sleep," said Tobias, "for I considered only the happiness of him whom I loved as my own son. There was no need . . ."

"The need has arisen," said the old man firmly. "We who were your father's friends have never lost sight of that likelihood, though i' faith we let you sink so deep into Oxfordshire mud that it has been hard to find you. That was the doing of our reverend brother Tobias. You have lived a score of years in a happy ignorance, but the hour has come when it must be broken. Your mother . . ."

He paused, and Peter's heart stood still.

34

"Your mother was no Sweetbread kin. She was the Lady Elinor, the eldest daughter of Percy of Northumberland."

Peter's heart beat again. He felt his forehead flush and a wild gladness in him which sent the tears to his eyes. He was noble then on the distaff side, noble with the rarest blood of England. What runaway match, what crazy romance, had brought him to birth?

"My father?" he asked.

"Be comforted," said the other, smiling back. "I read your face, but there is no bar sinister on your shield. You were born in lawful wedlock, a second son. Your mother is long dead, your elder brother is these three months in his grave. You are now the only child of your father's house."

"My father?" The tension made Peter's voice as thin as a bat's.

"Your father?" said the old man, and he rolled the words out like a herald at a tourney. "Your father was that high and puissant prince, Edward, Duke and Earl of Buckingham, Earl and Baron of Stafford, Prince of Brecknock, Count of Perche in Normandy, Knight of the Garter, hereditary Lord High Steward, and, in virtue of the blood of Bohun, Lord High Constable of England."

"He died in the year '21," said Peter, blindly repeating what he had heard in the Ram inn.

"He died in the year '21, a shameful and unmerited death. His lands and honours were thereby forfeited, and you have not one rood to your name this day. But in the eyes of God and of honest men throughout this land you are Buckingham and Bohun and the sixth man from Edward the Third. I and those who think with me have sought you long, and have planned subtly on your behalf, and on behalf of this unhappy realm which groans under a cruel tyranny. The times are ripe for a change of master, and there will be no comfort for our poor people till that change be accomplished."

"You would make me a duke?" Peter stammered.

The westering sun was in the old man's face, and it showed that in his eyes which belied his age. He was suddenly transfigured. He came forward, knelt before Peter, and took

35

his hand between his two palms.

"Nay, sire," he said, "by the grace of God we will make you King of England."

CHAPTER III

IN WHICH PETER LURKS IN THE SHADOW

Four weeks later to a day Peter sat again in his old eyrie, above the highway which descended from Stowood to the Wood Eaton meads. Strange things had happened meanwhile. Twenty-four hours after the meeting in the Abbot's lodging the heat had broken in thunderstorms, followed by such a deluge of rain as washed the belated riverside haycocks to the sea and sent Isis and Cherwell adventuring far into distant fields. In the floods a certain humble dependent of Oseney, Pentecost by name, had the ill-luck to perish. For two days he was missed from his accustomed haunts, and on the third news came up the river from Dorchester that he had been last seen attempting a crazy plank bridge over Thame which had been forthwith carried down by the floods. The body was not recovered, but there were many nameless bodies washed up those days. Perfunctory masses were sung for the soul of the drowned man in a side chapel of Oseney Great Church, and in the little chapel of St George in the Castle, and Brother Tobias wore a decent mask of grief and kept his chamber. A new master in grammar was found for the novices, and there was a vacancy in an Oseney corrody and an empty bed in the Castle garret. In a week a deeper tide than that of Isis had submerged the memory of Peter Pentecost.

"It is necessary to do such things cleanly," the old Lord Avelard had said. "There must be no Lambert Simnel tale that might crop up to our undoing." He was a careful gentleman, for Brother Tobias was sent to Wychwood to spread the news, so that those who had sat by Peter on the benches of Witney school might spare a sigh for a lost companion.

Then Peter by night was taken to Sir Ralph Bonamy's house at Wood Eaton. No servant saw him enter, but in the dark a clerk's gown was burned, and in the morning a young man broke his fast in Sir Ralph's hall, who bore the name of Bonamy, and was a cousin out of Salop. The manor-house of Wood Eaton was no new-fangled place such as fine gentlemen were building elsewhere. It was still in substance the hall of Edward the First's day, with its high raftered roof, its solar with plastered walls, its summer parlour, its reedy moat, which could nevertheless be speedily filled bank-high by a leat from Cherwell, its inner and outer courtyards bastioned and loopholed for defence. Sir Ralph was as antique as his dwelling. A widower and childless, he lived alone with an ancient sister, who spent her days amid the gentle white magic of herbs and simples. He was well beyond three-score and ten years, but still immensely strong and vigorous, and able to spend long days in the field with his hounds or on the meres with his fishing pole. He was short and broad, with a noble head of greying reddish hair, and he was clad always in coarse green cloth like a yeoman, while his boots were as massive as an Otmoor fowler's. He was a lover of good fare and mighty in hospitality, so that his hall was like a public house of entertainment, where neighbour or stranger could at any time get his fill of beef-pudding and small beer. It was an untidy place, murky in winter with wood-smoke and dim even in summer, for the windows were few and dirty. It smelled always of cooked meats and of a motley of animals, being full of dogs—deerhounds and gazehounds, and Malta spaniels, and terriers; likewise there were hawks' perches, and Sir Ralph's favourite tassel-gentle sat at his elbow. The stone floor was apt to be littered with marrow-bones and the remains of the hounds' meals, and the odour was not improved by the drying skins of wild game which hung on the walls. Sir Ralph had a gusty voice and a habit of rough speech, which suited his strange abode, but he was also notably pious, and a confrater of Oseney; a small chapel opened from the hall where the family priest conducted regular devotions, and he kept his Fridays and fast days as rigidly as any Oseney canon. He was an upholder of the old ways in all things—religion, speech, food and furnishing.

Peter, clad in a sober, well-fitting suit of brown such as

became a country squire out of Salop, breakfasted his first
morning at Wood Eaton with his head in a whirl. His host,
in a great armed chair, made valorous inroads on a cold chine
of beef, and drank from a tun glass of ale which he stirred
with a twig of rosemary. The long hawking-pole, which never
left him, leaned against his chair, and by his hand lay a little
white stick with which he defended his platter against the
efforts of a great deer-hound and two spaniels to share its
contents. Sir Ralph had welcomed his guest with a gusto
which he had in vain attempted to make courtly, and since
then had said nothing, being too busy with food and dogs.
"Eat, sir," he had said, "youth should be a good trencherman.
Now, alas! I can only pick like a puling lanner." Then he cut
himself a wedge of pie which might have provisioned a
ploughman for a week.

Peter turned his head at a sound behind him. Lord Avelard
had entered the hall, preceded by his body-servant, who
arranged his chair, procured him some wheaten cakes and
butter, filled a glass of sack which he mixed with syrup of
gillyflowers, and then bowed and took his leave. Seen for the
first time in the morning light, the face of the old man was
such as to hold the eyes. His toilet was but half made; he had
slippers on his feet and still wore his dressing-gown; his age
was more apparent, and could not be less than four-score;
nevertheless, so strong was his air of purpose that he seemed
ready forthwith to lead an army or dominate a council. A
steady fire burned in his pale eyes, a fire of enthusiasm, or,
it might be, of hate. Peter, as he looked on him, felt his
curiosity changing to awe.

But the old man was very cordial to the young one. He
greeted him as a father might greet a son who was presently
to be pope or king.

"We will call him for a little by your name, Ralph," he said.
"Master Bonamy—Master Peter Bonamy—I have forgot what
is his worship's manor t'other side of Severn. Wood Eaton will
be a safe retreat for a week or two, till I am ready to receive
him at Avelard."

"By your leave, my lord," said his host, "it is none too safe a sanctuary. Wood Eaton has a plaguey name as a house of call for all and sundry. It is as open as the Oxford corn-market. Likewise, I have lodging here my niece Sabine—old Jack Beauforest's daughter—you mind Jack of Dorchester, my lord? Come to think of it, Sabine is as near kin to your deceased lady as to me. She is gone for a week to the nuns at Godstow, where she went to school—Abbess Katherine was her mother's cousin—but will be home tomorrow. The secret with which you have entrusted me is too big for a maid's ear, and I do not want Mistress Sabine and this new cousin of ours to clap eyes on each other. You see the reason of it, my lord, though, as one with a hospitable name, I think shame to urge it."

"But I have a plan to offer," he continued, when he saw the old man's countenance fall. "Let him go into Stowood to a verderer's lodge. I, as principal ranger, can compass that. There is one John of Milton, a silent man, who lives deep in the forest, and to him I would send our cousin, my lord. There no eye will see him save that of gipsy or charcoal-burner or purleyman, and he will have leisure to perfect himself in arts in which I gather he is lacking. A month will pass quick in the cool of the forest."

Lord Avelard pondered. "Your plan is good, Ralph," he said. "Wood Eaton is a thought too notable because of its master." He looked at Peter and smiled. "How will you relish taking to the greenwood like Robin Hood or Little John? You are dedicated, my son, to a great purpose, and it has always been the custom of the dedicated to sojourn first for a while in the wilderness."

His face, as he looked on the young man, was lit for a moment with a strange tenderness, but the next second it had fallen back into the wary mask of the conspirator.

"How goes the country, Ralph?" he asked. "What does Oxfordshire say of the latest doings at Court?"

"Oxfordshire is very weary of the Welshman," was the answer, "and grieves for the fate of poor Hal Norris. It was well to cut off the Concubine's head, but why should Hal have been made to suffer for her misdoings—Hal whom I knew from boyhood and who was innocent as a christom babe? Wychwood and Langley forests had never a better keeper than Hal. Who is to have the post, think you? I heard talk of Jack Brydges."

"The King, as you know, has married the Seymour, so he has a new breed of wife's kin to provide for."

"The Welshman makes a poor business of marrying, for he has nothing to show for his pains. The Lady Mary is outlawed, and the Concubine's child is outlawed, and . . ."

"Nay, but there is a new conceit," said Lord Avelard. "Parliament has granted the King's grace the power to bequeath the Crown of England by will, as you or I might legate an old doublet."

"God's wounds!" cried Sir Ralph, "but this is sacrilege! If a pack of citizens can decide the disposition of the crown what becomes of the Lord's anointing? It is the tie of blood which God has determined. . . ."

"Do not vex yourself, for the thing works in our favour. If the King forget the obligations of lawful descent, England remembers them. What further do you report of the discontents?"

"There is the devil's own uproar over the King's extortions among the gentle, and the simple complain that they are sore oppressed by the inclosers and the engrossers and the woolstaplers. Likewise the pious everywhere are perturbed, since heretics sit in high places and the blasphemer is rampant in the land. Crummle's commissioners go riding the roads, with the spoils of God's houses on their varlets' backs, copes for doublets and tunics for saddlecloths. There are preachers who tell the folk that the Host is only a piece of baker's bread, and that baptism is as lawful in a tub or a ditch as in a holy font; and will allow a poor man none of the kindly little saints to guide his steps when God and His Mother have bigger jobs on hand. Certes, the new England they will bring upon us is good neither for Jack nor his master."

"Jack knows it," said Lord Avelard. "I will prophesy to you, Ralph. In a matter of months, or maybe of weeks, you will hear strange news out of the eastern and northern shires. There will be such a rising of poor Christian people as will

41

shake the King on his throne."

"Ay, ay. I have heard something of it. But Jack alone will never oust the Welshman. That is a job for Jack's masters. What of them, my lord? What of the nobles of England?"

"Their turn will come," was the answer. "First, the priests and the common people. Then, when they have fluttered the heart of the Court and drawn the King's levies into a difficult campaign, we shall strike in the western and midland shires, and the blow will not be by a bill in a clodhopper's hand but by a glaive in a steel gauntlet. First the commonalty, then the gentles—that is our stratagem."

"And of these latter more puissant folk what numbers can you command? Remember, my lord, I have been a soldier. I was at Flodden and Therouanne. I am not ignorant of the ways of war."

Lord Avelard consulted a paper. "Your walls are secret?" he asked.

"As the grave. Likewise I have no servant who is not deaf or dull in the wits."

"Of the plain country squires throughout the land, three out of four are on our side. For the greater ones—Norfolk is Harry's man, and Suffolk married his sister—we can reckon on neither. In the north there is hope of Northumberland. He was once affianced to the Concubine and weeps her death, and likewise he is your cousin's kin on the distaff side." He smiled on Peter. "Westmoreland and Cumberland are with us, and Latimer and Lumley. In the mid shires and the east we shall have Rutland and Huntingdon and Hussey and Darcy. We can count assuredly on the Nevilles. Shrewsbury we cannot get, but if we lose the Talbots we have the Stanleys."

"What of the west?" Sir Ralph asked. "What of Exeter?"

"I have good hopes. But the Courtenay blood is hard to judge, being in all things capricious, and my lord of Exeter is a grandson of Edward Fourth, and so himself within modest distance of the throne. He cannot love the Tudor, but he may not consent to give place to a son of Buckingham. Yet we shall see. What of you, old friend? Will you strike again for England against the Welshman the shrewd blow which you

42

struck against the Scot at Flodden?"

"I am aged," was the answer, "and am somewhat set in my habits. But I stand for holy Church, the old blood and the old ways, and not least for Ned Stafford's son. I will ride with you, provided your campaigning season does not fall athwart my other duties. Let me consider. In the months of August and September, I am engaged, as principal ranger of the King's forests of Stowood and Shotover, in thinning the deer. The fallow buck are already ripe for the bolt, and in a week the velvet will be off the red deer's horns. That brings me to October, when we take the wild fowl from the Otmoor fleets; a heavy task which needs a master's eye and hand. Then up to Yule I hunt the fox and badger and get the pike out of the river. January is a busy time with my falcons, seeing that the geese are on the wing if it be frost, and if it be mild the pigeons are in every spinney. February and March are the training months for the eyasses, while the herons nest, and in April and May there are the trout to be caught in the Fettiplace waters and the monks' ponds of Bicester. In summertime I have the young haggards to consider which my men take in the forest, and that, too, is the season when the *manège* must be looked to against the hunting months."

"You have filled up your year to the last minute," said Lord Avelard.

"By the sorrows of God, I have." He pondered in deep perplexity. "Let it be summer, then," he said at length. "I must leave the haggards to my falconer Merryman. I will mount and ride with you if your summons come on the first day of June. But, as you love me, not a day sooner, for Windrush trout rise heartily till the last moment of May."

So Peter had exchanged the gloomy halls of Wood Eaton for the verderer's lodge deep in the heart of Stowood, where the ground fell steeply from the chantry of Stanton St John to the swamps of Menmarsh. The lodge stood in a glade among oaks, beside a strong spring of water—a pleasant spot, for the dwellers there looked northward over dim blue airy distances and a foreground as fantastic as a tapestry. The verderer, John

43

of Milton, who came from the Milton hamlets in the east by Thame side, was all day absent on his own errands, and to Peter, as a cousin of the chief ranger, he behaved as a respectful servitor, sparing of speech but quick to execute his wishes. The boy was not lonely, for he went anew to school. Under Sir Ralph's direction he was taught the accomplishments of his rank. One of the Wood Eaton men, who had like his master confronted the Scottish spears at Flodden, taught him various devices in the use of the two-edged, cut-and-thrust blade, of which he already had mastered more than the rudiments. A hedge-captain came out from Oxford to instruct him in the new Spanish sword-play, where the edge was scarcely used and the point was everything. Peter had often marked the man in Oxford and had taken him for a lord from his fierce eyebrows and arrogant air—but he proved only a different kind of usher, who doffed his cap respectfully to Sir Ralph's kin. Likewise, Sir Ralph's chief falconer, Merryman, who was an adept at the cross-bow, made Peter sweat through long mornings shooting at a mark, and a Noke man taught him to stretch the long-bow. Peter was no discredit to his tutors, for his eye was true, his sinews strong and his docility complete. Besides, his training had been well begun years before on the skirts of Wychwood.

At last had come Brother Tobias, riding out on an Abbey mule, when the little wild strawberries were ripe in the coverts. Tobias liked these fruits, and had a bowl of them, lappered in cream from the verderer's red cow. He regarded Peter nervously, avoiding his eye, but stealing sidelong glances at him, as if uncertain what he should find. Peter himself had no shyness, for this old man was the thing he loved best in the world.

"You knew all the time?" he asked when he had settled his guest on a seat of moss beside the spring.

"I knew, and I was minded never to tell," was his answer. "You were born too high to find peace; therefore I judged that it was well that you should remain low, seeking only the altitude which may be found in God's service. It was not so decreed, and I bow to a higher wisdom."

44

But if Tobias was embarrassed he was likewise exalted. It appeared to him that his decision had been directly overruled by Omnipotence, and that his pupil had been chosen for a great mission—no less than the raising again of Christ's Church in England. He expounded his hopes in an eager quivering voice. The Church stood for the supremacy of spiritual things, and the King out of a damnable heresy would make it a footstool to the throne. The Church stood for eternal right and eternal justice; if it fell, then selfish ambition and man-made laws would usurp the place of these verities. Upon the strength of the Church depended the unity of Christendom. Weaken that integrity, and Christendom fell asunder into warring and jealous nations, and peace fled for ever from the world. Granted abuses many; these must be set in order by a firm hand. But Pope must be above King, the Church's rights above the secular law, or there could be no Christian unity. God and Mammon, Christ and Caesar—they could not share an equal rule; one must be on top, and if it were Mammon or Caesar then the soul's salvation was ranked lower than the interests of a decaying and transitory world. It was the ancient struggle which began in Eden, and now in England it had come to the testing-point, and Peter was the champion by whose prowess the Church must stand or fall.

The old man's voice ceased to quiver and he became eloquent. Forgotten was the Grecian, the exponent of new ways in learning, the zealous critic of clerical infirmities; he who sat on the moss was a dreamer of the same dreams, an apostle of the same ideals, as those which had filled his novitiate.

Peter said nothing—he spoke little these days. But he remembered the sinking revenues and the grass-grown courts of Oseney, the pedantries of the brethren, the intrigues and quarrels that filled their petty days. He remembered, too, the talk of Lord Avelard. Those who took the Church's side in the quarrel had, few of them, much care for the Church, save as part of that ancient England with which their own privileges were intertwined. None had such a vision as Brother Tobias. Peter had travelled far in these last years from his old

45

preceptor, and had come to think of the Church as no better than a valley of dry bones. Could those bones live again? Were there many with the faith of Tobias, life might still be breathed into them. But were there many? Was there even one? He sighed, for he knew that he was not that one. Disillusionment had gone too far with him, and his youth had been different from that of the old believer at his side.

He sat that August afternoon on his familiar perch above the highway, and his head was like a hive of bees. It had been humming for weeks, and had become no clearer. Outwardly he was a silent and reflective young man, very docile among his elders, but inwardly he was whirlpool and volcano.

He had got his desire, and he was not intoxicated or puffed up or strung to a great purpose; rather he was afraid. That was his trouble—fear—fear of a destiny too big for him. It was not bodily fear, though he had visions now and then of the scaffold, and his own head on that block where once his father's had lain. Rather it was dread of an unfamiliar world in which he had no part.

Lord Avelard's was the face that stuck in his mind—that wise, secret face, those heavily pouched eyes, the gleam in them of an unquestionable pride and an undying hate. He had treated him tenderly as the son of an old friend, and respectfully, as one of whom he would make a king. But Peter knew well that he was no more to Lord Avelard than the sword by his side, a weapon to be used, but in a good cause to be splintered. The man and all his kin, the ancientry of England, were at deadly enmity with this Welshman who had curbed their power, and was bringing in a horde of new men to take their places. They professed to speak in the name of the burdened English commons, but for the poor man he knew they cared not a jot; given the chance they would oppress as heartily as any royal commissioner; was it not they who had begun the ousting of tillage by the new sheep pastures? They claimed to stand for the elder England and its rights, and the old Church, but at heart they stood only for themselves. And he was to be their tool, because he had the blood of the ancient

46

kings in him. He was being trained for his part, so that when he came into the sunlight he should have the air and accomplishments of his rank. Peter sickened, for it seemed to him that he was no more than a dumb ox being made ready for the sacrifice.

They professed to fight in the name of Christ's Church. For a moment a recollection of Tobias's earnest eyes gave this plea a shadow of weight. Sir Ralph, too. That worthy knight, if he could be dragged from his field sports, would fight out of piety rather than concern for his secular privileges. But the rest! And was that Church truly worth fighting for? Had he any desire to set Aristotle and St Thomas back in their stalls? Was he not vowed heart and soul to the new learning which Colet and Erasmus had brought into England, and would not his triumph mean a falling back from these apples of the Hesperides to the dead husks of the Schools? Was it any great matter that the Pope in Rome, who had been but a stepfather to England, should have the last word, and not an anointed king? Was there no need of change in the consecrated fabric? Half the religious houses in England were in decay, no longer lamps to the countryside, but dark burrows where a few old men dragged out weary days.

He tried to recover that glowing picture of the Church of God which he had brought with him from Witney school, when Oseney's towers seemed to be bathed in a heavenly light, and its courts the abode of sages and seraphs. He tried to remember and share in Tobias's vision of Christendom. It was useless. He saw only the crumbling mortar and the warped beams of Oseney cloisters, and heard Brother Lapidarius and Brother Johannes disputing shrilly about the Kidlington dues, over their fried onions at supper. The glamour had passed. How could he champion that in which he had no belief or men who at the best were half-believers?

As he looked at the strip of highway passing through the canyon of the forest he recalled with a shock that evening a month before, when at the end of a day of holiday he had watched the pageant of life on the road beneath him, and longed for an ampler share in it than fell to the lot of a poor

47

clerk of St George's. He had got his wish. He remembered his bitter jealousy in the hot Oxford streets of a sounding world in which he had no part. He was in the way during the next few months of getting a full portion of that world. And he realised that he did not want it, that the fruit was ashes before he put his mouth to it.

Peter tried to be honest with himself. One thing he had gained that could never be taken from him. He was not born of nameless peasants, but of the proudest stock in England. He had in his veins the blood of kings. That was the thought which he hugged to his breast to cheer his despondency. But now he knew that he wanted that knowledge, and nothing more. He did not desire to live in palaces or lead armies. He wanted, with that certainty of his birth to warm his heart, to go back to his old bookish life, or to sink deep among country-folk into the primordial country peace. He had thought himself ambitious, but he had been wrong. His early life had spoiled him for that bustling fever which takes men to high places. He did not like the dust of the arena, and he did not value the laurels.

The opposite slope of the hill towards Elsfield was golden in the afternoon sunlight, and mottled with the shadows of a few summer clouds. He saw the brackeny meadow, and above it the little coppice which hid the Painted Floor. He had a sudden longing to go there. It was his own sanctuary, hallowed with his innermost dreams. It represented a world of grace and simplicity aeons removed from the turbid present. But he did not dare. He must go through with the course to which he was predestined. He had got what he had hungered for, but he felt like a wild thing in a trap. Yet he was Buckingham's son, and there could be no turning back.

A magpie flew down the hollow, but he had turned his head to the hill and did not notice it.

There was a hunt that day in Stowood. At dawn the slowhounds had been out to start the deer and the greyhounds had been unleashed before noon. They had begun by running a knobber in the Shabbington coverts, but in the afternoon the sport had been better, for they had found a stag of ten in the oak wood by Stanton and had hunted him through the jungle of the Wick and the Elsfield dingles, and killed in the hollow east of Beckley. As Peter made his way back to the verderer's lodge he had heard the mort sounded a mile off.

He hastened, for he wished to be indoors before he was seen by any straggling hunter. Such had been Sir Ralph's precise injunction; when the hunt was out he must bide indoors or in cover. But this time he was too late. He heard cries and laughter on all sides; a knot of hunt servants, whom they called Ragged Robins, crossed the road ahead of him at a canter. Worse, he saw two of the hunters coming towards him, whom he could not choose but pass. One was a woman on a black jennet, the other a young man on a great grey gelding. The first wore a riding dress all of white, with a velvet three-cornered cap, and a rich waistcoat of green velvet, the other had the common green habit of the woods, and was not to be distinguished from a yeoman save by the plume and the jewel in his flat cap.

Peter recognised the man first. He was the rider whom he had envied a month ago, first at the gate of Stowood and then in the Oxford street, because he seemed so wholly master of his world. The man had still that mastery. He passed the boy with a lifted hand to acknowledge his greeting, but he scarcely spared him a glance; nor were his eyes set on his companion, but roaming fiercely about as if to seek out matter of interest or quarrel. His weathered face had the flush of recent exertion, but his pale eyes were cool and wary.

These same eyes might well have been on the girl at his side. Peter had a glimpse of ashen gold hair under the white cap, a cheek of a delicate rose above the pale ivory of the uncovered neck. She bowed her head slightly to his salute, and ere she passed on for one instant the heavy lids were raised from her eyes.

Peter stood stock still, but he did not look after them. This was the white girl who had danced at midnight on the Painted Floor. Now he had seen her eyes, and he knew that there was that in them of which the memory would not die.

He continued his way in a stupor of wonderment and uneasy delight. He halted at the spring by the verderer's lodge, and turned at the sound of hoofs behind him. To his amazement it was the girl. She sprang from her horse as lightly as a bird. The jennet, whose bit was flecked with foam, would have nuzzled her shoulder, but she slapped its neck so that it started and stood quivering.

"I am warm with the chase, sir," she said. "I would beg a cup of water."

Peter fetched a bowl from the lodge and filled it at the spring. When he gave it her she sipped a mouthful. Her face was no longer rose-tinted but flushed, and she was smiling.

"Greeting, cousin," she said. "I think you are my cousin Peter from Severn side. I am niece of Sir Ralph Bonamy at Wood Eaton. My name is Sabine Beauforest."

She offered him her cheek to kiss. Then she drew back, and to Peter it appeared that she blushed deeply. She sank in a low curtsey on the moss, took his hand and carried it to her lips.

"I am your Grace's most loyal and devoted servant," she said.

CHAPTER IV

IN WHICH PETER GOES DEEPER
INTO THE GREENWOOD

Two days later came Sir Ralph Bonamy to the verderer's lodge in Stowood. He left his big-boned horse in a servant's charge half a mile from the place, and reached the cottage by a track among brambles and saplings, walking so fast that the sweat beaded his brow. Clearly Sir Ralph's errand was one of speed and secrecy.

"This is but a feeble harbourage," he told Peter. "I thought you were safe here as in the heart of Otmoor, but you have taken the air too freely, my lad. It seems you have been seen, and questions asked, for a youth of your shape and bearing is a scarce thing in the forest."

"There was a lady . . ." Peter began.

"Ay. That was my niece Sabine. If I ever trusted woman with a secret, it would be niece Sabine, for she is close as a hazel-nut. She had word of a cousin from beyond Severn who was sojourning in Stowood, and, being a quick-witted wench, put a name to you when she saw you. It is not Mistress Sabine that troubles me, for I can control my womenkind, but he that rode with her. Did you mark him?"

"A tall fellow with a stiff neck and a proud eye."

"That is he. That is Master Simon. I have naught against the lad, though my sire and his fought like cockerels. They both claimed for their scutcheons the barry nebuly of Blount, and they wrangled as bitterly over that device as Scrope and Grosvenor over the bend d'or. The lad himself is well enough, a good man to horse and hound, a keen eye for a cross-bow, and a strong hand for the sword. But he is not of our faction."

"Is he one of Crummle's men?"

"Nay, he loves Crummle and his rabble as little as I. But he is a King's man, and has been on some errand of the

Welshman's to the northern states of Europe. Also, he has been on voyages with the Bristol merchants, and has picked up some vile heresies in outlandish parts. My news is that he is asking questions about a stranger in Stowood, and when such an one asks he is likely to get an answer. He lives too plaguily near at hand for my peace of mind, for he is Simon Rede of Boarstall—his home is not five miles distant under Muswell hill. Also through his mother he has heired the manor of Headington, and his lawful occasions take him often through this forest. We must find you a safer lodging, friend Peter."

Sir Ralph removed his bonnet, and with his great brown face, and his ancient brown doublet, much soiled at the shoulders by his falcons, he looked not unlike a stump of oak.

"You are not due at Avelard yet awhile, and we must jealously observe my lord's instructions. But Avelard is the other side of Cotswold, and the nearer you are to it the better for my lord's purposes. My advice is that you move west in the company which I shall appoint for you. I had thoughts of sending you to Otmoor among the moormen, but Simon is a moorman himself after a fashion, and Boarstall is on the edge of the meres. You will be safer in Wychwood and Cotswold."

"I was bred there," said Peter. "There are many living who remember me. Mother Sweetbread . . ."

"Why, so much the better. Peter Pentecost is dead and masses sung for his soul, but Mother Sweetbread will not have forgot him and will welcome her fosterchild restored to her, whatever name he may choose to bear. She has all along been privy to your tale, for she was a serving-woman of your mother's. There you will be safe from the sharp eyes of Simon Rede, and the coverts of Wychwood are deeper than the coverts of Shabbington. But to make security certain I have trysted with one who will accompany you and never leave your side till you are safe at Avelard. He will be here before sunset to start with you, and 'twere well that you keep yourself privy till then."

"Who is this guide?" Peter asked.

Sir Ralph smiled and scratched his head. "That were hard

to say. The name he will give you is Solomon Darking, but he has many others. He is of the old race of these parts, the squat dark folk we call the Wens, who were here a thousand years before the Romans. He is a true man and a wise man, and if he seems strange to you, remember that wisdom is apt to cohabit with oddity. There are mannikins plenty who have seen something of oddity in *me*. This I can tell you. If I were fleeing for my life it is to Solomon Darking I would go, for he could call the beasts of the field and the birds of the air to my defence. Farewell and God bless you. I must get me to Beckley, where there is a gyr-falcon training for me at the Upper Lodge."

Off rode Sir Ralph, leaving Peter to an afternoon's meditation in the deeps of an oak coppice. Two days had worked a miracle in his mood. He was no more the doubter, proud only of his rediscovered race, but shrinking from the hazards and heartbreaks of the career into which others would thrust him. He now longed for it. He longed to set his foot on the wildest road so long as it led him to the hill-top. For he had seen someone for whom a hill-top was the only dwelling.

The girl, of whom he had had two glimpses in the afternoon sunshine of Stowood, whom he had seen dancing at midnight on the Painted Floor under the moon, had sent warmth and light running through a world that had seemed all frost and shadow. He had never since his childhood looked a woman full in the face. He had been aware of them as mysterious beings, sometimes old and witch-like, sometimes young and shining, but always to be shunned by him who would serve God and save his soul. Yet he had had his own fancies. He had seen in imagination the slim girls in Theocritus dancing to the shepherd's pipes, and he had exulted in the proud tales of old queens, for whom men had counted the world well lost. So he had come in time to make for himself pictures of a woman who should be fair as Helen and gentle as the Virgin Mother, pictures as vague as gossamer, for they rested on no base of human meaning. Sometimes indeed, when the sun was bright of a spring morning, his visions had taken a simple form, and he had felt strange stirrings of the blood, which he had not resisted as sin—which he had not even questioned, for they seemed as innocent as thirst or hunger.

But now, suddenly, all his imaginings and desires had become centred on a living woman. She had first come to him on his own Painted Floor, a fellow discoverer. Two days ago she had taken his hand and called him liege-lord. Surely in this there was a divine foreordering. What if the two of them were predestined to tread the road together? That road which seemed so grim would be different indeed if that white girl were by his side, and if at the end of it he could make her a queen. For a queen she was born to be; nothing less would content him, or be worthy of her magnificence. Peter, deep in the oak scrub, felt a wild hunger to be up and doing, to be treading the path to greatness which others had marked out for him. It was a fine thing to be Buckingham and Bohun; it would be a finer to lay England at Sabine Beauforest's feet. He thought of her with none of the tremors of a lover. He did not ask her beauty for his arms, but that principalities and powers should rest in her slender hands. He was in that first stage of love when it is divinely unselfish.

When the shadows began to lengthen he returned to the verderer's lodge, dressed himself for a long journey, and put a few simple belongings into his wallet. He was to be still in the greenwood, but a little nearer to the hour and the place where he would begin his new life.

Presently out of the thicket came an urchin. John of Milton was gone to Bernwood, so Peter was the only living thing in the place for the messenger to accost. The boy was about twelve years of age, squat and freckled and frog-like. He spoke in a tongue which was hard to comprehend, but his intention was made clear by a jerked thumb. He had been sent to lead him somewhither to someone. Peter picked up his wallet and followed.

The urchin led him, at a pace surprising in one so small, past the granges of Woodperry, and downhill to where a long tongue of Otmoor crept into the forest. After that the road lay in the dry belt of tall reeds along the edge of the marsh, till the slopes of Beckley had been turned and the rise of Wood

Eaton hill was visible, and the hovels of Noke, smoking for the evening meal, could be seen over pools now reddened with the sunset. Then they turned north, along a causeway which brought them to the little river Ray, which they crossed by a plank under the hamlet of Oddington, where geese were making a great clamour in the twilight. Once again they were in forest country, a long rough hillside full of hollows and thickets. Into one of these they plunged, and after a rough passage came into an open space in the heart of it, where a fire burned. There the urchin disappeared, and Peter found himself confronted with a man who rose from tending a pot and doffed his cap.

The man was short and burly in figure, his dress was that of a forester, and he carried a cross-bow slung on his back and a long hunting knife in his girdle. His face was sharp and yellow, like one who had suffered from the moor-ill, and a mop of thick black hair fell to his shoulders. His eyes, seen in the firelight, were like a dog's, large and sombre and steadfast.

"I seek Solomon Darking," said Peter.

"He is before you, my lord," was the answer. "He that you wot of has spoken to me. I make you welcome to a hunter's hearth. You will eat and then you will sleep, but dawn must find us many miles on our way. Sit ye down. No grace is needed for food eaten under the sky."

He made a seat for Peter on a heap of fern, and served him with stew from the pot on a little iron platter. He did not eat himself, but waited upon his guest like a servant. When Peter had finished he cleansed the platter in a well of water and made his own meal. The same water was the sole beverage. Not a word was spoken; the only sounds were the crumbling of the fire's ashes, the babble of a brook that ran from the well, and—very far off—the chiming of bells from Islip church. When he had finished the forester again washed the platter, cut some swathes of bracken and made two beds, and stamped out the embers. He stood listening, like a dog at fault, for a moment, and then, like a dog, shook his head and stretched himself.

55

"To your couch, my lord," he said. "You have four hours to sleep ere we take the road. A wise man feeds full and sleeps deep when he has the chance, for it may be long before that chance returns."

Peter asked no questions. There was something about this man which made them needless. He had the sense of being shepherded by wise hands, and laid his head on the bracken as confidently as he had ever laid it on his pallet in the Oxford attic.

He was awakened while it was still night, though there was a thin bar of grey light on the eastern horizon. Darking stood ready for the road, and Peter, rubbing sleepy eyes, did up the belt of his doublet and prepared to follow him. There was a thick dew on the ground, and Peter was soon soaked to the knees; also the air blew cold as if rain was coming from the west. Come it did before they had crossed the Cherwell, and Peter, empty and chilly, felt his spirits sink. Soon, however, he found that he had so much ado to keep up with his companion's vigour that he had no leisure to despond. Darking moved at a prodigious pace, so fast that Peter, who was half a foot taller and had longer legs, was compelled often to trot to keep abreast of his stride. Moreover, the road chosen seemed to be the worst conceivable. Anything like a path was shunned, even when it bent in the right direction. Open meadowland, the bare crest of a hill, a broad woodland glade were avoided as if an enemy's arrows commanded them. Darking did not even take advantage of the fords, for streams were crossed at their deepest and miriest. Presently, as they toiled through a thicket of oak saplings, the sun came out. Darking sniffed the air. "The rain has gone," he said. "It will be fine till sunset. We are nearing our breakfast."

They came to an outcrop of rock rising above the woods and thatched with wild berries. From a distance its bald head could not be distinguished from the oak tops; it looked like a patch of dead wood in the coppice. There was a hollow on the left, and this had been roofed with timber, now so lichened as to be indistinguishable from stone. The result was a narrow hut, discernible only at the closest quarters by one who knew

56

what he sought. In front of it a blackened angle of the rock showed where a fire had once burned.

Darking brought some dry billets and twigs from the hut, and laid and lit a fire. From the hut, too, he fetched a pan, some collops of deer's meat, a lump of deer fat, a loaf of rye-bread, and a leatherjack of ale.

"Strip," he commanded. "You will have ague in your young bones if you sit in a damp shirt. For me, I am so full of it that a wetting more or less does not concern me."

So Peter, stripped to the buff, sat warming his toes at the fire, while the meat sizzled in the pan, and his clothes, stretched on the rock face, dried fast in the sun.

"You have led me by a hard road," he said, when Darking filled his platter. "Why need it have been so secret? Are you a man of many enemies?"

Darking's gravity did not respond to the smile on the young man's face.

"It is well to be secret in such times," he said. "Households are divided within themselves and sons are set against fathers. No man knows his enemy. He who would live at peace must take the byways. I was told that it is most needful that you, my lord, keep out of men's sight yet awhile; therefore, while you are in my company we will court no questions."

He broke off and pointed to the south, where a flock of birds was wheeling. He stared till they were out of sight, and when he spoke his voice was solemn.

"That is the second portent within the week. Last Thursday in Horton spinney I saw a bramble with both ends growing in the ground. Know you the meaning of that? It is the noose the Devil makes for his next hunting. And now, behold these birds."

"They are only curlews," said Peter.

"Curlews and whimbrels—young birds bred on the hills. But what do they here in the tail of August? Two months ago they should have been on the salt beaches. Remember, the long beaks are no common fowls, but have foreknowledge of many things, and their lives are full as long as a man's. They tarry inland to see what they shall see. The old wives say that a curlew after June spells foul weather. Foul weather comes, not in the heavens, but in the ways of men. Therefore it were wise to go secretly."

They crossed the little streams of Dorn and Glyme and came out of the forest to wide downs of grass and furze. Bearing northward, they still ascended, Darking in the bare places showing as much precaution as if he were stalking a winter's hind. They never passed a crest except on their bellies, or crossed an open slope without a long reconnaissance. They had seen no dwelling or sign of man, but he behaved as if he were in a populous land. At last they reached a point which seemed the highest ground in the neighbourhood, for on every side the country fell away into valleys.

Peter recognised his whereabouts. He was on the skirts of Wychwood, the other side from where he had dwelt as a child, and so to him unknown country. Away to the south he saw the lift of the Leafield ridge, and that gave him his bearings. All about them the forest flowed in a dark tide, so that it seemed to cover the whole visible earth. The little clearings round the hamlets were not seen, and the only open patches were the marshy stream-sides far below, which showed bright green among the dun and olive of the woods. It seemed a country as empty of man as when primeval beasts had trumpeted in the glades and wallowed in the sloughs. And yet their journey had been as stealthy as if enemies had lurked in every acre.

"There are no folk left hereabouts," Peter said. "Why have we made so secret a business of this morning?"

"The hamlets are emptying, but the woods are filling," said Darking.

"But we have seen no sign of humanity since sunrise."

"*You* have not, my lord, but you have not the ears and eyes for the forest. I have seen and heard many."

Peter stared.

"There were charcoal-burners in the coppice above the Dorn. There was a camp of Egyptians a mile on—I smelt their cooking—a fawn, I think. A man with a long-bow was in the thicket this side of Glyme. I saw two of the Ditchley foresters pass on our left but an hour ago, and there was a horseman in a mighty hurry on the road from Woodstock to Enstone. Also the prickers were out among the hazels beyond Wootton. One way and another I have seen a score of mortals since we broke our fast."

"They did not observe us?"

"Of that I am certain." A slow smile lit his sallow face.

"But I have seen no smoke from cot or village," said Peter.

"You will see none. There are few cots, save here and there a forester's lodge, and scarcely a village. The land has become all wood and sheep-walks."

"And the people?"

"Dead or wanderers. England is full of broken and master-less men this day. They have gone under the ground, finding life too hard above it. Let us press on, and I will show you something."

They came presently to an upland meadow whence rose one of the feeders of Evenlode. Once there had been a village here, for there were the ruins of a score of mud-and-wattle huts. The baulks of the common field were still plain; likewise orchards running wild, and that rank growth of weeds which means abandoned ploughland. In one corner by the brook stood a heap of stones, which at first sight Peter took for a quarry. Darking stood for a little gazing at the scene.

"When I was a child," he said, "this was a thriving village. Bourtree was its name—Bourtree in the Bush, men called it. Half a hundred souls had their dwelling here, and it was noted over all the land for its honey. You must know that there was a miracle wrought here. Once upon a time a fellow stole a fragment of the Host that he might work magic by it, and set it by his hives to improve their yield. But the bees, the little pious ones, built round it a church all of wax, with altar and windows and steeple, to protect its holiness. You have heard the tale?"

Peter nodded. He had told the story to the novices at Oseney.

"Behold Bourtree today! The church is a heap of stones, most of which they have carried off to help build the new great church at Charlbury. What was once tillage and orchard is now sheep-walks for the graziers. The men and women that dwelled here are most of them under the sod, and if any still live, they are nameless folk drifting like blown leaves in the shadows."

He lifted his head and looked Peter full in the face with his odd melancholy eyes. "Much of old England is gone to ground, my lord," he said. "Keep that in your mind and ponder on it, for it may deeply concern your own business."

"I have brought you to a Pisgah-sight," said Darking an hour later. "The land is your own, so long as I am with you, and you are as secure as a badger in its earth. What are your commands, my lord? I can hide you so snugly till the summons comes that all the King's armies searching daily for ten years would not find you. But that might be but a dismal life for youth in sunshiny weather. Or . . ." He paused.

"Or?" Peter repeated.

"Or I can take you with me a little way underground—among the masterless folk who will soon be half our people. I ask no questions, my lord, but he at Wood Eaton warned me that you were a precious piece of goods that mattered much for the welfare of England. The gentles play their high games and the noise of them fills the world, but in the end it is the simple who decree the issue. Would you sojourn for awhile among the simple?"

"I was bred among them," said Peter. "I would first see my foster-mother, the widow Sweetbread, who lives below Leafield on the forest edge. Do you know the place?"

"Nay, then, since you are Mother Sweetbread's fosterling, you have already the right of entry among all the forest people. Well I know her. Her goodman, Robin Sweetbread, was my trusty comrade." He seemed suddenly to look at Peter with changed eyes, as if a special password to his confidence had been spoken.

When they took the road again, so as to ford Evenlode and come down the Windrush side, Darking, while still wary in choosing obscure paths, was no longer silent. Friendliness now

60

mingled with his dignity. He spoke to Peter like a respectful kinsman. He was quick to point out, here a derelict farm, there a ruined village, among the grassy spaces of the hills.

"'Twas the little granges first, and then the hamlets, and now, if all tales be true, 'twill soon be the proud abbeys. Nought of man's work in England is steadfast, not even the houses he has built for God. What sends an earl to the block sends a churl to the gallows' hill, and the churl's wife and children to eat nettles by the wayside. None is safe today save those who do not raise their noses above the covert, and the numbers in the covert grow fast."

"Are you among them?" Peter asked.

Darking lifted his head proudly. "No man can harm us of the old England and the older blood. Kings and nobles and priests may pass, but we remain. Ours is the *fallentis semita vitae*, which is beyond the ken of the great."

Peter cried out in surprise: "Have you the Latin?"

"A tag or two," and a smile wrinkled the sallow cheeks.

Mother Sweetbread welcomed Peter as one recovered from the dead. She strained him to her breast and wept over him. "They said you were drowned," she crooned. "Brother Tobias spoke a word in my ear that you still lived, but he warned me that I should never see you more. And now you come stepping like Robin Hood out of the woods, clad as a proper man and no clerk. Son Peterkin, you are now a man indeed."

She had been a tall woman till age had bent her, and she had none of the deformity of the old peasant, crippled with ague and incessant toil. Her petticoat was coarse but spotless, and on her head was the snowy curch which was Peter's clearest memory of his childhood. Out of her high-coloured old face looked two eyes as black as sloes. Merry eyes they still were, for mirth and she had never been strangers.

She prepared food for him, those dishes which she remembered him liking as a child, and set before him a jug of her own cowslip wine, heady as ale and scented of flowers. But she did not sit with him at meat, nor did Darking; they waited on him till he had finished, and then ate their meal.

Her eyes followed him hungrily, and now and then she would stroke his sleeve with her old fingers.

"You are still the lad I nurtured," she said; "but you are grown too mighty for this nest. I thought you were an eyass with clipped wings that would never fly far from me. That was the hope of Brother Tobias, too, but God has ordered it otherwise. Once you favoured your mother, and I took it for a happy omen, but now, childing, I see your sire in you. You have that kindly sullenness in the eyes which men spoke of in his grace. Heaven send you a happier fate." And she crossed herself and muttered a prayer.

"How long?" she asked of Darking. "Not till St Martin's day? You have come among your own folk, Peterkin, and we must make you ready for your flight. You are safe among us, and maybe we can do something ere that day to help your fortunes. You will soar out of our ken, but we can make certain that, if your wings tire, there is cover where you can clap down."

Darking took him to a hut in Wychwood in a patch of ashes above St Cyther's well, which had been used sometimes to give a night's shelter when the hunt was up in that quarter of the forest. There they made their dwelling, and it was as lonely as a hill-top, the new ranger not having yet taken up his office, and every verderer and forester being under the spell of Darking's strange authority. There Darking took Peter in hand and taught him much not commonly known by those who have in their veins the blood of kings. The boy was country bred, and started with some equipment of wild lore, but presently he understood that he had dwelt hitherto only in the porches of nature, and that he was now being led into the inner chambers. "Have patience, my lord," said his tutor. "Great folk live and move high above the common world. But now and then they come to ground, and it is well to have a notion of that ground where you must creep and cannot fly."

So Peter learned the ways of weather—what was portended by rooks flying in line, and mallards roosting in the trees, and herons leaving the streams for the forest pools. He learned to read what haze signified at dawn and sunset, and to smell distant rain. He was taught the call and cry of all the things that ran and flew, to imitate a stoat's whistle and a badger's grunt, the melancholy trumpet of the bittern, and the broken flageolet of the redshank, the buzzard's mewing and the grey crow's scolding. Presently he knew the mark of every pad in mud or herbage and the claws that patterned the streamside shingle. Something he learned too of the medicinal lore of the woods, how to make febrifuge and salve, what herbs sweetened foul water, or quieted hunger, or put a wakeful man to sleep. He was a ready pupil at this lore, for it gave his mind something to work on in those weeks of idleness. Also it seemed to marry the new strange world into which he was entered with that old world he was forsaking. It was pleasant to think that he, who might yet be a king, should go first to school with the ancient simplicities of earth.

Darking gave him another kind of tutoring. He made him discard the clothes he had worn, and put on the rough garb of a lesser forester. And then, enjoining on him to hold his peace at all costs, he took him far and wide through the neighbourhood. They visited the fairs in the little towns and sat in alehouses listening to the talk of peasants. They joined themselves to wool convoys on the highroad, and attended the great wool markets in Northleach and Burford and Campden. One day they would eat their bread and cheese in a smithy, the next in a parson's kitchen, and the third day in a cornfield with the harvesters at their noonday rest. Darking seemed to have a passport to any society, some word which set people at their ease and opened their mouths.

"You are school-bred and abbey-bred," he said. "It were well that you should learn of the common folk on whose shoulders the world rests. If you are to be Jack's master, it is time to know a little of Jack."

Peter, with his memory full of pinched faces and furtive talk of oppression, and eyes that spoke more eloquently than words, shivered a little.

"What has become of merry England?" he asked. "It is a sad world you have shown me, and a dark. Most men are groping and suffering."

63

"There is small merriment nowadays," he was told, "save among the gilded folk at the top, and those who have sunk deep down into the coverts. But it is a world very ripe for change."

Mother Sweetbread favoured a different kind of preparation. She was in her way a devout woman, but she believed in an innocent magic outside the sanctities of the Church. Like all peasants, she was a storehouse of traditional lore which had descended from days long before Christ came to England. Her special knowledge was of herbs and simples, some for medicines, but most for spells, since there was a motley of vague beings to be placated if one would live at ease. During Peter's childhood she had practised many harmless rites on his behalf. She had tried to foresee his future by fire and running water. The way of it was that you flung a blazing wisp of straw into a stream at midnight of a Thursday and repeated a benedicite and the rune "*Fire burn, water run, grass grow, sea flow*," and then finished with a paternoster. But she had gained nothing that way except a fit of ague. She had striven to ward off evil from her charge by sticking a knife into a plant of helenium at sunrise on Michaelmas Day, in the hope that the proper demon would appear, whom at that hour and with such preparation she would have power to command. But no spirit, good or bad, had made himself visible, though the awaiting of him had been a business requiring all her courage. But with her herbs she had been more fortunate. She had mixed the juices of dill and vervain and St John's wort, and it was to this application, accompanied by the appropriate words, that she attributed Peter's notable freedom from childish ailments.

Now she must go further, and the next step was for a true initiate. There was a woman lived at Shipton-under-the-Forest, Madge Littlemouse her name, who was reported to be learned in the old wisdom, and yet whose doings had left her on the sheltered side of the law and the Church. Indeed, there was no breath of discredit against Madge; she never dried up the ewes or the kine with the charm—

"Hare's milk and mare's milk,
And all the beasts that bears milk,
Come ye to me . . ."

or brought pains and death to her neighbours with nigromantic images, or fasted the Black Fast against her ill-wishers. She was a meek-faced old woman, whose garden was full of bee-hives, and to her bees she would talk as to a gossip. For certain, there was no such honey as hers in all Cotswold; but there were those who said that her bees were more than bees, that they were familiar spirits. The miller of Chadlington had found her asleep one summer noon, and had seen bees issuing from her mouth and ears, so that, being then in liquor, he had been instantly sobered, and had sworn off ale for a twelvemonth. But Madge's repute was not hurt by this tale. Beyond doubt she had power, but her magic was white and unhurtful—no trafficking with the horrid relics of dead men and foul beasts, no blasphemous juggling with the sacred chrism or the more sacred Host, but clean invocations to decent spirits, who might reasonably be called good angels.

This potent ally Mother Sweetbread desired to enlist on Peter's behalf, and she especially desired that Madge should make him a ring, the possession of which would attach to him a friendly guardian spirit. So she managed to obtain during Peter's visits some oddments of his belongings—a lock of his hair, the paring of a nail, a fragment of linen which had been worn next his body—indispensable things without which Madge would be helpless. The ring must be of silver, so for the purpose she sacrificed a precious buckle, the gift of her old mistress: and she offered Madge as her fee a gold noble out of her small hoard.

She spoke to Darking of what she had done. He was not less superstitious than she, but he shook his head.

"Remember what befell the lad's father," he said. "The beginning of the lord duke's calamities was the prophecy that he would be King. 'Twas one Nicholas, a Carthusian monk, that made it. There are some things too high for mortal men to meddle with."

"Nay, Solomon," she said. "I would not tempt God by such meddling. But I would make him a ring such as the great Cardinal had, which will assure his fortune and keep a good angel by his side."

"What sort of angel had Wolsey?" Darking cried. "I have heard of that ring. It brought a devil named Andrew Malchus to do his will, and all men know the consequence."

"This shall be decently and piously made, with prayers and paternosters," she pleaded.

But Darking still shook his head. "Many a man has sought to secure a good spirit, and has found a fiend answer his call. I like not this dabbling in forbidden things. But go your ways, mother, for you are wiser than me. I will tell you how you can best benefit my lord. Get Goody Littlemouse to tell him where treasure is hid and you will make his fortune secure. For, hark you, mother, my lord has nothing now but his name and his birth. He has no great estate to milk or vassals to arm; therefore he is but a tool in the hands of those who seek his interest just in so far as it serves their own. Give him his own privy purse, and, so it be large enough, he will be able to carry his head high."

The old woman pondered the words, which had been spoken lightly enough, and from a chance remark or two later it appeared that she had taken counsel with Madge Littlemouse on the matter. One day Peter and Darking were overtaken by a violent thunderstorm which split a great oak before their eyes. Darking laughed, as he wrung the wet from his cap. "Mother Sweetbread is busy about treasure-trove and is raising foul weather."

But one night he talked for a long time apart with the old woman.

"The hour of the summons is near," he said, "and soon the lad will be out of our care. I have taught him where and how to find refuge, if all else fails. Presently he will be set on a pinnacle, but a pinnacle is poor footing, and he will be alone. I am for showing him where to find allies, besides those great ones who will companion him. There will be a gathering soon of them we know of. I saw Catti the Welshman yesterday on the Burford road, and old John Naps was at the Rood Fair on Barton Heath, and there is word of Pennyfarthing in the Cocking dingle."

Mother Sweetbread opened her eyes wide.

"You would not take my lord into such company?"

"I would take my lord to any company that can strengthen his hands. Listen, mother. England is all of a turmoil nowadays, and no man knows which is the true road or who are his friends. There is dispeace in the King's Court, and disorder in the Council, and disquiet in Parliament, and everywhere divided minds. But far down below there are those who know their own purposes and hang together like a nest of wasps. I would take my lord to the only part of England that is stable."

CHAPTER V

THE PARLIAMENT OF BEGGARS

The first frosts began with October, and after the hot September suns the leaves yellowed fast and hung loose, waiting for the Martinmas gales. One evening Darking and Peter left their hut in Wychwood and took the road up Evenlode, while the forest behind them was a riot of colour, and the waterside meadows lay yellow as corn in the sunset. Both were shabbily dressed, Mother Sweetbread having obtained for the boy a suit which her husband had worn for twenty years at the winter woodcutting.

"You are my prentice for the nonce," said Darking, "and you have no name save Solomon's Hob."

"Where are we bent?" Peter asked.

"To Kingham Waste. There is a place in the heart of it called Little Greece, where we shall meet with company. You must not open your lips, but follow me and gape like a bumpkin."

"What company?"

"Strange company, my lord. I have told you that half England has gone to ground. This night you will see some of those who hold rule among the vagabonds. Little Greece is no common bowsing-ken. All trades have their laws and disciplines, and not less that which is the trade of idleness. You would think, maybe, that the limping rogue you meet on the road obeyed no law but his own desires and necessities. Yet you would be wrong. He is under as strict rules as any soldier of an army. Tonight you will see some of his officers. Twice a year they meet to take counsel upon matters that affect their living, and in this beggars' parliament you will see the men who govern all the vagabondage between Thames in the south and Severn in the west and Trent in the north."

"Tell me of this strange world. I know nothing of it."

"You could not. They keep wide of the King's forests for the most part, though I have known a batch of wild rogues raid the deer. Nor will you find them often in the Oxford streets or the lanes about Oseney. But elsewhere they are thicker than crows on a March ploughland."

Peter asked the origin of so great a multitude.

"The poor we have always with us," Darking quoted. "There have always been the unfortunates whose craft has failed them, or who have come to odds with the King's laws, and find it convenient to have no fixed habitation. But in the last fifty years there has been a breaking up of England, so that honest fellows, with generations behind them of laborious forbears, have not known where to turn to for the next crust. Such are now on the roads. Also the end of the wars both here and abroad has deprived many soldiers of a trade. Then there are those who take willingly to the life because of the restlessness of their bones or the corruption of their hearts. Every year sees a fresh hatch-out. The King's rabbling of the small religious houses has sent a new swarm abroad, and trebled the number of patricoes. Lastly, there are some who take the wallet for a deeper purpose at the bidding of great men. You must know that every vagabond must have his billet or licence duly signed and sealed, else he will be taken and whipped at the next town-end. Such billets can be granted by anyone in authority—justice, or knight, or noble, or church-man—and what easier for a great one, who wishes to know the truth of what is happening in England, than to equip his own men with such licences and send them forth to glean tidings? The device has not been practised by the King's Council, but some, who like not the King, have used it freely. There are many of my Lord Avelard's intelligencers abroad with the beggars."

"Tell me of these beggars," said Peter. "Are there several kinds of them?"

"As many as there are kinds of fly hatched out in summer. They have their own names, and their own manner of speech and way of business, and if I were to recite them all I should not have done by the morrow's dawn. There are those known

69

by the misdeeds they favour. Such are the rufflers and the rogues and the highwaymen, who use violence, and the coney-catchers and cozeners and hookers and horsepriggers and fraters who use guile. Some have their trades, like the tinkers and pedlars, the jugglers and the minstrels, the crowders and fortune-tellers and bearwards. Some are plain beggars; others practise different arts to excite compassion, as the palliards, who make sores on their bodies with ratsbane and spearwort—the abrahams who sham madness, and the cranks who counterfeit the falling sickness—the dommerers who are deaf and dumb, and the whipjacks who tell a lamentable tale of shipwreck at sea or have a father or brother made captive by the Turk. There are more varieties of calling in vagabondage than in honest trade, and more ranks and classes than at the King's Court. And at the top of all are those whom they call the Upright Men, that are their captains and justices. Them we shall meet at Little Greece."

"But for what purpose?" Peter asked.

"For many. These rogues have their ears very near the ground and hear much which other men miss. They have knowledge which the King's Council could not buy for gold. Also they are strong and secret, and throng as a swarm of bees, and they cover all England. If we win their favour they may come to your aid when you are hard beset and your great friends are powerless."

"Why should they bear good-will to me?"

"They will know nothing of you. To them this night you will be my servant, a gaping youth out of the forest. You will watch my movements and follow them like a lackey, and for the Lord's sake utter not one word, for your speech would betray you. A man's life would not be worth a moment's purchase if he broke in unwarranted on the Beggars' Parliament. In half an hour his throat would be slit and he would be six foot deep under a farm midden. For me, I have a name among them and certain credentials. They will not harm me and may even do as I desire. But for you, my lord, safety lies only in an owlish silence."

They were now traversing a flat moorish space where

narrow tracks ran through thickets of furze and blackthorn. Their goal seemed to be near, for Darking instructed Peter in a low voice.

"The captain of this parliament is one they call John Naps, an old whipjack who is in some sort the owner of Little Greece. No man gave him the title, but there is none who would dispute it with him. He is an ancient merry villain, and a kind of king among the vagabonds between Cotswold and Chiltern. For the rest I can tell you some who will be there. Mark well a little, black-eyed, beetle-browed ruffian with a long knife at his belt. That is him they call Catti the Welshman, whose special business is to rob travellers who go from Thames to Severn. He bears a woman's name, but he is not womanish. None knows so well every road and track and horse-path in south England. There will be a fat man whose jaws never stop munching so that he seems to be chewing the cud like kine. That will be Timothy Pennyfarthing, otherwise True Timothy, who is master of the palliards, that make their bodies foul with sores and cry their ailments at every doorstep. He is a longheaded rogue with a shrewd judgment, and, except in his trade, a certain honesty. Likewise, there will be Henry Hooker, chief of them that thieve with a crooked stick and prig the goodman's shirt out of an open window. He has special authority Warwick and Northampton way. Flatsole will be there beyond doubt—a lean man with a poxed face and eyes of different colours. He is a horse-thief to trade, and knows every fair and feast and market south of Trent. Do not engage him in sword-play, my lord, for Flatsole has been a soldier, and no court gallant can match him at the cut-and-thrust business. The rogue is well-mannered, too, for he is the by-blow of some noble house. Also, you will meet one Pierce the Piper, who travels farther afield than the rest, for he has carried his cow's bladder benorth of Tweed among the wild Scots and west of Severn among the wild Welsh. He is a scholar of a sort—some say of Balliol College—and when he is well drunk, can make music to wring a man's heart. None of the raggle-taggle following will be there, and the doxies will be left behind, for this is a high occasion for the rogues, and they are as solemn about it as a mayor and aldermen. Walk warily now, for we are nearing their sentinels."

A pole was suddenly thrust from the covert athwart Darking's breast, and he stopped in his tracks. A voice said something in what seemed to Peter a strange tongue, and Darking replied with like gibberish. The pole was withdrawn, and from the thicket came words which seemed to be a direction.

They were now in what was little better than a maze. High walls of furze and bramble and hazel, matted with wild clematis, stood up on each hand, and the path was no wider than a rabbit track. Also it twined and zigzagged and split into baffling sideways, so that more than once Darking hesitated. A second pole across his chest and another colloquy in jargon gave him the clue, and after a little the path widened, and the jungle was varied with patches of heath and now and then a tall tree. The moon had risen, and instead of a green dusk there was now an alternation of silver spears and inky shadows.

Three times more the travellers were brought to a halt and a password exchanged. The last time the sentinel himself emerged from the scrub—a slim boy whom Peter at first took for a girl. He made a sign by drawing his forefinger down the right side of his nose and then cupping his right ear, and Darking replied with a gesture which seemed to satisfy him. The boy looked sharply at Peter, and Darking explained his presence in words not one of which Peter understood. Then the boy preceded them and led the way to a space where the thicket ceased altogether. There was a paddock with several horses at graze and several more tethered to the paling; there was a slender stream issuing from a broad pool which was indeed one of the springs of Evenlode; there was a grove of tall ashes and oaks, and in the midst of it the dark loom of a dwelling. No light showed, but as they rounded the end of it the sound of human speech came from within. The place seemed once to have been the tithe barn of a manor, for fallen stones and broken walls showed all around. At the door stood two sentinels, tall men in beggars' rags, each with a curtal-axe held at guard.

72

Here again there was a halt and a parley. The boy who had guided them spoke in whispers with the sentries, and then entered the barn, diving beneath a thick curtain. He was absent for a minute or two, and when he returned he seemed to look at Darking with a new respect. He said something in his queer jargon.

"They have finished their council," Darking whispered to Peter, "and are about to feed. We are bidden to the banquet."

The boy raised the flap of the frieze curtain and they entered the barn. The place was dimly lit, smoky and very hot, for a fire had been made on the stone floor, and there were no windows except the vent in the roof. At the far end a covered lantern had a pedestal formed of two barrels on end, and another stood on a table on the near side of the fire, a table which appeared to be loaded with dishes and flagons. Ten men sat round the fire, sprawling on straw-stuffed cushions, their legs outstretched to the blaze. Each of them had a platter and a mug, and two ancient crones were acting as servitors, carrying food and drink from the table to the feasters.

Peter was sharp-set with his long walk in the chill evening, and his eye went first to the laden table. Never had he seen such a riot of coarse dainties. There were great dishes of tripe and cow-heel. One earthenware platter was loaded with pig-food, another with white and black puddings, while a third bore a gigantic haggis. A mighty copper kettle was full of a broth which from its odour had been made of various sorts of game, while another bubbled with hasty pudding. But the chief dish was a huge pie which contained the mortal remains of one of the King's deer. There was a plate of pippins to give refinement to the feast, and one of almonds and raisins. The drink was ale in blackjacks, no thin and common brew, but strong October, heady and ripe and dark as bog water. The ancient women hobbled between the table and the circle, replenishing platters and mugs, for the company seemed to have been starved for months, so resolutely did they set about the duty of feeding.

Suspicion woke in the eyes of several as the two strangers

73

entered, but a deep voice beyond the fire bade them welcome. It came from a little old man, who in spite of the heat of the barn wore a cloak; since, unlike the rest, he squatted instead of sprawled, he looked like a broody hen. He had a ragged white beard, and white hair which fell on each side of lean mahogany cheeks. His nose was long and his weak eyes seemed to be always weeping, but there was comedy at the corners of his mouth. The voice was magnificent—rich, fruity, sentimental, cajoling, capable of an infinity of gross humour and grosser pathos.

Peter looked with interest at the captain of the vagabonds of the south. John Naps, who at the first sight seemed only comic, improved at the second. The man had a magisterial eye, and in his voice was that complete self-confidence which is the best endowment for a leader. He cried out a welcome to Darking with his mouth full of pasty, but his jargon was beyond Peter's comprehension. He made room for him at his right hand, and Peter sat modestly behind, where he was served presently with broth and ale.

There were ten men at meat, but only nine in the circle, for one sat apart out of the glare of the fire. Peter, as he satisfied his hunger, let his eye rove among his neighbours. Some he made out at once from Darking's description. There was True Timothy, the king of the palliards, a vast browsing figure, whose paunch stuck out beyond the others like a flying buttress. Timothy was very serious about the business of eating, and gobbets of pasty were shovelled into his cavernous mouth as fuel goes into a furnace. No doubt either about Catti the highway robber. The Welshman was as Darking had said, small, swarthy, beetle-browed, and the haft of his long whinger, as he sat, was almost at his chin. Yet it was not a face to inspire fear, for, as it lifted and Peter could see the mouth and eyes, there seemed something elfin and mirthful in it. He remembered tales of this Catti, which had penetrated to Oxford taverns—how he robbed especially rich men and usurers and the King's servants, but spared the Church and the poor—a shabby Robin Hood with, instead of the green-wood humour, something of the wildness and magnanimity of his own hills. Flatsole, too, he made out, from his meagreness and pitted cheeks. The horse-thief did not sprawl but sat lightly, as if ready to spring to his feet at a word of danger. The face was turned from Peter, so he could not see the twy-coloured eyes. A by-blow of some noble house, Darking had said; and for certain there seemed to be breeding in the slim neck and the graceful poise of his head. The man had swordsman written in every line of him.

But the one that held Peter's eyes was he who sat outside the circle. This must be the piper Pierce, for, though his pipes were not there, a rude boxwood fiddle lay over his knees. He appeared to have no appetite for food, for a wedge of pie lay untouched beside him, but his tankard was constantly being replenished. The rest of the company had sober garments, like those of a small farmer on market day, but Pierce wore a jerkin of faded red and blue, and atop of his shock of black hair was set a damaged hat of black felt bound with a riband of the same colours. The hair fell over his brow and almost hid his deep-set eyes. His cheeks were shrunken and Isabella-coloured, he had no beard, and his lips were perpetually parted in something between a pout and a sneer. Peter remembered that, according to Darking, this man had once been a scholar, and decided that he looked more like a warlock.

Suddenly Pierce lifted his fiddle and began to play, accompanying the music with a voice of a curious softness and power. The crackle of the fire and the steady munching of human jaws seemed to hush as the clear notes mounted the air.

> "Peter sat at Heaven's gate
> Beeking in the sun
> While the souls came up the stair
> Limping every one.
> Like the weary homing rooks
> When the day is done."

The ballad went on to tell how kings and nobles and

bishops and mitred abbots presented themselves and got but a dusty answer from the Keeper of the Gate, but how when the beggarman appeared he was welcomed as a boon companion. It was the kind of ribald song popular at a time when men had lost much of their awe of the divine mysteries. He followed it with a piece of naked uncleanness, which won much applause, and then—with a startling suddenness—broke into a sad old catch with an air like a wandering wind and the patter of raindrops.

"Godsnigs, Pierce," John Naps commanded, "put more mirth into your music. That tune gripes one like sour ale, till I feel the cart moving beneath me and the rope at my weasand."

The piper obeyed and broke into a song, of which everyone took up the chorus.

> "When is the time to drink with a friend?
> When is it meetest thy money to spend?
>   O now, now, now.
>   O now, now, now.

> "When should a man fill his belly with meat,
> Cool his hot throat and anoint his sore feet?
>   *O now, now, now.*

> "When are most honied the lips of a lass?
> When tastes the sweetest the foam on the glass?
>   *O now, now, now.*"

There were a dozen verses or more, and the revellers swelled the chorus *O now, now, now* like a kennel of full-throated hounds.

Then came toasts, mostly in the beggars' patois, at which tankards were emptied and refilled. The company, heads of oak all of them, seemed to get no drunker in spite of their potations. But jollity increased and suspicion departed, till Peter found himself meeting the gaze of others and exchanging friendly grins. His body was far from comfortable, for he was not accustomed to squatting or lolling, and the heat of the fire and the heavy flavour of food and ale had made the place like a limekiln. Soon he felt he must drop off to sleep. But suddenly he was shaken into wakefulness by a hush in the babble of tongues. Darking was speaking and every face was turned to him.

Solomon was not using the beggars' jargon, and he treated that odd gathering as if it were the most dignified assembly in the land. He was honoured, he said, with the right of entry to the councils of the Upright Men. He had missed the consultation of that evening, when doubtless matters of great import had been decided, but he craved permission to bring them again into council. No doubt after a feast the wits of most men were slow, but this company was different, for with such seasoned vessels the malt was never above the meat.

Permission was granted by general assent, for Darking seemed to be in favour with these kings of vagabondage. Even True Timothy propped himself on a bulky elbow to listen.

"I have often come to you for counsel, my masters," Darking said, "and sometimes I have given it to you. We have been benefactors to each other, I think. Tonight I have something to give you and something to ask from you. You, whose life passes like a shuttle through England, can tell better than any other the maladies of the land. How is it with England today? What says the lord of Little Greece?"

Old Naps shook his head. "Badly. We touched on that matter at our consult. The skies are darkening, and presently a thunderbolt may fall. Let Master Flatsole speak, and after him Master Pierce, for they go farthest afield."

He spoke no longer in jargon, nor did Flatsole. The latter set down his mug, stiffened his back, and in a slow crooning voice testified to things which drove from Peter's head every atom of drowsiness. The King's levies were proving more burdensome, and in all the land there was discontent. The new rich were becoming richer and the poor poorer. He who had been a squire with ten free tenants was now himself a tenant on other men's lands, hard put to it to snatch a living. He who had been a free farmer, with two yokes of plough oxen, a good horse, a dairy cow and a score of sheep, was now a labourer

77

for daily hire. And he who had been a labourer was now on the roads or dead of hunger. The land was full of men broken in the wars, and trained to arms. There were concealed weapons everywhere. None loved the King, save his pensioners, and the plain man groaned to see his substance wasted on royal harlots and jacks-in-office.

"As for us of old England," he said, "we like not the Welshman nor his ways. He is making our trade too throng for a man's comfort. And now he is laying hands on God's houses, and soon there will be a horde of abbey-lubbers and unfrocked priests to cumber the roads and milk the charitable."

"What of the abbeys?" Darking asked. "Will the people at large approve the King's doing, or will fear of Hell and hope of Heaven set them in a ferment?"

"It is hard to say," was the answer. "Most men today think of their next meal before their hopes of Heaven, and their bellies before their souls. Holy water will not wash a foul shirt clean. But beyond question the devout are perturbed, and it would take little to bring them into the streets with staves and pikes. I have heard of a stirring Lincolnshire way, and Pierce will tell you that a very little spark would fire the northern moors. But I have been in too many wars to set much store by what the commonalty alone can do. There are plenty of foot-sentinels, but 'tis the captain that matters."

"Ay," said John Naps, "'tis the captains. What say the great folk, good sir? The poor knave whose back is broke with beating hemp has no guts in him to strike the first blow, but he may lay shrewdly about him if he find a trusty leader."

"Granted such a leader," Darking asked, "with what cry could he raise England?"

There was no answer. Each man seemed to be puzzling over the question.

"The safety of the Church?"

"'I faith, no. The Church has bled 'em too hard and has stirred up too many grudges. Here and there a pious soul might risk his neck for his salvation, but most would leave the business to the churchmen. It is not Christ that is in jeopardy, but his holiness of Rome and a score or two of plump abbots."

"The redress of wrongs?"

"Ay. There you have a cock would fight. Let some great one offer to ease the burdens on the poor and hang the rich who oppress them, and the trumpet would sound from Devon to Berwick."

"And the great one—who would be such a leader? My lord of Exeter?"

Catti the highwayman spat vehemently and his eyes blazed. "I'd liefer slit his weasand than follow him," he growled.

"Talk to Saint Peter of cockerels but not to friend Catti of that lording," said Naps. "He once suffered lamentably from his justice."

Darking ran over other noble names, and all were received with doubt or disfavour.

"None will fight," said Flatsole, "to make Neville or Percy King save their own men. If you are to oust the whoreson Welshman you must have a prince indeed, and one of the old blood, for the English have long memories."

"Such an one as Buckingham was?"

Flatsole considered. "Ay, such an one as Buckingham, for he was of the ancient kings, and had the bearing that the plain man loves."

"If such an one appeared—of Buckingham's house and kindred, say—and with Buckingham's art to charm the people and bade men follow him that merry England might come again—would he succeed, think ye?"

"Yea. 'Tis a salmon to a gudgeon that the Welshman goes."

Pierce broke in, having hitherto not opened his mouth except in song. He spoke as he sang, in a voice so soothing to the ear that it compelled attention. Unlike the others, he said, he had no terrestrial bounds, not even south England, to limit him. He had penetrated beyond Severn and threaded his way among the green foothills of Clun and Wye into the stony Welsh vales till he had looked from the Dyfi mouth on the Atlantic. He had been in the north among the great seas of heather that lined the track for days and days, and had talked with their hard, heather-bred folk. He had been in the south-west among the tin-miners of Cornwall and the rich Devon pastures, and round the coast from the Dorset dunes to the Kent chalk-cliffs and the Essex marshes and the sea-meres of Norfolk. And inland he had carried his pipes and his fiddle from the Malvern hills to the Cambridge fens, and from the Hampshire wolds to the fat meadows of Trent and the dark glens of Derwent. For the great he could not speak, though he had made music in castle halls, but he could tell of a thousand taverns and hamlets and granges where his playing had enlivened the cheesecakes of the simple.

"It is a dim land nowadays," he said. "The blanket of the dark lies heavy on it." (Peter started at the phrase.) "But there is an uneasy stirring, and that stirring may soon be an upheaval that will shake down crowns and mitres. There is a new world coming to birth, good sirs, though men know it not and crave rather to have an older world restored."

"That is truth," said Flatsole, "as I can bear witness. Only a leader is wanted."

"Ay, but what leader?" the piper asked in his soft far-away voice. "If it is a great one he will only lead the nobles against the King, or some of the nobles against others. Who will lead the people against both?"

"I care for none of your new worlds," said Naps. "We of the road want the old world with its wealth of cakes and ale, and we are for anyone that will give it back to us."

Peter, at Darking's shoulder, looked round the circle where the faces had become dimmer as the fire declined. It was hard to believe that this was a gathering of the kings of wastreldom. Each face, on which time and hard living had written curious tales, seemed to be sunk in musing. No doubt it was only the effect of October ale, but it looked like profound meditation.

Darking was speaking. "If such a thing should come, and a prince of the old blood should appear with a strong following to ease the people of their discontents, could he reckon on your support?"

Naps replied for the others. "If you vouch for him, Master Solomon, we are his men. That is, up to our capacities. We are not an army, though we have fighting men among us, and we are poor folk, though now and then we can sup like gentles."

I ask no more," said Darking. "But such an one might well call for help from those who know our England to the roots and who have their folk in every square mile of the land. What token can he give so that such help will be forthcoming?"

The old man's face took on a sudden shrewdness.

"Is such a business in train?"

"Maybe. And I would make all things ready against the hour."

"'Tis well. You know yourself the pass-words of our different orders. But I will give you a masterword and I will warn the troops so that, on its presentation, every wayfaring man in England is bound to honour it, though it put his neck in a halter. Are we secret here, think you? Who is he that sits at your back?" And he looked hard at Peter.

"A forest lad in my service," was the answer. "I brought him with me because it was more convenient than to leave him behind. He is thick as an oak-log," and he tapped his forehead.

Old Naps considered.

"Hearken, sirs," he cried. "The master-word I appoint is this. The question will be asked, 'How far is it to the skirts of Wychwood?' The answer will be, 'As far as to Peter's Gate.' Upon which says the questioner, halting between each word— 'Alack—I—shall—not—be—there—in—time.' Whoever hears such question and reply, must put his all at the disposal of him who asks it. Let that go out to the troops as my command. Another jug of ale, gammer, for I am dry with talk, and do you, Pierce, give us a stave."

The tankards beside the dying fire were refilled and the fiddle woke. But it was no drinking song that came from it, but an air as slow and solemn as a Gregorian chant. The words seemed to be a comment on the piper's last speech, and, in that place of strange faces and crooked shadows, they sounded as ominous as the owl's complaint before a stormy dawn.

81

"Worm at my heart and fever in my head—
    There is no peace for any but the dead.
    Only the dead are beautiful and free.
    Mortis cupiditas captavit me."

John Naps flung an empty ale-pot at his head.
    "God's curse on your snivelling, Pierce," he cried. "Give us
Kind Heart or *Banbury Babby*—summat to warm our blood."

CHAPTER VI

IN WHICH PETER EMERGES INTO THE LIGHT

I

Cotswold lay asleep in the October afternoon under a haze like the bloom on a plum. Long before the western rim of the uplands was reached Peter and Darking had entered the pale of Avelard. Its stone walls began before they passed the upper waters of Coln and came out on the high bleak tableland where all the tributaries of the young Thames have their source. It was now a country of pasture, with the short sweet bite for sheep, but here and there rank patches showed where there had once been ploughlands. There were no hamlets or farms, only shepherds' cabins, and the ruins of former habitations from which the walls of the pastures had been built. The sheep were small and shaggy to Peter's eye, accustomed to the heavier animals of the lowlands; the shepherds were wild-looking folk, with their swathes of rags for footgear and their long hazel crooks, and the dogs were savage and noisy.

"These are my lord's flocks," said Darking. "He has been a great pasture-maker, and most of his wealth comes from these dirty hides."

But at the scarp the pasture ceased, for the land fell not in gentle shallow vales as on the east, but in a declivity of a thousand feet to the huge hollow of a river. The slope was a wild park, full of fern and furze and seedling thorns, with here and there clumps of scrub oak and holly and hazel. In places there were acres of greensward among the bracken.

"See there," said Darking, pointing to one of the clearings. "This has not long been forest land. A dozen crofts were sacrificed to make my lord's park."

But Peter was not listening, for the breath was taken from him by the vast prospect, the widest he had ever beheld, since

83

the western scarp of Cotswold was the highest ground which his feet had yet trod. The slope ended far below in a champaign of meadow and woodland, but mainly woodland. A wide river looped itself through the plain, and on its banks he saw the walls of more than one town, and the spire of a great church. Beyond he could see foothills, for in the Severn valley the upland haze had gone, and the western skies were darkening for rain. And far away, a spectral blue against the rain-clouds, loomed a field of black mountains, higher than anything that the lowland-bred Peter had dreamed of, menacing and yet inviting with their promise of unknown worlds.

"The hills of Wales," said Darking, with a jerk of his head. "Ill neighbours for peaceable folk."

Half-way to the valley below, and a little to the right, was a broad shelf of ground, partly terraced with gardens. In the midst rose a great house, clearly new, for the yellow Cotswold limestone was not yet grey with lichen and weather. It was built in the form of a double L, and from where they stood above it could be seen the green of the lawns enclosed in the half quadrangles. To Peter it seemed more immense than any dwelling he had seen—far bigger than Stanton or Woodstock or Ewelme, greater than any college except the unfinished Cardinal. His heart beat faster, for he knew what it was without Darking's words.

"That is the castle of Avelard. It is also new built, save for the keep on the left, which in its time stood many sieges in the Barons' Wars and from the wild Welsh. Now my lord is rich and peaceful, and he has built him a house without defences. Let us make haste before the storm breaks."

There was a postern gate in a battlemented wall abutting on the hill. The travellers had been seen, for a serving-man awaited them there. Darking spoke aside to Peter.

"Here I leave you, my lord. God prosper you in your venture. Remember that you have a bodyguard in the forest. You have but to speak the word old John Naps taught you to command their aid. That way, too, you can send me a message if you have need of me."

Peter wrung his hand. The kindness in the sombre face

84

brought tears to the boy's eyes.

"Your goodness is beyond my gratitude," he stammered. "What have I done to merit it?"

"I was your father's man," was the answer. "In old days there was never a Bohun rode to the wars but a Darking ran by his stirrup."

Solomon slipped into the thicket after he had given Peter's satchel into the servant's hands. The man bowed low and led the way through the postern. Peter found himself in a demesne enclosed from the wild park, a place of wide lawns set with clumps of foreign bushes. Then came a sunken garden running the whole length of the terrace—a pleasance still in the making, for the containing walls showed recent marks of the chisel, and the long pool in the centre was empty of water and its bottom littered with heaps of quicklime. Two fountains were spouting, one of white marble shaped like a pyramid, on the apex of which sat a marble bird, and one a cluster of sea nymphs around Neptune. Here there were trim walks of grass, and fantastic plots of withered flowers. A marble staircase led to the terrace, a quarter-mile of sward a little browned with the September drought, edged by a parapet of blue Forest stone. Above it rose the southern facade of the house, all a dazzle of high square-headed windows surmounted by cornices moulded in the Italian manner, but ending far up in Gothic gables. In the centre was a great porch set with columns and capitals of the Tuscan order, and carrying a shield carved in deep relief with the lion rampant of Avelard.

A tall grave man was waiting in the porch. He bowed low.

"My lord has not yet returned," he said, "but all is ready for your lordship's reception."

He led Peter into a hall, the height of two storeys of the house, with a gilt and painted plaster ceiling of dolphins and gorgons and the Avelard lion. It was panelled half-way up with small squares of oak, new and not yet darkened by smoke, and the immense chimney of white stone looked like a work of yesterday. Peter stared in bewilderment, his eyes running from the sober hangings of black and gold velvet to the rich hues of the plaster, the brilliance of a Spanish foot-cloth below the central table, the silver sconces and the great carved silver chandelier, the huge buffet laden with silver and gold plate, the Avelard lion, sable on or, ramping above the fireplace, set between two mighty alicorns. He had not believed that such magnificence dwelt even in kings' palaces.

The yeoman of the hall handed him over deferentially to the yeoman of the chambers. Behind screens of Spanish leather they entered a lesser hall, whence rose a broad staircase of oak on the newels of which sat the Avelard lion. On the first floor he passed through a narrow gallery full of pictures into the Great Chamber, hung with Flemish tapestry, where stood a state bed of scarlet and sky-blue, and a raised chair of state under a silk canopy, cabinets of ivory and tortoiseshell and ebony, stools covered with velvet and embroidered fustian, and a medley of musical instruments, including one of the new upright spinets, called a clavicytherium, which Peter had heard of but had never seen. From this he passed to a nest of lesser chambers, in one of which a wood-fire burned on the hearth. It was a bedroom, for there was a great bed with Ionic pilasters and brocaded valance and curtains. Here a groom awaited him.

"Your lordship will bathe before he sups?"

Peter assented, with his head in utter confusion. He suffered himself to be undressed, and bathed in a tub with a curtain-like covering. The water was perfumed and warm. Then he was clothed in a new suit, the like of which he had never seen—a shirt of delicate white silk, a doublet of purple velvet slashed with yellow satin, and a surcoat of heavy silk lined with marten's fur. His trunk hose were of silk, and on his feet were soft fur-lined slippers of cherry velvet. This done, he passed into the adjoining room, which was fitted up as a winter parlour. There he found a table covered with fine linen, and two grooms waiting to serve his meal. He had not broken bread since the morning, and, in spite of his bewilderment, fell to with a will. The grave man who had first received him again made his appearance.

"My lord has not yet returned," he said. "Meantime we

wait your lordship's commands."

Peter made his supper off sausage served with a sauce of almond milk, an omelette of eggs and chopped herbs, a slice of a venison pasty, and a tart made from warden pears. He was offered a variety of wines, white and red, but chose the mild beer made bitter by hops which was just come into England. This he drank from a tankard fashioned in the shape of an Avelard lion, in the bottom of which was set a piece of unicorn's horn. When he rose from meat he drew back the curtains and looked out. The night had fallen dark and wet, with a howling wind.

Again the old usher appeared.

"My lord still tarries. Maybe he is storm-stayed and will stay the night at his house of Minster Carteron. Has your lordship any commands?"

"I am weary," said Peter. "I go to bed." He had risen two hours before sunrise.

A groom undressed him and put on him a nightgown of quilted satin lined with ermine. There was a table beside the bed with spiced wine in a gold posset-dish and a silver lamp burning scented oil. The air in the room was as heavy as that of a chapel at high mass. As soon as the man had withdrawn Peter pulled back the curtains, opened one of the lattices and let in a breath of the soft western wind. Then he turned the lamp low, for he felt that a night light would be a comfort in this strange place. He flung from him his night-robe, and dived between the cool cambric sheets, which to his naked body were as grateful as spring water. Such a bed he had never known, for he seemed to sink deep in down and yet float on air. The sheets were as fine as silk, and the Chalons blankets as soft as fur—far different from the rude Witney fabric which had hitherto been his only covering. The strangeness and the luxury, maybe too the rich supper and the posset, sent him forthwith to sleep.

Presently he awoke. The wind had freshened and the open lattice rattled noisily. He came back slowly to consciousness and struggled for a little to discover his whereabouts. He had been dreaming, and had thought that he was in Wychwood, crawling through a covert which grew thicker with every yard and pressed down on him from above. He tossed the blankets from him, and stuck his legs out of bed, where a cold draught from the window brought him to his bearings. The lamp was flickering in the wind, so he shut the lattice, and as he did so he noticed his right hand in the light, the middle finger of which wore a broad silver ring. That had been Mother Sweetbread's gift, the work of the wise woman at Shipton-under-the-Forest. It was the talisman which was to bring him safety and fortune on his new road. The sight of it cheered him in the midst of this unfamiliar magnificence, for it seemed to him a link with his old world.

Then, above the riot of the gale, he heard music. It came not from without, but from somewhere within the house, for when he opened the lattice again he did not hear it. He sat on the edge of the bed straining his ears. The thing was fitful like a wind, now dying away, now rising into a perceptible air. He believed that it came from the Great Chamber, and that someone was playing on the clavicytherium. Had Lord Avelard returned and brought company?

Whoever played accompanied the music with the voice. For an instant the melody came strong and full, and he could almost catch the words. A girl was singing, and by some strange wizardry the voice was familiar. The sound of it brought pictures before his eyes—the summer midnight and the dancer on the Painted Floor—an August afternoon in Stowood, and the white girl who had called him cousin and offered her cheek to kiss. Then the music ceased and the only sounds were the night wind without and the hoot of an owl.

He breathed freely now, for ever since he arrived he had had the sense of walking in a stifling dream. Out there in the darkness was the world he knew, the world of simplicity and bare living and old silent things. A mile or less distant, in the straw of a cowshed or in a dell of the woods, were men who, when he spoke the word, would do his bidding. He had felt imprisoned—but only a sheet of glass separated him from the most ancient freedom. Meantime, this magnificence was his; he was born to it; he commanded servants; soon he might command all England; and there was a girl with a linnet's voice waiting for him to set a crown upon her head.

He snuggled again into the sheets. "I am Bohun," he told himself. "I am even now in God's sight a duke, and soon I may be a king."

But he did not sleep, for the music had been resumed, nearer it seemed, perhaps in the next room. This time the voice of the singer had lost the note of a wild bird. It was seductive music, languorous, rousing strange tremors in his body. It seemed to invite to new and lawless delights. Peter shivered, for he knew that whoever sang was calling him, was awaiting him. They two were alone in that great dark house. He had a moment of wild exultation, succeeded by sheer terror. He was being tempted, and was in the mood to yield. He buried his head under the clothes and said a prayer. When he uncovered his ears the music had stopped, and to his horror he found himself longing for it to begin again.

When he was wakened by a lackey, who drew the curtains and proffered a morning draught in a gold cup, Peter found himself in a new mood of pride and expectancy. He had forgotten his scruples. This fantastic world into which he had fallen was full of strange delights, and, if some were unlawful, the deeper their witchery. "I am Bohun," he repeated. "I must assuredly remember that, if I am to keep my back stiff in this palace."

II

Lord Avelard had returned and received Peter in a little room which opened from the Great Chamber. He was dressed as ever in plain black and silver, and he sniffed a gold pomander, for October was the month when men feared the plague. His lined waxen face and the dark pouches beneath his eyes gave him in the cruel morning light an air of immense age, but the eyes themselves were keen as a hawk's, and there was none of the impotence of senility in his delicate stubborn jaw. He took the boy's hands in his.

"Welcome to Avelard," he said. "You are master here, and

89

my servants will do your bidding as they would my own. But your rank and name must still be secret. You are a kinsman from the west country whom I would make my heir, and I have seen to it that whatever is needed for that station has been forthcoming. Here you will stay till the times are ripe, and I think that the days of waiting will pass pleasantly. I am too old to be a fit companion for youth, but there are those here who will better suit your age. Young Messynger will arrive tomorrow, and my dead wife's niece, Mistress Beauforest, will provide the graces. She is niece too to Sir Ralph Bonamy whom you know. Meantime, I have news for you. Yesterday morning there came a post out of Lincolnshire. The commons are up in the eastern shires and the King's agents are hanging like crabs on every wayside tree. The church bells are ringing, and the priests are on the march, and ten thousand men are moving on Lincoln under the banner of the five wounds of Christ."

The voice in which he spoke had no fervour in it, but rather a cool irony, and his waxen cheek puckered in a smile.

"All goes as I foresaw," he said. "Soon the trouble will spread north beyond Trent and fire the Yorkshire dales. I learn that the King is hurrying every man he can muster to this peasant war. Suffolk has clomb into the saddle, and Norfolk is on the road, and Beauchamp and Russell and Fitzwilliam. Presently there will not be a stand of arms left in the Tower of London, or a vassal of the King's lords who is not tramping Lincolnshire mud. The King purposes to use the eastern shires as he used Wales, when five thousand rebels decked the gibbets. I have not been slack in my loyalty," and again the smile flickered, "for a troop of my Gloucester lads is on the way to join my lord of Shrewsbury. Crummle will have no word to speak against the name of Avelard. I shall have a letter from the Welshman commending his affectionate cousin. And in the meantime . . ."

He broke off and his eyes seemed to burn into Peter's soul, while every line of the old face spoke of a consuming passion.

"Meantime," he went on, "behind the cover of this eastern revolt our preparations ripen. When the King is embroiled

90

deep with priests and commons, we of the old houses will strike. It is time to let you deeper into our plans, for they touch you nearest of all. When we take the field our banner will not be any monkish device, but the silver knot of Stafford and the swan of Bohun."

He spread some papers on a table. Shire by shire, demesne by demesne, he took Peter through the details of the rising. This lord was good for so many mounted men, this squire for so many footmen. Peter found himself enthralled by the vision of great numbers waiting under arms from the Cumberland lakes to the Devon moors till the word was given, and then moving like a river fed by many streams towards London and victory. His cause was strong, it seemed, along all the western shires of England, with outposts in the midlands and the south. They lay on the flank of the royal army, and the farther that army was beguiled north of Trent the more deadly their blow. There were the Welsh, too, twenty thousand of the mountaineers, who would fight for a mercenary wage, but with something more than a mercenary's fury, since they had a long tale of wrongs to avenge. They passed to minute computations of armament, wagons, horses and supplies. Wales would furnish a reserve of horses, and at various key-points provisions had been long accumulating. Serpents and culverins were making in the Dean forest.

"Who will command?" Peter asked, and was told himself. "Only a son of Buckingham can keep such a concourse to its purpose. Never fear. You shall have skilled marshals to assist you. We do not look for the arts of war in one clerkly bred. There are with us many old captains of the French and Scottish wars—men accustomed to order a battle—no mere carpet-knights and jousters like the King."

Peter asked one last question. Whence came the funds for this great venture? Lord Avelard smiled wryly.

"You have set your finger on our weakness. We have somewhat, but not enough. Some, like myself, are ready to pledge their private fortunes, and there will be certain payments coming from the Emperor, who wishes us well. But we cannot do as the King does, and order requisitions in the name

91

of the law. We must depend on the good-will and ardour of our followers, who will venture their substance knowing that victory will repay them a hundredfold."

"But if the King has bled the land sore, will there be any recompense for those who overthrow him? He has plundered the Church and the poor, and such a course is barred to us."

Lord Avelard glanced sharply at Peter.

"A way will be found," he said. "There are many resources for the victorious."

Peter's life at Avelard was not to be idle. His mentor was satisfied with his skill in swordsmanship and something more than satisfied with his prowess with long-bow and cross-bow. But the boy had no more than a peasant's knowledge of a horse, and he spent long hours that afternoon at the *manège*, where Lord Avelard's master of horse, a Walloon from Ghent, proved an exacting, albeit a respectful, tutor. For the rest he seemed to be solitary in that immense echoing house. Lord Avelard did not show himself after the conclave of the morning, and there was no flutter of skirts in doorway or corridor to reveal the girl who had sung to the clavicytherium.

Peter watched the dusk gather over Severn valley, and roamed from the terrace to the pleasance and to the edge of the outer curtilage. The smell of wet bracken and rotting leaves drifted up to him from the woods, and a whiff of wood-smoke from the fire of some tinker or forester in the dingles. He had lost his sense of strangeness. He felt that this world of power and riches was his by right, and he looked on the lackeys with a possessing eye. His imagination was fired by what he had heard that morning, and he burned to see the argent and gules of Buckingham marshalled against the Tudor verd and argent. He must learn—learn savagely, for there was but little time in which to become a leader of men. He must be wary, for he stood alone. He was a pawn in the game, but when that pawn became a king it would be no more a pawn. His followers would fight for him only because he might help them to satisfy their own desires. There had been kindness in Lord Avelard's face, he was well-disposed to the son of his old friend, but kindness would never be the overmastering motive with such a man. That old face, with the shadows blue as in a snowdrift, was like white fire. He stiffened his back, and felt a sudden access of manhood. These men should not use him save in so far as his will consorted with theirs. Money—that was what he lacked, what the whole enterprise lacked. Had he but wealth behind him he would assuredly call the tune. As it was, he would play high for fortune. He was Bohun—of that pride none could deprive him.

But, indoors again, his thoughts were suddenly switched to a different world. "Mistress Beauforest begs permission to join you at supper"; the yeoman of the hall told him, and his cheeks burned foolishly. He was to see for the third time this lady who had become the constant companion of his dreams.

He ransacked his new wardrobe for a suit which took his fancy, and finally chose one of rose-coloured silk taffeta, with a surcoat of primrose velvet. Boy like, he was first of all delighted with his magnificence, and then abashed. He wore a sword—he was entitled now to that, since he would soon have an army behind him. And then, with his heart beating hard, he entered the Great Chamber, where he proposed to sup. "My lord keeps his room," the usher told him, and his heart went faster.

He had not long to wait. A girl entered, followed by her tire-woman, who carried her comfit-box, a gold pomander, and a little pied Italian greyhound. She swept Peter a curtsey so deep that her knee almost touched the floor. She did not offer him her cheek; instead she took his hand and carried it to her lips. The tire-woman withdrew, the lackeys, after placing some dishes on the table, also left the room, and the two were alone.

A girl, so he had thought of her. But this was no girl, no woman, but the very goddess of love, Venus sprung from the foam. She wore a gown of black satin bordered with black velvet, an ebony sheath for her dazzling whiteness. There were jewels with a frosty blue sparkle on her hand and in her hair. To Peter's fascinated eyes it seemed that her gown was scarcely a covering, for the snow of her neck and bosom was revealed, and, as she moved, the soft supple lines of her body. But it was her eyes that held him in a spell. This was a woman whom he had never seen before, and such eyes he had never dreamed of, coaxing, inviting, challenging.

She waited his permission to sit down. The fire on the hearth was burning brightly, and its flicker caught her jewels and the sheen of her satin. The heavy curtains shut out the world.

She toyed daintily with her food, but Peter's meal was a farce, for he could not swallow, though he drank a goblet of wine in answer to her pledge. She fed the little greyhound on scraps, and talked to it wooingly. To Peter she spoke in a soft voice like music, with an air of tremulous respect. But she was wholly mistress of herself, and in her eyes was a strange seductive boldness. Her every movement was voluptuous—the turn of her limbs when she switched her train beside her chair, the sudden glimpse of a shapely arm outstretched to take a pear from a platter, the occasional fall of her cloak which revealed more of a white bosom.

Peter was in a tremor, in which there was as much fear as delight. Dimly he perceived that this woman was his for the taking, that she was part of the appurtenances of one who was Bohun and might be King of England. But he had not bargained for such a goddess. He had thought of her as a difficult Artemis, and now, behold, she was Aphrodite. Something monastic and virginal in him was repelled. He suddenly found his self-possession and the power of speech. But, as he recovered his tongue, she lost hers and she answered only with her eyes. And gradually into her eyes, which had been so full of lure and challenge, crept something different—was it disappointment, anger? Peter could look steadfastly at her now, and he observed that these eyes, which with her ashen blondeness should have been grey or blue, were the faintest hazel, like a shallow moorland stream running over white sand. The light in the limpid waters seemed suddenly to grow hot and sullen.

It was she who rang the silver bell which brought the servants and concluded the meal. Her tire-woman caught up her greyhound and her trinkets, and the lackeys bowed her to the door. She offered her cheek to Peter in a cousinly good-night, and to his lips it was cold.

As Peter went to bed he passed Lord Avelard in a furred night-robe and it seemed to him that the old eyes opened a little wider as if in surprise.

He fell asleep with his head full of the strange beauty which might be his, but he did not dream of her. Instead he saw a great army trampling over England, with, in the van, the silver knot of Stafford and the swan of Bohun.

III

Next day came Sir Gabriel Messynger out of Wales. It had been rough weather beyond Severn, but that morning Sir Gabriel had made a fresh toilet, and was as trim and bright as if he had never left the Court. He was a young man not yet thirty, high coloured and ruddy, with reddish hair cut close to the bone after the new fashion, so that his round head flamed like a noontide sun. His clothes had the extravagance of the town—a shirt of fine laced silk, a doublet of cloth of gold, and sleeves puffed and slashed in a magnificence of rose and purple. Peter's forecast proved true. This was the gallant he had seen that evening in Stowood when he had first set eyes on Lord Avelard.

Sir Gabriel showed that he was in the secret by treating the boy with an elaborate respect, while his shrewd pale eyes— blue in one light, green it seemed in others—sought his face furtively, as if hungry to appraise him. He had news of importance for Lord Avelard's ears, and was closeted with him till the dinner-hour. At that meal Sabine Beauforest appeared—to be the recipient of Sir Gabriel's loftiest courtesy. Yet the two seemed to be old acquaintances, for they shared together many covert jests, and their eyes would often meet in secret confidences. Her manner to Peter was one of stiff decorum; to the other she unbent like a friendly child.

After dinner they rode in the wild park in a brief clearing of the weather. Sabine and Sir Gabriel rode like madcaps, and

Peter, still in his novitiate, found himself often in these gallops half out of the saddle and only saved from falling by an unseemly clutch at the mane. Happily his horse, Spanish blood crossed with the nimble Welsh, was wise and sure-footed, and needed little management, for Peter had none to give. While they walked their beasts, Gabriel and Sabine yielded place to him as to a superior, consulting his wishes, and falling a little behind like dutiful servants; but, once let them swing into a gallop in some aisle of turf, and Peter was forgotten. He pounded precariously in their rear, while their laughter came back to him above the beat of hoofs, and sounded like mockery.

The consequence was that, once indoors again, with his blood brisk from movement and weather, Peter found himself in a mood of jealous irritation. He had been excluded from a world which should have been his own, he lagged last when he should have been foremost. Before supper in the hall they played games—Pope July, shovelpound, imperial, and the new French deckles—and he played badly, for his temper was sour and his self-consciousness extreme. Sir Gabriel—in a fresh suit—was in a merry mood, and Sabine was prepared to condescend, but Peter's sulks kept the air tense. He was ready to quarrel with Sir Gabriel, whose fine clothes offended him, his idiot laugh and aggressive geniality. With Sabine he could not quarrel, for she regarded him not; only by a respectful inclination or a humble dropping of the eyes did she acknowledge his presence. She had some grievance against him, and barred him resolutely from her world. But Sir Gabriel refused to quarrel; he accepted Peter's contradictions meekly, and turned his rudeness with a pleasant laugh, so that the boy for very shame was forced to civility.

At supper a new Sir Gabriel was revealed. When the servants had gone and a bowl of spiced wine had been mixed against the damp, they talked of the King, half under their breath, and with many glances at the doors. The goblets were all of crystal, a new device to guard against poison.

"You have his colouring, Gabriel," said Lord Avelard. "Were your mother's virtue not notorious, you might be reckoned his son."

"He never begot anything so sound of flesh," the young man laughed. "My lord, have you not observed that his blood is tainted? When he is bruised in a tourney, he shows black for months. If his skin is broke, he will bleed for many hours. The nature of his body is all evil humours."

"In his youth he was like Phoebus," said the old man, "rosy and effulgent, so that the commons on whom he beamed hailed him as half divine. Never was such a bewitcher of empty heads. But to those who marked him close there was something of ill-breeding in the little eyes near set in that vast shining face. He seemed something less, if something more, than man. There was a devil, too, in his vast appetites."

Sir Gabriel cracked a walnut. "There are tales not seemly for a gentlewoman's company, which would bear out the truth you have spoken. He is of another breed from the old, rugged, hard-faced masters of England. As you know, my lord, I am of an ancient but modest house, and so, being in a middle place, am well situated to note the heights and the hollows. I go not in my judgments by a man's countenance. The ancient nobility had as many different visages as coats, but were all large-featured and lean, the body being but a sheath for a strong spirit. Their colour was dusky or wan, since their flesh was in close subjection. But now comes the King and his race of new men, and they are all much cumbered with fat and overfull of blood. There was the Cardinal of York, with his cheeks like a Martinmas boar. There is this Crummle with his litter of chins and his swine's eyes. There is Russell and Wriothesley and Fitzwilliam, all fair of flesh like apple-women. Above all, there is the King's grace. The Beast has come to rule in England and it is ousting men made in their Maker's image. But mark you, if they have boar's cheeks and boar's eyes, they have also boar's jaws which do not easily slacken their hold."

Lord Avelard smiled. "You have wits in that popinjay's head of yours, Gabriel. The Welshman has indeed the lust to acquire and the lust to retain. That is the devil in his blood, and it will not be subdued save by blood-letting."

97

"Ay, my lord," said Sir Gabriel, "but let us remember this for our comfort. If you let clean blood, you free a man from surfeits and make him whole, but if you let tainted blood you kill, for the wound will not heal. There is some nice chirurgeon's work in store for England."

Lord Avelard retired early, and the others sat in the Great Chamber. Sabine had withdrawn into a distant stateliness, and was fingering a lute as if it burned her fingers. "Music, music," Sir Gabriel cried, stretching himself on a long stool. "Music to dispel the ugliness of our table talk. Sing of bright and jolly things. Hark to the wind! Winter is on us, and God knows what that winter will be. Sing of summertime."

"I am in no mood to sing," said the girl, but she plucked softly at the lute's strings.

"Tush, my lady, you are always singing. Your face is a madrigal, and your hair is a mesh of sweet notes. You are all music to the eye, so make music also for the ear."

The girl sighed, cast one sombre glance at Peter who was standing by the hearth, and then let her eyes rest on the smouldering logs. She touched a chord or two and began to sing:

> "Summer is come with love to town
> Throstle in bush and lark on down
> Merrily tell their tale O
> Folk that pine
> Now drink sunshine
> More strong than winter's ale O.
> Sweet mistress, why so pale O?
> I hie to thee
> As river to sea
> When the deer draw to the dale O."

It was a rude thing of several verses, each ending with the refrain about the deer and the dale. But, as the girl sang it, it was no longer a country catch, a thing for milkmaids and shepherds, but the paean of youth and spring with the bravado of all lovers since the world was born. Into that shuttered and curtained chamber, outside which the wet October winds blew, it carried a fragrance like flowers. Sabine sang soft and slow, her eyes on the fire, her face abstracted from Peter. She repeated one verse, and then broke into a flight of grace notes, a fantasy which she followed with her voice, a rich eddy of curious music twisting in and out in an aerial dance. She was singing to please herself, for she had forgotten Peter by the hearth and Sir Gabriel on his couch. Presently a gentle snore broke in on the music. Sir Gabriel, tired with his Welsh journey, was asleep.

It was the fantasia, rather than the singing, which stirred Peter's heart. For the rhythm it made was the rhythm of the dance which he had watched in the midsummer night on the Painted Floor.

She fell silent at last, and let the lute drop, while she sat with her hands between her knees, her head bent forward.

"I thank you." Peter's voice sounded intolerably harsh in his ear—the words of Mercury after the songs of Apollo. "You sing like the blessed angels. . . . I have heard that song before."

She bent her face slowly towards him, and he noted that her eyes were blind, as if turned back in some inward absorption. "That cannot be," she said.

"Nay, but it is so. Not heard it, maybe, but felt it. For I watched you dancing to that very air one July night on the Roman floor by Wood Eaton."

Her absorption was gone. She flushed rosily to the tips of her little ears. "You know the place?" she stammered. "You saw me? . . ."

"I first found the place, being guided thereto by the words of an ancient deed, and with my own hands I cleared it. We are twin discoverers, mistress."

She rose and held out her hands, and in her eyes was a sudden wild abandonment which made their cool shallows a molten fire. She was giving herself to his arms—she was inviting him to her breast—and an answering passion awoke in the boy. But at that moment Sir Gabriel rolled off his couch and woke. He saw Peter holding Sabine's hand to his lips, and speaking words of gratitude with a warmth which he had not looked for in one so fish-like.

Peter was roused before dawn next morning by Lord Avelard standing by his bed. The collar of his furred night-robe stood about his head like a crest, so that to the boy's sleepy eyes he had the air of an immense gnome.

"The devil is in this business," he said. "Who think you are here? One of Crummle's wolves—Plummer his name, a Middle Temple lawyer—on his way to take reckoning with the Gloucester monks. He has a secretary with him, and four armed servants, and as a companion young Rede of Boarstall, who once saw you and inquired concerning you. What brings them here? They are ten miles out of the straight road to Gloucester, and there is no religious house in these parts to stir their greed. It may be that Crummle has got a hint of our doings and would spy out the land. I like not this young Rede's presence, for he has been known as a King's man, but no Crummle's man, and yet here he is playing fugleman to the worst of them."

"Must I get me gone?" Peter asked.

"Nay, that would be to make suspicion certainty, if, as I believe, they know of your presence here. But, while they know of your presence they do not know who you are. Mark well, my son. You are no more than my cousin and destined heir, Master Bonamy from Dyston in Salop. My servants have been instructed, and Sabine and Gabriel will keep up the play. God send our guests do not tarry long. It behoves us to treat the rogues like princes and welcome them like May flowers. Haply we will get from them some later news out of the east and north."

It was a clear mild October day, and at breakfast in the hall the sun shone full on the company. Master Plummer, the commissioner, was a black-avised man of middle age, with a yellow parchment skin, a quick eye like a fowl's, and the voice of the hectoring lawyer. He was servile to his host, civil to Gabriel and Peter, fulsome to Sabine, but always with an air of one who condescended, and could at any moment change

100

the velvet glove for the iron hand. He ate a breakfast of a size miraculous for one so slight, and, as he gobbled noisily, he babbled of his doings at Court, of his purchase with his master and his power with the King, and of the noble work he had wrought already in curbing the vice and gluttony of the religious. "Honest men must come to their own," he cried so often that it sounded as if he demanded from the company some proof of honesty.

The other traveller, Simon Rede, for the most part kept silence. Three times Peter had seen him—once on the mid-summer night in Stowood when he had envied his conquering air, once in Oxford streets, and once on that afternoon when he had ridden with Sabine from the hunt. Now, in his travelling dress which bore the stains of the road and was scarcely richer than a yeoman's, he looked more formidable than ever. There was power in every movement of his limbs, the small shapely head set on a strong neck, the breadth of the shoulders, the gnarled brown wrists beneath his cuff-bands. His face appeared to have been weathered by hotter suns than England's, for, except below the eyes and ears, it was the colour of dark oak, and seamed with the fine lines which come only from the glare and the spray of the sea. It was a hard face, and yet prepossessing, for its arrogance was a clean thing like a north wind, not the fussy pride of the commissary. He met Peter's eye with no sign of recognition, though he had had him in full view on that afternoon in Stowood, and, according to Sir Ralph Bonamy, had set afoot inquiries about him. Sir Gabriel was a stranger to him, but Sabine was plainly a friend. She had greeted him as such, and at breakfast his eyes were always travelling towards her, and whenever she spoke, he seemed to bend to listen. Peter had a sudden conviction. This man was in love with her. He had come here because of her, using the commissary's visit as an excuse to enter Avelard. And with this conviction came a spasm of furious jealousy.

Master Plummer, having ridden through part of the night, was weary, so he retired to his chamber to sleep, announcing that he would push on towards Gloucester in the late afternoon. So far so good, but it was necessary to dispose safely of Master Rede. Sir Gabriel took upon himself the duty of master of ceremonies. There was a heavy buck harboured in Dainton wood, which would for certain run towards the river, where the going was good even in a soft October. So horses were brought and the four young people rode out into the sloeberry bloom of the autumn wilds. For three hours they ran the buck, but the mort was never sounded, for he took to the water and found sanctuary beyond the flooded Severn. By midday, too, the weather had changed, a torrent of rain descended, and long ere they won the shelter of Avelard the four were soaked to the bone.

Peter had been all morning violently out of temper. The thought of Simon Rede as a lover of Sabine had thrown him into a mood of deep disquiet. Sir Gabriel's intimacy with the girl had not perturbed him, but there was that in the other's air of mastery which struck fear to his heart. What woman could resist one who had the face of the god of battles, and treated the world as his own demesne? Before such assurance Peter felt raw and impotent. This galling sense of inferiority was increased by the incidents of the hunt. Where the others leaped their horses easily over ditches and pales, he was compelled to make an ignominious circuit. The result was that he fell far behind, and the stag had taken to the river while he was still ploughing a mile away through swampy thickets.

From a knoll he saw the others turn, while the prickers' horns sounded to recall the hounds. The rain had begun, and in deep disgust he too swung his horse round for home. Below him in a hollow were some charcoal-burners at work, and one of them, a young man, followed him, and touched his stirrup.

"How far be it, master, to the skirts of Wychwood?" he asked in a broad Gloucestershire burr.

For a moment Peter was taken aback, and could only stare. Then he remembered.

"As far as to Peter's Gate," he replied.

"Alack!" said the man, stumbling between each word, "I shall not be there in time." Then he grinned. "I have a message for ye, brave sir. Mas'r Darking be mighty eager to see ye. Ye will get news of him at Goody Sweetbread's. The word given me to pass on was that there was summat in the ground as concerned your fortunes." The man pulled a forelock, and went back to his companions.

To Peter the message was like a breeze to dispel the fog of his discontents, since it reminded him of the high road on which his feet were set. What was Simon Rede to him who would soon be the master of ten thousand men? His ambition rekindled, and burned side by side with his passion for Sabine, for the two were one.

After dinner, while the rain pelted on the windows, came word that the commissary, fearing the swamps of the valley in such weather, had resolved to postpone his going till the morrow. So the good-humoured Sir Gabriel set himself to devise amusement for indoors. Little Welsh horses were provided, their feet cased in monstrous shoes of felt, and he and Simon held a miniature tourney on the black-and-white marble pavement of the hall. Sir Gabriel won, and was crowned by the laughing Sabine with a wreath of ivy. There was sword-play, too, in which Peter could hold his own, and a nice show of dagger-and-buckler work by Sir Gabriel, who at the French court had learned to be a master of games. Then, as the wet dusk drew in, they sat around the big hearth and talked, the commissary being engaged with Lord Avelard elsewhere.

It was curious talk, in which Peter, restored to good humour, joined but little, sitting apart and watching the others. It began with the foreign wars, and it seemed to him that Sir Gabriel was bent on discovering, with adroit courtesy, something of Simon's past life and present ventures. But, with equal courtesy, the other put the questions by. He had been much about the northern courts on errands for the Council, but such business was not for gossip, as Sir Gabriel well knew. Peter observed that the latter's manner had lost its bravado, and that his face had become that of an older and shrewder man. Almost it seemed to him that it had acquired something of the hardness of the commissary upstairs.

To the girl Simon was more forthcoming. "There is a wider

world than Europe, my lady," he said, "and I have ventured some way into it." And then, in response to her questions, he began to tell tales, drifting casually into them, smilingly disclaiming any importance for them, and, as he spoke, his face too seemed to change. It became gentler, less wary and assured, and he smiled as if his memories were happy. He told how, as a boy, he had journeyed in the Bristol gabbarts to Gascony for wine, to Portugal with salted fish, to Ireland, and once far north, involuntarily, with a storm behind him, into icy seas. And, when come to man's estate, he had sailed with Cabot of Bristol in the service of the King of Spain to the new world beyond the Western Sea. For a space all hung on his words, and Sabine, with her head bent forward and her lips parted, never took her eyes from his face. He told of great rivers so wide that a man in midstream could see neither shore, of forests with their feet in the salt water, of strange bright fruits and birds, and dark-skinned people a touch of whose arrows brought death.

"Gold and jewels?" she asked breathlessly. "Did you find them?"

He laughed. "A little of each, mistress, such as a hasty seafarer can carry on board. But those lands are rich beyond mortal dreams. There is a dark blanket which covers Europe, but beyond it there are open skies and the sun."

She looked at him with wide eyes.

"How can you endure to sit at Boarstall and look out on Otmoor mud, when you know that there are such brave lands for the finding?"

Again he laughed.

"I am an Englishman," he said, "and I may wish to give a hand in raising the blanket that covers us."

At that all fell silent, for they realised that they had come very near forbidden things, and each wondered what was in the other's heart.

Lord Avelard broke in upon the conclave, and with him came the commissary, now rested and refreshed and in a mellow temper.

"We have another guest," said the old lord, "and an ill-boding one. There is a fellow here, one of the new gospellers, who has been working mischief among the Oxford clerks. He is Cambridge bred, but the devil sent him to sow tares in the Oxford fields. The proctors laid hold on him, but he escaped, and his grace of Lincoln, having a mind to end the evil, sent his men after him, and he has been taken while attempting to cross the marches into Wales. He has been brought here, and it is required that I keep him in safe custody and send him guarded to Oxford for the Bishop to deal with. They are bringing him in that I may have a look at him. Master commissary, we know well that the King's grace, though he has a grudge against certain of the religious, has an ardent mind to pure religion and will tolerate no heresy-making."

The commissary nodded and blinked.

"The King's grace is a good Christian. And so likewise is his grace's Vicar-General." But he seemed uneasy, and shot a sharp glance at Simon, which Peter intercepted.

"'Tis a difficult time for a Christian," said Sir Gabriel airily. "If he have a liking for the Pope he may be hanged for treason, and if he like not the mass he may burn for heresy."

The commissary frowned, and Lord Avelard shook a warning head. Simon had risen and Peter observed that his face had become grim.

"What is the man's name?" he asked, and it was clear that he strove to keep his voice soft.

"One Sturmy or Sturdy," said Lord Avelard. "His grace of Lincoln writes a plaguey bad hand. But here comes the fellow."

The outer door of the hall was thrown open by an usher, and five men entered. Four wore the Bishop's livery and carried halberts. The fifth was the man Peter had met with the gipsies in the Stowood covert—he could not mistake the thin face and the burning eyes. He was no longer in rags, but wore a sober clerk's garb much splashed with mire. He had damaged his left arm, which hung in a dirty sling. There was a chain round his middle, the other end of which was locked to the wrist of one of the warders.

The prisoner seemed in no way perturbed. He looked weary

and famished, but he held his head erect, and his eyes met Lord Avelard's bent brows with a scornful composure.

"You are one Sturmy, Nathaniel Sturmy, a clerk of Cambridge?"

The man bowed. "I am that one."

"Who after working mischief in Oxford fled to Wales, but was taken on the bank of Severn?"

"I was stayed by the Lord's hands. He sent His floods as a sign that He had still work for me to do in England."

"You are charged with speaking against the holy mysteries, and with distributing certain books among the common people whereby their hearts are seduced?"

"The charge is true. I have spoken against mummeries which pervert the truth, and I have laboured to spread the knowledge of God's own word."

"You have already been found guilty of like blasphemies, and have confessed and repented. At Uxbridge you carried a faggot in a procession of heretics, and did penance on the altar-steps?"

A spasm of pain crossed the man's face. "Woe is me, it is true. The flesh was weak and I was afeared. Now I have gotten strength to endure all things."

The commissary spoke out, and his tone was harsh. "A plague on such ignorant lubbers. When the King's grace is bent on reforming Holy Church, you must needs step in with your follies, thereby delaying the good work. Know you the penalty, fellow, for your errors, the penalty established by the law's wisdom? To be drowned in a sack or to be burned in a public place."

The man looked scornfully at his inquisitor.

"Threaten those things to rich and dainty folk who are clothed in purple and have their life in this world. Thanks be to God, I care not whether I go to Heaven by land or water or fire!"

As he spoke, he looked round the company, and his eyes fell on Simon. Some intelligence seemed to pass between them, for of a sudden his face lightened, and when Peter glanced at Simon he saw that his mouth was set hard. And then Peter

106

had a strange experience. As he looked, the world seemed to go small. The noble hall with its carvings and gildings and escutcheons suddenly shrank into a little bare place. Lord Avelard seemed a broken old man with deathlike cheeks, Sir Gabriel a painted lath, the commissary a hollow thing like an empty barrel, Sabine a pretty mask with nothing behind but a heart ticking foolishly. Even Simon looked wooden and lifeless. But this wisp of a man, manacled to his jailer, seemed to give out life as fiercely as a furnace gives out heat. There was such a convincing purpose in him that in his presence all the rest of them with their brave appurtenances dwindled and withered.

The mood lasted but for a second. When he looked again he saw only a shabby prisoner, and heard Lord Avelard saying: "Take him away. I will furnish two extra guards to carry him tomorrow to Oxford."

The rest of the evening was all discomfort. The commissary was out of temper, and suspicious of everybody, notably of Sir Gabriel, whose persiflage fell as flat as rain-water in a strong sun. Simon was moody, and seemed to be thinking his own thoughts, while Lord Avelard laboured in vain to play the genial host. Sabine, too, was in an odd mood, dropping her eyes, chary of her smiles, forgetful of her graciousness of the night before. She spoke only to Simon, who gave her short answers. Peter's jealousy burned fierce, for it had much to feed on. He went to bed angry with the world, angry with the girl, and with the conviction that in Simon Rede he had found a rival and an enemy.

Lord Avelard came to him in his chamber. He at any rate was not out of temper, for his cheeks puckered in smiles.

"That was a pretty play," he said. " 'Tis well known that Crummle is the blackest heretic in the land, and this young Rede I fear is no better. They are walking on difficult ground, for with one hand they are plundering the Church and with the other must smite all who deny the Church's creed, because their thick-witted master still hopes to save his soul. They cannot quarrel with my urgency to oblige the Bishop, since 'tis their King's wish, but you could see what gall and wormwood it was to them. But Avelard is no place for you at this moment. Both Rede and that black commissary have been examining my servants concerning you. Best go back for a little to Stowood till this visitation be past. There is good news from the east, where the stubble is ablaze, and soon Crummle and his crew will have their hands full in that quarter. You had best leave at dawn tomorrow. I am sending two of my fellows to strengthen the Bishop's guard—needless enough, but a proof of my good-will—and what more natural than that my young kinsman should accompany them, as a pledge of the holy zeal of the house of Avelard?"

"Does Master Rede go tomorrow?"

"He rides with the commissary to Gloucester. What brought him here, think you? I have my guess that it was the bright eyes of Mistress Sabine. But that dainty flesh is not for him." The old eyes looked at Peter with that in them which restored his confidence and set his heart beating.

He did not tell Lord Avelard of the charcoal-burner's message. That side of his life had nothing to do with Avelard, and at the moment it did not seem to him of much importance.

CHAPTER VII

HOW A WOULD-BE KING BECAME A FUGITIVE

Sleep banished the dregs of Peter's ill-temper. The sky had cleared after the rain, and he set out on his journey in a world all blue and golden. Master Plummer, too, made an early start, and to his surprise Peter found that Simon Rede had made a still earlier one, having left before dawn for Gloucester to prepare the way for the other's reception. The sour-faced commissary was therefore a witness, as Lord Avelard had intended, to the zeal of the house on the Church's errands. The Bishop's four servants wore sad-coloured liveries with a cross on their shoulders, but the two Avelard men were splendid in Avelard's yellow and black. As they started uphill towards the crest of Cotswold the Severn vale swam in a clear morning light, and the far hills rose blue and wraith-like against the pale sky. Every thicket was a riot of autumn gold and crimson, the pools left by the rain were alive with wild-fowl, and a great wedge of geese was winging across the valley. Peter drew long breaths of the sharp, scented air. In such a world it was good to be alive.

His heart had lightened as a boy's will at the coming of a new pleasure, and his head was filled with two pictures. One was Sabine, as he had seen her that night when he had revealed his knowledge of the Painted Floor, and her arms had opened towards him. Fool that he had been not to accept his fortune! A malediction on Sir Gabriel for his inopportune awakening! She had invited him to a deeper intimacy, since they two were sharers in one secret. She had invited him before. He remembered her appealing music on his first night at Avelard, and the night when they had supped together and her eyes had been like a siren's. Now he saw these incidents in a different light, and he recalled Lord Avelard's words the evening before. He was the unicorn who, according to the tale, could only be captured by the wiles of a virgin's lap. This girl was destined for him, was his for the taking—and she was not unwilling. A delicious tremor shook him; he exulted, yet with fear. What mattered Simon Rede when her heart was his? He told himself that he had already conquered. And then another picture took the stage in his brain, inspired by the quick movement and the jingle of harness in the diamond morning. He saw himself riding at the head of an immense concourse—all England—with the swan of Bohun above him. The picture fairly ravished him. What, forsooth, mattered Simon Rede to one born to such a fortune?

Ay, but what of Simon Rede? There was that in the man's face which could not be put aside, and Peter's high mood suddenly fled. The man was stronger than he. He had travelled far and wrought mightily and mastered his world, while he was still in his tutelage. The thought brought back all his uncertainties. He was but a tool in the hands of others and his power and place was only on sufferance. He was the painted flag men sent before them into battle—a thing valued not for its own sake but because it was a symbol of their pride. And, as he looked back on the company at Avelard, the picture seemed to darken. The old lord with his waxen face fought for the antique privileges of his order, and since Peter was of his order and a comrade's son he had a kindness for him. But nothing more. Sir Gabriel was a squire in the same cause—a crusader with a very mercantile interest in his crusade, for he had studied his face and seen the cool calculation behind the gaiety. Sabine was the delicate lady of the order, the prize for the man who should be its champion. But Simon Rede was of a different world. Whatever course he followed would have daylight and honour in it. He was the spending, not the getting, kind, and would fling his cap over the moon for a gallant whimsey. Curses on that high air of his! It might leave Sabine cold, but for Peter it had an ill-boding sorcery.

And that rag of a man, the gospeller! He had spoken strange words the night before, when he had scorned the commissary's threats, and had bidden him use them to those "whose hope was in this world." Peter had been bred to think that this world at its best was a perishing thing, and that man's first business was to save his soul. But now all his thoughts were on mundane glory and mundane joys. There was small relish of salvation in his new life. He was to be the champion of the old Church against the King, but what cared Lord Avelard and his like for the Church, save as a prop to their own fortunes? He was now engaged in the repression of heresy, but there were some who had called both him and Brother Tobias heretics, because they had followed Erasmus and the new learning. This gospeller's offence was spreading knowledge of the Scriptures, a thing which Tobias had long urged and which the King's grace himself had toyed with. Acute doubts assailed him, doubts not only of his own powers, but of the merits of his cause. Was he fighting only for the lust of the eyes and the pride of life? If so, his cause smacked somewhat of damnation.

Hitherto he had ridden ahead, but when they were descending the long slopes to the Coln, with Cirencester town smoking below on their right, he fell back on the party. The gospeller rode between two of the Bishop's servants with the two others behind him, and the Avelard men bringing up the rear. He was no longer manacled, but a stout thong joined his bridle hand to the belt of one of the servants. Peter ordered the thong to be loosed that he might ride abreast of the man, and bade the others fall back a little. The Bishop's servants, ill-looking rogues all of them, sullenly obeyed. At first it seemed that they might refuse, for they knew nothing of Peter, and the old clothes which he had resumed did not suggest rank, but a word from the Avelard men brought their compliance.

The gospeller looked ill and weary. In the daylight his skin had the yellow tinge of one who had suffered much from ague, and the same colour showed in the whites of his eyes. He drooped in the saddle, and his wounded left arm seemed to pain him. He stared in front of him, while Peter adjusted the cavalcade, and when they rode forward together he did not raise his eyes. He seemed to be repeating a prayer, for his lips

111

moved continually.

"You are a sick man," Peter said. "I will call a halt, when you wish, that you may rest. There is no need for haste."

"Nay, friend, I am well enough," was the answer. "Like the Psalmist, I pass through the valley of misery and find springs therein."

"We have met before. In July at midnight in the hollow below Stowood as you go to Wood Eaton. You were with a troop of gipsies, and I tumbled by chance on your encampment."

At last the man raised his head and looked at his companion. "I remember. An Oxford clerk in a poor gown. What does such an one in the halls of the great? I saw you yesternight among the gentles, clothed as they. What part has a scholar in that magnificence? What has a poor Grecian to do with the rich and the oppressive?"

"You said, when you looked in my face that night, that I was no churl's get."

The man set his penetrating eyes on his companion. "I spoke truly. So you are of the blood of Avelard. Well, 'tis a high stock to them who value such vanities, but 'tis a strange taproot for a Grecian. Yon old fox is the steeliest bigot in all the west country. He loves not the King, but he will compound for treason by being hot against heresy."

A bank of cloud had obscured the sun and the wind blew suddenly sharp from the south-east. The gospeller shivered, for he had no cloak.

"I like not the weather," said Peter, sniffing the air. "The mallard are flighting low, too. It smells like the first snows."

The gospeller muttered to himself. "When it is evening, ye say, 'It will be fair weather, for the sky is red'; and in the morning, 'It will be foul weather today, for the sky is red and lowering. O ye hypocrites, ye can discern the face of the sky, but can ye not discern the signs of the times?'"

Then he lifted his hand. "You are abbey-bred, young sir?"

"Ay," said Peter. "Oseney."

The man's face softened. "Well I know it, and 'twas once a noble palace of God. But it is falling, falling, like all the

112

others. I looked on it again this very summer, and my eyes watered as I gazed on that noble tower which would make a fit resting-place for archangels, and my ear heard its myriad of chinking rivulets. When I passed through its courts I saw old men mazed in foolish worldly toils, and the stones crumbling, and grass growing in their cracks. There are few sins in Oseney save those of omission, but its feeble innocence will not save it. It goes the way of the rest, for the Lord is purging His threshing floor. You are doubtless one who would save such relics, even when they fester."

"Nay, I would reshape them. There are abuses enough, God knows, and some of them I have seen with my own eyes. But I would not plunder God to enrich Mammon."

"So that is your way of it." The man seemed to have lost his weariness and sat straighter in the saddle. "Where then should the abbey spoils go when the folk are sent packing? If you say 'to the service of a purified Church,' then you and I think the same. Strange, if you are kin to Avelard!"

"I would not send the folk packing. They have not oppressed the poor, like many of the great ones, and the poor in these days have few friends."

The man bent his brow. "Stranger still for Avelard blood! Why, man, your ancient kinsman has been in his day the harshest oppressor this side of Severn! You are right in one thing. The poor man needs every friend who will stand between him and the bitter blasts that blow from the high places. But the abbeys were not protectors. No nursing mothers they, but harsh stepdams."

"Then what is this news from the eastern shires?" Peter asked. "It would seem that the commons of those parts are ready to risk their necks for the religious houses."

"That is the lovable simplicity of poor folk. But it is not for the monks they fight but for their hope of salvation.

> "'Christ crucified
> For thy wounds wide
> Us commons guide
>   Which pilgrims be!'

113

That is their song. The hearts of Englishmen are not turned from God, but their eyes are dim. But God is preparing His own salve for their blear eyes, and soon they will see clear. England will be merry again when she has turned from the glosses and corruptions of man to the plain script of God. To that great purpose many contribute, though they know it not. The King on the throne, for one, and the broad-faced scrivener Crummle who gathers treasure for his master. They are but instruments to win the world back from the Church to Christ."

"They are strange instruments for a strange end," said Peter. "And the same instruments will bear hard on you, my friend."

"Though He slay me yet will I trust in Him," was the answer. "The bodies of many will be dung for the fields before the new grain springs."

Peter rose in his stirrups to look behind him. There were the Bishop's four servants, but what had become of the Avelard men? They must have fallen far back and be beyond a turning of the road which lay straight to the eye for a mile and more. For the party was now on the great Fosse Way, the Roman highroad which ran from south-west to north-east across England. The six of them stopped at the tavern of Fosse Bridge to eat, where the road crossed the Coln, but they finished their meal without any sign of the truants. Peter, intent on his own errands, saw no reason to delay for them, since the Bishop's men were a sufficient posse, so presently they were jingling up the hill towards the town of Northleach, where the road branched off for Oxford. But before they came in sight of its great church, as big as many a minster, and heard the rattle of the windlasses in the wool-sheds, another horseman on a bay gelding struck in from a by-path on their right and joined them. To his surprise and disgust Peter recognised Simon Rede. The gospeller too recognised him, for his pale face flushed and a sudden light came into it.

Simon ranged himself on Peter's other side.

"A fair day for the road, my friend, but 'twill be snow ere night." His face was ruddy with the weather, and his pale eyes were merry.

"I thought you had gone to Gloucester," said Peter glumly.

"I have done my errand in that direction, and now business calls me back to Boarstall. I and my horse are used to long and sudden journeys. It appears that you are shedding your convoy, Master Bonamy. I passed two of my Lord Avelard's men five miles back, drunk as swine in a hedge alehouse."

Peter cried out. "They were sober fellows as ever I saw."

"They are most marvellously unsober now. Strong ale and strong air go fast to a man's head. But the Bishop may do very well without them. Four lusty rogues are sufficient to carry a feeble man to jail."

How it was managed Peter did not know, but at a nod from Simon the escort closed up, and the gospeller fell back among them. "Secure that thong," they were told, and the prisoner was again bound up to the belt of the lackey. Thus Peter found himself riding ahead with Simon as his companion.

All his antagonism had revived. This man had taken charge of the party and ousted him from the command, without so much as a word of explanation. The arrogance of it left him speechless, and rankled the more since it seemed so natural. The intruder made no question of it, for he assumed that no question could be asked.

Yet they had scarcely left Northleach when he found himself forced into conversation with the interloper, and they had not gone a mile before that conversation had driven all other thoughts from his head. For it was clear that this man did not despise him—nay, that he might even fear him. He seemed disposed to friendship, and felt his way towards it with a careful diplomacy. He accepted him as Lord Avelard's heir, a cousin, too, of old Sir Ralph at Wood Eaton. But his curiosity did not seem to be about Lord Avelard's affairs but about Sir Gabriel. Who and what was Sir Gabriel? What did he at Avelard? An unwilling admiration seemed to lurk in Simon's voice, and dislike too, as for one too showy and foppish, a distaste which he flatteringly assumed Peter must share.

But Peter had little to tell him. Sir Gabriel was of the Court,

115

and had been useful in going to and from the King of France. And then he guessed at the cause of Simon's interest. He feared Sir Gabriel as a rival with Sabine, and would probe his quality. But he did not fear Peter. . . . And at the thought his vexation returned, and he gave short answers.

But Simon's good humour seemed unbreakable, and it was hard to be short with him. For, presently, detecting his companion's mood, he swung off to different topics. He spoke, as he had spoken the night before, of a widening world. The man had scholarship of a kind, for he could quote a phrase of Aristotle and a line of Seneca to the effect that one travelling towards the sunset would in time come round to the sunrise. Peter's interest was acutely stirred, and there might have been confidences between the two had not the weather suddenly turned to the vilest. The road, strung high along open wolds, ran eastward, and the riders were met by the full force of a blizzard of snow. It drove with the violence of the first precursor of the winter's storms, whipping their faces, blinding their eyes, and shutting out the Windrush vale with a screen of leaden mist.

"If we would enter upon this new world," Simon was saying, "we must purge our baggage. A man must travel light." Then he flung a fold of his cloak around his throat. "A murrain on this weather," he cried, "for I must be beyond Otmoor ere I sleep. There is promise of a heavy fall. You will be well advised, Master Bonamy, to seek a shelter for the night, since in your errand there is no need of spurring. It matters little when the wretch behind us lies in the Bishop's prison so long as he duly reach that haven. In an hour the night will fall. Best look for a lodging while there is a spark left of daylight."

The counsel was good, and Peter was conciliated by this deference to him as leader of the party. But it was no easy task to find port in such a place in such weather. The road ran solitary among downs, now piebald with snow, and the prospect on either side was only a few yards of driving vapour.

Peter had decided to push on to Burford, which he judged to be but a few miles distant, in spite of his aversion to lying

116

at a tavern on such an errand, when in a sudden clearing of the snow he saw a light flicker on his left. He decided that they were close to Barrington woods, which were outliers of Wychwood. This must be some forester's hut, and where a forester lodged there would be an outhouse of some kind where they could camp, and fuel for a bivouac. So he gave the order to turn north, and, after a hundred yards of rough pasture, they reached the light and smelt the smoke of green boughs.

The place proved to be a wretched hovel of logs and mud, through the chinks of which came the gleam of a fire. In the dim light there could be seen around it broken walls and one large ruinous barn.

"This was once a snug farm," said Simon. "Now some waif squats in the ruins, as a bird builds its nest in the nettles of a stoneheap."

A shout from Simon brought someone to the door, a half-naked boy in his middle teens. Simon flung himself from his horse and pushed past him into the hovel, while Peter followed. It was a single room with an earthen floor, on which the snow, melting on the wattled roof and drifting through the holes, was making deep puddles. There was no light in the place but a new-kindled fire of wet wood, the smoke from which filled the air and set the eyes smarting. Furniture there was none except a three-legged stool and in a corner a heap of straw on which it seemed that a human figure lay. This was no forester's hut, but a hovel of the very poorest.

On the stool sat a man who seemed to be engaged in cooking something in a broken pot. He was a bent creature with tangled tow-like hair. A ragged sack was his only garment, and through the rents of it showed ribs as sharp as the bars of a harrow. At the sight of the strangers he let the pot drop so that some of its contents spilled and fizzled in the ashes, while his face was drawn in an extreme terror. Yet it was a vacant terror, a physical rather than a mental passion, for, while his cheeks and mouth were contorted, his eyes remained dull and blind.

Simon sniffed, for the spilled food sent out a vile odour.

117

"We want lodgings and kindling for a fire," he said. "What of the barn? Is the roof reasonable tight?"

The man only muttered, and it was the boy who answered.

"Tighter than this, master. There be store of faggots, too, against the next deer-drive. But we have nought to do with the place, for it belongs to Master Lee, the verderer."

"We will take Master Lee's permission for granted, for we travel on the King's business. What have you in that pot?"

The man now spoke, his thin jaws working with a great effort, and his voice was like a bat's squeak. But his speech, like the boy's, was not that of an ordinary churl.

"Nothing, gentle sirs, but some nettle broth, with the thickening of a dead partridge, half-plucked by a hawk, which Dickon found in Waterman's Acre."

"The bird must have been dead a week," said Simon, screwing up his nose.

"You speak truth, sir," said the man eagerly. "'Twas only carrion, and therefore honestly come by for a poor man." And, all the while his lips and eyes seemed to be twisting towards the pot, as if he were in the last stage of famine.

"What is that on the straw?" Simon asked.

"My wife, noble sir. She has been dead twelve hours, and Dickon and I wait for the snow to pass to bury her."

"Of what sickness?" Simon demanded in a sharpened voice, for the whole world feared the plague.

"Of none. Of a lamentable lack of food. Dickon did not find the partridge in time, and we have had nought for our bellies this past sennight but hips and haws and beechmast."

Simon swung round. "Go on with your meal, brother. We will camp in the barn and make use of Master Lee's faggots. We carry food with us, so need not borrow yours."

Peter, whose stomach was turning at the stench of the pot and the spectacle of the dead thing on the straw, followed him hastily out of doors. The men were soon settled in the barn, which proved to be tolerably water-tight, a fire was made and a lantern lit, and the food wallets unpacked; while the horses were tethered among some straw at the far end. When the meal was eaten, Simon resaddled his beast.

"I must get me onward," he said, "for the storm seems to abate. Farewell, Master Bonamy, and good speed to your journey! If you will honour my humble dwelling of Boarstall I will show you the work of the Italian chart-maker whom I spoke of." Then to the men, "See you truss up that fellow when you lie down. If you sleep like hogs, and he is unshackled, he will be over Severn by the time you wake."

Peter's first intention had been to pass the night with the others. But the sight of a patch of clear sky and a few stars made him incline to follow Simon's example. He was not concerned to deliver the gospeller to the Bishop's charge: that was for the Bishop's servants, and the two Avelard men, now lying drunk many miles in the rear. His business was to find Darking, and for that he must get him to Mother Sweetbread. The distance was not more than five miles, and he knew every cranny of the countryside.

So he, too, resaddled his horse, and with a word to the men to go on to Oxford next day as they had been bidden, he opened the door and flung his cloak about his shoulders. It had an odd feeling, and, when he took it to the lantern, he realised that it was Simon's cloak of grey frieze, and that his own, which was of soft murry-coloured woollen from the Stour, was now on Simon's back on the road to Boarstall. There was small loss in the exchange, for the two men were much of a height.

Then another thought struck him. He picked up some of the remains of the food, a piece of loaf, a knuckle of salted beef, and a fragment of pie. There was enough left for the men to breakfast off, and they would be in Oxford for the noontide meal. He slung the viands in a corner of his cloak, and led his horse to the hovel door.

The couple had finished their meal, for the pot was empty. The man was picking his teeth with a bit of bone, and the boy was scraping the pot. The fire had sunk, and the light was so dim that he could not see the dead woman on the straw.

"Here are some broken meats," he said. "And see here, friend. Here are also three silver pennies, that your wife may be decently put in the earth."

119

The man scarcely lifted his head, but the boy seized eagerly on the gifts.

"If I were found with those monies on me I would hang," said the man.

"Nay, father, I know where I can spend them secretly," said the boy. "And here be enough food to keep us for a week. God bless ye, my lord."

The man cast one look to the corner, and shook his matted head like a puzzled animal. "Would that God had sent him twelve hours sooner, or that Dickon had been quicker in finding the bird." He hunched himself again on the stool, and stared into the ashes. There was neither sorrow nor regret in his voice, only bewilderment.

The snow had gone, and there was sufficient clear sky to permit of a faint starlight. Peter put his horse to a trot, for he wished to put miles between him and that place of death and famine. Fresh from the splendour of Avelard, he felt like a man in thin raiment coming from a warm and scented room into a bitter wind. To one brought up in the homely comfort of the Wychwood cottage, and the simple abundance of Oseney, this sudden glimpse of unimagined poverty was an awful revelation. He could not banish the picture from his mind, as he rode through the slush of the highway and the sprinkled meadows to Mother Sweetbread's cottage high up on the skirts of Wychwood.

There he found the warm fire, and the lighted lamp, and the old welcome. He stabled his horse in an outhouse commonly occupied by forest ponies, and supped off a stew of game and a cup of Mother Sweetbread's famous sloeberry wine.

"Solomon Darking left word that you were to follow him without delay to Oxford," he was told.

"You will find him, he said, at the Swan tavern over against the Ox Pens. You were to go secretly, and only under cover of night. Now to bed with you, Peterkin—for I will call you by no other name. You look as weary as John Gowglass when he fled home from the night-riders on Bartholomew Eve."

But Peter had not been three hours between Mother

120

Sweetbread's blankets, when he was roused by voices at the door, and found a lean urchin gabbling a message to his hostess. At the sight of him the boy slipped to his side, and in his eagerness took him by the hands. It was the boy from the hovel, and his errand was urgent. Someone had attacked the posse in the barn and released the prisoner, setting him on the best horse. The Bishop's men had been overpowered in their sleep . . . bound with ropes, too, and had only freed themselves after the fugitives had been half an hour gone. They had been in a great taking, and had gone to Squire Fettiplace at Swinbrook, who was a zealous King's man and would for certain mount his servants and scour the country. "They think it was you that done the deed, master," the boy added, "for they swear they recognised the cloak of him that mishandled them. . . . I heard them say that the villain was one Bonamy, who had ridden with them from Avelard and decoyed them to their undoing."

Peter's first impulse was to laugh. Simon Rede with the borrowed cloak had bested him nobly.

"Haste ye, master," said the boy. "I followed ye here by your horse's tracks. There is a powdering of snow and others can do the same."

CHAPTER VIII

HOW PETER SAW DEATH IN THE SWAN INN

In the light of Mother Sweetbread's rush candle Peter stared at the sparrow-like child, and the sparrow-like child stared at Peter.

There was no manner of doubt as to his peril. If the Fettiplace men laid hands on him, he would have the evidence of the Bishop's servants against him—honest evidence, for it would rest upon the sight of his own cloak on the back of the man who had freed the gospeller. To rebut it he must proclaim his connection with Avelard and reveal the details of his journey, and that meant that he, who for the moment must court obscurity, would stand out glaringly to the whole shire—nay, even to Oxford and the Bishop of Lincoln. The thing was not to be thought of.

"I am trysted with Solomon in Oxford," he told the woman, "but not till the dark hours, so I must get me to cover. I am for Stowood. Feed the child, mother, for he has earned it well." Then to the boy, "What is your name?"

"They call me Dickon," was the answer. "Dickon of the Holt!"

"Then, Dickon, get you back the road you came. Put yourself in the way of the Swinbrook men and let them drag from you news of me. You saw me on the Witney road with the prisoner, riding like one possessed. This horse of mine, mother, you will send into the forest till I can recover him. Hide him where no Fettiplace can penetrate, for he is a damning link with Avelard. Then give me some provender for the road, for I will be hungry before tomorrow's e'en."

"This is the vigil of Hallowmas," said the old woman anxiously. "'Tis an ill night to take to the greenwood."

"Better Hallowe'en witches than the rough hands of Squire Fettiplace. Haste you, mother. I must be beyond Cherwell ere daybreak."

Ten minutes later Peter—cloakless, for he must travel light—had slipped from the hut, where a hungry lad was supping bear-meal porridge, and an old woman was saying spells by the fire for his protection. The snow had ceased to fall, but it lay an inch and more deep on the ground. The wind had dropped, a few stars showed, and on the horizon there was the prelude of moonrise. It was bitter cold, so he ran— first across the slushy pastures, then through the scrub of the forest bounds, and then by a path he knew, which in the shadow of the trees was almost bare of snow, and which took him down the southern ridge of the Evenlode vale.

Now that he had leisure to think, his anger surged up against Simon Rede. The man was a foe to God, for he had freed a heretic—Peter made the reflection mechanically and without conviction, for it seemed to set his grievance on higher grounds than his own pride. Simon was certainly an enemy to himself, for he had deforced the Bishop's men in such a way as to lay the blame on his innocent head. Doubtless, too, he had earlier in the day made the two Avelard men drunk. For what purpose? To free the gospeller? But why incriminate Peter?

He was of the opposite party, and must suspect something—Lord Avelard had feared this—Sir Ralph Bonamy had feared it—that was why he himself had had to take the road again. The man was as cunning as he was bold. Peter thought bitterly of how he had thawed to this enemy, and a few hours ago had looked on him almost as a comrade. He remembered ruefully his admiration of the man's carriage and conversation. And he had been nobly duped. The stolen cloak, the tale of a journey post-haste to Boarstall, the friendly parting— every incident rankled in his memory. Well, it was for him to defeat Master Simon's conspiracies. He had something against him—the knowledge, the certain knowledge, that he was in league with those who defied the King's grace in matters of religion. And then he laughed sardonically, for he himself was about to defy the King's grace in things of greater moment.

He strove to keep his mind on the notion that Simon's

hostility to him was because of state policy. But it would not stay there. The unpleasing reflection would edge its way in that the cause was Sabine Beauforest. The man had not come to Avelard to please Crummle's commissary, but to be near the girl. Of that he was as certain as that he was now stumbling through the scrub oaks above Evenlode with owls hooting like lost souls around him. Presently the thought became a conviction, and the conviction an oppression. Simon was a rival, a deadly rival, and he had won the first bout by turning the heir of Avelard into a mockery. He saw that lean face puckered with mirth, and those cool, arrogant, contemptuous eyes, and he had a miserable consciousness of weakness in the face of such an antagonist. Decked with the pomp of Avelard he could condescend on one who was no more than a squire of modest estate, but now Simon was mounted and fronting the world, while he was afoot and a fugitive.

In his depression the picture of Sabine seemed to limn itself on the dark night—Sabine, not as he had last seen her, distracted and sullen, but Sabine on that night when she had opened her arms to him, her pale loveliness suddenly become a fire. Once he had thought of a fair woman as something dim and infinitely distant, like a sickle moon in an April twilight. Now he had seen the fairest of all, her eyes dewy with kindness, her lips tremulous with surrender. The picture entranced and maddened him, but it also drove Simon Rede from his head. He was Bohun, and his business was to win in the lists which had been set for him. To victory there all other things would be added, chief of which was a laughing girl.

Before dawn the snow returned, big powdery flakes with no wind behind them. In a crook of Bladon heath, just outside the deer-park of Woodstock, he stumbled upon a small encampment of horse-priggers, round a hissing fire. Half a dozen weedy garrons, with their heads muffled in sacking, were tethered near by. John Naps's watchword saved him a slit throat, and secured him a bed of moderately dry bracken and enough of the fire to warm his toes. There he slept till an hour after daybreak, when he was roused by the

124

encampment shifting ground. He breakfasted on some of the food he had brought from Mother Sweetbread, distrusting the stew of the priggers. The ruffians were civil enough and a little abashed in his presence, for Flatsole ruled the clan with an iron hand. They showed some relief when he prepared to leave them, and they gave him a useful bit of news. Catti the Welshman was in the alehouse at Gosford, lying hid because of a broken rib. Peter must find a place to spend the daylight hours, and in such weather he preferred the shelter of a roof to a cold hollow of Stowood. Where Catti lay he might reckon on a safe sanctuary.

The snow grew heavier as he crossed the open moorlands towards the sharp spire of Kidlington church. He skirted the village and came to the tiny hamlet of Gosford, hard upon a ford of Cherwell. He remembered the alehouse, a pleasant place where, in a garden beside a colony of bees, he had had many a summer draught. Now the bush at its door was turned upside down—the innkeeper's sign that there was sickness in the hostelry and that no guests could be entertained. There was an utter silence in the hamlet, not a soul showed or a dog stirred, nothing but the even descent of the snow. But behind doors and windows he seemed to catch a glimpse of furtive faces.

Peter made for the back-quarters of the tavern. There he found a sluttish girl plucking a cockerel, and tossing the white feathers to mix with the falling snow. "Will you carry a message, Mother Goose," said Peter, "to him who lodges here?"

"There be no one lodging here, master," she said. "Feyther has the autumn sickness, and mother is new brought to bed."

"Nevertheless, you will take my message and give it to whom you will," and he spoke the first part of John Naps's watchword.

She looked up at Peter, and, seeing him young and well-favoured, relaxed her stubbornness. She flung the half-plucked fowl to him with a laugh. "I dar not idle, master, with all the work of the house on my hands. Do 'ee finish my job and I will carry your word indoors."

In an instant she was back, giggling.

"Feyther he says, 'Far as to Peter's gate.' What play be it, master? Wychwood's no more'n six miles."

"Say, 'Alack, I shall not be there in time.'"

She nodded. "Ay, that was what I was bidden wait for. Come 'ee indoors, but first shake the clots from your feet, lest you muck up my floor."

Catti was not in the house, but in a chamber, the remnant of an old priory, which was connected with the building by a vaulted passage. There he lay on a couch of straw and rags in a darkness illumined only by a brazier which burned beside him and such light as came from above through the slats of the roof. But even in the dimness Peter saw the beetle brows and the fierce black eyes and the hilt of a long knife.

The man was genial and open, for Naps's pass was clearly a master word. When he heard that Peter—whose name he did not ask—was on his way to meet Darking and in some peril from the law, he became reassuring. Peter was safe for the daylight hours, and what easier than to slip into Oxford by the east gate in weather which would keep the inquisitive at home? Thereafter Solomon would see to him, Solomon who could, if he wanted, pass a red-handed felon through the guards of a palace.

He had got his own hurt on the Worcester road. It was near healed, and he proposed to move towards London, where trade would be brisk, since the King's law was gone Lincoln way. Peter, with Lord Avelard's talk in his head, was amazed to find how well informed this bandit was on every matter they had spoken of with hushed voices. He knew what was stirring on the western marches, and named the very numbers which Neville and Latimer had under arms.

Peter asked about Simon Rede, and Catti scratched his head.

"He is a ready man with his blade," he said, "as some of us know to our cost. But he is merry, too, and Boarstall has a good name among us wandering folk. They say he is hot for some new thing called Gospel, which the King mislikes. There are many that hate him, but more that fear him, and

126

he goes his own road unquestioned. Nay, he is not one of us. They say that Gospel is harder on an honest man than the King's justices. Job Cherryman that took up with it fell to groaning and weeping and died of a wasting in a twelvemonth. 'Tis some madness of the gentles, and not for the poor."

Peter ate the rest of his food in Catti's company, and noted how messages came all day to the recluse—a head thrust past the door, a question asked and answered, all in the jargon which he had heard at Little Greece. When the time came for him to leave, Catti appointed a ragged urchin to show him the road down the right bank of Cherwell.

"You are well served," said Peter.

Catti laughed. "Needs must in a trade like mine. This morning, master, you came from Brother Friday's priggers on Bladon heath. I had news of you before you passed Kidlington granges, and, had you not come from honest company, you had never had speech with Cis here, and gotten entrance to this cell of mine."

An hour after dark Peter entered Oxford by the side-gate adjoining Magdalen College. The snow had passed, and the air had sharpened to a still frost, but a light fog held the upper heavens, and there was no moon or star. There had been a glow by the east gate, which lit up everything, for Magdalen College, which was without the city wall, had fired a great bonfire to drive away the plague. The High Street was dark in patches, but opposite University College there was a glare also, for in its quadrangle was another bonfire. Though the hour was yet early, the place seemed empty and quiet. Farther on, where Peter had to grope his way to avoid the swollen gutter, there came the music of an organ and young voices across the way. Peter remembered that it was the Eve of All Souls, and that, according to custom, masses were being sung in Chichele's college for the repose of the dead fallen in France. There was an echo of singing, too, from Brasenose, and Haberdashers' Hall had lights in all its upper windows. But beyond that it was very dark. The Ram inn had shut its outer door, so that only a narrow thread of light escaped to

127

the cobbles. The flesher near by had shuttered his shop, but the carcase of a buck from Shotover was hanging outside from a hook of the balcony, and Peter's forehead took the beast's rump with such force that he sat down heavily in the slush.

At the place called Quarvex, where the church of St Martin hung above the meeting of four streets, stood a stone seat called the Pennyless Bench, built for the comfort of the market-folk. The little square was deserted, and Peter stepped out with more confidence, for he was now on the confines of the west part of the city, which was his own quarter. But from the shadows of the Pennyless Bench a voice spoke:

"'Tis a raw night to go cloakless, friend," it said.

Peter started and slipped in a puddle of snow. He understood now that the faint glow from the east window of the church must have illumined his figure to one sitting in the shadows. Moreover, he knew the voice. He took a step forward, and saw in the corner of the bench what seemed to be the figure of a tall man.

Even as he stared the figure twitched a cloak from its shoulders and tossed it towards him.

"Take it, friend," said the voice. "You have the better right to it." And Peter caught in his hands his own murry-coloured cloak of woollen.

The voice spoke again.

"You would fly at my throat, but I pray you consider. This is no place to brawl for one or t'other of us. Also you are unarmed and I bear a sword. Doubtless I used you scurvily last night, but I had weighty reasons, which some day I may recount to you. Thank God for a restored garment, and go in peace."

Peter's anger flared up at the cool air of authority.

"I have no sword, but, if you are a man, you will unbuckle yours. Come with me across Bookbinders bridge to a corner I know of where we may be undisturbed. There I will fight you with the weapons that God gave us both at birth, and bring you to task for last night's work."

A laugh came from the shadow.

"'Twould be good play, doubtless, and would warm our

128

blood in this nipping weather. But I have no time for such sport, nor, methinks, have you, Master Bonamy. I am within easy hail of Boarstall, but you are very far from Avelard. Get you to Oseney and your supper."

There was a noise farther down the Cornmarket street and a sudden gleam of light, which announced the watch.

"I have but to wait," Peter said, "and proclaim that you are he that loosed the heretic from the Bishop's men."

Again the man laughed. "You would not be credited," he said. "I am better known in Oxford town than the reputed heir of my Lord Avelard out of the west country. Besides"— he paused—"bethink you what, if so minded, I could proclaim of you. Begone, my priestling. A cell at Oseney is healthier for you than the cobbles of Quarvex on a November night."

The sound of the oncoming watch grew nearer, and Peter let prudence govern his temper. This was not the place or hour for a reckoning with Simon Rede. He flung the cloak round his shoulders, and turned down a lane that led to the Castle. He was angry and shamed. Once again his enemy had had the laugh of him, and at the thought of the scornful merriment in Simon's voice he shivered, but not with the cold.

It was darker and quieter among the lanes beside the Castle which sloped to the river. Down in Fisherrow there were moving lights, and high in the sky Peter saw the lamp in the bell-tower of Oseney. Even as he gazed Thomas began to strike the hour of eight. He passed no one except a lay brother hurrying to Rewley, and a party of young bloods from one of the colleges, who had come from hawking in Botley fen, and had been making a great clamour at the west gate. At the said gate a band of west-country clothiers were setting out, hoping to lie the night at Witney, so as to make Gloucester on the morrow. Peter slipped round the shaggy cavalcade, and found himself without the walls, on the Oseney causeway.

From there it was but a step to the Ox Pens, a piece of open ground where a cattle-market was held of a Tuesday. Beyond it was a cluster of small houses, huddled round the approach to the river bridge called the Fennel. It was rough going, for the ground was slippery with dung and offal, and there were many miry puddles now crackling with frost. The Swan tavern was not hard to find, for it had an open door from which slanted a broad band of light that illuminated a white swan on a scarlet ground on a board surmounting a pollarded willow. The place, now that Thomas's strokes had died on the night, was as silent as the heart of Wychwood. Even the lit tavern made no sound.

It was a very humble place, but the rushes on the floor were fresh and the logs on the hearth crackled cheerfully. There was no one there.

Peter shook the powder of snow from his cloak, stamped his feet clear, and warmed himself at the blaze. The place had the air of a room much frequented and expecting guests. He called loudly for a drawer.

A little girl peeped round the corner of an inner door, and laid her finger on her lips, her eyes wide with apprehension.

"Whisht!" she said. "Ye manna make no noise—he be near his dead-throes."

"Master Darking?" Peter began, but the child had gone. He noticed that at least a dozen lights, besides that of the fire, were burning in the little room, so that the place was as bright as a high altar at Candlemas. There was no sound except the logs crackling. The door was pinned open to its widest, and from the silent tavern an eerie radiance flooded out into the silent night.

Peter felt a spell creeping upon him. He took off his cloak, sat down on a stool, and stared into the fire. This was the place that Darking had appointed, and his task was done in coming here. Meantime he could rest, for he felt listless and out of temper.

A hand was laid on his arm, and he saw that it was Darking, who had come in by the door through which the child had peeped. He wore a townsman's clothes, so that he looked like some prosperous trader, save for his lean, outland face.

"God's mercy has brought you here, my lord," he said. "I feared my message would not be in time, or that you might have some pressing business at Avelard. But indeed no business could be more pressing than this. One lies dying in this house that has something to say to you.

Darking pulled another stool to the hearth.

" 'Tis the outcome of Mother Sweetbread's care and the spells of Madge of Shipton. They have sought treasure for you, and maybe they have found it. You have heard of the great Lord Lovell?"

Peter nodded. "Him that died after the Stoke battle— drowned in Trent?"

"Nay, he did not drown in Trent. He came in secret to his own house of Minster Lovell, and what befell him after that is known only to God. But he is dead long since, for that is fifty years back. But mark you what manner of man was this Francis Lovell. With Catesby and Ratcliffe he ruled the land under King Richard. You have heard the country rhyme:

" 'The Cat, the Rat, and Lovell our dog
Ruled all England under the Hog.'

He brought your grandsire, Harry of Buckingham, to his death, and got his office of Constable. He had the plundering of the whole nation, and, being no spender, he amassed uncounted riches. Where, think you, has that wealth gone? Harry the King had never a groat of it. 'Tis buried somewhere among the ruinous courts of Minster Lovell, and it may be yours for the finding. A third of it, my lord, would give you the sinews of war, and make you master indeed, for you would have your own privy purse, and be dependent on none."

Peter was stirred to the liveliest interest.

"But what hope? . . . Who can know? . . ."

"Listen! My tale goes on. At Minster Lovell there was one household thirled above all others to the wicked lord. Its name was Blackthorn, and Giles Blackthorn was at my lord's bridle hand in all his iniquity. Where Lovell pricked Blackthorn slew, and where Lovell pinched Blackthorn skinned. Well, this Giles died beyond question on Stoke field from an arrow in the throat, but he left a widow more evil than himself. 'Twas to Mother Blackthorn at Minster Lovell that my lord fled after his cause had gone down, and Mother Blackthorn alone knew what end he made. She lived for but a month after Stoke, and died in the terrors of hell, screaming that she could not leave her lord, and, as I have been told, being held down in bed by four men to control her frenzy. With her an ugly stock passed out of the world, save for her son Jack. He had been page to Lovell, and had been at Stoke with him and had accompanied him home, and, though only a stripling, was as wicked as his master. Whatever black secrets Lovell had this Rustling Jack, as they called him, was their sure repository. After his mother's death he disappeared, like my lord, and was believed long since to be in the devil's hands. But it seems the world was wrong. He was in far countries, fighting for the Spaniards, and a prisoner for years among the heathen. Now, by the arts of Goody Littlemouse, he has been discovered."

"Where?" Peter asked breathlessly.

"In this very house, where he is now at the point of death. The priest of St Thomas awaits to shrive him. But he cannot save his soul by confession like a Christian, for it seems that he has done things which cannot be told even to holy ears. Also he has some restitution to make, and till he make it his soul will not leave his body. He has a horror of darkness on him, and that is why these lights burn. Also he has a horror of sound, and cries that the pealing of Oseney bells are the yells of the damned."

"What has he to restore?"

"My guess is that it is the clue to Lovell's treasure. Mother Littlemouse, who has her own ways of getting knowledge, is assured that he has such a secret in his keeping. But he will not surrender it to any chance comer. He cries out for one of the blood of Lovell to help him die. You, my lord, are of that blood, for Lovell and Stafford and Bohun were all inter-mingled. They say, too, that you are the living image of your grandsire, Duke Harry. Maybe, when he sees you, he may be moved to make you his confessor. But we must make haste, for his thread of life wears thin."

The boy's mood in a violent revulsion was now one of excited triumph. It seemed like God's hand leading him by strange paths to recover that heritage of which he had been harshly robbed. Lovell's treasure was Buckingham's treasure, since Lovell had clomb to power on Buckingham's ruin. A sudden memory gave him assurance. The sign of this place was the swan, and the swan was the badge of Bohun.

The frontage of the tavern was narrow, but the building was deep, since behind it lay a nest of small rooms, dug out of a fragment of old masonry which may have gone back to Norman days. Peter found himself in a crooked passage, blazing with tallow dips in iron sconces. There was a little window with a broken hasp, through which came eddies of air that set the lights smoking. As he passed it he had a glimpse without of swollen rushing waters. This place abutted on the river—a fine strategic point for lawless folk.

Darking ushered him into a big room which looked like the girnel of an ancient mill. Here, too, many lights blazed, which revealed the cobwebbed rafters, the floor deep in dust, and a vast rusty pin projecting from the wall. On a pallet in the centre lay the dying man, with beside him an old woman, the inn-wife, who from time to time moistened his lips with sour wine. A man in a priest's gown stood by the far wall, a timid youth who was busy with his beads. As they entered Darking fell back, the old woman rose and withdrew to the priest's side, and Peter found himself alone by the pallet, looking down at a grey face distorted with fear.

The man whom they called Rustling Jack was very old. His neck was a mere string of sinews, his cheeks were fallen into ghastly hollows, and the lips he moved incessantly were blue like the blackthorn fruit. A great scar ran athwart his brow, and the wrists which lay on the coverlet were grooved deep with the manacles which had once attached him to his oar in the Moors' galleys. The eyes were shut, and through his clenched teeth came a slow moaning.

Peter stood awestruck, regarding the tortured face. He had never seen a man die, and this one was having a cruel passage. In spite of age and weakness the man on the pallet seemed to him a fearful thing, for on his face was printed as in a book a long odyssey of evil.

133

Suddenly he saw that the eyes had opened and were staring at him, and so hungry was their stare that he stepped back a pace. A voice filtered painfully between the lips.

"Who is it?" it croaked. "In God's name what are you that vexes me? Your name? Your name? You have eyes I mind of. . . ."

"I am Bohun," said Peter, and he was not conscious of what he said.

There came an exulting laugh.

"There is no Bohun in England—not these fifty years—it is Lovell I see—Lovell."

"I am the grandson of Henry of Buckingham."

A gleam of intelligence came into the frenzied eyes.

"You are Henry of Buckingham. . . . I saw him die at Salisbury . . . his head rolled a good yard beyond the sawdust, and I sopped my kerchief in the blood of it. Yea, you have his eyes . . . he had pretty eyes to beguile hearts, but they could not save him. Harry Stafford . . . my lord liked him ill."

A last spasm of life galvanised him into action. He half raised himself, and Peter saw the neck muscles knot like eggs.

"Be you from Heaven or Hell I care not. Lovell slew you, but you have Lovell's blood, and I summon you to give my master peace. If you are a blessed one, I plead in Christ's name. My lord never leaves me . . . his voice whinnies and sobs in my ears, and I cannot go to meet him till I have done his commands. Angel or devil, I charge you to lay his spirit. Listen. . . . Bend down, ghost, for my breath is short. . . ."

Peter bent till his ear was close to the dying man's lips. The words came slow and faint but very clear. "*The west court,*" it said, "*the corner under the dovecot. . . . Three paces from the east wall.* . . . Haste ye in the name of God the Father and God the Son and . . ."

He fell back choking on the bed, and at the same moment all the lights in the room swayed and flickered as if from a rush of wind. Peter, white with awe, thought it was the waft of death, till he saw that the door by which he had entered had opened, and that the scared little girl he had already seen was standing in it. There was a noise beyond as of men's heavy

134

feet and men's speech.

At the same moment he felt Darking's hand on his arm. "You have the word?" was his excited whisper. "Then this is no place for you and me. There are men here seeking Jack, and they will find only clay. Quick—follow me."

Someone in a hurry blew out the lights, all but two at the bed head and one at the foot. Peter found himself dragged by Darking into a passage, narrower than that by which they had entered, and dark as a pit. Presently cold air blew in his face, and he was at a window, through which he was made to clamber. "Drop," said Darking's voice, and he was sprawling in the bottom of a wherry, riding on a rough current. A second later Darking joined him, untied a mooring rope, and took up the oars, and the boat shot under the bridge called the Fennel.

"You heard the words clear," Darking asked, and made Peter repeat them. "God be thanked, my lord. 'Twas a race between us and the Devil, and we won by a hair."

CHAPTER IX

THE ROAD TO DAMASCUS

Darking drew in to a corner of the upper Fisherrow which made a tiny wharf, and shipped the oars. The flurries of snow had ceased, and the air had become still and very cold. Thomas of Oseney rang the hour of ten, and his notes lingered long in the black vault of night. When they had died away, there was no sound in the world but the swirl of the flooded river.

"We must get a bed for the night," said Darking, stamping his feet against the chill, "and be off by dawn for Wychwood. Goody Littlemouse must lend her aid, for this is a dark business, my lord, and must be done very secretly and in the night."

Peter shivered. He could not banish from his memory the possessed face and the tortured eyes of the dying man in that room of many lights.

"I do not venture near Minster Lovell except in holy company. Brother Tobias goes with us, or I stir not a yard. God save us, Simon, but there is a fearsome relish of damnation about this business."

Darking looked at him sharply. "So be it. Your purpose is honest, my lord, and you but recover your own, but it is true that the Devil walks wherever Lovell trod. Now for bed. We can lie at Mother Shabbit's in Titmouse Lane."

Peter did not dare himself to enter Oseney. Though his clothes were no more clerkly, and his recent life had changed his colour, yet he could not hope to conceal himself from those who had seen him daily in chapel and fratry. So Darking did his errand, and brought him word that Tobias was engaged with the holy business of All-Hallows day and could not leave Oxford till the next morning. The weather was setting to heavy frost, and Peter had no mind to spend the day shivering

in the bed-loft of Mother Shabbit's tavern. He left Darking
to make the necessary arrangements for the morrow, since
Tobias was an old man who must ride and needed a sober
beast to carry him. Darking should bring him to Mother
Sweetbread's before dark on the following day, while Peter
would go on ahead and await him there.

So early in the forenoon he took the road on foot, out of
the west gate and along the Botley causeway to where the
highway to the west country ran between Wytham hill and
the shaggy slopes of Cumnor. The sky was an icy blue, and
an east wind blew sharp into his back, and on the flood-waters
skeins of wildfowl squattered among the crackling cat-ice. The
high-road was busy that day, for, besides the usual pack
trains, and a variety of religious padding it between Oxford
and Eynsham, he passed three armed companies swinging in
from Gloucestershire. These men were the King's levies, on
their way to the King's army in Lincoln, and the sight of them
cheered him. The fewer of that breed left in the west the better
for his cause.

From Swynford bridge, where he crossed a swollen Thames,
he took a short cut over the downland and forestland which
make a barrier between Evenlode and Windrush. His head
was full of war, for the tramp of horses and the clatter of
harness had power to intoxicate him. He had forgotten his
scruples and his qualms; the dying face in the Swan inn was
no longer an ironic comment on human glory. The biting air
and the free movement of his limbs on the winter turf had
revived in his blood the pride of life. Lord Avelard was the
master strategist! Peter saw, as in a view from a hilltop, the
King (he pictured him as fat and buxom in a suit of gold tissue)
sore pressed in the fenlands by a horde of churls who
welcomed death in their certainty of heaven; and all the while
a vast silent gathering drawing from north and west and
creeping like a dark shadow ever nearer the doomed tyrant,
who for his lusts had made England sorrow. He saw pallor
steal over the ruddy cheeks and fear dawn in the witless eyes.
And at the head of the shadow he saw the swan of Bohun.
What was his own place? Was he no more than a watchword,

137

a badge, an oriflamme? That had been his dread, but the dread was gone. If he were the paymaster he would be leader, not in name but in deed. It seemed as if God had moved in the matter to make plain his road, and the hot blood of youth and the clerk's conscience were alike at peace under this assurance of celestial favour.

He came to Mother Sweetbread's cottage just before the sun sank in a fiery haze over Cotswold. As he forded Windrush, where the ice was forming on the edge of the slack water, he saw, a mile behind him, the towers of Minster Lovell glowing blood-red in the sunsetting. He halted to gaze, and the sight made him uneasy. Somewhere in that maze of dark stones lay the treasure which was to ensure his triumph—that was what he told himself, but he found his heart incredulous. The place, a jumble of ink and blood and murky gold, seemed too fantastic for earth—unhallowed, too, a thing founded on lust and death and lit terribly by the fires of hell. He remembered how in his boyish days the name of Lovell had been a dark spell, and how, except in bright weather, no one had dared to go near that castle by the stream. In its shadow even Windrush lost its speed, and flowed stagnant and dim under the battlements. He was thankful that he had summoned Tobias to his aid, for he needed all that was of good report behind him.

To his amazement there was no sign of life in Mother Sweetbread's cottage. There was no candle, no fire on the hearth, no food on the table, though the door was unbarred according to the forest custom. Mother Sweetbread had clearly gone a-journeying.

Peter lit a fire, and found food in the cupboard, on which he made his supper. Then, for no reason which he could give, he dropped the heavy bar over the door, and clamped the window shutters. He was ill at ease, for he could not rid himself of the memory of that grim tower not a mile off, where none had dwelt for half a century. Nothing human, at least, but God knew what things of the night had made their lair in it. The picture of it as seen in the cold twilight filled his mind. It had seemed to be awaiting him, beckoning him, offering some dark commerce. Thank God, he was above it now, three hundred feet nearer Heaven, and close to the friendly beasts of the forest. He stretched himself on his foster-mother's bed, close to the hearth, and fell instantly asleep, but he had ill dreams. Door and windows rattled, though the night was bound still in frost. The first time he woke he started at a crooked shadow which ran towards him, till he saw that it was caused by the dying spurt of a log on the hearth. Twice he woke again and each time he seemed to hear the beating of great wings without, and had much ado to compose his mind with prayers. He commended his soul and his cause to God.

"I am only His instrument," he told himself, "I follow where He leads, and, whether it be His will to break me or to exalt me, I am content." But in his heart he knew that he lied.

Morning brought a heavy sky and a fiercer cold, but it brought to Peter some peace of mind. He unbarred door and windows, and let in the grey light. With his teeth chattering, he revived the fire, fetched water from the well which rarely froze, and made himself some porridge. He laved his face and breast and arms, and set his blood moving by a brisk run in the forest clearing. He returned to the cottage to find that Mother Sweetbread had returned, and with her an ancient woman whose face was waxen with age, but whose eyebrows and the hair on a mole on her chin were black as jet.

His foster-mother clasped him in her arms. "Woe is me," she cried, "that you should come to my house and get so cold a welcome! You found food and firing, you say? But you had to get it for yourself, Peterkin, and that is no task for a great man. I durst not sleep the night here, for there are devils unloosed—I could hear them whimpering in the dark—so I took shelter with Mother Littlemouse, and Madge has come back with me to bear me company."

The little old witch-wife looked him over with eyes like pits of bog-water.

"You have my ring on your finger, my lord," she said, "so no ill can hurt you yet awhile. When do the others come?"

Peter told her that Darking would appear before evening, and with him Brother Tobias. At the name of the latter Mother Sweetbread cried out with delight, but Madge looked grave. "He cannot go where you must go, my lord. It is decreed that he that would challenge the spirits of earth must challenge them alone. A priest will scare them and wound their dignity. The Church, on which be blessings, has its own land, and these spirits have theirs, and God has ruled that for the time the boundaries shall be fixed. You were no more than in time at the Swan inn. It was needful that you saw him they call the Rustler before his death, and I sat at Shipton sweating with fear lest you should be too late. He died three minutes and twenty seconds after you left him."

"How did you learn? . . ." Peter began.

"Hush, sir, and ask not," said Mother Sweetbread. "Madge here has her own ways of knowledge."

The witch-wife regarded him with placid eyes.

"The day before yesterday I followed your every step after you left the priggers' camp at Bladon. I watched you visit Master Catti, and saw you creep into Oxford and have words with a certain one at Quarvex. I could have wept with vexation at every minute you tarried, for I saw also the Rustler with the breath choking in his throat."

"You saw?" Peter stammered.

"I saw, but with the eye of spirit, not the eye of flesh. I have woven a chain 'twixt you and me, which keeps me aware of all your doings. Ask me not how, for that is my secret."

"And with Rustling Jack?"

"With him I have long had such a chain, for once we were lovers."

"Tell me of tonight. Is there indeed treasure at Minster Lovell? Shall I harvest it?"

"I cannot foretell what God decrees is to come to pass. My knowledge is only of things that already are in being. But this I can tell you. There's that in Minster Lovell which the Rustler valued as dear as his own life, and which the Lord Lovell valued no less. 'Tis for you to guess what that can be."

She flung a sort of cowl over her face and withdrew to a

corner. "I would be alone now, that I may be busied with arts for your safety this night. Yon earth is as full of dark spirits as there are rooks in Shipton copse, and, Tobias or no, it behoves us to go warily. Many a time the earth devils have played their pranks upon a holy man."

Peter walked the woods that day, the favoured haunts of his childhood, and his mood was high. He had no doubt as to what the coming night would bring forth. He saw himself able to speak with Avelard and Exeter, with Neville and Latimer, as a potent equal. As one who supplied the sinews of war he would have a final word in that war's purpose. He told himself—this to his clerk's conscience—that thus he would keep pure the purpose of the crusade—for God and His Church and the poor commons of England. But deep down in his heart he knew that he had other thoughts. Ambition welled fiercely within him. The nipping air wrought upon his head. His imagination was full of trampling horses and bright swords and banners, the mad cheering of multitudes, thrones and palaces and soft raiment, the soft eyes of fair women. From a high point in the forest he looked down on Wychwood and saw the blur of Minster Lovell among its trees. The place had no longer any power to affright him. The old pale ghost of its dead lord was an obedient shadow, waiting to surrender its charge before it fled to its appointed torment.

As the day drew to evening the clouds mounted in the east, clouds like foul wool with leaden shadows. "Winter is early upon us," said Mother Sweetbread; "there was not a swallow in the eaves by mid-September, and they are the birds that know." The dark had fallen before Brother Tobias's cob, led by Darking, came up the road from the ford. Tobias was in a sad humour. The journey had tired his bones, and the lowering weather depressed one accustomed to sheltered Oseney, for in his old age it was not his custom to go abroad except when the sun shone. Also he mistrusted his errand, for Lovell was a name of ill omen. "God's blessing never went with aught of that breed," he told Peter, "and belike it will not go with their gear."

"But it will be spent for an honest purpose," said Peter.

"Pecunia non olet."

Tobias wrinkled his nose, as if he doubted the truth of the adage.

Mother Sweetbread set supper before them, and drew Madge of Shipton from her solitary communings. The little old witch-wife went on her knees to Tobias and sought his blessing, which was given with a doubting face. Then she seemed to take command of the party. Her toothless mumbling changed into a tone of authority; alone of them she seemed to know not the goal only but the road to it. She bade Darking get mattock and pick from the Sweetbread store, for, said she, "The frost has bound the earth, and earth lies heavy on that which we seek." The keys of the outer curtilage and the keep had been long in Mother Sweetbread's care, and these were sought out, a mighty bunch of rusted iron strung on a strip of cowhide. "But these are not the keys we seek," said the witch-wife. "There are deeps in Lovell's castle which no mortal key will unlock. For these we have the Rustler's word." Nor would she allow them to start till she gave the signal. "Let the daylight get out of the earth and the night currents begin to move. We can work only under the blanket of the dark."

When at last they left the cottage the night was thick as a cloak round them, windless and piercing cold. Darking had a lantern and guided them by a track down a shaggy slope, among scrub of thorn and holly. The old women marched like soldiers, but Brother Tobias stumbled often and leaned heavily on Peter's arm. "I am afraid, son Peter," he murmured. "This is no work for a priest. I doubt if it be work for any Christian man, but in these days a Christian must have a stout stomach."

They skirted swampy meadows fringed by elders, which rustled eerily, though there was now no wind. Then suddenly they came on a little church, where the altar had long lacked servers; the slats were falling from its roof, and its north door stood open to the weather. There were roofless huts beside it, and nettle-grown heaps of stones, and beyond a dark mass like a mountain.

"There is no entrance this way," said Darking. "We must

seek the Water-gate." So with difficulty they picked their way through ruinous closes till the lantern caught the tides of Windrush, which here drowsed in long lagoons. There was a postern half blocked by a fallen lintel, through which they squeezed. "This is the west court," said Darking, and an owl seemed to echo the whisper.

It was a strange place, grown thick with grass, with on three sides of it walls which beetled like crags. Fifty years had worked a ruin. The paving was broken into hollows, and every now and then a trickle of falling masonry sounded above them.

"Now where in God's name is the dovecot?" Darking asked, flashing his lantern upon the precipitous sides, and was told by Madge Littlemouse, "The northeast corner." Sure enough in the far angle the echo which their feet awoke was answered from above by a sound of wings. There were still pigeons making their home in that round tower on the roof which no man had entered for half a century.

"This is the place," said Darking. "Three paces from the east wall was the Rustler's word." He started back. "Others have been here!"

What they saw was an opening in the ground made by the removal of a heavy slab. Steps ran down, green with ferns and slime. Darking turned the lantern on them. "Nay, these have not been trodden for a hundred years. This is some ancient doing." He descended as far as the steps allowed. "Something has fallen," he announced out of the depths.

"Reach me a mattock. It is only soil and rubble."

He wrought for some minutes, flinging out shovelfuls above their heads. Then he stopped. "There is a door," he said. "I think it opens inwards." There came a sound of heavy blows, then a splintering and rending, and the falling forward of a heavy body. Presently Darking emerged spitting earth from his mouth. "The door is gone rotten with age. Beyond is a passage in which a man may creep. The Rustler no doubt spoke truth. But let us clear our wits before we take the next step, for we may be on the edge of dangerous things."

Peter shivered violently. His eagerness had not died in

143

him, but it was blanketed by a weight of nameless fears. The black night, the echoing cavern of the court, the cold which froze even his young blood, seemed to lay a palsy on his mind. He had pictured an adventurous journey among vaults, a treasure-hunt in brisk company; instead he seemed to be standing on the brink of a noisome tomb.

He screwed up his courage.

"I go," he said. "I am the chosen one."

Madge Littlemouse croaked. "He goes. He is the chosen one. And he goes alone."

But Tobias broke in. "Nay, that he does not. I go with him. Whatever is beneath ground we face together."

The witch-wife protested. "Ye will anger the spirits, holy sir. They are lost spirits who obey not the Church. They are biddable, if they be taken wisely, but if ye anger them they will flee to the abyss and take Lovell's gold with them."

"Avaunt thee, woman!" Tobias's voice had gained assurance, for his wrath was stirred. "If it be devil's gold, it is not for us, who be Christian folk. I tell you, it is the treasure of one who was mortal man, and is now a lost soul. Our purpose is honest, for we would use in a holy cause what now festers idly in the earth. In the name of God, I go forward."

He would have led the way, but Peter prevented him. Darking had lit a second lantern, which burned clear in the windless air. With this in his hand Peter descended the steps.

"Give us as much time," he called to Darking, "as a man may walk a mile. After that come and seek us."

The passage sloped downward, and was so low that the two had to bend double. But after the first few yards it was dry, as if cut from solid rock, and it was powdered with a fine dust. Soon the roof lifted and they could walk upright. Peter stopped now and then to take his bearings. "We are going north," he whispered. "We must now be under the keep. The air is fresh. Doubtless there is some vent from above."

But presently they reached a subsidence which almost blocked the corridor. Above the rubble there was a gap through which a man could squeeze, and Peter managed to enlarge it so that Tobias passed. Beyond they found steps which descended steeply. The air smelled damper and closer, and there was a sound of dripping water behind the containing walls. "We are in the bowels of the earth," said Peter, "and that flow I take to be the Castle well. Wary is the word, lest we plunge into the pit where Lovell is said to have made an end of his ill-wishers."

But the road straightened itself, the roof rose, and the lantern showed a door bound with rusty iron. This was no such rotten thing as Darking had broken down at the entrance to the passage. Peter flung his weight on it, and it held like a rock. Then he had recourse to Mother Sweetbread's keys, which he had carried on his left arm. He tried one and then another in the great lock, and the third fitted. But as his fingers moved to turn it, he was taken by a second fit of shivering. He turned to Tobias.

"Pray," he said between clenched teeth. "This is the last stage. Pray that we be given strength to face what may be beyond this door."

Tobias's voice was calm. "*Expectans expectavi Dominum,*" he said, "*et intendit mihi, et exaudivit preces meas, et eduxit me de lacu miseriae, et de luco faecis, et statuit super petram pedes meos.* Lead on, my son. He who has brought us thus far will lead us to a secure place."

Peter's fingers trembled so that he fumbled for long with the key. At last the bolt lifted with a shriek like an animal in pain. The door opened towards them, and as they drew back to let it swing it seemed that a foul wind, smelling of a charnel house, blew for an instant in their faces. Then the lantern gave them a view.

It was a little chamber hewn out of the living rock, and there must have been an entrance of air from above, for after the first noisome blast the place smelled pure and cold. And it was empty. There were none of the chests and strong boxes which might be looked for in a treasury. Rather it was like an anchorite's cell. There was a table and a chair, and in one corner a pallet heaped with rotting bedclothes. There were objects scattered on the floor, and on the table a sconce for candles, and some mildewed parchments. There were other things, for as Peter stepped in he tripped over something which lay close to the door. With horror he saw that the something had once been a man.

For a moment he thought it lived, that it was creeping to catch his foot. He cried out and dropped the lantern. Fortunately, it was not extinguished, and Tobias caught it and turned it on the body.

It lay huddled and crooked, as if it had been struggling with the door, and had used its last flicker of life in a hopeless assault. It was the body of a tall man, and it was not yet a skeleton. There had been no rats or worms to deface it, and, though the eyes I had shrunk to things like dried berries, the skin, grey I and wrinkled, still hung on the bones. The beard had become like lichen, and so had the fur collar of the surcoat. The teeth had mostly dropped from the withered gums, but two protruded over the grey lips, with an awful air of ravening and pain. The man had died of hunger and thirst, had died in mortal agony, for he had gnawed his finger-tips and bitten deep into his left wrist. Wrinkled at their feet, every limb contorted, the garments disordered in the last extremity, the body was an awful parody of the image of God.

Peter, deadly sick, leaned on the table. Tobias touched the jewel at the belt, and it fell from the decayed leather. He took a broad ring from a clawlike finger.

"This is not Lovell's treasure," he said softly. "It is Lovell himself. See, here is the barry nebuly and the chevronels. So passes the world's glory. We will seek no more gold, son Peter, for God this night has shown us a better thing. He has shown how sure and righteous are His judgments. *Qui fodit foveam, incidet in eam, et qui dissipat sepem mordebit eum coluber.*" He signed himself with the cross, and stood with downcast eyes.

Peter's bodily sickness was passing. He could look now at the thing in the gloom. He saw the dreadful panorama of the man's death as if he had been an eye-witness. The fugitive from Stoke battle, with the avenger of blood at his heels, had sought refuge in his own house, where Mother Blackthorn hid him beyond the reach of any pursuit. She alone knew the secret of his lair, and had the means of entrance. There Lovell waited till a way could be found of moving himself and his ill-gotten wealth overseas. But the woman had fallen sick, a mortal illness, and, since she was the sole guardian of the hermitage, the refugee deep in the earth had no one to give him food and drink. She had grown delirious, men had had to hold her down in bed and check her frenzy, for she knew that her master below was dying by inches; presently she had passed into stupor and death. Meanwhile, he who had been a great prince and had ruled England had grown hourly weaker, impotent as a babe to save himself. He had licked up from the floor the crumbs of his last meal, he had eaten the candle-ends, he had gone mad and chewed his hands, until at the end in his ultimate mania he had beaten on the unyielding door till he dropped with death in his throat.

The first emotion of horror had left Peter. He had now only a great pity and a great clearness, as if some cloud had lifted from his brain. In that subterranean cell he seemed to view the world from a high hill.

He turned the lantern on the crumpled vellum pages on the table. He saw that it was an account-book. Lovell had been passing the hours of his confinement in counting his wealth. Perhaps the book would give a clue to its whereabouts? With a spasm of nausea he dismissed the notion. Lovell's treasure seemed to him a thing accursed, and any motion to win it a sure plunge into damnation.

"Let us be gone," he said faintly, "and seal up this place so that no eye may ever look on it again."

"Nay," said Tobias gently, "we must first give this body Christian burial. We are bound to the dying man in Oxford who pledged you to lay the wandering spirit of his lord. I will have masses sung in Oseney for his soul's repose. Do you go and bring Darking to help?"

"I dare not leave you alone in this place."

"Nay, I have no fear. What is there to affright me in a handful of bones and parched skin? His spirit will not hurt me, for I do it a kindness. Haste you, son Peter, while I meditate on him who once was Francis Lovell."

147

Peter made his way back to the outer air, fumbling in the dark, for he had left the lantern in the cell. It seemed an age till he caught a speck of light, and saw Darking's face peering in at the tunnel's entrance. When he emerged into the bitter night, a new faintness came over him, and he leaned, choking, on Darking's arm.

"You have found the gold?" Darking asked.

"We have found its master," he gasped.

The witch-wife cried out. Her curch had slipped and her grey locks hung loose like a maenad's.

"Lovell is there! I dreamed it! White and picked like an ancient crow! But what of the gold he guards, my lord? Let us deal mercifully with his bones that his ghost may be kind. See, I have brought a deadcloth, that he may be decently and piously planted in holy earth."

She drew from her bosom a coarse shroud, which fluttered ghoulishly in the night.

"Come with us," said Peter to Darking, "that we may get him above ground."

They broke off the table legs and made a bier of the top, wrapping what had been Lovell in his rotting surcoat. Once in the open Madge Littlemouse shrouded him in her linen, and Peter and Darking bore him to the graveyard of the ruinous church. There, among the broken headstones, they dug a grave with the mattock which had been destined to unearth treasure, and into that grave, before the earth was shovelled back, Peter flung the vellum account-book which might contain the clue to Lovell's hoard. Tobias said the prayers for the dead, and it seemed to Peter that as he spoke the air lightened, and the oppression lifted from the black trees and mouldering walls. There was a sudden rift in the clouds, and the moon rode out into clear sky.

"*Nihil enim, intulimus in hunc mundum,*" rose the voice of Tobias; "*haud dubium quia nec auferre quid possumus. . . . Nunc autem Christus resurrexit a mortuis, primitiae dormientium. . . .*"

As the voice ceased, the witch-wife plucked at Peter's arm.

"The gold!" she croaked. "We have laid the ghost. Now

the road is plain. Where Lovell laired the treasure cannot be far distant."

"I have found it," he answered, "for I have got me a new mind."

CHAPTER X

OF THE CONCLAVE AT LITTLE GREECE

At Mother Sweetbread's he found the lean urchin Dickon of the Holt, whose rags now hung on yet barer bones. He greeted Peter with a pull of his forelock.

"They be after ye, master," he said. "The other of you two, a tall man, him that set free the prisoner three nights back, has been at his tricks again. Maybe 'twas he set the Fettiplace men after ye, forbye that ye were seen this day in the forest. In less than an hour they'll be here, for they know that this is your hidy-hole. They were to muster at Asthall crossroads, for I was dobbing down in a chump of furze and heard them plan it."

"Are you hungry?" Peter asked, and the boy's wolfish eyes answered.

"Give him food, mother," said Peter. "There is a bare cupboard at the Holt."

"There be no cupboard there," said the boy, "and there be no Holt. When I followed ye t'other night, father he set the place afire, and hanged himself to a rafter, and him and mother was all burned to cinders." He spoke calmly as if such doings were trivial, and his eyes followed Mother Sweetbread as she brought food.

"Then you have no home? Where do you sleep?"

"Where there is a chance of meat. Outside Martin Lee's kennels, where I can pick up scraps from the hounds' dish, or beside the swine-troughs up Swinbrook way. That's how I come to hear the talk of the Fettiplace folk."

"You will come with me, Dickon lad, for it seems you are destined to serve me. Have you any old garments of mine, mother, to amend his raggedness?"

"We must be on the move," said Darking. "Little Greece is the best shelter. I know not if John Naps be there, but I

150

have the right of entry, and no Fettiplace durst follow."

Madge of Shipton took up the tale. She was in a sullen mood, and had sat mumbling to herself in a corner.

"What of Lovell's gold, young sir? The gold I have tracked by my spells through air and earth and water? What of the treasure that will set you among kings?"

"Let the first comer have it," said Peter. "I have no longer need of it. I am beholden to you, Mother Littlemouse, but I am done now with spells and treasure. I have a path to tread where it would only cumber me."

Peter's tone, solemn and resolute, woke Brother Tobias from the half-doze which the fatigues of the night had brought on him.

"And you, Father," said Darking, "will sleep here the night, and tomorrow I will send a man who will lead you back to Oseney."

"Not so, friend," said the old man. "My bones are rested, and my horse can carry me to Little Greece, which I take to be no great journey. I have a notion that my son Peter will need my counsel, and Oseney can well spare me."

"Then let us haste," said Darking, "or we shall have the Fettiplaces on our backs, and I for one am in no mood for a mellay. Food, mother, for there may be no larder at Little Greece. Make speed, Dickon, with that new jerkin."

When they left the cottage, Dickon in the frieze of Peter's boyhood, Tobias stiff and weary on his ambling cob, Peter and Darking striding ahead, the clouds had for the most part lifted, and the moon was riding in mid-heaven. There was no sign of pursuit, as they entered the forest aisles, and in ten minutes, through Darking's subtle leading, there was no fear of it. They were back in an ancient world where Darking, and indeed Peter himself, could baffle any Fettiplace lackey. The cold had lessened with the dark, and the wind seemed to have shifted, for it blew in their left ears now and not in their right. Darking sniffed the air. "Winter has taken a step back," he said. "St Martin will not forget his little summer. The moles were throwing up fresh earth, so I knew that the frost would not hold."

151

Few words were spoken on that journey, and none by Peter, for he was in the grip of a great awe and a new enlightenment. The tortured dead, sprawled by the locked door, had tumbled down his fine castle of dreams. What was the glory of the world if it closed in dry bones and withered skin? Lovell had been, next the King, the greatest man in all England, and he had died like a rat in a trap, gnawing his fingers in his agony. The starved peasant gasping out his last breath in a ditch had a better ending. And, as Lovell, so had been his grandsire, Henry of Buckingham, and his father, save that their threads of life had been shorn by a clean axe in the daylight for all men to see. It was not death that he feared, but the triviality of life. He had the awe of the eternal upon him, and he saw mortal things as through an inverted spy-glass, small and distant against the vast deserts of eternity. Only a few hours back his head had been full of trumpets and horsemen, and his blood as brisk as a March morning. Now they all seemed little things, short-lived and weakly. The song of Pierce the Piper came to his mind—

> "Worm at my heart and fever in my head—
> There is no peace for any but the dead.
> Only the dead are beautiful and free—
> *Mortis cupiditas captavit me.* . . ."

But no, he had no craving for death, as he had no fear of it, and he did not yearn for a peace which was rottenness. It was the littleness of life that clouded his spirit.

He had known these moods of disillusion before, when light and colour had gone out of everything. At Oseney, often, when he was tempted to forswear his gods, and the solemn chants of the choir in the great abbey church and the manuscripts of Plato in Merton library alike seemed foolishness. Since his new life began, he had scarcely felt them; rather he had been filled with a young lust of living. But now he had seen the world grow suddenly small, once at Avelard when the gospeller spoke his testimony . . . once when he saw the dead woman in the hut at the Holt . . . and two nights ago

152

when he had looked at the dying face of the Rustler. And if earthly greatness had shrunk for him, he was not recompensed by any brighter vision of celestial glory. Was it *accidia* that troubled him, that deadly sin? Or was it illumination, the illumination of the King Ecclesiast, who had cried *Vanitas vanitatum et omnia vanitas.*

Nay, there was one thing that was no vanity. In the atmosphere of decay which surrounded him one thing shone fresh and bright and living, a star among clouds, a rose among the graves. The beauty of Sabine came over him like a benediction. He had got a new mind, he had told Madge of Shipton, and he had spoken the truth. In the last hour he had become very old and wise. He had sacrificed all his whimsies. He would do whatever work God called him to, but he asked no reward. He did not seek kingdoms or dukedoms, or purple and fine linen, or trampling armies behind him. Such pomps he renounced as willingly as any monk. But in his revulsion from death he hungered for life, and to him Sabine shone as life incarnate, youth *in excelsis*, beauty sanctified. A great tumult of longing filled him. A line of some forgotten wandering poet came into his head—

> "*O blandos oculos et inquietos!*"

It was true; her eyes were both lovely and wild, unquiet and kind. He searched his memory for more. *Illic*—how did it go?—yes—

> "*Illic et Venus et leves Amores
> Atque ipso in medio sedet Voluptas.*"

He tried to turn the couplet into his own tongue:

> "For there dwells Venus, and the tiny Loves,
> And in their midst Delight."

The word *Voluptas* offended him. It should have been *Desiderium*.

153

They threaded without challenge the maze of thorn scrub which surrounded Little Greece, and when they reached the great barn there was no light in it. But the door was unlocked, as Darking had told them was the custom, and within there was plenty of kindling, and on the rafters a ham or two and the side of a fat buck. Darking and Dickon, who showed himself assiduous in his new duties, made a fire on the stone floor, and from the bean straw in the far end shook out four beds. "We will rob old John's larder," said Darking, and he cut slices from one of the hams and fried them on Naps's griddle. But of the party he alone ate, and Dickon, who had vast arrears to make up. Peter would have flung himself on his pallet that he might dream of his love, but Tobias detained him. The old man lay couched on the straw, his head on his hand, and the firelight on his face revealed an anxious kindliness.

"There are no secrets among us, son Peter," he said. "For certain you have none from me, for I read you like a printed book. This night you have seen a vision, such as befell St Paul on the Damascus road. You have seen the vanity of earthly glory, and your soul is loosed from its moorings. Speak I not the truth?"

"It is the truth." Peter spoke abstractedly, for he had been called from the deeps of another kind of meditation.

"I have wondered sometimes," Tobias continued, "whether of late months you had not forgot your upbringing, and had become over-worldly for one of your high calling. The lust of the eyes and the pride of life were new things to you, and I have often feared that you were dazzled. But this night you spoke words which were balm to my heart. You said you had got you a new mind, and that you trod a road where Lovell's gold would only cumber you. If you meant what I take it you meant, you have indeed had a baptism of grace. I would have had you get treasure that you might be the more free to work a noble purpose. But if you sought it only to hold your head higher among worldly men and attain more readily to worldly honour, then your purpose was evil and God in His mercy has frustrated it."

Peter made no answer.

"For you are a soldier of Christ, my son." The old man's voice had a crooning tenderness. "If you fight in your own strength and for your own cause, you will go down—I know it as if God had whispered to me. You will be the third of your house to die a violent and a futile death. For you may drive out the Tudor and yet go the way of Duke Harry and Duke Edward, for he who draweth the sword in his own quarrel will himself be slain by the sword. But if you fight as the champion of God's Church and His poor folk you cannot fail, for if you fall you fall a blessed martyr, and angels will waft you to Paradise—and if you win, your crown will be like the crown of Israel's High Priest, with the words writ thereon, 'Holiness to the Lord.'"

Tobias had raised himself on his couch, eyes and voice had become rapt like a prophet's, and he held out his arms to Peter in an ecstasy of appeal. Then he sank back, for the fire blazed up in a sudden draught, and there was a bustle at the doorway.

John Naps had entered. The master of Little Greece was wrapped up in several ragged mantles, as if he had found the night chill. From these rags there protruded only some wisps of white hair, the long coppery nose, and the moist magisterial eyes.

"Ho, masters!" he cried, and his voice boomed like a bittern's. "What a Christ's mercy ha' we here? Godsnigs, but you are at ease in another man's house!" Then his eye fell on Darking. "Solomon, my love, is't thee? Welcome, old friend, and I prithee present your company!"

Then he caught sight of Brother Tobias, and doffed his hat. "A brother of Oseney, i' faith? My greeting, holy sir. Lardy! It is the good Tobias that never denied alms to a poor man. May your reverence feed high and sleep deep in John Naps's kennel!"

His rheumy eyes next covered Peter. "Your 'prentice, Solomon—the honest lad that attended ye at our parliament a month back?"

"Know him by his true name," Solomon laughed. "To the king of the Upright Men I present Master Bonamy, out of the west country."

The old whipjack's face underwent a sudden change. The comedy left it, and it fell into the stern lines which Peter remembered. His voice, too, became hard and grave.

"Him that has the Word—our Word, Solomon! 'Twas passed to him a sennight back at Avelard, and he passed it to Catti the Welshman t'other day at Gosford. Bonamy, you say? Well, one name will serve the present need as well as another, but maybe the true one also spells with a B. Say, friend," and he spoke low, "is't the one we await? In the words of Holy Writ, is't him that should come or must we look for another?"

"You have said it," was Darking's answer.

Naps cast off his ragged cloak and revealed a very respectable suit of brown frieze and leather. He bobbed on his knee before Peter, looking like some king of the gnomes with his domed skull, his mahogany cheeks, and his wisp of white beard. He took the young man's right hand, and laid it on the crown of his own head and on his heart, mumbling all the while a thing like a paternoster. He took a water-jug which stood on the floor, and sprinkled some drops on his palm. He picked a half-burned stick from the fire, and quenched the glowing end with his wet fingers. Last, he plucked a knife from his belt, and drew the edge over the back of one thumb so that a drop of blood spurted. What he had done to his own left hand, he did to Peter's right.

"I swear you the beggar's oath of fealty, sire," he said, and the whipjack had a sudden hierarchic dignity. "The oath by water and fire and cold steel and common blood. Whenever your call sounds, the beggars will rise around ye like an autumn mist out of every corner of England."

Then his eyes became anxious.

"We be all true men here?" he asked. "The reverend father?"

"Be comforted, John," said Darking. "'Twas he that had the bringing up of my lord. He knew his secret first of any."

The whipjack's humour changed, and he was again the jovial ruffian. He got himself some food, and made himself

156

a bed of straw by Darking's side.

"What brings this high and mighty company to Little Greece? Few, save ourselves, come here, unless the King's law be troublesome."

"'Tis the King's law troubles us," said Darking. "My lord has his own business about the land, and for the moment must lie as close as a badger in snow. But some nights ago there was trouble at the Holt about the setting free of a gospeller, who was captive to his grace of Lincoln, and through a trick the deed was blamed on my lord. This day we come again into this countryside to find the cry still out and the Fettiplace hounds hot on the scent. Wherefore we seek refuge in a place which no Swinbrook man dare enter."

Naps laughed long and loud. "Behold the foppery of the world!" he shouted. "He that will soon be the first man in England is at the mercy of a loutish esquire who thinks to curry favour with Law. The good Tobias, a pillar of Holy Church, is privy to an offence against that Church, and must needs go into hiding. And these two great ones seek shelter from old John Naps, who all his days has had little favour from Church and none at all from Law. But the cream of the jest ye have yet to hear."

He lowered his voice.

"There is another seeking sanctuary. He knows the road hither, and may be here any moment, and his need is greater than yours, for he is the guilty man. Ye have heard, maybe, of the young lord of Boarstall, him they call Simon Rede, him that has been fighting overseas ever since his beard sprouted. It seems he has took up with the thing Gospel—though what this Gospel be I know not—some say 'tis a fetter to bind the poor and others a club to beat the rich. 'Twas he that freed the gospeller at the Holt, and hid him for the time in a place which I know but will not tell. This day he returned to put the man in still safer hiding, and get my help on the job, for Boarstall has ever been a kindly door to wandering men. Nay, Solomon, fear not. He is not one of us, as you are—as this lord is. He has not the Word. Well, he succeeded, and the gospeller, a sour, starveling fellow with no stomach for ale,

157

was hid away as snug as a flea in a blanket. But Esquire Fettiplace's long nose was smelling out the business, and, if he came on the scent of my lord here, he comes plump and fairly on the footprints of Master Rede. Wherefore these last hours the said Master Rede has been hard put to it to shake off the hounds. With my aid he has done it, for he doubled back in the forest, and I sent one of my lads on a horse to draw the hunt towards the Glyme, so that by this time the Fettiplace dogs are giving idle tongue in Wootton or Glympton. And Master Simon will presently be here, if he remembers my guiding and does not fall into Borney marl-pit or drown in Capperton mere. He will be a weary man, sore in need of bed and supper."

Darking looked grave.

"There is no love between him and my lord. Also, he is said to be of the King's faction, though he has a taste for this Gospel. Above all, he is not in the secret. We must be wary, John, and guard our speech, and do you, my lord, let wrongs be forgot for this night."

The name of Simon Rede had stirred Peter into complete wakefulness, for it was with Sabine that he chiefly associated the squire of Boarstall. All his old jealousies revived. The theft of the cloak, the arrogant air of superiority—such offences now seemed trivial compared with the fact that he dared to raise his eyes to the girl at Avelard. Was he certain? Might it not be only his fancy? He longed to have Simon face to face to make sure. And yet he dreaded the meeting, for the man rasped his soul like a rough cloth on a sore.

But Simon was long a-coming. That was a restless night in Little Greece, for midnight was past, and Naps was snoring like a trumpet, and Peter mazed with the wheel of thought that spun in his brain, and Tobias sleeping the light sleep of old age, when the door opened, and the dead embers of the fire blew up in spirals of cold ashes. Thereafter there was no more peace. Dickon set the fire going again, and further rashers were set to broil, and Peter, elaborately incurious, at last raised his eyes to see on the straw opposite him the tall figure he knew so well.

Simon had had a rough journey. His boots were wired above the knee, and his hose and doublet had suffered heavily from the thorn scrub. But his dark face seemed content. He had a mug of ale in his hand—for Naps had revealed a secret store—and when he caught Peter's eye he raised it to him.

"Greeting, Master Bonamy," he said. "We are fated, it seems, to forgather in strange places. That cloak of mine, now? You have your own back, and I would welcome my own old mantle."

He laughed, but there was no malice in the laugh. He seemed a new being, a boyish, friendly figure, that played pranks and frankly avowed them. Peter answered in the same strain.

"The frost has gone, so you will need it the less. But 'tis at Mother Sweetbread's by Leafield under the Forest when you care to seek it."

"I thank you for your stewardship. I make you my compliments, too, on the speed of your travels, for you cover the countryside like a Welsh cattle-lifter. I leave you by the Burford road, and twenty-four hours later meet you on the Oxford plainstones, and now I find you thirty miles off by the springs of Evenlode. You must have weighty business on your hands."

"Weighty enough, but less urgent than yours, it seems. Have you gotten yon gospeller into safe hiding at last?"

The man's face hardened.

"Please God, he is now where no Bishop's jackal will ever unearth him!" He stopped, for he saw the eyes of Brother Tobias fixed on him, and he realised for the first time that Tobias wore the Oseney habit.

"What does a monk in Little Greece?" he asked sharply of Naps, and his eye was stern and wary, while his hand travelled to his side.

"Be comforted, master," said Naps. "None that shelter here dare speak what they learn beyond these walls. That is the first of our laws, and it is death to break it. These gentles know your tale. They, too, have had trouble this very day from the Fettiplace folk that hunted you. We be all comrades, and

159

secret as a stone tomb."

Then Tobias spoke. He had had all the sleep he needed, and now sat up, very wakeful.

"In spite of my habit, friend, I am not against you. I am not of those who would punish man for giving the Scriptures to the commons—in truth I laboured myself in that cause long ere you were born. Today there is a sad confusion on the matter in the Church's rule and the King's laws. I wish yon gospeller relief from his tribulations. My hand would never be lifted against such as he."

Simon looked at him harshly, till the gentleness in the old man's face and voice seemed to thaw his suspicions.

"Is it so?" he said. "Then there is one honest Christian in the abbeys?"

"There be many," Tobias answered. "And there be many kinds of Christian. You are young and I am old, and youth is a hard judge. God has not made all His servants of one mould."

"That is strange doctrine for an Oseney brother. The Church would have every man and woman conform to its own rusty pattern, and those that jib at such antique moulds and seek the liberty of God's children she dubs heretics and would consume with fire."

"You are harsh to the Church, good sir. Maybe, you have met too many worthless clerks."

"I have met worthy and worthless, but they are alike in bonds. See, father. I have been wearing my youth in far lands where there is no room for cloistered virtues, and I have learned the greatness of God in deep waters and on desperate battlefields. I return to find those who call themselves His servants in this land making a mockery of His service—babes mazed in childish mummeries or hucksters selling God's mercies for gain. Wherefore I say—and I will cry it on the housetops—that there is need of a harsh broom and a strong broom in England."

"Doubtless," said Tobias. "I have long pled for such a broom. But see that it truly sweeps out the foul corners, and does not hurt the tender and gracious things."

"In such a sweeping frail things must be broke. It is a cheap price to pay for a cleaner land."

"When you have emptied the sanctuary and burned its old furniture how will you furnish it anew?"

"With the plain truth of God's Scriptures," said Simon.

"That were well. I have preached for thirty years that man must go back to the Scriptures. And yet—and yet. The Church is a fold for all, rich and poor, learned and unlearned, the child and the grown. If she do no more than preach the bare and difficult sentences of God's Word, her meat will be too strong for her little ones, and her poor ones. The Word must be tempered and translated for the weaker lambs of the fold."

"It must be the truth," said Simon, "the truth, the naked truth, without human trimmings."

"The truth!" Tobias dwelt long on the word. "No doubt such fare would be fit for your puissant youth. But for the simple and the unlettered? . . . Moreover, what is the truth? 'Tis a question no philosopher has yet answered. What is the truth of the Scriptures? There be many commentators, and they are not agreed, for Clement says one thing, and Athanasius another, and Austin a third, and the great St Thomas may differ from all."

Simon shook his head angrily. "That is a monkish subtlety. The truth is plain to read for all that have eyes and an honest heart."

"The truth may be, the truth of man's salvation, but men are a diversity of creatures, and it must present itself to them in different forms. I have lived in this world nigh three-score and ten years, and I fear to circumscribe by mortal dogma the infinite ways of God. I incline to the belief that in the light of eternity all our truths are shadows, and that the very truth we shall only know hereafter. Yet I think that every truth in its own place is a substance, though it may be a shadow in another place. And I think that all such shadows have value for our souls, for each is a true shadow, as the substance is a true substance."

Simon looked long at Tobias, and something melted in him under that innocent gaze.

"I think you are a good man," he said. "But what would you do in the present discontents? You will not deny that the Church has fallen from its high estate, and that the religious houses are too often haunts of lechery and greed."

Tobias smiled. "I would use the broom—a stiff broom. But I would not burn down an ancient dwelling whose walls are sound because there is filth in some of the rooms. I would not give the worldly man what was destined for God, and I would not, like the King's grace, slay men because they account that to be a shadow which some hold truth, and truth what many call shadow."

"Ay. That's the rub and a plague on it! I am a man that loves clear courses. I am for the King against the abbeys, but I am most vehemently against the King in this matter of heresy. I am of those that the Spaniard calls Luteranos, who would have God's revelation rewrit for simple men. But for the one faith the Bishops would burn me if they had the power, and for the other the King would assuredly hang me. 'Tis a hard choice, yet on the whole I am for the King's way of it. He has men around him who may guide him into wiser roads. But if the Church and the Pope once again put their foot on his neck, then farewell to all hope for England."

He cast his eye round the company. Peter lay on the straw, his eyes half shut; Naps was busy with the blackjack; Tobias sat erect with his hood fallen back from his bald head; Dickon was asleep, and Darking's sombre face was heavy with its own thoughts.

"We here in Little Greece," Simon cried, "are for the moment of one company. We can speak freely, for our lips hereafter are sealed. There is word of a great revolt preparing against the King, with the Church behind it, and the Church's serfs, and many great ones whom Harry has flouted! What know you of it, John Naps? Your ear is very close to English ground."

"Look Lincoln way," said the whipjack. "The trouble has begun there, and there is word that it is spreading northward."

"There is more in it than that. The rising in the east is an affair of peasants, which the King's men-at-arms will crush.

162

But strange tales come out of the west, and that is a graver matter."

He suddenly dropped the guarded tone he had been using and spoke out like a soldier crying a command.

"Who is this Master Bonamy that spends his time on the road between Oxford and Avelard? What part has he in those doings? I have heard a whisper of strange tales."

Peter's head buzzed like a hive, there was heaviness about his eyes, and pain in the back of his neck. He had scarcely listened to the talk, for his wits were wool-gathering. But he pulled himself together at the challenge.

"Little Greece is a sanctuary," he said, speaking his words slowly and with difficulty, "but it is not a confessional, and you, Master Rede, have no warrant as an inquisitor. I am the Lord Avelard's heir."

"Doubtless," said Simon. "But what does the heir of Avelard do so far from his manor west of Severn? What does he at Avelard itself and at Stowood and Wood Eaton?"

"I will answer you of my courtesy," said Peter. "I am in those parts because I am paying court to a lady—my lord's niece."

Simon started as if a whiplash had stung him.

"Sabine! Mistress Beauforest! Man, she is affianced to me. We were boy and girl together in the Boarstall woods."

Then his face flushed deep and his temper broke.

"The devil take you for your insolence! . . . By God, you will never get her. If yon old fox at Avelard play false to me and her dead father, I will wring his neck though all Severn side were at his back."

CHAPTER XI

HOW PETER CAME AGAIN TO AVELARD

Of the later events of that night Peter had no clear memory. He was conscious of trying to speak and finding utterance hard; his mouth was dry, and the words stuck to his lips; also his head ached. After that came a blank, and the next thing he remembered was lying, not on straw, but on a rough pallet bed with wet cloths on his temples. There seemed to be a pool of water in front of him which glimmered in the darkness; it was a belt of sunlight coming through the half-shuttered window in the barn. There was a woman there, an ancient woman whose face seemed familiar, and Darking sat beside him on a three-legged stool. The pain in his head had gone, but a wheel was still turning dizzily inside it, and his eyes pained him so that he could not look at the pool of light.

Then, after another spell of oblivion, he heard Darking's voice, and made sense of his words. He was speaking to John Naps—he could not mistake Naps's parrot-like white head.

"No more than a common fever," Darking was saying. "He went down like a felled ox—that is the way of youth that knows nothing of sickness. 'Tis this soft weather. When St Martin starts his summer before the feast of Simon and Jude young blood must suffer. Also he may have got a whiff of some malady by the Rustler's bed or in that crypt where Lovell died. God knows there were foul airs enough in that hole to sicken an army."

The whipjack laid his horny claw on the wet clouts on Peter's brow.

"He burns like a lime-kiln," he said. "Heaven send the holy one make haste and bring a leech, for there is need here of drenching and purging and blood-letting."

After that came confusion again. His next memory was of Tobias with a grave face, sitting by his bed and conning his breviary. Then came a new figure—a wisp of a man with a small head and a sharp nose, a figure like a heron, that stooped and pecked at him. He was conscious of little stabs of pain, and of spasms of great weakness, after which he floated away on clouds into forgetfulness.

These were hard days for Brother Tobias. To see the lad, whom he had never known sick or sorry, lie helpless in fever, wrung his old heart and put amazing vigour into his old bones. There was a wise man at Banbury, one Pyramus, who had studied medicine at Palermo; so to Banbury went Tobias, and, having his own means of persuasion, brought the leech straightway to Little Greece. Dr Pyramus pronounced it no common autumn fever. He suspected poison, and finally amended his diagnosis to an infection by evil breath, whence breathed he could not tell. He bled his patient with such vigour that the boy's face became like tallow and Tobias could not look at it without a heart pang. He compounded noxious draughts, made out of foul things like wood-lice, and spiders, and powdered deer horn, and the dung of white doves, and these, mixed with hot ale, Peter was compelled to swallow. They did one thing effectively, for they made him deathly sick, thereby relieving his body of evil humours.

One day Mother Sweetbread stood beside him weeping, and with her Madge of Shipton, who, to the scandal of Tobias, made spells with well water and a lighted candle and the tail hairs of a black mare. Tobias's own part was to keep the brow cool and the lips moist, to prevent him tossing the blankets off him, and to hold his hand when Peter clutched at the air in a feverish dream. Also to pray, incessantly, to God and God's Mother, and to all the saints who furthered the healing art—St Blaize and St John the Almoner, St Timothy and St Michael the Archangel, St Anthony who cures heats of the skin, and St Lazarus who was himself once a youth raised by our Lord from the dead.

The fever was stubborn, but whether it was the purgings and bleedings, Goody Littlemouse's spells or Tobias's prayers, there came a day when it left Peter, and he lay as weak as a kitten, while the tides of life began to drift back slowly into his body. Dr Pyramus came from Banbury for the last time, and pronounced over him the curative benediction, half Latin and half Arabic, of the Palermo physicians. Then it was the task of others to speed the patient up the slopes of health. Goody Littlemouse came from Shipton, and this time she did not weave spells. A big fire was lit, and a pot boiled, and she washed Peter in scalding water, and wrapped him in a skin new stripped from a heifer calf. Also her cunning hands, strong as a bear's paws, picked out and kneaded his flaccid muscles, and soothed the tormented nerves of neck and face, and pounded his breast so that vigour should return to his heart. Mother Sweetbread took up her quarters in Little Greece, and made him broths of game and wild herbs, and frumenty spiced with ginger, and, to quench his thirst, a gruel of barley mixed with her own sloeberry cordial. Also Tobias came again from Oseney, and, having given thanks for a son restored, read to him the *Colloquies* of the great Erasmus, as well as the Scriptures, and gave him the news of Oxford. It was now long past St Martin's day, but the good saint's summer still held, and presently Peter was carried to a chair and looked out on blue skies and smoke-brown coverts, and sniffed the sweet wild odours of the winter woods.

"God has sent you this sickness, my son," said Tobias, "for His own purpose. *Deus nobis haec otia fecit.* You have had peace to make your soul before the hour of trial comes. First came that night at Minster Lovell which was a purging of your heart, and then the needful purging of your body, and last these days of quiet reflection. The ways of the Lord are altogether wise."

For a little, while his strength crept back to him, Peter lay in a happy peace. He felt himself purged indeed, a chamber clean and swept for a new life to fill. But presently, as his vigour renewed itself, the peace became cloudy. He remembered dimly Simon Rede's last words, but very clearly he was conscious of his challenge. Sabine's figure returned to haunt his memory. He would lie for hours dreaming of her, sometimes happy, sometimes vaguely unquiet, now and then in the midnight hours uncommonly ill at ease. While he was tied by

166

the leg in Little Greece, what had become of the girl—what was Simon Rede doing? He had forgotten his greater task. For him Avelard was only Sabine's bower and Lord Avelard only her guardian.

But little by little his old life rebuilt itself in his mind. What was a-foot in the world beyond the oak shaws? One day John Naps arrived, and he listened to his talk with Darking, who had come the night before from Oxford.

"There is word from Avelard," said the latter; "my lord here is bidden hold himself in readiness for a sudden call. I had a message in Stowood."

The whipjack nodded.

"There is a mighty to-do among the great folk," he cried. "Flatsole is in Bernwood, fresh from the north, and he says there is a fire alight in Yorkshire that the King's men cannot put out, and a running to and fro of dukes and earls and King's messengers like the pairing of partridges in February."

"There is a kindling in the west, too," said Darking. "The priests are broidering a banner with the Five Wounds, and Neville is gone to Wales. The hour is near when he of Avelard must stir himself, and that means work for our young lord. King Harry, who has been looking east and north, is beginning to throw a glance westward. I had news in Oxford yesterday. Crummle, they say, is more anxious about Severn than Trent, and is turning his pig's face this way. That spells danger. Is my lord safe here from prying eyes?"

The whipjack spat solemnly. It was his favourite gesture of contempt.

"As safe as if he were in Avelard with all the armed west around him. Since the hour he fell sick, my posts and pickets have been on every road. 'Twould be harder for one unbidden to enter Little Greece than to kill and cart a buck in Windsor Forest under the castle walls, and any Peeping Tom would soon be an acorn on the highest oak. But if there be war coming, I fear it may get foul weather. I like not this false summertide which stretches towards Yule. The sky curdles too much of an evening, and the wild geese are flighting in from the sea."

"What do you fear?" Darking asked, for the whipjack was famous for his weather lore.

"Snow," was the answer. "Wind, maybe, but I think snow. There will be deep snow by Andrewmas."

But the feast of St Edmund the Martyr came, and still the weather held, and on St Catherine's day the sky was still clear, though the wind was shifting by slow degrees against the sun to the north. By now Peter was on his feet, and able to walk a mile or two with comfort, right down through the alleys amid the thorn scrub to where Naps's sentries kept watch. Indeed, he could have walked farther had not Mother Sweetbread commanded moderation, for he felt his limbs as vigorous as ever, and had that springing sense of a new life which falls only to youth recovering from a fever.

On the night after the festival of Catherine, Darking came to Little Greece—in a great hurry, for he was in the saddle and not a-foot.

"How goes it, my lord?" he asked. "Are your limbs your own once more? Can you back a horse for a matter of twenty miles?"

"I am strong enough to stride that distance in four hours," said Peter.

"Well and good. The word for you is mount and ride. You must be in Avelard by tomorrow's noon."

So there was a furbishing up of Peter's raiment, and the horse he had brought from Avelard was fetched from its stable in the forest, where it had been bestowed after the loosing of the gospeller at the Holt. And next morning he set out with Darking, who conveyed him only a little way, since he had business of his own on Cherwell side. The sky was still bright, though the air stung when they left the Evenlode vale for the wolds of Stow. It was wintertime clear enough, for there were no larks rising on the hills or swooping plovers—only big flocks of skimming grey fieldfares, and strings of honking geese passing south, and solemn congregations of bustards, and in the wet places clouds of squattering wildfowl. But the grass was still green, and, though the trees were leafless, the

168

bushes were so bright with fruit that they seemed to make a second summer.

"Heaven has sent a breathing space to the world as well as to me," thought Peter. "I wonder what it portends. Maybe a wild Christmas."

That morning's ride was to dwell in his memory like a benediction, for it seemed that from his sickness he had won a new youth. Every sight and sound and scent charmed his recovered senses, and his thoughts had again the zest and the short horizons of the boy. He schooled his spirits to temperance. He reminded himself that no more for him was the foolish dream of worldly glory. He was a soldier vowed to a selfless cause. But he found a substitute for drums and trumpets in this very abnegation. He recalled the many who had lost the world to gain it, and found exhilaration in the thought of a high dramatic refusal. The verse of Boethius ran in his head—

> *"Ite nunc fortes ubi celsa magni*
> *Duci exempli via."*

He sung it aloud to the empty wolds:

> "Go forth, ye brave, on the high road
> Where honour calls to honour's wars;
> Strip from your back the craven load;
> Go spurn the earth and win the stars."

In his new mood he wove for himself delicious dreams of a world where the philosopher would be the king, and Christ and Plato would sit at the same table, and the Psalmist and Virgil would join their voices in the celestial Marriage-song.

But the mood could not last, and before he had come to the last edge of Cotswold and looked down on Severn, he had different fancies. Down in the valley was Sabine, in an hour he would be under the same roof, in an hour he would see her eyes. He was no longer the seer and the dreamer, but the common lover, with a horizon bounded by his mistress's face.

169

The verses which now filled his head had no taint of sanctity, but were the snatches of wandering goliards, to whom women and wine were the sum of life. He would make for her songs of his own—her eyes should be hymned as Catullus had hymned the burning eyes of Lesbia; he would make her famous among men as Peter Abelard had made the Abbess of the Paraclete, so that, like Eloise, men would speak of her beauty long after it was dust.

Arrived at Avelard, he was taken straight to my lord's chamber. Lord Avelard wore a heavy furred robe, for his blood was thin, and a fire of logs made the place like an oven to one fresh from the sharp out-of-doors. The old man kissed Peter on both cheeks.

"You have been ill, my son? Only stern business kept me from your bedside, but I had constant advices, and you were in good hands. My faith! but sickness has made a hero of you. You look older and sager and more resolute, if still a trifle over-lean. Sit, my son, for you must husband your strength. The moment is very near. The Welshman is most deeply entangled in the north, and from what I hear both heart and guile are failing him. Our plans are on the edge of completion, and the word has gone forth that on St Lucy's day our folk begin to draw together. After that we move swift. You shall eat your Christmas dinner in Oxford, and, if God please, you shall sit in London ere Candlemas."

The waxen face had now more colour in it, and the approach of the hour of action seemed to have put fresh life into his blood, for he moved briskly, and fetched from a side table a mass of charts and papers.

"Now for your own part. In the next week you will visit some of the centres of our rising and show yourself to those who will follow you. 'Faith, they will think you St George himself, if you are properly habited, for sickness has made you like a young archangel. . . . Meantime there are these parchments for you to put your hand to. They are, in a manner of speaking, the pay-rolls of your army, only you pay not with coined gold but with assurances. Your followers will spend much substance in your cause, and doubtless much blood. If

170

you win, it is right that they should be recompensed by some increase to their estate."

The parchments were many, and they made a most comprehensive pay-roll. To his horror Peter saw that they related mainly to Church lands. There were one or two royal manors to be apportioned, but most were the property of the abbeys and priories of the Thames and Severn vales. The lists made very free with the estates of the greater houses—Gloucester and Tewkesbury and Malmesbury and Evesham—and bore somewhat less hard upon the smaller foundations. Eynsham and Bicester and Hailes and Winchcombe were left with a larger proportion than Pershore. His own Oseney was to be comprehensively despoiled and all her rich lands about Bibury were to be taken from her. The abbeys themselves were to remain, apparently, but they were to remain with less than a tithe of their old wealth. It was a spoliation more drastic than Crummle's.

Peter read on with a darkening face. Even the revelation here given of the strength of those who followed him woke no response in his heart. He was shocked to the bone that he, the champion of the Church, should be her chief despoiler. To each piece of land was attached the name of the new owner. The great lords had the lion's share—Avelard himself, and Exeter, and Rutland, and Neville—even Northumberland. But there was good provision for the lesser gentry, and the names of Sudeley and Boteler and Tracey and Lacey and Noel bulked large. Even Fettiplace, his late pursuer, was there. Also the wool merchants of the Calais staple, who were doubly valuable, since they could contribute good money, as well as stalwart prentices. Not one of them seemed to be absent— Drury, Midwinter, Cely, Bartholomew, Grevel, Hicks, Marner, Tame, Sylvester, Whittington—representing every stone town from Stroud to Witney, from Fairford on Thames to Stratford on Avon.

Peter conned the documents with an angry heart, and took so long over it that Lord Avelard tried to turn the leaves faster.

"You are mistaken in me, my lord," he said at length. "May God forgive me if I put my hand to any such parchment! Are

171

we the devil's scriveners to hack and whittle at God's inheritance and break down the carved work of the sanctuary?"

The waxen face did not change, or the steely regard of the pale eyes.

"Patience, my son. There is no purpose of malevolence against Holy Church. But her possessions have grown somewhat cumbersome for her handling. The wiser abbots and bishops are of the same mind, and the people of England are set on the freeing of the religious lands. Think you that otherwise the Welshman could have done what he has done? Crummle would have had his throat slit in the first week of his visitations if England had not approved the purpose, though condemning its executors."

"Maybe you speak truth, and the abbeys need pruning. I know well that some of them fester like cesspools. But that pruning must be done with a single eye to the glory of God and the comfort of His people. My lord, your plan is common banditry. You would plunder God to enrich the proud, and that were a deed accursed of Heaven."

Peter's wrath had given him assurance, and he faced the elder man with a firm chin and a glowing eye.

"These same proud," Lord Avelard said quietly, "are the men who will fight for you and set you in a high place. Hear reason, my son. An army must be paid, and where is your war chest? You have not a groat which you can call your own. I and some few others are willing to risk our substance in your cause, which is also the cause of England. But for the others— the rank and file—they will venture only if they see their profit. Consider the interests of Holy Church herself. The Welshman will wholly root her out of England and give her possessions to those who are sharers in his iniquity. That is the avowed purpose of Crummle and his kind, and it is they who control the King. Is it not better to stablish her securely, even if she herself have to pay in part for that security? Consider, my son. We dwell in a fallible world where great deeds can only be compassed by reckoning with the foibles of mankind."

"Nevertheless," said Peter stubbornly, "I will not set my

172

hand to these parchments. There must be some purging of the Church for the Church's sake, but it cannot be done in such fashion. I will not be privy to giving what is dedicated to God and His poor to those who have abundance. Let us make a hazard, my lord, and if we win, then is the time to effect a decent and orderly reformation. There be Church lands which have been ill guided and may well be entrusted to better hands. There be royal manors to repay my army. There be . . ."

It was Lord Avelard's turn to flush, and his voice was no longer quiet, but full of a cold passion.

"A murrain on all clerks!" he cried. "You have the accursed taint in your blood, got I know not how—'tis not the strong wine of Bohun. I had thought Solomon Darking would have put more wisdom into your skull. Duke Edward and Duke Harry would have burned every monkish rookery in the land if it would have furthered one ell their march to the throne. You are a priest, it seems, and no soldier, and who will strike a blow for a peevish priestling, even though he have Buckingham's blood?"

Then he seemed to put a check on his temper, and his voice softened.

"Forgive me, son. I am an old man, and do not love to have my plans questioned. We will let these parchments sleep for the moment. Maybe, when you have seen something of those who follow you, you will come to another mind. Trust me, I am no less devout a son of the Church than you, though I was not bred in a cloister. I am too near the grave to do aught to imperil my salvation."

In the afternoon came Dickon to Avelard, having been delayed at Little Greece till his new suit arrived from the Witney tailor. With some weeks of good feeding behind him he looked a different child from the starved urchin at the Holt, and in his servant's livery of sober brown he cut a personable figure. When Peter went to his chamber to change his clothes before supper, he found Dickon in waiting, handling curiously the rich garments of silk and taffeta and velvet.

"We are in a lord's palace," said the boy, "and you yourself

173

are now a lord. With what softness the great ones clothe themselves!" And he laid a satin doublet against his hard cheek.

Peter had not yet cast eye on Sabine. She did not appear at dinner, and all afternoon he had ranged idly through the park, hoping to catch a glimpse of her gown or hear the feet of her horse. That evening the northern sky had banked up ominously with clouds, and the wind had settled fairly into that quarter—a steady wind blowing through leagues of ice. So Peter had been fain to seek the hearth of the great hall, and let his cheeks grow hot in the glow of it, while he reflected upon the events of the morning. Once more he was lapped in the luxury of Avelard, and it moved him little; for certain boyish weaknesses seemed to have been burned out in his recent fever. He was no longer thrilled by dainty fare and fine raiment, as he had been a month before. Now he was conscious of a stronger purpose in his heart, of more masterful blood in his veins, of that power to command which was his birthright. Today he was doubly Bohun. Also he realised that he had that first of a leader's gifts, a fine carelessness of self, so that if need be he could stand alone. He was prepared to fling soul and body into the arena, to be exalted or trampled under as God ordained. And then he was forced to confess to himself that this boasted self-sufficiency was a lie. He did not stand alone; there was one in this very house who could tumble him from his pinnacle by a glance of her eye.

At supper Lord Avelard kept his room, but Sabine appeared. The meal was served in the Great Chamber, as on the first occasion, and when the food was set on the table the servants withdrew. This time the girl had discarded her black robes for a wonderful gown of silver tissue, and her jewels were not sapphires but stones that darted crimson fire. She gave him both hands at her entrance, but not her cheek. Tonight she seemed not kinswoman or friend, but possible mistress, certain queen. Her pale beauty had authority in it, and her eyes a possessive pride.

"Have you brought your lute?" he asked. "Once you ravished the soul out of me with your singing."

She laughed and looked at him from under drooped eyelids.

"Tonight we take counsel, my lord. The matter is too grave for music."

At first they spoke little. The girl's eyes smiled on him, but not with common friendliness. She seemed to be appraising him, to be striving to read something in a face which his recent fever had made keener and finer, for there were little puckers of thought on her brow. Also—or so it seemed to him—there was a new respect in her air, and with it a certain hesitation. Once or twice she appeared to be nerving herself for words which she found it hard to utter. There was between them a thin invisible veil of ice.

It was Peter who broke it.

"Has Simon Rede been here in the past month?" he asked abruptly.

"He came three weeks since," she answered, "a week after you left Avelard." There was no sign of discomposure in her face.

"He came to pay court to you?"

She laughed.

"Maybe. We were sweethearts as children, but that is long ago. Does my lord do me the honour to be jealous?"

"I would be glad to learn that he got a flat denial."

She shrugged her white shoulders. "There was no need. Master Simon's love-making did not stretch thus far. I am the ward of my lord Avelard, who has something to say in the disposal of my hand, and he does not look kindly on Master Rede."

"But you yourself?"

"I am a woman grown and a woman must think of many things. I am no green girl to be led captive by a plumed bonnet and a long sword and a soldier's airs. What has Master Simon to offer but the mouldering walls of Boarstall, or more likely a wet bed in the forest, for he is ever at odds with those in power. We women, who would be wives, love peace and surety." There was a curious sudden hardness in face and voice.

"Yet I have heard that a woman will risk all for love."

175

"Ay, for true love." Her eyes did not melt. "When true love rides the road, some women will sell their shift and follow him. But I do not love Master Simon, though I have a tenderness for an old playmate."

She paused. There was honesty, a kind of boyish frankness, in her tone.

"I do not think I was born for such love. I have never felt those raptures, which youth calls passion and eld green-sickness. Maybe 'tis a sore lack, maybe good fortune, but so we Beauforests are made. We are good wives to those we choose, for we are loyal comrades and can play high and bold like a man. There burns in us a fierce ambition, and it is no idle fancy, for we have the power in us to deal with high matters and the courage to use that power. Make no mistake, my lord. We are no common housewives to tremble at a husband's nod, and bear a child once a year, and see to his cordials and pasties."

The veil of ice between them had gone and so had the rosy mist of sex. Peter felt that a human soul confronted him, a soul fierce and candid, earthy and gallant, and no mere lovely body shrouded in silks and jewels.

"You were meant for a queen," he said, and there was reverence in his voice.

"Maybe. Assuredly I was not meant for a squire's lady."

In that instant of intimate revelation Peter's love blazed to its height, and yet at the back of his head he realised its hopelessness. Here was one more starkly contrary than Lord Avelard.

"I would make you a queen," he said, and he lingered over the words, for he knew that he was nearing an irrevocable choice.

She rose and curtseyed, gravely, without coquetry. I am honoured, my lord, she said.

"I love you, Sabine. It is true love with me, for I live with your face in my heart—I cannot see the light for you—I cannot pray for the thought of you—I desire you more than my salvation."

"Than your salvation?" she echoed. "Then you are indeed

176

a lover and no clerk."

For one moment it seemed as if his ardour awoke in her a like response. Her face grew gentler, her eyes softened. Peter realised that her arms were waiting for him. And yet he did not move. The word "salvation" held him. Was he honest with her, as she had been with him?

She saw his hesitation, and attributed it to the true motive, for her voice was cool again.

"I am willing to be a queen . . . I am willing to risk all hazards by your side, and if you fall to fall with you like a true wife. But I must be certain that that is indeed your purpose, my lord. I will not link my fortunes to one who is half-hearted, for in this cause it must be venture all."

He did not answer, for he was in the throes of a great temptation. Never had she seemed more desirable. This was not the shimmering girl with some of the airs of a light-in-love, who had first enchained his heart, but a woman with greatness in her, a true queen, a comrade to ride the fords with were they agreed about the road. His longing was less to have her in his arms than to see the light of confidence and affection in those clear eyes. But were they not poles apart? How could he, who had set common ambition behind him, keep step with one whose heart was set so firmly on earthly magnificence?

"I will venture all," he said. But as the words left his mouth he knew that he lied.

She knew it also.

"Your clerkly scruples?" she asked. "My uncle has told me of them. You would lead an army and yet refuse to provide its reward. That is mere folly, my lord. This is no perfect world, and he who believes it such is doomed to fail."

"I will venture my life—my hope—my peace—but not my chance of Heaven," he said, and his voice in his own ears sounded small and far away. He realised miserably that he had crossed the stream and that there was no returning.

Her quick mind saw that here was finality. She laughed bitterly.

"What kind of gage are these? Life, hope, peace! A common soldier will risk as much. It is as I thought. You are a clerk

177

to the bone, and had better get you back to your cell. Nay, I do not blame you. You have been honest with me, as I with you. But you are not the one to upset the Welshman. A strong man will risk soul as well as body, and look to make his ultimate peace with a God who understands our frailties, since He ordained them."

She rang the silver bell to summon the servants.

"I will never be your queen, my lord," was her last word, "for you will never be a king."

Peter went to his chamber with a chill at his heart. He felt that in the last hour the youthfulness of the morning had fallen from him and that he had grown very old. The room was warm and perfumed, but its comfort deepened his chill. He flung open the lattice and stared into the night.

Snow was coming. He smelt it, and saw it stored in heavy clouds under the fitful moon. An owl hooted by the wall, and from the valley came the sound of wild swans travelling with the wind. There was a light far off burning in some hollow of the woods. He drew in his head, and the cold at his heart was lightened. The splendour of Avelard was not for him, but he had still a share in the wild elemental world.

CHAPTER XII

OF THE VISION IN THE SNOW

Next day they were in the saddle soon after dawn, Lord Avelard muffled in three cloaks and wearing an extra surcoat. The snow had not begun to fall, but the world lay under the spell of its coming. The sky was leaden grey and, though there was no frost, the earth seemed to be bound in a rigor like an ague; nothing stirred, not a leaf on the tree or a bird in the bush; the very streams seemed to hush their flow in a palsy of expectancy. Even on Peter's young blood the cold smote like a blow.

The old man said not a word of their talk of yesterday. He seemed to cherish no resentment, and, so far as the discomfort of the weather permitted, to be in a cheerful humour.

"I am taking you to Neville," he told Peter. "My lord of Abergavenny is the greatest man on the Marches and can horse five thousand spears, besides what he can bring from his Welsh dales. The man is sick—has long been sick—but his spirit burns the more fiercely in his frail body, and he is also a skilled soldier. What he lacks in bodily strength will be supplied by his brethren Sir Thomas and Sir Edward. My lord is your near kin, for he married your sister by blood, the Lady Mary, now dead."

"Why is he one of us?" Peter asked. "He stands high at court."

A laugh like a frog's croak came from the old man.

"He has some matter of private grievance against the Welshman. Likewise he would increase his estates. He is the richest man in the west country, for he heired the broad Beauchamp lands, but he would leave his son still vaster possessions. Speak him fair, my son, for he has a temper spoiled by much dealing with slippery Welsh." And he shot at Peter a glance of many meanings.

179

"Bethink you, my lord, while there is still time," said Peter, for in the night watches he had been pondering his position. "Am I the man for your purpose? Would not my lord of Exeter better serve it?"

"May the mercy of God forbid!" Lord Avelard cried. "The Nevilles would be posting to London to lay their swords at the King's feet. The name of Courtenay is not the name of Bohun, and has no spell to summon England."

They found the chief of the Nevilles in his house of Marchington by the Severn. He was of the old school, wearing the clothes of another age, and eschewing the shaven fashion of the Court, for he had a forked grey beard like the tushes of a boar. His massive figure had grown bulky, his legs tottered, the colour of his face was that of his hair, but he had the old habit of going always armed, and supported indoors a weight of body armour that might have been at Agincourt. The house had not been changed since the time of the Edwards, and was a rough draughty place, very different from the comfort of Avelard. There was a pale woman flitting in the background, his latest wife, who had once been his mistress, but she did not come near the strangers, and the party of three sat in the chilly hall on bare stools, as if they had met at a leaguer.

Neville looked at Peter long and searchingly.

"Ned's son, by God!" he exclaimed. "I would know that nick in the upper lip out of ten thousand. You have kept him well hidden, or some spy of Henry's would have unearthed him, and he would have tested Henry's mercies. Hark ye, lad, you are my brother, child though you be, for in your sister, now with God, I had as good a wife as a man of my habits deserves. You are abbey-bred and no soldier? So much the better, say I, for you will leave the business of war to such as understand it. Half Henry's bungling has come from his belief that he is a new Caesar."

To Peter's surprise this man, whom, according to report, greed spurred to action in spite of age and sickness, spoke no word of those ill-omened parchments at Avelard. He was new back from Wales, and had much to say of the levies due from

180

thence; they would march on a certain day, so as to be at the meeting-point in Cotswold by St Lucy's eve. His brother, Sir Thomas, would lead them; he was even now busy on Usk and Wye. All Gwent and Powysland would march, and many of the new-settled English would wear saffron. There was still good fighting stuff in the dales—bowmen like those of the old wars and squires like Sir Davy Gam. The grandson of old Rhys ap Thomas was with them, him who had put Harry's father on the throne—he had seen at Dynevor the great stirrups used at Bosworth—and as the grandsire had set up the Tudor so the grandson would help to pull him down. Then he outlined the plan of campaign, and Peter listened with some stir in his heart. They would march swiftly on Oxford, which would at once be surrendered, for they had friends within. It was altogether needful for their security to have a docile Oxford in their rear, for the city was the key of the route between Thames and Severn. But they would not tarry there, though it might be necessary to hang a few rogues for the general comfort—some of Crummle's dogs—Dr John London and others. After that they would not take the valley road to London by way of Windsor; but would move on the capital in two bodies, one going by the backside of Chiltern and coming down from the north, the other keeping the Berkshire and Surrey downs and attacking from the south.

"We must have hard ground for our march," said the old campaigner, "for at this season the valleys are swamps. Also by this device we achieve two mighty ends. Our northern force cuts in between London and the King's armies in Lincoln and York, which by all tales are already in some straits, and it will hinder Henry, too, from drawing support from Suffolk and Norfolk. Our southern force will sever London from the King's friends in Kent and on the sea-coast. We shall build a dyke on each side of him, and the only open country will be to the west, which is the road of our own folk."

There was immense vigour in the speech and eyes of the old man, but the strength of his body soon ebbed, and he had to be laid every now and then on a leathern settle till his breath came back to him. At the end of one of these bouts Peter found the sufferer's eyes fixed on him.

"The new brother you have brought me is to my liking, my lord. He is as handsome a babe as you will see in a year of Sundays. Have you found him a wife?"

"It is proposed," said Lord Avelard gravely, "that if our venture succeed, he shall marry the King's daughter, the Lady Mary."

The old man chuckled.

"Policy, policy! A wise step, doubtless, for the commons have a weakness for the lady and her sad mother. Also, if she has the Tudor in one half of her, she has the high blood of Emperors in the other. But, by the rood of Asseline, she hath an ugly face and the tint of Cheshire whey. Yet cheer up, brother. 'Tis no bad thing to have a plain wife, for it whets a man's zest for other and fairer women. I, who speak, have proved it."

As they rode homeward in the late afternoon Peter's thoughts were busy. He believed that he read Lord Avelard's purpose—to allow the matter of the parchments to sleep, but by this very silence to let Peter commit himself unconsciously, so that, in the event of victory, he should find over him that stiffest of compulsions, the will of a victorious army. He had accompanied him to Marchington to prevent undue candour on his part towards Neville, though, as it had fallen out, Neville's thoughts had been on another bent. But why this tale of the daughter of Catherine, who was devout among the devout?

"You would marry me to the Queen's daughter?" he said to his companion after a long spell of silence.

"Ay," was the answer, and there was a dry bitterness in the tone. "You are unworthy of beauty, so we fall back on piety. We must reap what vantage we can out of your monkish tastes."

The other journeys Peter made alone, for in them it seemed that Lord Avelard scented no danger. Some were to the houses of strong squires, who received him as Buckingham's son and would have kissed his stirrups. At Stanway the family priest,

182

a man like an ancient prophet, blessed him solemnly, and old Sir John Tracey and his five sons knelt as at a sacrament. At Burwell he found a lord so bitter against the King that he asked for no reward except the hope of seeing the Tudor green and white in the mire. At Abbotslease he was met by a hundred men of those deep pastures, all girt for war, and the banner of the Five Wounds was consecrated and exalted, and in the burr of Gloucestershire he heard the old recruiting song of the Crusaders,

"O man, have pity upon God."

As he travelled the roads, he realised that Lord Avelard knew but little of one side of the movement he controlled. The great lords might rise for worldly profit or private vengeance, but here in the west, in outland places and among plain men, there was smouldering the same passion which in Lincoln and the Yorkshire dales was now bursting into flame. They were ready to fight, not for the abbeys, maybe, or even for the Church, but for what they deemed their souls' salvation. In the churchyard of Ashton-under-Bredon he had listened to the parson chanting to a pale and weeping crowd of armed peasants the tremendous prophecies of Zephaniah, and had felt in his own heart the solemn exaltation of a crusader.

"*Juxta est dies Domini magni,*" the hoarse voice had risen and fallen like a wandering wind, "*dies tribulationis et angustiae . . . dies tenebrarum et caliginis . . . dies tubae et clangoris super civitates munitas et super angulos excelsos.*"

For certain these were *dies tenebrarum*, for the snow still tarried, though its shadow darkened. On his journeys Peter was accompanied by six of the Avelard men-at-arms, and by Dickon, mounted on a grey palfrey, and wearing the black and gold Avelard liveries. The hill country lay in a gloom, which was not a fog, for distances could be perceived, but everything was drained of colour and frozen into a tenebrous monotony. Daily the sky seemed to sink nearer the earth. The first utter silence had gone. Now, though there was no wind, the trees and grasses shook and shivered eerily as if some tremor had

183

passed through the ground. It was weather to lie heavy on a man's spirits, for not only was the cold enough to freeze the marrow, but there seemed to be in the air a dull foreboding. The Avelard varlets never whistled or sang; there was no merriment at the wayside taverns; the horses, well fed on grain and therefore likely to be fractious in the cold air, now plodded like oxen; the sheep had been brought in from the wolds to wattled shelters, where they huddled shivering with scared eyes.

One afternoon on the road between Avelard and Colne Peter saw an encampment by the wayside—half a dozen shelters of boughs and straw around a great fire which burned cheerfully in the brume. Tending it was a man with a vast fat face and a paunch like a promontory, in whom he recognised Timothy Pennyfarthing, him whom they called True Timothy, the master of the palliards. Peter bade his men ride on with Dickon, and turned aside to the blaze.

It was as if he had trod on a wasps' nest. Timothy, unperturbed, continued to feed the fire, but from the beehive shelters appeared a swarm of foul faces and verminous rags, and the glitter of many knives.

Peter sat his horse and waited, till Timothy turned his face towards him, which was not till he had adjusted properly an iron kettle.

"How far is it to the skirts of Wychwood?" he asked.

"As far as to Peter's Gate," came the answer, delivered cavalierly, almost insolently.

"Alack," said Peter, "I . . . shall . . . not . . . be . . . there . . . in . . . time."

The words wrought a miracle. Every foul head disappeared into its burrow, and Timothy's flitch of a face assumed an expression of gravity and respect. He came forward from the fire, and bent his forehead till it touched Peter's left stirrup. Then he led him a little way apart.

"You have the Word, master. Have you also the message? Solomon Darking told us that the hour for it was nigh."

"Nigh, but not yet. My command is that you and all wandering men be ready against the feast of St Lucy."

"Your command, my lord? Then are you he we look for?"

"The same. The same who with Darking attended your parliament at Little Greece."

"Yon forest lad! Soft in the wits, said Darking. 'Twas a good jape to put upon the Upright Men." Timothy chuckled. "Have you any orders for us palliards?"

"Not yet. How go things underground in England?"

"We be awake—awake like badgers in April. When the hour comes, there will be a fine stirring among our old bones. The word has gone out among the Upright Men from the Black Mountain to Ivinghoe Beacon, and south to the sea-shore, and north to the Derwent dales. There be much ado, likewise, among the great folk, but that your lordship knows better than me. There is one piece of news I had but this morning. They say that the King's grace is disquieted about the westlands, and may come himself to cast an eye over them. They say it is his purpose to keep Christmas at Woodstock."

Peter cried out. "I had heard nothing of that."

The palliard shook his head wisely. "True it may be, natheless. I had it from a sure hand. 'Twill serve our purpose nobly, my lord. 'Tis better if the fox blunder into the hounds than to have to dig him out of his earth."

"Let the word go out," said Peter, "that any further news of this be brought to me at Avelard."

Timothy nodded.

"It shall go by Solomon Darking." Then he sniffed the air. "There is but one danger to your cause, my lord. This devil's weather may upset the wisest plan of lording and vagabond, for there is no striving against the evil humour of the skies."

"What do you make of it?" Peter cast his eye over the darkening landscape, which seemed void of life as a sepulchre.

"There will be snow," was the answer, "a cruel weight of snow. Look ye, the hedgehog, when he snuggles down in winter-time, makes two vents to his cell, one north, one south. He will stop up neither except for the sternest need. Now he hath stopped up the north vent. We have seen it in every wood, for we know his ways and often dig him out for our supper, since a winter hedgehog will fry like an eel in his own

185

fat. That means snow such as you and I have not known, for the thing has not happened in my lifetime, though I have heard my father tell how he saw it in the black winter of '87. I will tell you another thing. The dotterels have all gone from High Cotswold. When they come in flocks it means good weather, but when they leave it means death to beast and man."

"Snow might serve our purpose well," said Peter.

"Ay, a modest snow, with a frost to bind it. That were noble weather for armed men. But not mountains of snow which smother the roads, and above all not melting snow. Your folk will come from far places and must ford many streams. I dread the melting wind which makes seas of rivers and lakes of valleys. Robin Hood feared little above ground, but he feared the thaw-wind."

That night came a message from Darking, who was in south Cotswold near the Stroud valley, and begged that Peter should go to him to meet certain doubting squires of those parts. Lord Avelard approved. "They are small folk in that quarter," he said, "and therefore the more jealous. 'Twere well to confirm their loyalty by a sight of you."

So early next morning Peter set out—this time unattended, for the journey was short, and he proposed to return well before the darkening.

To his surprise Sabine declared that she would accompany him for part of the road. She wished to accustom two young eyases to the hood, and to try the mettle of a new Norway falcon. So, with a couple of falconers in attendance, the two rode out of Avelard towards the scarp of the hills and the open country. It meant for Peter some slight deviation from his route, which should have lain nearer the valley bottom. The girl was muffled in furs, her horse had a frieze blanket beneath its saddle, and on her head she wore a close-fitting bonnet of white ermine.

The weather was changing. The clouds hung closer to earth than ever, but it was no longer a still cold. Something which was less a wind than an icy shiver seemed to be coming out of the north. There was a deathly oppression in it, which weighted Peter's spirits and kept the chattering falconers dumb. Sabine alone did not appear to feel it. Her cheeks glowed, her eyes sparkled within their ermine cincture. She looked the one thing alive in a world of death.

The hawking proved a farce. For one thing there was no game. Not a rabbit stirred from the clumps of furze, or hare from the bracken; there was nowhere the flutter of a wing or the rustle of a moving beast. The hawks, too, behaved oddly. The eyases clung dully to their leashes, as if they were mewing, and seemed to have no wish to get rid of their rufterhoods. The splendid Norway tiercel, when cast free, instead of ringing up the sky, returned to its perch after a short wavering flight, as if it sought the protection of man. There was no chance of serving it by showing a quarry, for there was no quarry to show. The cold bit into the bone, and every now and then came that ominous shudder from the northern sky.

Even Sabine's youth and health were not proof against the oppression.

"The world is dead," she said, and there was awe in her light tones. "I and my hawks must needs go home, for they cannot hunt in a desert."

Then something in the muffled sky and the menacing air frightened her.

"This is no weather to be out in, my lord," she turned to Peter. "Come home with us, for there is mischief afoot. I can hear its hoofs drumming on the hills." There was anxiety in her eye, almost kindness.

"I must keep tryst," said Peter. "But I will be back at Avelard within four hours, and I think I will forestall the snow."

"At any rate, take one of my men with you," she pled.

He shook his head. "I thank you for your kindness, mistress. But he would only delay me, since I am better mounted. But do you go back to the fireside, and have a hot posset ready for my return. I am like to be chilly enough."

"A wilful man must have his way," she said, as she swung her horse round. "Heaven send the snow tarries. If it come, take the valley road home, for these hills will be death."

Peter set spurs to his horse, and as his pace quickened the air cut his face like a file. But he did not regard it, for his heart was hot within him. Longing for Sabine engulfed him like a flood. The sudden kindness in her eyes, her glowing figure, instinct with youth and life among the drooping hawks and pinched falconers, her soft voice which was like a fire in the winter cold—these things made him sick with regret. Here was a woman who was life incarnate, and he had renounced her for a scruple. Here was one who would be like a lamp in the darkness that awaited him, and he had rejected that light. He choked down the thoughts, but they made a weight on his heart and a confusion in his brain.

He reached the appointed place by noon, and found Darking in the company of a half-dozen loutish squires who had been passing the time with dice and strong ale. It is likely that the sight of Peter was well fitted to impress them, for he came among them ruddy from the road, and his preoccupation made his manner high and his speech peremptory as befitted Buckingham's son. There was no trace of the Oseney clerk in the young lord who spoke as one accustomed to obedience, and gave orders as sharp and clear as a huntsman's call to his hounds. Nor was he without graciousness—the graciousness of one who is ready to give favours since he is too great to seek them. He could see Darking's eye on him in the conclave, and in that eye there was a pleased surprise.

Peter drank a cup with the company, and then called for his horse. "I must haste me back to Avelard," he told the gaping squires, "for there are many tasks before me, and the weather threatens."

Darking looked anxious. "I will accompany my lord," he said. "I think the snows will break ere the dark."

The others disputed. One older man maintained that there would be no fall for twenty-four hours, and his neighbours agreed with him. "The heavens have been frozen," he said, "and now they are melting, but the drip of them will not reach us before tomorrow."

"You will stay here," Peter told Darking, "and complete the business of which you have told me. These are not the times to think about weather."

Darking was still anxious. "You will take the low road, my lord? There are woods there which will give shelter if the snow overtakes you."

Five minutes later, his horse refreshed by a mash of grain and hot ale, Peter swung out of the manor gates and rode south along the lower slopes of the hills. He was back again among the bitter thoughts of the morning, but their sting was less sharp. Sabine was no longer the melting figure that had tortured his fancy on his outward ride. He remembered now the hard agate edge of her. She sought that which he could not give her—the giving of which would mean the loss for ever of his peace. That was the naked fact, and there was no road round it. And yet, if she were only a Delilah to tempt him, why did the memory of her so hearten him? Why did the thought of her seem to brace him to a keener life, a manlier resolution, if to love her was to lose his soul?

He was in a wood now, one of the patches of native forest which clad the western slopes of Cotswold. He knew that the hour was no more than two o'clock in the afternoon, but already the darkness seemed to be falling. The sky, seen through the leafless canopy of oaks, was the sky of night, though below there was light enough near the ground to discern the path.

A memory cut like a sunbeam into the entanglements of his thought. It was the memory of some words of St Augustine. How did they go? *Nondum amabam et amare amabam; quaerebam quid amarem, amans amare*. The wise Father had known his mood. Was not this his own case? "I did not yet love, but I sought something to love, for I was in love with love." And then there flowed in on him other recollections, the tale of Eros and Psyche, the wandering soul and the wandering heart brought at last together. He had been hungering for something of which Sabine had been only a shadow.

A strange solemn joy took possession of him. He was being weaned from the lesser that he might attain the greater. The sight of Lovell's bones had shattered one kind of earthly ambition, and now in the girl he had renounced another. He

189

felt a great tenderness warm him so that the cold, which he had felt acutely at the start of the afternoon's journey, seemed a trivial thing.

He noticed that the snow had begun. A thin powder was filtering down through the branches.

The road left the patch of wood for open hill, and there he rode into a new world. It was dark with a misty white gloom, for the air was thick with snow. The powder had changed to heavy flakes, but he saw them only on his horse's neck and on his saddle, for what descended seemed to be a solid thing, as if a cloud had taken material form and enveloped the earth. The weight of it pressed down on him like a blanket, and he noted that the ground seemed to be rising towards him. Already his horse's feet were sunk above the hocks. "At this pace," he thought, "there will be six feet of snow in an hour, and I shall assuredly be buried."

Presently the wall did not drop vertically, but seemed to sway towards him, as if under the compulsion of a secret wind. The impact took the breath from him, and his horse stumbled. He felt himself encrusted with ice, which filled eyes and mouth and nose, and sent cold fingers under his garments. These swaying onrushes were intermittent, but at the impact of each his horse crouched and slipped, and he bent his head as if to avoid a blow. There was as yet no wind—only a shivering of earth and sky. "It looks as if I must find a shelter," he thought—and there was no fear in his heart, but a comfortable confusion—"for another hour of this will destroy me."

He was among trees again, but he only knew it by the struggles of his horse among the lower scrub and the scraping of laden branches in his face. And then the shuddering, which had bent the snowfall against him like a billow, changed to a fury of wind. He was in a patch of forest at the foot of a cleeve of the hills, and the northern blast, from which the slopes had hitherto sheltered him, swept down the cleeve as through a funnel. The trees bent on him and shook off avalanches. He felt himself smothered, stifled, his wits dazed by the ceaseless lashing of boughs and the steady buffets of

190

the snow. His horse was in desperate case, for the track had long been lost, and the two floundered among dead trunks and holes, with no purpose except to escape, though it were only for a moment, that torturing blast.

He tried to think, to plan. Progress was impossible—was there no chance of a shelter? . . . But this wood seemed to be swept to its roots, for the turmoil in the air was matched by a like turmoil on the ground, where the snow was being swirled by the wind into fantastic heaps and hollows. His head was confused, but his heart was calm. "This looks like death," he thought. "This beast of mine will soon go down, and we shall both lie cold in a drift."

What time he parted company with his horse he did not know. The struggle for mere breath was so cruel that he was scarcely conscious of the rest of his body. But somewhere in a drift the animal slipped and did not rise, and Peter must have been thrown, and gone forward on foot, under the impulse which demanded movement to escape from torment. At any rate he found himself engulfed to the middle in whirling snow, every step a task for Hercules. He had a pain in his left shoulder, where some branch had struck him. Of this he was dimly conscious, and he was conscious too of a great weakness. It would have been despair if he had had any fear; but fear there was none, so it was only weakness—a creeping lassitude which bade him drop down and sleep. But as there was no shelter anywhere he could not sleep, because of the sting of the gale, so he kept moving like a marionette whose limbs are jerked by some alien power. "If I once lie down, I shall never rise," he told himself, with conviction but without panic. It did not seem to matter greatly—if only this blizzard would stop scourging him.

He stumbled into an aisle of the forest where, by some freak of the wind, the ground had been swept almost bare of snow. Here his limbs moved more freely, and this freedom brought a momentary clearness to his brain. He knew that he was very near the end of his strength; if he dropped here on the bare ground he would freeze to death, if in the drifts he would soon be buried. His spirit seemed to hover above him, careless and

191

incurious, watching the antics of his feeble body. The misery now was less acute, for his senses were numbing. It occurred to him that this was an occasion for prayer—occurred merely as a notion of the mind, without any tremor of the heart. The prayer which came to his lips was that invocation to the Mother of God which had been his favourite in childhood:

"*Imperatrix supernorum,*
Superatrix infernorum."

Suddenly there came a great peace in the world. The inferno of the gale seemed to be stilled, and the darkness to lighten . . . something lifted from his brain and his eyes opened. He saw that he was in a forest aisle like a cave in an ice-wall, and before him a light was glowing. And in that light was a figure.

Once a Florentine, who had come to Oxford to study a codex in Duke Humphry's library, had told him of the great statues of the Greeks, destroyed these thousand years by barbarian hands. The Athene of the Parthenon, he said, had been no colourless pale marble, but had had a face of ivory, and eyes of flaming jewels, and delicate tresses of wrought gold. Peter had dreamed of this marvel, and now in this icy place it stood before him. It was a woman's figure, a woman with a celestial face, helmed and panoplied with gold, her garments shining with other colours than those of earth. In her face was a great peace and a great gentleness. He had one half-moment of clarity. "Am I dead?" he asked, "and in Paradise?" He told himself that that could not be, for he was conscious of an aching left shoulder, and the blessed do not suffer pain.

Then his soul lost its frozen calm, and life of a kind returned to the channels of his heart. For suddenly it seemed to him that what he saw was no statue, but a living presence. The gold and jewels dimmed and shone again in a milder light, the face melted to a human softness, and in the unearthly radiance that surrounded her he saw that the draperies about her breast were that heavenly blue which it is given to one alone to wear.

192

He knew that he was looking upon the Mother of God.

He stood, or lay, or knelt—he was beyond consciousness of the body—and gazed upward with wondering rapture. He had heard it said that the Blessed Trinity ruled in turn, and that the reign of the Father and of the Son had passed, and that now was the reign of the Holy Spirit. But, since men must have their special worship, his had always been for the Virgin, who stood between man and the harshness of eternal justice. She was Woman, Mother and Queen alike, who loved beauty and simple things and did not greatly relish the cold cloisters of piety. She was divine, but like Prometheus she had brought fire to men. Her face was grave, for she had known infinite sorrow, and it was proud, since she carried the keys of Heaven; but it had tenderness and humour, too, for she had been human and loved humanity. She was stronger than the greatest warriors, and wiser than the wisest, the woman enthroned to whom all men must bow in the end. She was the hope of the world, for she made even mortality divine; she was the Power above the Law, who brought mercy into justice and tenderness into the sublimities of Son and Father. She was the protectress of man against fate, his one way of escape from the punishment of soul and body.

As he gaped, it seemed to him that in that face he saw every dream of his childhood and youth—the dim heights of devotion to which in Oseney Great Church he had mounted on waves of music—the glory of the fields in May—the joy of young blood—the vision of shimmering nymphs and slim goddesses out of old poets—the solemn rapture of the philosophers. Sabine, too, was in her, for she was very woman—Sabine's witchery and Mother Sweetbread's tenderness; queen she was, but peasant too—peasant and gipsy. To those immortal eyes the little conventions of mankind were folly, but even to folly they were kind.

As his senses slipped from him, he thought clearly for one moment, "I have seen the Queen of Heaven. Now I know that I shall not die, but live."

It took True Timothy and his palliards, who were encamped

in the wood, a good two hours to bring life back to Peter, though they wrought hard with strong hands and rough cordials.

" 'Twas lucky that the grew-bitch went hunting," said Timothy, shivering under his mountain of rags, for fat chills fast. "Else there had been a stiff lording in Batt's Wood and a newcomer at Peter's gate."

CHAPTER XIII

THE UNLOOSING OF THE WATERS

Peter lay two days abed at Avelard, while the snow muffled the land, made plains of villages, and built new mountains on the levels. Recovering from a great fatigue is in early youth a pleasant thing. Weakness, after a man has slept his fill, passes into a delicious languor, hourly the blood runs more strongly in the veins, hunger revives, the scents and sounds of a recovered life come with a virgin freshness. Peter lay in a delectable dream, while Sabine brought his meals—first possets of ewes' milk and white claret, then eggs beaten up with cordials, till his restored strength demanded solider fare. He looked at her without embarrassment—nay, with a kind of cool affection. She was part of the beatific vision he had seen, but part only: now he had gotten a divine discontent and had his mind on the stars.

He rose on the third day, a whole man in body and a new man in spirit. He had come suddenly to maturity, and all the hesitations and doubts of his youth had dropped from him like an old cloak. He felt himself in the mood for command. He could now bend men to his will, for his purpose was a clear flame. No hazard was too great, for he had lost fear. The word of the Israelitish prophet rang in his ears: "Who art thou that thou shouldest be afraid of a man that shall die, and of the son of man which shall be made as grass?"

When on the third day he met Lord Avelard he found that the awe in which he had always held him had gone. This was an old man he looked on, an old man near the end of his days, tramping wearily in the world's mire. Such an one could not mould the fates of the land; it was very necessary that he himself should be up and doing. Peter felt his youth and vigour surge within him like springtide.

"You are like Phoebus new-risen," said the old man, and

there was that in his eye which wondered. This man that stood before him was not the stripling he had known.

"I feel within me the strength of ten," Peter replied. "In four days, my lord, it will be St Lucy's feast. I must be stirring. What news of the King?"

"Darking came here yesterday. The Welshman will pass Christmas at Woodstock. He leaves Windsor tomorrow, and will travel by Reading and Watlington and Hasely. That is his accustomed road, but hitherto he has made his progresses in the height of summer, or in September when the buck are fat. What is his purpose, think you? By the rules of common wisdom he should sit snug in Windsor, or, if he move, go north to the Yorkshire dales, where the trouble waxes daily. 'Tis said he has pardoned the chief rebels there, but his clemency has not abated the discontent."

"He must have news which makes him fear the west more than the north."

Lord Avelard nodded.

"Doubtless. And that is the doing of Crummle and his vagabond commissaries. They have been into every abbey on Thames and Severn, and though our plans are well guarded we could not hope that some rumours of them would not escape. The Welshman wishes to learn our condition for himself and, if need be, to strike the first blow. I think that purpose will miscarry."

"What force does he bring to Woodstock?"

"No more than a hundred mounted men of my lord Shrewsbury's. Elsewhere things go happily for us. As I told you, Henry has broke with the Emperor and is now hotly abetting the French King. Therefore the Emperor is with us, and he is sending money—his legate Reginald Pole, him that is Clarence's grandson, is even now awaiting a ship on the Flanders coast. Also James of Scotland is moving on the northern marches, and his holiness of Durham will find it hard to stay him. There is good news, too, of my lord of Exeter. It seems that the Cornishmen would make him king, but my lord's heart fails him for such a flight. All he seeks is the Welshman's downfall, and at the word from us he will march on Bristol."

"But what of the King at Woodstock? He may be at Avelard gate while we are busy with our muster."

Lord Ayelard smiled. "That is not the way of the King's grace. He will sit snug in Woodstock and send out intelligencers, and it will be odds against those intelligencers ever returning. Besides, the snow will hamper him. You cannot ride fast on muffled roads."

Then the two fell to the study of papers and plans. What had hitherto been to Peter a half-understood game which he was content to leave to others had now become a passionate absorption on which his mind worked with precision and speed. He asked a hundred questions; he pressed for exact answers; he made computations of his own, and questioned some of the details of Neville's plan. Lord Avelard opened his eyes. "These last days you have become a soldier, my son," he said. "No doubt the gift was in your blood, but what has brought it to birth? Whence got you the light?"

"As Paul got it on the road to Damascus," said Peter and turned again to the papers.

"I must go abroad," he said at last. "There are loose nails which need a hammer to drive them home, and the time grows scant. There will be many of the commons that cry out for the Five Wounds and the Holy Blood of Hailes, while the watchword of the lords will be God and the Swan. I must be the one to blend the two into a single army."

"Then God prosper you, for you will find it no mean labour. There is much wild stuff about in this west of ours. There is a mad Carmelite, who claims that his order descends from Elijah and that he is Elijah reincarnate, sent by God to hew down the groves of Baal—by which groves he signifies the King's Court and Council. He and his like will need a stout spur to break to harness."

"I must be that spur," said Peter.

Lord Avelard looked at him curiously.

"There are ill tidings from Marchington," he said. "It seems that my lord Abergavenny is mortal sick and like to die. He has been frail these last months, and has ridden his body too

197

hard. He was to be our leader in the field, for he has more skill of war than Norfolk and Suffolk and Shrewsbury joined together. His brother, Sir Thomas, is in Wales, bringing in the hill levies. If my lord should die, the other brother, Sir Edward, must take his place."

"Nay," said Peter, "there can be but one commander, and I am he. I, and no other, am Bohun. . . . This afternoon I ride to Marchington."

A smile, mingled of humorous surprise, respect and kindliness, broke over the waxen face.

"I commend your spirit, my son. You have assuredly seen a great light. . . . But you cannot yet ride to Marchington. The snow has ceased falling, but it lies twelve feet deep in every hollow, and Marchington is in the river meadows. You must wait for friendlier weather. I think the change is nigh, for the wind is shifting. What we want is a binding frost which will last till the new year, to set a crust on the snow and make easy travelling. For, as you well know, our people have far to come."

But that afternoon the wind moved not to the east as some had foretold, but against the sun into the west. Out in the drifts of the park, which had been hard enough for a man to walk on, Peter noted the thaw beginning before the dark fell. In his bed that night he found his blankets too heavy and the room airless, and when he opened the lattice a mild wind fanned his face. At sunrise he saw a strange sight. A black thundercloud swamped the sky, from which the lightning flashed, and the waning moon in that strange radiance showed red as blood.

Then, in one unbroken and relentless deluge, came the rain.

Never in the memory of the oldest man had the fountains of heaven been thus unloosed. It fell as the snow had fallen— as if the clouds were bags of water which drooped near the ground and then discharged themselves in an even torrent. Under the red dawn the earth had been one vast white counterpane, running into hills and ridges, but otherwise unfeatured. By midday it was already piebald. Forests were showing sodden crests, the scarp of Cotswold had resumed its

198

normal shape, every lane was a rushing river where nothing mortal could live. The silence of the snowbound world was exchanged for a devil's kitchen of sound—the unending beat of the falling rain, the rumour of cascading waters, the sudden soft crush which told that a slope had melted into mud or that a tall tree had slipped down to join the chaos in the valley.

In such weather no man durst tempt the roads. With bitten lips Peter sat in his chamber, watching the grey mists droop over Severn. In two days the hour of destiny would strike, and how could men muster in a dissolving world? . . . Again and again he essayed the out-of-doors, only to be driven back by the deluge. He had a horse saddled, but the beast could not progress a hundred yards on what had once been dry Cotswold slopes but were now a slippery glacis of mud. . . . What would the rivers be like in another day and night? The air was too thick to give him any prospect, but he could hear Severn— miles away—roaring like an ocean. And what of Usk and Wye and Teme and Clun, which the Marchmen must cross? What of Avon which guarded Warwickshire? What of the little rivers which barred the road to Oxford? What, above all, of the northern streams which lay in the path of Westmoreland and Cumberland and the Stanleys?

It rained for seventy-three hours, till the eve of St Lucy, just before the darkening. There was not a speck of snow left except some dirty streaks in the lee of walls and ditches. Every inch of soil was sodden a yard deep, and when the sky cleared towards sunset Severn was seen to be the better part of a mile wide, a turbid lagoon like an arm of the sea.

At dawn on St Lucy's day Peter rode to Marchington. The air was as mild as June, the sun shone through a watery mist, and everywhere rose pale exhalations from the infinity of floods. Often he had to swim his horse across meres which had once been Cotswold meads, strange waters indeed, for instead of clumps of rushes to stud them they had the tops of thorn trees. Marchington moat was a swirling torrent, and Peter had to leave his horse on the near side, and make a perilous passage of the drawbridge on foot.

He found death within. The old lord had given up the ghost two days before, and now lay in grim state in the hall under a splendid mortcloth till such time as he could be moved to the family sepulchre. The pale wife flitted in the background like a shade. Beside the dead stood an angry man whose lantern jaws and drooping nose proclaimed his kinship.

"Here is the confusion of Hell," the man cried. "Brother George is a corpse and brother Thomas is in Wales and Noah's flood roars between us. The new lord—my nephew and yours, young sir—is with his cousins in Kent. The house of Neville is most plaguily scattered at this hour when it should be bound tight together, and they tell me that Henry is in Woodstock waiting to pounce like a crow on our broken meats. God's wounds, but the Devil has come to his own these days!"

"There will be no crossing Bran or Towey or Usk or Wye for a sennight," Sir Edward went on, "and that only if the rain holds off, and a man might as well hope to swim the Narrow Seas as to ford Severn. And there is still rain to come. So says my armourer, and he can smell it a week off in the sky."

It was long before Peter could divert him from his passionate maledictions, uttered often in a strange tongue, for he had lived much with the mountain folk.

"Our spearhead is the Welsh," he ended, "who can march thirty miles in a day and then fight like wild-cats; and where in God's name are the Welsh? Sitting by smoky fires on the sodden ground watching the rivers roar to the sea. Sorry am I for him that comes within a mile of brother Thomas, for his temper will be like a flaming oven. Ay, they could march a circuit by the river heads, but 'twould take them a month to reach us, and by that time all England would be agog. Our blow was to be secret and swift, and now 'twill be as slow as the stumbling of a woman in labour. 'Tis no better up north. If Severn is swollen, so likewise will be Avon, and Avon, flowing through the marshlands, will not decline till Easter. And what of Shropshire and Cheshire and Lancashire and Westmoreland? We are islanded here on a knuckle of Cotswold and cut off from all England. The King has got a better ally in this devil's weather than a thousand Norfolks. 'Tis your family blight, my lord. Duke Harry, your grandsire, in Richard's day perished because of the same accursed floods."

In the end Sir Edward's passion spent itself, and he spoke soberly.

"My counsel is to let our levy dissolve, even as the hillsides have melted in the rain. The weather, which has frustrated it, will also conceal it. For a month this west country will be a secret land, with none coming or going, and Henry at Woodstock may guess as he likes, but he will have no proof to offer Council. I will contrive to get word to brother Thomas and to the northern lords. Let my lord Avelard make haste to Woodstock to forestall gossip, and invite his liege lord to a merry-making at Avelard. The Cotswold men, you say? Nay, they are too few, and without the Welsh behind them they will not stir. Sudely and Boteler and Noel are shrewd folk, and the wool-staplers are shrewder. Here and there you may get a mad squire or a mad priest to run his head into the noose, but not the solid men. As for you, my lord, my counsel is that you get you back to Avelard, and lie as close as the fox till the King goes eastward again. You may thank the mercies of God that you have not yet shown yourself in the light of day."

Peter argued and pled, but the man was stubborn. He had his nephew to think of, whose guardian he now was, and he would not fling away the Neville and Beauchamp lands on any wild hazard.

From Marchington Peter rode north to the squires that lived on the slopes looking toward Avon. From the Traceys he got some comfort; that stout house would mount for God and the Swan though not a Welshman crossed Severn. But the Traceys were alone in their careless valour; elsewhere he found only long faces and heads cautiously shaken. From one spur he got a prospect which confirmed his worst fears. The vale of Evesham was a sea from which the tops of trees and church towers rose like foundered ships. With Avon and Severn thus swollen the road from the north was securely barred.

On his way back to Avelard he fell in with a white friar,

201

the very Carmelite who claimed to be Elijah's successor. The man sat beside a sheepfold, sodden and travel-worn, muttering prayers. By some strange divination he seemed to recognise Peter—or perhaps took him for some local leader—for he seized his bridle, and poured forth a torrent of ravings, mingled with texts from the Apocalypse.

"Fear not, my son," he cried. "The word of God is with me, His prophet, to bid you go up against the evil city—the city which is spiritually called Sodom and Babylon, where also our Lord was crucified. The windows of Heaven have been opened, but not in your despite, for the waters will cumber the evil ones, but for you they will be cleft apart as the Red Sea at the command of Moses. I say unto you that a handful will put to flight ten thousand, and three banded in God's name will become a multitude."

The man was mad, but there was method in his madness, for he preached what to Peter seemed good strategy. Let them go up at once against the city—whether Oxford or London was not clear—for every delay would enable the ungodly to assemble, whereas, if taken by surprise, they would be shepherdless sheep. The wild figure in that lonely hollow of the hills, rugged as a tree against the twilit sky, affected him strangely. He dismounted, and knelt to receive the Carmelite's blessing. And, as he cantered through the soaked Avelard meadows, he felt his resolution grow more desperate. If the odds were weighted against him so much the more work for God's hand. Besides, were the odds really increased? What crippled them and shore their levy of its strength would likewise cripple and lull their enemies.

At Avelard he found Darking. He had come from the east, and reported mighty floods in the Oxford rivers. Nevertheless, they could be passed by men who knew the ways of them. The King had reached Woodstock. He had with him an escort of Shrewsbury's men, but he had also called for levies from the local lords, avowedly for the Yorkshire campaign, where the rising of peasants and gentry might at any moment be increased by the advent of the King of Scots. Meanwhile he was hunting in the great park, so far as the weather allowed,

202

since the open winter had kept the deer in season. Crummle had been with him, but had now returned to London. He had a posse of secretaries, but none of the great lords of the Council. And then he added a piece of news which made Lord Avelard frown. Sir Gabriel Messynger was with him, specially summoned out of Kent.

It was plain that Lord Avelard was in deep perplexity. He was of a stouter heart than Sir Edward Neville, or maybe had more to gain and lose. He was not ready to give up an enterprise which had been so long the chief preoccupation of his brain. On the other hand, he had none of the simple passion of the Traceys, and had no mind to go crusading unless there was a reasonable chance of victory. He laughed to scorn the Neville advice that he should go forthwith to Woodstock and seek the King's favour. "I shall bide here," he said. "The next move is for the Welshman to make. He knows nothing of what we have done, and will know nothing, unless he clap all the west country in prison and put it to the rack. Our secret is confined to true men."

"What of Sir Gabriel?" Peter asked.

Lord Avelard replied with a laugh in which to Peter's ear there was a trace of disquiet.

"Sir Gabriel is the deepest involved of any. He was our go-between to the northern lords, and has twice followed Neville into Wales. There is nothing new in his going to Court. He was bred there as a youth, whence the touch of the popinjay in his manners."

"We cannot sit idle," said Peter. "Either we must do as Sir Edward advises, send word to Wales and the north, and call off all preparations. Or we must strike now, trusting to win such vantage that, when the floods abate and our army arrives, we shall be able to use it to deadly purpose."

Darking nodded, as if in agreement, but Lord Avelard flung up his hand impatiently.

"How in God's name can we strike? We have nothing at our command but our Cotswold neighbours, and you have seen their mood today. We might take Oxford by a bold stroke, but we should be scattered long before we were twenty

203

miles on the London road."

"Assuredly," said Peter. "My mind was not on London, for it is certain that we must revise our plan."

"Then where? Oxford is useless, except as a step. Windsor is seventy miles off. . . ."

"It has come nearer these last days. I think Windsor is now in Woodstock park."

The old man stared and Darking smiled.

"See, my lord," Peter went on. He had risen from his chair and stood in the glow of the hearth, tall and straight, tense as a strung bow. His face had lost all the softness of the boy's, and was set in hard lines.

"See, my lord. I am Bohun, and it is right that I run the chief hazard. The King is at Woodstock by God's grace, and has but a small force to guard him. What of the Oxford squires?" He turned to Darking.

"Sir Ferdinando Fettiplace with twenty men rode to Woodstock this morning, but he was sent back to Swinbrook to wait further commands. With the waters out the muster will be slow."

"That is well. The King has but the Shrewsbury men around him and the park rangers. Give me a hundred spears, and, so be they are true folk, I will engage to bring the King's grace captive to Avelard. Then, when our own men muster, we shall confront a leaderless enemy. We have the chance to seize on the very keep and citadel of the foe, and there are enough stout fellows in Cotswold for the work. If the venture succeed, then we are three parts of the road to the freeing of England. If it fail, some honest lads will go to Paradise, among them a nameless clerk of Oseney."

The old man gazed at the speaker, and into his face came a sudden flush which told of something deeply stirred in his heart.

" 'Fore God," he cried, "you are true Bohun! True Bohun and true Percy, for old Hotspur has come to life in you. God go with you, my son. There is a madness that is better than wisdom."

CHAPTER XIV

HOW PETER STROVE WITH POWERS AND PRINCIPALITIES

St Thomas's eve was quiet and very mild. There had been no winds to abate the flood-water and dry the sodden meadows, so the valleys were still lagoons and every rivulet an encroaching mere. The rendezvous was in the distant hollows of Wychwood, and thither the little bands from the western Cotswold moved under cover of night.

Peter, with Dickon and a dozen picked Avelard men, took the road by Stow, where the wolds made easy travelling. Word had come that the bridge at Charlbury could be passed, the only crossing of Evenlode, and such a route would take them over Windrush near its source. All were to move slowly and secretly, keeping to cover by day, and making the next stage in the darkness. There were to be no liveries or badges among them, but each man as drab as a deerstealer.

At cockcrow, when they stopped for meat on Naunton downs, the Carmelite came out of the shadows, his white gown showing in the half-light like a monstrous owl. He knelt and mumbled Peter's hand, and then his wild eyes scanned his following, and he cried out like a man in pain:

"Where is the trampling of the horsemen?" he screamed, "the mighty array that should sweep the hosts of Midian into the deep ocean? I see but a handful of country folk! Where is your army, my lord? Remember, you go up against the great city of Babel, and her towers are iron and her battlements of hewn stone."

The man was not easy to soothe.

"The others will come in good time, father," Peter told him. "We are only like the scouts sent out by Joshua to spy the land. Get you back to your cell, for you can help best by your prayers. We travel secretly and your exhortations may do us a mischief."

In the end he flitted off, his arms waving and his voice falling and rising in what seemed now a chant and now a moan; but Peter noted with disquiet that the road he took was not west but east.

At Slaughter, where the little river was ill to ford, there was a mad woman in the hamlet who found their camping place in the woods. She seemed to divine their purpose, for she cried around them like a lost soul. It seemed that she was come to warn, and the Avelard men's faces blanched at the sight of her.

"Back to your homes, my darlings," she cried. "I see blood in Evenlode, and blood in Glyme, and blood in Cherwell, which all the floods will not wash away. That road there are pretty lads hanging on every tree. Back to your sweethearts, for there are no honest maids where you be going."

Over Peter's shoulder she flung a ragged wreath of holly and ivy, such as are made for the Christmas pleasantries.

"May your lordship's grace be decked with no harsher crown!" she cried, and then fled babbling into the covert.

It was clear that strange rumours had gone abroad in the countryside, for, stealthy as was their journey, they seemed to be expected. If in the twilight they skirted a village street, the doors were shut, but there were curious eyes at the windows. The children had been forewarned; they stared with open mouths, but spoke no word, and did not run away. The Avelard men, who had been advised of the deep secrecy of the journey, were perturbed by this atmosphere of expectation, and spoke aside among themselves. Peter scarcely noticed it. His thoughts had flung ahead, out of this sheepwalk country to the glades of Woodstock, where somewhere a ruddy man was breathing his horse and looking doubtfully towards the west.

At Chadlington in the early hours of the night Darking met them.

"Evenlode runs like a mill-leat," he said, "but the causeway holds. I can guide you across, my lord. Others are before you, and I have left those who will lead them to their appointed places. Pity you have drawn your folk from High Cotswold, where there is nought but thorns a man's height. Our work will be in a forest, and these Tracey lads have never seen the tall trees and are easily mazed among them."

Darking brought news of the King. "I have passed the word among the Upright Men," he said, "and there are many quick eyes in the Woodstock coverts. See, my lord, yon spark of light in the valley. That is Little Greece, where old John Naps now sits at the receipt of custom. He will be eyes and brain to us. King Harry is snug at Woodstock with my lord Shrewsbury's men to guard him. He hunts daily, but only in the park, for the floods have narrowed his venue. Glyme is a young ocean, and Evenlode below Wilcote fills the vale to the brim. I doubt if we have seen the end of this overflow. The snowcap on High Cotswold is still melting with the mild air, as your lordship has seen this day, and that will prevent the streams abating. Nay, they may rise higher yet, for in certain valleys lakes have formed through the damming of trees and sliding earth, and any hour the dams may break and send down a new deluge. It is fickle weather for our enterprise, and we be terribly at the mercy of God.

"What keeps the King in keeps us out," he went on. "There is nothing to be done inside the pales of Woodstock, where every furlong has its verderer. We are like a troop sitting round a fortalice which it cannot enter. Heaven send the weather let Harry go forth. That is what he longs for, since the hunting in the park is a child's game to the hunting in the forest. 'Tis the great yeld hinds of Wychwood that he seeks. Pray for a cold wind and a drying wind, so long as it do not freeze."

Darking guided them skilfully across the Charlbury bridge. A causeway of hewn stone led up to it at either end, but this was hidden in the acres of eddying water. A man who did not know the road would have slipped into the swirl, but Darking kept them on the causeway, where the stream was not beyond the horses' withers. Presently they were on the arch of the bridge, and then on the farther causeway, where the eddies were gentle, and then on the hard ground of the forest slopes. By midnight they were encamped in a dingle of dead bracken, hidden as securely as if they had lain in the Welsh hills.

There were five such encampments within the forest bounds, and by the next morning all the men had arrived—a hundred picked spearmen, some of them old soldiers of the French wars, all of them hard and trusty and silent. For the present their task was to lie hidden, and they were safe enough from prying eyes, for the King had appointed no new keeper of Wychwood in the place of the dead Norris, and every ranger and verderer was Darking's man. Also there was an outer guard of the vagabonds under the orders of John Naps at Little Greece.

Peter inspected the five companies and approved, but Darking shook his head. "They are lithe fellows, but they belong to the bare hills. Stout arms, no doubt, in a mellay, and good horsemen in the open, but I cannot tell how they will shape in our forest work. They are a thought too heavy-footed for that secret business. God send our chance comes in the open."

It was a blue day, mild and sunny, with but a breath of wind, and that soft from the south.

"We are for Woodstock park, my lord," said Darking. "You and I alone, and on foot, for we go as spies. Follow my lightest word, for your life may hang on it. And shed most of your garments. The air is mild and there is swimming before us."

In shirt and hose and deerskin shoes they made for the old bridge below Finstock, which a week before had been swept down to Thames. Here Evenlode ran for ordinary in a narrow stream which spread into a broad mill-pond. Now it was all one waste of brown torrent. Darking led the way to the end of the broken pier of the bridge. "The current will bear us down to the slack water beyond the hazels. Trust your body to it, and swim but a stroke or two, enough to keep your head up. Then, when I give the word, strike hard for the other shore. The rub is to get out of the stream once it has laid hold of you."

So Peter found it. The torrent swept him down easily and pleasantly, till he was near the submerged hazel clump. Then Darking struck off left handed, and it was no easy task to get

208

rid of the entangling current, which would have carried him into a maelstrom of broken water. It plucked at his shoulders, and gripped his feet with unseen hands. But, breathless and battered, in five minutes they were shaking themselves among the rushes of the farther bank.

"Let us stretch a leg," said Darking, "or we will chill, and maybe be late for the fair. The King's grace on a day like this is early abroad."

They were now within the pale of Woodstock, but they had four miles to go before they reached the wilderness of green glades and coppices which was the favourite hunting-ground. An hour later Darking had his ear to the ground, and then stood like a dog at gaze. "I can hear horses," he said, "maybe a mile distant. I could hear them better if the earth were less full of rain. Also the hounds are out. I judge they are in Combe Bottom. If they unharbour a deer there, with what there is of wind it will come our way. Let us harbour ourselves, my lord. No, not on the ground, for that might give our scent and turn the deer or lure the hounds. This oak will be screen enough."

He caught a spreading limb of the tree and swung himself into a crutch. Peter followed, and found that he had a long vista down an aisle of rough grass. Now he could hear the hounds giving tongue in some thicket, but that was the only sound. He might have been listening to mongrels hunting alone in a covert, for there were no horns, or human cries, or the jingle of bridles.

Presently the hounds seemed to come nearer. A cloud of pigeons rose from the opposite trees, and a young buck, a two-year-old at the most, stuck out his head, sniffed the air, and proceeded to amble up the glade. He may have caught a whiff of their wind, for he turned back to covert.

Then the world woke to life. A big old hind, barren by her grey muzzle and narrow flanks, broke from the wood, and behind her the covert was suddenly filled with a babel of noise. The first hounds streamed out, fifty yards behind; and two sweating beaters in blue smocks, who had been stationed there to turn the hind to the open glades, stumbled after them and promptly flung themselves on the ground. In a second they

209

were up again, for a horn was blown behind them.

From an alley in the opposite woods the huntsmen appeared, debouching into the broader aisle. There were five of them—three in livery, with badges in their hats and horns at their saddle bows; one young man with a doublet of crimson velvet, a plumed cap and a monstrous jewel; the fifth a big man who rode first and waved his hand and shouted hoarsely. Peter, from his crutch in the oak, craned his head through the leafless boughs and watched intently. For he knew that he was looking upon the King.

He was plainly dressed, with trunk hose of brown leather and a green doublet with a jewel at his throat. A heavy silver-handled hunting-knife hung at his belt. His horse was a big-boned Fleming with a ewe-neck, and he handled it masterfully; for all his weight his seat was exquisitely balanced and the big hands were light on his beast's mouth. The face was vast and red as a new ham, a sheer mountain of a face, for it was as broad as it was long, and the small features seemed to give it a profile like an egg. The mouth was comically small, and the voice that came from it was modest out of all proportion to the great body. He swept like a whirlwind up the glade, one hand pawing the air, screaming like a jay. In every line of him was excitement, an excitement naive and childish, but in his very abandonment there was a careless power.

Peter's eyes narrowed as he watched the broad back above the flat rump of the Fleming lessen in the distance, till the men behind blocked the view. He had seen his King—his rival—his quarry. Many a picture had he formed of Henry, but none like this. He had looked for gross appetites, cruel jaws, lowering brows, eyes hot with the lust of power. In all his portraits the man had been elderly. But what he had now seen was more like an overgrown boy. There was a preposterous youthfulness in this ageing creature, whinnying like a puppy with the ardour of the game; there was something mirthful in his great, glowing, fleshy face. There was more. One who, with his kingdom afire in the east and north and smouldering in the west, could fling his whole heart like a child into his play, had greatness in him. There was about him an insolent security. What he desired, whether it were deer or gold or kingdoms, he desired so fiercely that he was likely to get it. Peter felt as if some effluence of power had struck him, like a wind in his face.

"What think you of his grace?" Darking asked, as they stole back towards Evenlode.

"I think that he will not easily go down, and that if he falls much will fall with him."

Darking looked up into the sky.

"The wind freshens, and it has moved back to the south-east—a good wind for the forest. Tomorrow belike the King will hunt in Wychwood, and kill a yeld hind. There is a great she-devil harbouring in Finstock brake."

Darking's forecast was true. Next morning saw a dawn of lemon and gold, and a sharper tang in the air, while, instead of the spring zephyr which had blown for two days, there was a small, bitter easterly breeze. Peter was abroad at the first light, placing his men. If the King crossed Evenlode and entered the forest it would be by the bridge of Charlbury, for the best harbourage for deer lay to the west of Leafield in the thick coverts above Shipton. He would have an escort, since he was outside the Woodstock pales, but it was certain that, if a strong quarry were unharboured, he would soon leave that escort behind him. With the wind in its present quarter, the deer would run towards Ramsden and Whiteoak Green, where the ground was broken and the vistas short. There, at strategic points, his men would lie hidden, while in the undergrowth would lurk some of Naps's scouts to pass the word to the posts. Peter and Darking had planned every detail like the ordering of a battle, and had their alternatives in case any item miscarried. "Send the wind holds," said Darking. "The King will not stay abed today, and if the slow-hounds are once out in Shipton Barren, his grace in an hour's time will be among the Ramsden oaks."

The King was late. Word came by a lad of Flatsole's, who had swum Evenlode and stood dripping like a water-rat, that he was on the road for Charlbury, with five huntsmen and two

211

companion lords, and a score of men-at-arms mounted on beasts that would soon founder in the heavy bracken of the forest. But it was noon before Naps sent a message that the cavalcade was passing the Charlbury causeway. Peter, on an Avelard bay, whose strain of Welsh blood made him light and sure-footed as a mountain goat, rode west on the high ground to prospect, while Darking kept ward in the eastern forest.

From the Leafield crest he looked down on Shipton Barren, and soon his keen eyes detected the whereabouts of the hunt. The King was an epicure that day, for no chance beast was to his liking. Peter saw deer break cover unregarded, and once the hounds were flogged off a trail on which they had entered. By and by the horns sounded a rally, and there came the wild notes which meant that the chase had begun. Peter swung his horse round, ready to follow east at a higher level, for it was certain that any deer would at first keep to the riverside ground.

But to his amazement the hunt went otherwise. He got a glimpse of the first hounds with a verderer riding furiously on their flanks, and then, well behind them, a knot of men. They were going westward, upstream—westward or south-west-ward, for, as he looked, he saw them swing towards Fulbrook Gap. Then he saw the reason. The wind had changed, the sting had gone out of it, and it had moved to west of south, and was now blowing softly down Windrush.

He watched in deep perplexity the hunt wheel towards the high ridges, where the forest opened up into downs, and rose to the Hallows Hill. Beyond that the trees began again, the deep woodland country above Barrington. A yeld hind would need to be the stoutest of her breed to make those distant coverts. More likely she would soon be pulled down in the open, and then the huntsmen would return to draw another of the Wychwood harbours. There was that famous beast in Finstock brake.

Naps's men were fewer at this end, but he found a prigger lad cutting himself a switch from a hazel. Him he sent back hot-foot to Darking to report what had happened. It was now afternoon, and there were but two hours left of daylight. If the King was benighted, and he could get up his men in time, all might yet be well.

Peter set spurs to his horse, and galloped for the Taynton wolds. The land lay spread out like a map beneath him, pale as the country of a dream, with far down on his left the smoke of Burford town making a haze in the hollow. Soon he had come to a point which gave him a long view. That yeld hind must be a marvel, for she was still going strongly, having puzzled the hounds in the Fulbrook coppice. She was not bound for Hallows Hill, but had turned downward to where the Windrush floods drowsed in the valley. That would mean the end of her. She would never face the water, and if she kept down the left bank she could be brought to bay among the Burford garths. Could she but cross the stream, then indeed she might find sanctuary in the dense thickets above the little valley of Leach.

He had lost sight of the hunters, but presently the hounds came into view, running strongly at gaze. The hind was making for Windrush. Peter was now on a tiny promontory, and had the valley clear beneath him. The river at this point was less of a barrier, for the floods were dammed by fallen timber at Barrington. It might be passed. . . .

It was passed. He saw the head of the swimming deer, and then after an interval the dark beads which meant the hounds. Where were the huntsmen? The hounds had outrun them, and they were now stranded on the Taynton downs. He heard far off the thin but furious notes of the horn. They would return the way they came, and they had far to go, and the dusk would presently fall. The fates were kind to him, if only Darking moved his men west in time.

He had turned his horse to gallop back the road he had come, when over his shoulder he took one last look at the Windrush vale. What he saw made his heart stop. The deer and the hounds were now beyond the river, but all the hunters had not been left behind. One was still following. He was even now crossing, his horse swimming strongly. The light was too dim to see clear, but some instinct gave him certainty. That man was the King.

213

Peter went down the hill like one possessed. He had no plan or purpose except to keep touch with this lone horseman. There was a furious ardour in him, and awe too. It seemed that the stage was being set otherwise than he had expected, set for a meeting such as he had not dreamed of. Somewhere in that dim land beyond the waters the two of them were destined to come face to face.

He crossed Windrush without trouble, for the dam at Barrington had so shrunken the floods that the stream was little more than its turbid winter flow. But once on the far bank he was at a loss. The light was growing bad, and there was no sign of hounds or hunter. They had not pulled down the quarry, for in that still air he would have heard the savage rumour of the kill. He looked behind him. Dusk had crept down the Taynton slopes, and there was no sign there of following hunters. Even the angry horns had ceased to sound.

He rode a little way up-hill into the coverts, and then halted. Presently the King would find himself benighted, and would give up the chase. He had hunted in Wychwood often, and must know something of the lie of the land. He would make his way downstream, and cross at the Burford bridge, which was intact. Again Peter clapped spurs to his horse. He must watch the southern approaches to the crossing, from Westwell, and by the track from Lechlade.

He took his stand on a piece of high ground, from which he could see in the dusk a light or two beginning to twinkle in the Burford hollow. But he did not wait long, for far on his right he seemed to hear the baying of hounds. They were still hunting, and his ear told him that they were running east by Shilton. The King would still be following, for rumour said that he never left the chase so long as there was hope of a kill. Again, he spurred his horse. In half an hour at the most the dark would have fallen thick. Then the King would give up. He would cross Windrush at Minster Lovell, and take the quickest road to Woodstock. If the Burford bridge still stood, so would that of Minster Lovell, which was sound Roman work.

In an agony of uncertainty he resolved that the only chance

214

was to risk all on the likeliest happening. His horse was still fresh, and he covered the four miles of ground in little time. The bridge was whole. The shell of Lovell's castle rose black among the trees, and Windrush lay eerie and dim in its wide lagoon. He noted that the isle in the lagoon, which held one of the castle dovecots, was but little diminished in size. The dam at Barrington was doing its work well. He dismounted, and tied up his horse to a stump on the slopes of the south bank. If Henry came this way, he would let him cross the bridge, and then follow him up the Leafield road, where his own men were as thick as owls in the night. God had wrought a miracle for him, for his enemy was being guided relentlessly into his net. Peter set his teeth hard to curb his impatience. If he only came! . . . But he must come, unless he wanted to lie wet and cold in the Shilton woods.

Come he did. A weary horse, lame in the off foreleg, stumbled down the track. On it sat a bulky man, who leaned back to ease his beast in the descent, and whose great hunting boots stuck out from its sides like the yards of a ship. The man had lost his bonnet, and even in the dark Peter could recognise the round head, baldish at the top, the vast square face and the bull shoulders. It was beyond question the King.

Had he been less intent on the sight he would not have missed a sound like a grumbling thunderstorm which seemed to fill the valley and grew every moment in volume. The horse heard it, for it jibbed at the entrance to the bridge. The place was high-backed and narrow over which two men could not ride abreast, and which the wool-staplers' pack animals could not cross. The rider dug deep with his spurs, but the horse again refused. Then with a groan of weariness he rolled out of the saddle and attempted to lead it.

Still it refused. He was in front of it and dragging it by the bridle—he stood on the keystone, while the beast was still plunging on the bank. Then came a sound which broke in even on Peter's preoccupation. It was like a gale in a high wood, or a mighty snowslip on a mountain, with a rumbling undercurrent of thunder. Something huge and dark reared itself high above the stone arch, and the next second Peter was struggling in the side eddies of a monstrous wave.

He had been able to swim like a moorhen from childhood, and he had no trouble in shaking off the clutch of the stream. As he dashed the water from his eyes he knew what had happened. The dam at Barrington had burst, and Windrush, half a mile wide, was driving a furrow through the land— Windrush no more a lagoon but a rending ploughshare.

The King! Was this God's way of working His purpose? Was that mountain of royal flesh now drowning in the dark wastes of water? The bridge had been swept clean—the very horse was gone—nay, the bridge itself must have been broken, for only a swirl in the dimness marked where a fragment of pier still stood, submerged under three feet of flood.

Peter strained his eyes into the gloom. The coming of the water seemed to have lightened the darkness a little, for he could see the black loom of Lovell's castle on the far shore, and, downstream, the top of the island dovecot. There was no sound now except the steady lift and gurgle of the tide; the crested wave with its thunder was now far away down the valley. Only the even swish and swirl, with close at hand the murmur of little sucking eddies.

And then in the stillness came a cry. It seemed to come from the island, which was fifty yards below the bridge. It sounded again, a choked cry as from something in panic or pain. Peter knew that it could come from one throat only—of him who some minutes before had ridden down the hill. He had been plucked from the bridge like a straw and borne down, and was now by some miracle washed up like flotsam on the island shore. He was not drowning, for no drowning man could have sent out so strong a cry, but he must be in instant peril of death.

Peter was in the water before he knew, striking transversely across the floods so as to make the island. He did not stop to consider his purpose, for that oldest instinct was uppermost which of itself quickens a man's limbs to save another's life.

He swam strongly and cunningly, and forced his way to midstream. Then he let himself drift and listened. Again came the cry—now very near, and it was a cry of desperation. The

216

man was clinging to something which he could not hold. Peter's long arms in an overhand stroke devoured the waters, and his speed was thrice the speed of the stream. Again a cry, but this time with a choke in it. Peter butted into a tangle of driftwood among the island rushes. Where in God's name was the King?

Clearly he had lost his hold. Peter stood up in the shallows and shouted. Was that an answer from the dark eddy now sweeping towards the northern bank of Windrush? There seemed to be a sound there which was not the stream. Again he launched himself on the flood, and as his breast caught the current he heard again a cry. This time it was the strangled gasp of a drowning man.

In ten strokes he had overtaken him. The man could only swim feebly, and every second he dipped under the rough tide. A very little longer and he would dip for ever.

Peter raised his head and shouted lustily. The man heard him, for he made several feeble, hurried strokes. Then Peter was on him, and his hand was under his chin.

"Get your breath," Peter spluttered, for he had swallowed much water in making haste. "I will support you."

Then: "We must get out of the stream. Hold by my girdle and I will tow you."

It was a harder business than the crossing of Evenlode the morning before. Happily the main weight of the flood was on the other side of the island, and the stream between the island and the castle ran with less power. But the man was as weighty as a tree-trunk, and his clutch on Peer's belt was like shackles of lead. The muscles of shoulder and thigh were cracking, before the deadly plucking of the current eased off and they came into slack water. Then the other, who had manfully striven to obey his rescuer's orders, promptly let go and sank. Peter clutched him by some part of his garments and waded ashore.

He pulled the water-logged body through the selvedge of drift to what had been the quay of the castle. The man was in a swoon, but as Peter rolled him over his senses returned, and he was very sick.

Presently he sat up, coughing.

"God's name!" he gasped, "that was a rough journey. I am beholden to you, friend, whoever you be. You will not be the worse for this night's work. I am woundily cold and empty, save for flood water. Likewise my wits are somewhat dazed, and I know not where I have been washen up. Get me to bed and supper, and I will repay you well."

The man, bone-weary, dripping and chilled to the marrow, still kept a kind of dignity. He tried to rise, and sat down again with a groan.

"A murrain on my leg," he moaned. "'Twas already sore with the day's work, and now it has failed me utterly. I cannot put foot to ground, and my horse is drowned long ago. Can you find a way to move me, sirrah, for if I bide here I will freeze and starve?"

Then Peter spoke.

"Your grace must make the best of it. This is the ruin of Minster Lovell, and there will be no leaving it before the morrow. Supper I cannot give you, but I can find you a rough lodging. Kings have slept before in these towers."

"You know me?" came the sharp question.

"I recognise the King's grace," said Peter.

"Majesty, man, majesty," came the correction. "That is the new word I have commended."

"The King's majesty," Peter assented.

"I have often slept hard and supped bare. Had I but a dry shirt and a cushion for my cursed leg I would be content. But tell me, sir, does aught inhabit that shell? I had heard that it had been long tenantless."

"Nought but owls and bats and the twittering ghosts of old Lovells."

The other shivered.

"Like enough. What then can Lovell's castle offer me?"

"A shelter for your head. With luck I may also get you fire and food and dry raiment. But you must be guided by me, since I have plucked you from the water."

"I know not who you be, but you seem a good Christian. Give me your shoulder, lad, and I will make shift to hobble."

Leaving a trail of puddles behind them, they made their way through the blocked postern, called the Water-gate, into the west court, which, since there was no moon, was a trough of ink. They groped among the broken flags to the northern corner under the dovecot, where was the shaft which led to Lovell's prison.

Suddenly almost under their feet a spark of light flew up, followed by the crackling of twigs. In the glow Peter saw the bent back and elf locks of Madge of Shipton.

"What do you here, mother?" he asked.

She peered at him.

"Your errands, my lord. Since you will not seek your treasure yourself your well-wishers must seek for you. I was casting the runes of the burning ash-cross, for this was in old days a holy e'en."

Peter's intention had been to leave Henry and to borrow from Mother Sweetbread on the hill above the means of supper and bed. Now fate had sent him a helper.

"You will first do me a different service, mother," he said. "Go to Gammer Sweetbread, and bid her bring clothing and food for two starving men. You and she can bear it down the hill. We will await you here by your fire. Bring a lantern, too, and a tinder box.

The old woman rose to her feet. "You are white, my lord, and there are strange things writ in your face. I do your errand, for you are like two kelpies from the river, and will have ague in your bones in another hour."

There was a small heap of kindlings, with which Peter fed the fire.

"Get yourself warm, sire," he said, "and presently you will be better served."

Henry hunched himself close to the blaze.

"She called you lord," he said. "Who may you be, lad?"

"'Twas an idle word," said Peter; "my name is not worthy of your grace's hearing. I am a common man out of the forest."

"You are uncommon strong. Not ten men in this nation could have dragged my bulk from that stream. Ugh, the

219

majesty of England came near to being food for eels! A cold ending at which my belly turns. You have put Harry of England deep in your debt, young sir."

The man was clearly in deep discomfort. Seen in the firelight his face was mottled and streaked, a strong shuddering would take him, and he moved his leg continually as if in pain. Yet there was a rude fortitude in his air. His small, sharp, watchful eyes showed a spirit that would not bow to weariness.

He toasted his steaming body, and for an hour he only spoke twice.

"I have fifty lackeys within two miles," he groaned, "and not one lubber at hand. That is God's jest with royalty."

The second time he said, "I may ride a bushel or two lighter for this. They say cold water lessens weight!" And the strange man laughed.

By and by the two women came out of the darkness, with a bobbing lantern. They had brought blankets, and two deerskin cloaks lined with fustian, and a basket of broken meats. There was a flagon, too, of Mother Sweetbread's sloeberry cordial. They looked curiously at the great figure crouched by the fire as they laid down their burdens, and Peter followed them back into the shadows.

Madge of Shipton plucked at his arm.

"The half-drowned one will bring you fortune," she whispered. "I read it in your pale face and the sign on your brow when you wrinkled it. But beware—beware! The burnt cross of ash has called spirits out of the deeps, and there is a strife among the Powers. All night on your behalf I will say the paternoster of the Brethren." The clutch of her fingers on his arm was like the clutch of an eyas on the falconer's fist.

Mother Sweetbread said: "You will get the ague, son Peter. Come back with me, and I will bed you both, and roast the fever from your veins."

Peter put an arm round the old woman's neck. "I will get no ague, mother of mine. But hearken to me, for a kingdom hangs on it. Get a message to Darking, who is somewhere in the Ramsden bracken. The forest is full of Naps's folk, and

220

any one of them will carry the word. Say to Darking that I am in Lovell's castle with him he wots of, and that my men must meet me here an hour before dawn. Say, too, that there is no bridge left on Windrush, and that we must home by the road we came."

The woman nodded.

"Your message will be carried, my son, though I should have to bunch my skirts and stir my own old bones. Solomon shall have it ere midnight."

The King grumbled.

"I am no fox to kennel in a hole. Whence came those women? Have they no dwelling near where I may bed me?"

"A mile and more of rough ground distant. And miserable cabins at that, with a plague of rats and the stars shining through the thatch. You will be better in Lovell's cell."

"Let me lie by the fire."

"It is already dying and there is no more fuel. There will be frost ere morning and you will get a chill at the heart."

"But I will stick in that hole, and you who have dragged me from water may have no power to drag me from earth."

"The place is wide enough. Two months back I made the passage with a brother of Oseney."

"A holy man has entered it! That gives a flavour of grace to as graceless a spot as ever my eyes beheld. It looks like some werewolf's lair. But lead on, sir. Maybe you are right, and I shall be warmer if I have some yards of stone and earth for blanket."

Peter led the way down the slimy steps and over the prostrate outer door. The first part of the passage was narrow, and in bending the King had some trouble with his leg. When he jarred it on a knuckle of stone he would bellow with pain, and Peter, turning the lantern, saw the great face flushed and furious. Then the roof rose, and Peter's arm could give him support. At the subsidence it was hard to get the King through, and Peter had to clear away much rubble. Then came the sound of falling water.

"Have we escaped one flood to drown in another?" the

King asked tartly.

The corridor broadened, and at last came the ironbound door. It had been left unlocked on the last visit, and a pull set it creaking on its hinges. The little chamber smelt dry and fresh, and it had the chill neither of the water-logged outer air nor of the mildewed passage.

Peter set the lantern on the floor and dropped his burden.

"Behold your majesty's lodging for the night," he said, while Henry sat himself heavily in the chair which had once been Lovell's.

Peter flung the rotting bedclothes from the pallet, and laid on it Mother Sweetbread's blankets. He helped the King to strip off his soaked doublet and hose—a task of delicacy owing to the ulcer on his leg, and wrapped his great body in one of the deerskin cloaks.

"Get you among the blankets, sire," he said, "and I will serve your supper."

He fed him with Mother Sweetbread's provender, and he gave him to drink of Mother Sweetbread's sloeberry cordial. The King made an ample meal and the strong liquor warmed his blood. "Ha!" he cried, "I begin to thaw, and the ice has gone from my belly. This is a rough inn, but the entertainment might be worse. Give me another cup, and I will compose myself to sleep. What mountain is above me?"

"Lovell's castle," said Peter. "The abode of the last lord of that house."

The King cried out and crossed himself.

"It has an ill name," he murmured. "You say you came here with a brother of Oseney? Did the holy man lustrate this chamber, for wherever Lovell trod Sathanas walked in his tracks?"

"Set your mind at ease, sire. It was lustrated by prayer and tears, and the bones of Lovell were laid in hallowed earth."

But the King was not at ease. Some notion had arisen to vex him. He watched Peter strip off his clothes, wrap himself in the other cloak and make a bed beside the door.

"Oseney," he muttered, "what have I heard of a brother of Oseney?" and he raised himself on his elbow, and stared

222

at his companion.

Peter, ever since he had dragged the King ashore, had had a mind empty of thought. He saw the clear hand of God, and let himself follow blindly as it guided. There could be no failure now, for events had turned miraculously in his favour. Before dawn Darking and his men would be at Minster Lovell, and by noon the King would be safe at Avelard. The household at Woodstock would be hunting high and low for its lord and master, but here in this dungeon of Lovell's he was hidden more securely than if he were in the heart of Wales with all Neville's pickets to guard him. He had not troubled to think of Henry. The man with his gross body and his ulcerated leg was no more to him than a derelict log plucked from the water.

"Compose yourself to sleep, sire," he said; "on the morrow I can promise you better fare and a softer bed."

He was himself very weary, but before he lay down he raised the lantern to see to the candle within. Then he set it and the tinder-box on the floor beside him, blew out the light, and turned to sleep.

But in the moment when his face had been clear in the lantern's glow, Henry had seen in it something which made his cheek, now ruddy with the cordial, grow mottled and pale again. "By God, it is he," he whispered. "The Oseney clerk! He is Buckingham's get, for he has the Bohun lip. . . ." There was no drowsiness now for the King.

Peter slept lightly, as was his custom, for one trained in the Oseney services, which broke the night into short stages, was not likely to be a sluggard. He was awakened to sudden consciousness by the sound of a creaking pallet. The King was restless; nay, the King was rising.

He lay and listened. He heard Henry fumbling among his discarded clothes, and the clink of something hard—metal or stone. Then he heard the stealthy movements of the heavy body, which seemed to be coming towards him. He had that consciousness of imminence which comes neither from touch, nor sight, nor hearing, but from some subtler sense. He slipped

223

from under his blanket, and rolled very softly a few feet to his left.

The King was approaching the bed. He was close on it, leaning above it. . . . And then there was a rapid movement, the sound of an arm descending, a sudden jar of metal driven through woollen on to stone.

Peter's brain worked fast. The King had recognised him, had hoped to rid himself of a rival by the speediest way. Had he been sleeping heavily where he had laid himself down, the King's hunting-knife would now be in his heart.

Wrath plucked him to his feet and hurled him on his enemy. He felt the kneeling King topple over under his impact, and found himself grappling with something as soft and unresisting as a bolster. He wrested the knife from his grasp and sent it spinning into a corner. His hands found the thick throat, but there was no need to choke it, for the man was without strength. Instead he felt along the floor for the tinder-box and relit the lantern.

The King sprawled on his side, almost black in the face, his lips contorted with pain, while one hand groped at his leg. Peter dragged him back to his pallet, and set the lantern on the chair. In the struggle the deerskin had half fallen from Henry, and revealed his misshapen limbs and huge paunch and unwholesome elderly flesh. Peter looked down on him with a shiver of disgust. Then he filled a cup of cordial and put it to his lips, which greedily drained it. The King lay panting for a little while, while the darkness passed from his face, leaving it mottled and pale again. The pain in his leg seemed to have gone, for he opened his eyes, and they were bright and wary with fear.

"That was a foolish enterprise, sire," said Peter. "We two are alone here in this cell. One is old and one is young, one is sick and one is hale. If two such contend there can be but the one issue. He whom you would have slain has a few hours back saved you from death. I would remind you likewise that murder is a deed on which Heaven frowns."

The King had recovered his bodily ease, and with it his wits. He lay with the blanket drawn up to his chin, and his little eyes as sharp as a bird's. There was still panic in them, but also cunning.

"*Peccavi*," he said. " 'Twas a sudden tempting of the Devil. May God and His saints have mercy on me! I ask your forgiveness, young sir—I, the King of England, abase myself before you."

"You would have slain me. Why?"

"A sudden madness. I feared you. . . . I took you for one who was plotting my hurt."

"Whom do I favour? I, a nameless man of the forest! What enemy of your majesty's have I the ill fortune to recall?"

"None that lives," said the King, "but one that died long ago."

"Even so. It seems I bear on my face the proof of my begetting. Your majesty is right. I am the son of Edward of Buckingham."

The King's face did not change, but his lips moved.

"You have come into the west to seek me. I, too, sought you, and God has prepared a meeting. I deserve some favour at your majesty's hands for this night's work. First, I saved you from the floods, and second, when your majesty would have knifed me, I forbore to strike back."

There was a new light in Henry's eyes. His panic was now under command, and he was back in a world which he understood.

"You talk reason, my lord. I bear no ill will to your house— I have ever admitted its splendour. Your father stood in my way, and I had to thrust him aside, but I have no malice towards his son. You speak truth—I am most deeply beholden to you for what has befallen this night. I will make you the second man in the kingdom. The lands and dukedom of Buckingham shall be yours again, and you shall ride by the King's bridle and sit high in his Council."

Henry's eye was alert and watchful, but his smile was that grave and kindly smile that had often beguiled men's hearts.

Peter lifted his hand.

"Let me tell you of this cell where we now lie," he said. "Hither after Stoke battle came one who had been the second

225

man in the kingdom, who had ridden by the King's bridle, and had sat high in his Council. He was a fugitive, but in this place he was safe. Here he could lie till the hunt had passed, and he could get himself and his wealth abroad. But only one other knew the secret of the place, and that other fell sick and died. So the great lord Lovell was left to starve like a rat whose hole had been stopped. Two months back I entered this place, and stumbled over his bones. I came seeking treasure and I found it."

The King pulled the blanket from his chin. "'Fore God, I knew it," he said. "'Twas not Neville nor Avelard that paid for this mischief in the west. . . ."

"You mistake me. I said I found treasure, but it was not Lovell's gold. I found the philosopher's stone, the touch of which dissolves earth's ambitions. I no longer seek what Lovell sought."

The King sat up, and as he moved his leg he squealed with pain.

"That is an honest thought," he cried. "You would go back to Holy Church? I commend you, my lord. I will rejoice to further your purpose. You may have the choice of any abbey in this land. Nay, you will be bishop as soon as I can make room for you."

"Your majesty misreads me. I will never be clerk again. But I will not rest till there is a new England, for I am a fighter on God's side. I would save my soul."

"By the rood so would I!" The King's face had a serious bewilderment. "I am the devoutest man that ever wore ermine. If I have broken with the Pope, I will defend the faith better than he. No heretic shall breathe freely in this land while I sit on the throne. I have confuted in argument Luterano and Sacramentary alike. My chief study in my closet is holy learning. Every day I serve the priest at mass, every Sunday I receive the holy bread, every Good Friday I creep on my knees to the Cross."

There was a strong passion in the King's voice. This man, who a little before had been a murderer in intent, believed devoutly that he was on the side of virtue.

226

"You would serve God by putting yourself in God's place?" Peter said quietly.

The King looked puzzled.

"I am God's vicegerent on earth," he said, "therefore I sit in God's place. But the creature abaseth itself before the Creator."

"Is it God's purpose that you burn honest folk for a little deviation of faith, and likewise send to death those who hold in trust God's estates because they will not surrender them to your minions?"

The King's face lit up. Here was ground with which he was familiar.

"*Distinguo*," he cried. "No man suffers under me save for denying the catholic faith in which is alone found salvation. You are a strange clerk if you contemn that duty. I am the guardian under God of my people's hopes of Heaven. I am determined to make this realm one in faith as it is one in law. If I have shouldered his Holiness of Rome from the headship of Christ's Church in England, the more need that I perform the task in which his Holiness was somewhat negligent. Listen, my lord. Law is above all men, king and peasant alike. Of that law there are two branches, the law of God and the law of England, and both are in my care. The first is based upon God's Word and that inherited practice of God's Church which, being inspired by the Holy Ghost, is likewise canonical. I would make the Scriptures free to all in the vulgar tongue— you may have heard of my efforts thereto—but I would not permit ignorant men to interpret them as they please. The interpretation is laid down by Holy Church, and he who rebels against it will burn, be he bishop or noble, clerk or cotter."

There was no fear now in the small bright eyes. Henry spoke with a fierce authority, and his broad low brow had set in weighty lines.

"As to the second law, the law of England, I am its most devout and humble servant. I have never acted save in obedience to that law. 'Twas that law that shook off the Pope's burden. 'Tis under that law that I have taken order with certain religious houses. I have made it my care that the blessing of law shall be free to all, the poorest as well as the greatest, and that all shall stand equal before the royal tribunals. That law is not my private will, but the approved judgment of the wisest men. Maybe I have guided it into new channels, but the flow is that which came down through six centuries. I have sworn before God, that if any man, be he never so great, outrage that law I will make his head fly for it, and by God's help I will keep that vow so long as there is breath in my nostrils."

"Yet you have made an England," said Peter, "which is in some sort a stye and in some sort a desert."

"In what respect, sir?" the King asked sharply. "I have given it peace."

"That peace which is a desert," was the answer. "Your loans and benevolences have bled it white. There is as much suffering as in the days of the Black Death. The rich grow richer, and the poor die by thousands in the ditches."

"Ay," said the King. "No doubt there is much misery abroad. But mark you, young sir, 'tis a shallow philosophy which judges on what exists but takes no account of what has been prevented. I have had to steer a difficult course among the plots of the Emperor and the French King. Had I steered less skilfully a new Duke William might have landed on English earth. To defeat my enemies cost money, and that my people have cheerfully paid, for they knew it was for them that I fought. For the rest, I say again that I have given them peace. But for my strong hand the nobles would have been at each other's throats, and at mine, as in the old Wars of the Roses. I have shed blood, doubtless, but, had I been weak, every drop of that blood would have been a river. *Quicquid delirant reges*, says the poet, *plectuntur Achivi*. By curbing the madness of the kings I have saved the commons from stripes. Think you that is a small thing? By God, I am the man in all England best loved by the commonalty."

"I read it otherwise. What know you of the true commonalty of England? Your counsellors are the new men who have risen to power by the oppression of the poor."

To Peter's surprise the King assented.

228

"I do not altogether deny that. Hark you, my lord. These be strange and perilous times in which we live. Men's minds everywhere and in all things are in a confusion. Europe is a whirlpool because of the ambition of kings and the unsettlement of the Church. Here in England is the same strife in lesser degree. Not in things religious only, but in the things of Mammon, for it would appear that a new world is coming to birth. It is a hard world for many, a kind world to a few, but it needs must come as spring must follow winter. Everywhere in the land men are following new trades, and old customs are passing away. We grow rich, and in growing rich we doubtless grow hard, but that hardness is needful in the narrow portals of a new world. Had I been a slack-mouthed king, this England of mine would have been booty to the proud. Had I summoned to my councils only the ancient nobles, a promising growth would have been nipped in the bud. In a time of unsettlement one thing is needful above all others, and that is a strong hand and an iron law. That law I will give to England, though every shire be in flames against me!"

The man was great. It was borne in on Peter that this vast being, wallowing among Mother Sweetbread's homespun blankets, had the greatness of some elemental force. He hated him, for he saw the cunning behind the frank smile, the ruthlessness in the small eyes; but he could not blind himself to his power. Power of Mammon, power of Antichrist, power of the Devil, maybe, but something born to work mightily in the world.

The King was speaking again.

"I will have no treason in this land," he said, "for it is treason not against my person—which matters less—but against the realm of England. In Europe there is Caesar who has empire over men's bodies, and the Pope who has empire over men's souls. I have sworn that I too shall be imperial, and England an empire. No foreign Caesar or foreign Pope will issue edicts over this English soil. There will be one rule within these isles, not of Henry or Henry's son, but of English law. The Church will acknowledge its headship. Even now I am bringing my turbulent kinsmen of Wales inside its pale. There is not a noble but will be made to bow his stiff neck to it. Before I die I hope with God's help to make Scotland my vassal, so that the writ of England shall run from Thule and the Ebudes to the Narrow Seas. Only thus shall my people have peace, and as a peacemaker I shall be called the child of God."

"It will be a peace without God. You may preserve men's bodies, but you will damn their souls."

"Not so. In time the new wealth which this land is getting will spread itself so that the poor will benefit. Some day there will be an England prosperous and content, and what better soil for the flourishing of true religion and sound learning?"

Peter shook his head.

"There may be nobleness in your dreams, but in the meantime you are burdening your soul with evil deeds. Can piety and graciousness spring from what is evil? You are imperilling your salvation in a proud venture."

The king laughed—a low rumbling laugh, with mirth in it.

"I am willing to run the hazard. Listen, my lord. There is an old tale of a mighty Emperor who died and came to Peter's Gate. The devil's advocate had much to say against him— sackings and burnings and politic lies and politic slayings. 'But,' said the Emperor, 'I have had a hard task, fighting all my days with desperate men to put a little decency and order into my world. It is not fair to judge me by the canons of the cloister.' And the Lord God, who knows how difficult is the labour of government, admitted the plea, and the Emperor passed into Paradise. I am content to leave my own judging to the same wise God."

"You walk in Lovell's path," said Peter. "Would you had been with me when I first came to this place, and had seen the end of Lovell's glory."

"Tush, man, I have made account of that. All earthly splendour ends in rottenness. This body of mine is half-rotten already. But the flaming spirit of man outlasts his dust, and till God send for me I will rule England."

He yawned.

"I am weary and would sleep, for my leg is now at peace. Take you that knife into your bed, if it comfort you. You are an honest lad, but you are a monk in bone. Return to Oseney and I will make you its abbot."

CHAPTER XV

HOW THE SWAN OF BOHUN WENT DOWN

The prigger lad whom Peter found above Shipton Barren duly carried the message to Darking, and about the time when the former was crossing Windrush his men had drawn by secret ways towards the Fulbrook gap. Some of Naps's scouts were in the river bottom, and presently to Darking, hidden on the heights, they brought strange reports. A hind had crossed the stream with the hounds in full cry after her, and one man after the hounds. Darking guessed that this man might be the King, but he sought confirmation. It came with the first hour of twilight, when the royal escort, guided by the verderers, arrived in hot haste below the Barrington dam. Their master had gone out of their ken, and they had the task of finding him, knowing well that there would be the devil to pay if, when the heat of the chase was over, he found himself without attendants. They roamed the north bank of Windrush like hounds at fault, and at last a party crossed by the Burford bridge to explore the forest on the south shore.

Darking was in doubt about Peter till he got news from one of Flatsole's people that he had been seen on the high ground towards Westwell. This made his course clear: Peter was following the hounds and the King. His order was for every man to cross, but only half a dozen succeeded. For at that moment came the bursting of the Barrington dam, which drowned two of the Avelard troopers, and put an unfordable width of water between him and the farther bank.

He had now a new problem. The King and Peter were, he believed, somewhere in the thick woods that clothed the ridge between Windrush and Thames. A dozen at the most of the King's men had followed, and the remainder were aimlessly beating the Taynton slopes. He learned that every bridge on Windrush had been swept to the sea, and that the river could not be forded except far up its valley towards Bourton. This seemed to make his task simpler. The rest of the Woodstock men would doubtless aim at the fords of the upper valley, but he and his folk would outpace them. The dozen who had already crossed—Shrewsbury's men-at-arms—would make slow going in a land of which they knew nothing. The King was islanded for the better part of the night, cut off in a wild place with Peter on his trail; he himself had men with him who could move fast and sure in the dark; and behind him were Naps's vagabonds, every man of them skilled like wild things to thread the woods; it would be strange if before morning he did not join hands with Peter and have the King safe. After that a swift ride for Avelard with not one flooded stream to compel a circuit. Things had befallen—or should befall—as if the fates were their eager allies.

So the word was passed to ride west for the Bourton crossings. This was an easy task for the men of High Cotswold, who were now in familiar downland, where they found secrecy an easier matter than in the tangled woods. But the last twelve of them saw something which brought them off their horses and huddled them in the shelter of a coombe. A large mounted force came spurring from Charlbury way. Word of the King's disappearance must have already fluttered the Woodstock dovecots. "Soon," thought Darking, "they will have the countryside roused and every squireling will be out to succour majesty. By that time, if God will, majesty will be looking down on Severn."

They found a crossing under Rissington, and about the time when Mother Sweetbread was bearing food and clothing down the hill, had come by way of Sherborne to the great heath which lined the highway between Witney and Gloucester, the main road to the west. They left it when they saw the Burford lights, and plunged into the shaggy forest which lay between Shilton and the Windrush, the landscape which five hours before they had looked at from the other bank. It was very dark, but they had guides who knew the ground like their wives' faces, and could see like wild cats in the gloom.

It was a vain quest. Twice they ran into oddments of the

King's escort who had crossed before the bursting of the dam—men lost utterly and wandering blind in the night. These they could have easily made prisoner, but they let them stumble past unharmed. No clue was to be got from such as to the King's whereabouts. The hounds must have long ceased to hunt, and were probably now snuggled together in some dell. What would the King do when the dark descended? Make for Windrush and Woodstock? But the rise in the river would prevent his crossing, and what would he do then? Maybe sleep cold in the bracken. Maybe ride for Witney village. One of Naps's lads was sent on to Witney to inquire, and brought word that no man had come out of the forest from the west since nightfall. Slowly Darking came to the conclusion that the King was now in Peter's charge. Somewhere the two were together, and he and his men would find them at daybreak. He wished that it could have been in the night, for he had hoped to start for Avelard before dawn, since the daylight would bring half the countryside seeking the King. He took up his headquarters on the track between Asthall and Brize Norton, and sent out pickets who all night fruitlessly searched the coverts. There was not a man of Darking's that night in the original rendezvous in the Ramsden brakes, except a lame horseboy who had been brought to cook for the Stanway troop.

Mother Sweetbread bundled up her petticoats and bestirred her old legs to some purpose. The vagabond folk, who for a week had filled the forest around her cottage like woodcock in the first frost, had now mysteriously gone. She tried all their familiar haunts, she gave the beggars' call in her cracked old voice, but there was no answer. Then on her own feet she set out for Ramsden. The forest at that part lacked tall trees, and was mostly scrub oak, thorn and holly, but there was a track she knew of. She knew also, she thought, the very dingle where she would find Darking.

But she found that she had presumed on her strength. It was very dark and the lantern burned badly, so that she often tripped over the roots of trees. A badger had made its earth on the little-used path, and in it she wrenched her ankle. Long before she was at the moorish tract which dipped to Ramsden brakes, her legs and breath had begun to fail her. On the hilltop she sank on the ground in despair. She could never herself reach Darking, and the underworld of the forest, lately so populous, had become a desert.

A man was coming up the track. She cowered into the dead bracken and shuttered her light till he came close, and she saw from his garments that he was a friar. A white friar, for, when she lifted the lantern, his robe fluttered in its glare like the wings of a moth. Her hope revived. Here was a holy man, and holy men everywhere were on Peter's side.

The Carmelite was speaking to himself like one in a frenzy, and it was not till she cried out that he halted and looked towards her. His eyes blinked in the light like those of a great bird, and she saw that they were hollow and wild.

"Father," she cried, "I ask your mercy. I have an errand to do, and my strength fails me. Know you one Solomon Darking?"

"Who speaks that name?" he boomed. "Solomon Darking is busy on God's tasks. Who would stay him by carnal errands?"

The old woman was comforted. Here was one who was privy to the business.

"It is of these tasks I speak. I have a message to him from him whom he calls master."

"Mean you the young lord whom God has sent to deliver His people?"

"Even so. This night there is high work afoot, and he we know of has a word which must be gotten straightway to Darking's ears. Darking is somewhere in Ramsden brakes, but I cannot stir my feet another yard. Have pity, father, and be my messenger."

The Carmelite mused.

"I have but now passed through Ramsden brakes," he said, "and I saw no sign of man or horse. They were there four hours back, two-score stalwart lads from my own nook of Cotswold, but now the fires are cold ashes. Yet I will find

235

Solomon Darking, though I should have to borrow the wings of a bird. Speak on, sister. What is the message?"

"He whom we wot of would have Darking know that he is now in Lovell's castle, and with him is one whose name he did not speak, but of whom Darking is well aware. Darking is bidden bring his men to the place an hour before dawn. My lord said also that I was to tell him that they must hence by the road they came, since there was no bridge left on Windrush."

The Carmelite sunk his head on his breast and shut his eyes. When he raised it these eyes were glowing.

"That is the great news, mother," he crooned; "Minster Lovell! A fitting place for God's revenge upon evil! Who think you is he that is with my lord? None other than Antichrist, the man of blood. God has wonderfully guided His frail people. I have wept and fasted and prayed against this day, and in my folly I despaired, because I saw no great array, as I had dreamed, trooping from the west. But God follows His own secret ways, and those ways are not as ours. If we have gotten the Antichrist, we have gotten what is better than Oxford town or London city."

With upraised hand he blessed the old woman, and then turned and fluttered back the road he had come.

His zeal was his undoing. There was no one in Ramsden brakes nor yet in Finstock. He tried to plan, but his sick and fevered brain was incapable of thought. Instead he prayed, and it seemed to him that God answered his prayer, and made him take the road to Shipton. "The good Darking," he told himself, "will have gone there to greet the further levies from the west."

Till long after midnight he wandered between Leafield and Shipton Barren, running often in the exuberance of his purpose, and leaving rags of his white clothing on the briers as sheep leave tufts of wool on the downland thorns. But he found no Darking, nor any of Darking's men. Sometimes he flung himself on his knees and poured out a torrent of prayers; he waded through marshes and scrambled among marlpits, and always his lips were working and he was communing with his mad heart.

236

An hour before dawn, as the skies in the east lightened, he had a sudden assurance. "Presently I will find him," he said, "for God tells me so." And he fell to crooning the message which Mother Sweetbread had given him.

He was above the track from Charlbury to Burford, and he saw men—a dozen and more—riding fast up from Evenlode. The Carmelite was now at the very limit of his strength, but the sight roused some wild remnant of power. He could not see clearly, but he saw enough to know that these men did not wear royal liveries, nor were they Shrewsbury's squat midlanders. Beyond doubt they were Darking's folk—for that he had God's assurance.

He ran down the slope and stayed the cavalcade with uplifted hand. One who seemed to lead turned aside to him.

"I have a word for Solomon Darking," he cried.

"Ay. What word for Solomon?" asked the leader.

"He must go forthwith with all his men to Minster Lovell. Haste you, for you should have been there even now. It is not an hour till daybreak."

"And what is toward at Minster Lovell?" came the question.

"The young lord is there . . . and that other whom ye seek."

The man turned to his followers.

"Fortune is with us," he cried. "This is the mad friar who has come out of the west, and he is deep in rebellion. I do not know what his ravings mean, but there is something at Minster Lovell to be looked into. Forward, lads. Then turn to the left up the hill by the old gallows."

When Peter woke the King was still asleep. He could not be certain of the time, for in that deep cell those tides of air ceased to work which made a clock in his brain, but he believed that it must be close on dawn. Mother Sweetbread could not have failed him. Darking and his men would be without in the west court, with the hoar frost on their bridles, beating their breasts against the cold.

The King slept with his mouth open, his breath coming stertorously from his great chest. What a man! He slept carelessly beside one whom a few hours back he had tried to murder, one whom he knew to be the leader of a plot against his throne. There was the arrogance of greatness here. The man was a king beyond doubt, for power was the one lust of his life. He was the embodied new England, an England that had forsaken God. Peter repeated the phrase like a password. It was a sedative to his doubts. This man was against God, and God himself, not mortal man, would overthrow him.

He almost pitied him. In a little he would be bumping westward with a hundred stout fellows to guard him. And then, while he lay tight at Avelard or maybe in some fortalice of Wales, the vast delayed army would be mustering, hampered no longer by the floods—mustering from north and west and south, to sweep east upon leaderless forces and defenceless cities and courtiers that lacked their master.

A grunt and a succession of volcanic sneezes told him that the King was awake. He lit the lantern.

Henry was at his most vigorous in the morning. He rubbed his eyes, propped himself on one arm, and called for a draught. Peter gave him the last cup of Mother Sweetbread's cordial.

Recollection slowly flooded back on the King. He frowned and narrowed his eyes.

"What is the order of the day, monk?" he asked.

"I will escort you to breakfast and a more comfortable lodging."

For an instant suspicion and fear like an animal's woke in the small eyes. Then he laid some restraint on himself.

"You will guide me to Woodstock," he said. "Then you will be rewarded for your good deeds and . . ."

"Punished for my ill ones." Peter smiled. "Get you ready, sire, and we will taste what weather the morning has brought us."

Henry, with many groans occasioned by his leg, got himself into trunks, hose and doublet, still damp and wrinkled. He followed Peter's lantern down the corridor, grumbling at the stiffness of his limbs. The man to Peter's admiration seemed to have no fear, and to be concerned only with his discomforts.

The open greeted them with a mild frost, which lay white on all the west court, save one little strip which the sun had warmed. The place, to Peter's surprise, was empty and still. He had looked at least for Darking at the tunnel's mouth. "Solomon is with the others," he told himself. "I will find him at the Water-gate."

He gave Henry a hand as he limped over the broken flags of the court, and squeezed through the choked postern. They came into the little space of flat ground which bordered the river. Windrush had shrunk since the night before, and the jagged piers of the broken bridge stood out of the water, but, though the current was less strong, it was still some furlongs wide.

He saw men and horses. But where was Darking? He looked again. The men wore livery—red and white, it seemed. These were the Howard tinctures. . . . He was seen, and a cry was raised. A man, who sat his horse stiffly like a sentinel, turned and moved towards him.

The man shouted and was answered by a cry from the King.

"To me!" Henry cried, his voice hoarse with the morning chill. "Treason! Treason! I am the King. To me, all honest English!"

The men, a score at least, moved like a flock of rooks scared from stubble, those who had dismounted scrambling into their saddles. The sun caught their faces and Peter knew them for enemies. He turned and ran east down the river bank, under the great southern keep of the castle.

His first impulse was to swim the river—that impulse which comes upon all fugitives to put the greatest immediate barrier between them and pursuit. But he remembered that Darking and his men must be in the Ramsden coverts, and that with them lay his only safety. Had he followed his first instinct he would have been wise, for Darking and every man of High Cotswold were at the moment beyond the river, searching the thickets fruitlessly for traces of Peter and the King.

Instead, by a path between the castle wall and the floods, so narrow that no horse could pass, he turned the eastern

239

buttress and came out on what had once been Lovell's chase, a broad hillside dotted with thorn and furze. On the crest was the dark loom of Wychwood's skirts; once there he would be ill to follow. His pursuers could not know the place, and would take time to pass the ruined closes and granges of Minster Lovell, so as to reach the chase from the west. He was right in his guess; for he was nearly at the top of the slope, keeping always the scrub between him and any man looking up from the valley, before he saw horsemen emerge into the open.

He had no fear of capture. How could Norfolk's men hope to take him in a land of which they knew naught, and which he had conned since childhood. But it was not of himself that he thought. God's plan, aforetime so miraculous in his eyes, had miscarried. The King was back among his friends. He was no longer lost and derelict and alone, but must now be plucked from the heart of a troop. Peter's confidence flagged. And meantime where were his folk? Had Mother Sweetbread failed in her errand? Or had Darking been overpowered somewhere in the night and his troop scattered? Peter grew sick with apprehension.

He had learned from Darking all the calls of the vagabond folk—the dull whistle of the palliards, the broken whinny of the priggers, the owl's hoot of the rufflers, the snipe's bleat of the whipjacks. He tried each in turn, but there was no reply. Yesterday this forest had been alive with secret dwellers, but now it seemed as lifeless as a tomb. The birds that answered him were not breeched fowls, but pigeons that broke with a crash from the high tree-tops, and owls lumbering in the low coverts, and the soft swish of zigzagging woodcock. Where in Heaven's name were the vagabonds? What had become of John Naps's scouts? Where, above all, was Darking?

But if there was no sign of his friends, there was proof of the presence of others. As he crossed the forest road from Charlbury to Witney he saw that it was puddled with fresh hoof marks. A body of mounted men had passed here not an hour before, and the horses had been heavy lowland beasts, not the light mounts of his own people. And then he had a

240

sharp surprise. There were men in the forest, riding like prickers to unharbour deer. From a nook in the scrub he noticed several pass, men with a purpose, men looking for something other than buck, for they were not hunt servants. All wore livery or badges, and on one he recognised the Talbot colours. The enemy had taken the offensive. He was no longer the pursuer, but the pursued.

At last he was in the Ramsden dingles, and there he found only cold ashes. Anxiety for Darking had now fevered his thoughts. Had he and all his folk been driven out of the forest? Somehow, somewhere, there had been a great rallying of the King's men. He strove to think clearly. Darking in the night watches must have been disturbed, and prevented from receiving Mother Sweetbread's message, or, if the message had found him, from reaching Minster Lovell. It must have been a strong force that dispossessed him, but dispossessed he must have been—he and all John Naps's crew. The forest was now full of the King's folk. Whither had Darking gone? There was only one way—west by the high downs to their own country. Some violent compulsion had made Darking leave without a word of guidance to him; doubtless he trusted to his wits and woodcraft to make the right deduction and follow. . . .

And then came a ray of light in the darkness. In a deep hollow stood a verderer's hut, which had been the stable of the horse Peter had ridden from Avelard, what time he left it behind after the loosing of the gospeller. There it had remained during the weeks of his fever at Little Greece. He had left it fourteen hours back tied to a stump on the far side of Windrush. Now he was greeted with a whinny, and found the bay ranging in its stall, sniffing after stray grain and chaff in the corners. It had broken its tether and swum Windrush, for its flanks and belly were wet. There was some hay in the rack on the rafters from which he fed it. The stirrup irons and bridle were dark with frost.

His hopes rose. Here was a means by which he could overtake Darking. This was his first business, for the whole plan must be re-ordered. The King was alive to his peril,

241

but that peril might still be turned into doom. Whatever reinforcements he had got at Woodstock—and, since the forest was alive with men, these reinforcements must have been ample—they could be overmatched by the levies from the west. War had been declared, and there could be no turning back. Never had Peter felt such a heat of resolution. Every nerve of mind and body was constrained into one conscious purpose. He had seen his enemy and had understood both his power and his maleficence. His soul seemed now to be drawn to a fine edge of burning light.

They were beating the eastern forest for him; the troops at Minster Lovell, with Henry behind them, would follow hard on his tracks from the south; north lay Woodstock; his only course was westward. He summoned all his remembered lore to his aid. He knew a secret track which would bring him by Leafield to the open land above Shipton Barren. Once there, it would be strange if he could not ride fast by Taynton and Barrington and be past Northleach by midday. His enemies were not likely to have anything in the way of horseflesh that could vie with his bay for speed. He dug in his spurs, and galloped for the high woods of the Leafield crest.

About the same moment Darking, who after two hours of daylight had realised that the King and Peter were not south of Windrush, had issued orders to troops and vagabonds alike to get back to the north bank. Every mile Peter moved was separating him farther from his friends.

In an hour he was looking down on the road from Charlbury to Burford, at almost the point where, in the early dawn, the Carmelite had met the horsemen. A small army was encamped there—not less than a thousand men, and a chain of posts north and south along the highway barred all access to the Taynton downs.

Peter crouched and reflected. If he tried to pass by he would be seen. He might break through at a gap in the posts, but he would certainly be pursued. Was there hope of escape? His hawk eyes scanned the picketed horses, and he saw that they were of a different breed from the heavy beasts now lumbering behind him in the forest. They looked like southerners—

Norfolk's men, maybe, from his Sussex lands. Had he any chance of out-distancing such in open country?

If his soul was on fire, his brain was cool. Calmly he calculated his chances. They were quartering the forest behind him, and if he went back that way he would have to discard his horse and take to crawling in thickets. He might escape discovery, but there was no hope there, with Darking spurring somewhere on the road to the west. Besides, he would presently starve. He thought of sheltering with Mother Sweetbread, but only to discard the notion. Whatever befell him, he could not involve her in his danger. But indeed the forest was useless now. The campaign had moved to a different country. It was the west, High Cotswold, that mattered, the place where Darking had gone.

At that moment John Naps's men were filtering back into Wychwood. Darking and half his force had fetched a circuit, crossed Windrush below Witney, and were even now approaching the Ramsden brakes. One company of the King's men had been surprised by them, disarmed, and dismounted, and were now, mostly with broken heads, sitting in Finstock meadow.

All quarters seemed shut to Peter but the north. An idea came to him. What about the road he had ridden three days back? Charlbury bridge was indeed on the direct track from Woodstock, but for that reason it would be the less closely guarded. The bold road might be the wise road. He moved farther north on the crest. The pickets only occupied the higher ground, and did not extend to the meadows by Evenlode. He could not see the bridge nor the causeway, but he could see the track winding down to within half a mile of it, and it was empty.

His mind was made up. He would cross at Charlbury, where he was not looked for, and take the high road by Stow to the west. He had worn no sword the day before, for he had not looked for fighting, and had feared lest any weapon might obstruct his passage in the thickets. But a weapon he needed now. With his knife he cut and trimmed a great cudgel from an ash tree, and made it sing round his head. "If there is a sentinel on Charlbury bridge he will get a cracked skull," he thought. He felt strangely exalted. An issue would yet be found out of his perplexities.

Very carefully he made his way, leading his horse, round the butt of the hill till Charlbury bridge came in view. Evenlode had ebbed and the current no longer swirled over the two causeways; it barely lipped them. There was nobody at the near end of the bridge. The far end he could not see, for the high central arch blocked it. There was a hovel or two there, he knew, but the little town lay well to the right on the hill. He could see the smoke going up straight from its chimneys in the windless morning.

He came to the edge of the forest, beyond which some furlongs of meadowland separated him from the bridge. Less than a mile lay between him and safety, but he knew that that mile held the crisis of his life. He had the exaltation but also the anxiety of a great purpose. He knelt and prayed to the Virgin, her of whom he had had a vision in the snowy wood, but he had no answering comfort. "The Blessed Ones have left me to face this business alone," he told himself. "Well, here's for fortune!"

He mounted his horse and rode towards the bridge with his great cudgel carried at the rest, as a man might ride the lists at a tourney. Not a soul was visible in the wide landscape.

There was a little rise of ground before he reached the first causeway, and there his eye could just surmount the high bridge back. Something he saw beyond, and that something was like the summit of a pleached hedge. He knew it for the tips of spears. There were men stationed on the other side.

His eyes dimmed and then cleared, and out of his heart went all carefulness. That awoke in him which had sent his forbears rending the Scottish footmen and driving through the mellay at Poictiers. He felt light-hearted and unconquerable. His great stick was like a straw in his hands. He had in him the power to subdue thousands. He was singing to himself, singing small and low, and the words were Sabine's song.

The spurs were in the bay's flanks, and in a mad gallop he

was on the causeway. . . . *Summer is come with love to town* . . . . The light lip of the tide flew around him in spray. . . *Sweet mistress, why so pale O?* . . . With a bound he was on the bridge's keystone. . . . *The deer draw to the dale O!*

He saw below him a blur of men . . . and spear-points. Their faces seemed strangely white. They blocked the path, most of them dismounted, and they stared—stared with blank eyes. Could such feeble folk stay him? He saw one man on a horse with a blue surcoat over mail, and he saw him draw his sword. Down the steep descent from the arch to the far causeway he thundered, and men gave way for him and two fell sprawling. The horseman took his cudgel on his sword arm and promptly rolled from his horse.

Peter was not humming now, for the fury of an older England was on him. For the last time men heard a cry once more terrible than trumpets—the cry of "God and the Swan." . . . They divided and some ran, for the ash stick was breaking their heads and snapping their spear-shafts.

But there was a stout man at the back, one Jonas Turph, the Swinbrook armourer, and he bore a great hammer. Likewise he had a steel cap under his felt bonnet. On his head the ash stick shivered into a dozen pieces, and the hard skull beneath took no scaith. Peter was almost through—in three strides more he would be beyond the causeway with the road open for the west. But the armourer, shaking his head like a dog coming out of water, swung his hammer. It struck the bay's rump, there was the squeal of a beast in pain, and down it came with a palsied back. A great hand plucked at Peter's neck from behind, and in an instant he was on the ground with a press of men atop of him.

Sir Ferdinando Fettiplace, nursing a broken arm, looked at the trussed and half-senseless figure with a wry face.

"Curse on the madcap," he said. "'Twill be a month of Sundays ere I can sup broth again. This day will be worth a capful of gold to you, Jonas Turph, for beyond doubt 'tis the lad the King's grace is seeking. Well-grown, they said, and comely, and habited in russet and green. By the Blood of

Hailes, but he is ripe for hanging, for with such abroad there can be no peace in England. He came down on us like the lightnings of God."

CHAPTER XVI

HOW PETER RETURNED TO THE GREENWOOD

He was brought next morning before the King. Henry sat in the banqueting-house at Woodstock, with every window open, for the day was mild and he heated quickly. The guards were no longer Shrewsbury's hundred spears, for Norfolk had sent a thousand men under Surrey his son, and Sir John Denton had brought his Epping riders, and half the squires of east Oxfordshire and Berkshire had hastened each with his mounted lackeys to honour the King. The park was like a tented field in the foreign wars.

Peter had been well enough treated by the Fettiplace men. They had forborne to question him, and one, who knew something of leechcraft, had tended his bruises. That morning he had been heavily manacled and handed over by them to the royal guards, after listening to a stammering speech of loyalty from Sir Ferdinando and Henry's gracious reply—Sir Ferdinando whose name had been on the Avelard muster-roll. Peter did not grumble. He hoped that no thick-witted country lording would suffer in his cause, since that cause was now doomed and destroyed. Darking would know of his capture, and, he trusted, would lead his men safely back to High Cotswold. Avelard would hear of it, and Neville, and all the rest, and the levies would melt like snow in an April sun. Only he himself would suffer, which was just, since he was Bohun and might have been king.

He was in a strange mood, equable, almost happy.

A load of care seemed to have fallen from him. He had no longer to think of others, only of himself, and that was a light task. For him there was but the one fate. The great mill of destiny with which he had conversed two nights before, would grind him small. A miracle, and he might have overthrown it, but that miracle had miscarried. God had other purposes. It

247

was His celestial will that the Beast should rule a little longer in England. But he would not see that rule, for he would be under the sod. "Only the dead are beautiful and free"—why should fear vex any man, when so easy a gate gave upon a land where fears were at rest?

He looked curiously at the tall guards on each side of his settle, at the mob of Woodstock townsmen who thronged the doors in lively terror of the yeoman of the hall with his silver wand, at the dust-motes dancing in the sunlight which slanted through the windows, at the King in his crimson chair at the table on the dais, and the councillors about him. He saw Sir John Denton, and Chartley, and a red-faced ecclesiastic whom he knew for Dr John London of Oxford. One other, too, a stout man in a furred black gown, with a large pale face, a host of chins, a low voice, and steady ruminant eyes—a familiar face, it seemed. He asked one of the guards, and was told "the lord Crummle."

Henry was in a high humour. He had had an adventure out of which he had come with credit and safety. He felt confirmed in his self-confidence and in the approbation of God. That morning he had served at High Mass, and the odour of the black ropy incense which he loved still clung to him. He had eaten for breakfast the best part of a pasty of quails, and a great dish of buttered kidneys. The glow of conscious holiness and good feeding was in his veins.

He had many despatches to read, which he passed among his lords. Then he looked round the hall and saw Peter.

"Ha!" he said. " 'Tis the mad monk. Bring the man forward that my lords may see him. This is he that threatened the majesty of England, and held it in durance for a winter's night. But for your timely appearance, Sir John, it might be now lying in a ditch with a slit throat. Mark the fellow—he has thews like Goliath and the eye of a wrestler. Dangerous stuff to be abbey-bred!"

The lords looked at Peter incuriously. Battered and pale, his clothes torn and soiled, he looked a common vagabond, of whom the land had many. He had fallen in with the King, when lost a-hunting, and had threatened him. For that he must

248

swing, but it did not concern them. The King's story might or might not be true—he was a ripe liar on occasion—but it mattered little whether there was one unfrocked priest the less in the world. Only Crummle looked at him sharply. The guards would have led Peter away, but Crummle motioned to them to withdraw to the side of the hall.

"Will your majesty see the other?" he asked, and Henry, who was telling the young Howard of a new falcon, nodded.

Peter was in the dusk now, out of the way of the sunbeams. He saw the crowd cleared at the doorway, and a tall man enter with a rope at his wrists. His face had a great gash on the left cheek, from which blood still oozed. He held his head stiffly, and Peter saw for the first time since Little Greece the high bold countenance of Simon Rede.

Henry knitted his brows.

"This is the Luterano," he said. "A pest on the fellow for a crack-brain! Once he promised well, you say?" And he turned to Crummle.

"He carried letters, your majesty, for the Council to the Court of Denmark," said Crummle in his soft even voice.

"And now he must needs abet the traitors who would have England godless, and blaspheme the holy mysteries." Henry, with the incense of the mass still in his nostrils, grew hot. He consulted a paper. "He assisted the escape of one of the most pernicious of the foul brood called gospellers, deforced the servants of King and Church, and, when taken at last, broke sundry honest skulls and was heady in his impenitence. He has uttered blasphemies, says this indictment, too shocking to reiterate to godly ears, and he has altogether refused to confess his sins. . . . Hark you, sirrah!" Henry's face was mottled with passion. "I will have no heretics in England, be they gentle or simple. You are born, they tell me, of an honourable house, and have served with credit in the wars. The more shame to you for your errors! I have said it, and I say it now, that I will root out of the land every seed of false doctrine, till this England be the very apple of God's eye for its sweet and united faith."

"What is your majesty's will concerning him?" Crummle

asked. He seemed to be about to put forward some plea on the prisoner's behalf. But the King's face was stern.

"He will go to the court of my lord Bishop of Lincoln. He will be given the chance to acknowledge his errors and to recant them. If he continue obdurate, he shall burn, by God, burn as if he were a common blasphemer from the kennels."

Henry signed to Sir John Denton, his temporary marshal. "I would be alone with my Vicar-General. Have the rabble cleared from the door, and do you, my dear lord, wait on me again in an hour's space. . . . No. Remove the Luterano, but leave the monk. I may have a word to speak to him."

The hall was emptied, and the great door shut on the curious Woodstock townsmen. Henry sat in his crimson chair, with the portly Crummle beside him, and he signed to Peter to come out of the gloom. "Get you to the door," he told the guards, "and wait till you be summoned. The fellow is safe, for he has a load of iron on his wrists."

It was a different Henry. The complacency, the jollity, the sudden passion had all gone out of face and voice. He looked infinitely wary, and cunning, and wise. He smiled upon Crummle, who smiled also, craftily.

"It is he," said the King, "he we were told of. Nay, man, there is no need of proof to one who has seen Edward Stafford. Every inch of him is Buckingham's get."

The fat man looked Peter over slowly, shrewdly, not unkindly.

"He is a child," he said.

"No child, by God!" said Henry, "but one with more wits than any six Bohuns since William Conqueror. My lord, this realm has escaped a great peril. We know something of what is afoot in the west. But for the blessed weather, sent by God's own providence, all Severn might have been on us. This stripling was their hope, and without him they are scattered sheep. How great were Heaven's mercies usward! First the floods, and then this lad in some wild folly stumbles upon me, and puts his neck into the noose."

"I have heard your majesty's tale," said Crummle. " 'Twas a most happy deliverance."

250

"Well may you say so. Our troubles thin, my lord, and the sky clears. The east is quiet again. Aske in the north sues for mercy, and the mischief in the west dies still-born."

"What fate have you decreed for him?" Crummle asked.

"He will hang comfortably and quietly," said Henry, purring like a great cat. "No new Lambert Simnel tales—only a nameless monk who dabbles in hedge-treason and dangles for it. I purpose to send him into Berkshire with Sir Miles Flambard to hang at Reading. He is condemned of English law under the sanction given to a commander in the field, such as at this moment am I. The name in the death record is that which he bore at Oseney—Peter Pentecost."

"Your majesty has gone deep into the matter," said Crummle. "That is a name none of my intelligencers told to me."

Henry smiled and whispered something in the other's ear, and Peter thought that he caught the word "Messynger."

"You are confident that the danger is overpast?" Crummle asked.

"As I hope for salvation. I have sent one post to Avelard and another to Marchington. There will be a hasty spurring of horses eastward to make peace with a merciful King, nor will the suppliants be repelled." Again Henry smiled, and again he spoke low in the other's ear, and this time there was no doubt that Messynger was among the words he uttered.

"Leave me now, friend Thomas," he said. "I would have one word alone with this youth before he is sent to the judgment of an offended God."

Crummle arose and moved slowly from the hall, limping heavily, for he had a fit of the gout. The guards were back at the door out of earshot. Peter and the King were as secluded as they had been in Lovell's castle.

Henry was grinning. Peter's eyes dazzled, and the winter sunlight seemed to darken. It was dusk now, and in it the great red face glowed like a moon.

"You are he that would have ruled England?" The words came with a rich gusto of contempt. "Man, you had me at your mercy. You could have squeezed my life out with these strong hands of yours, and Henry would have been as lost to

251

the world as the rotting bones of Lovell. What brain-sick whimsy made you dream that you were the metal of which kings are wrought?"

The glowing face mesmerised Peter. It was like that moon of blood which he had seen at Avelard when the thundercloud broke at dawn.

"I offered you an abbacy—with the reversion of a bishopric," the voice went on. "You heeded me not, which was wise, for a promise wrung under durance is no promise. But that was due to no wit of yours, but to your pride of dreams. 'Faith, you will presently have peace to dream—the dream from which there is no awaking. In the space of twenty-four hours you will be carrion. You will learn what is the penalty of sinning against Henry of England."

The countenance was no longer a moon, but that of a great cat tormenting its prey. It seemed that the cat was disappointed, for the brows knitted in anger. There was no answering shadow of fear in Peter's face, for to him the whole scene was like some crazy mumming-play. His eyes regarded the King as incuriously as if he were a guizard at Hallowmas. What they saw was the blanket of the dark rolling over all England, not this angry glow in the heart of it.

"I am merciful," said the voice. "You saved my life in the floods for your own purpose and out of no love for my person. Nevertheless, for that I will make return. There will be no blazoning abroad of the treason of Buckingham's son. You will die decently in the name you bore as a monk, and you and your race will be forgotten utterly. Nay, nay—there will be no cherishing in the west of a tender memory. Avelard and Neville and the rest will be on their knees to make their peace with me, and will be glad to banish the very thought of you. You and your proud stock will have vanished out of the world like the flood waters which are now draining to the sea. In a little men will not know how to spell the forgotten names of Stafford and Bohun."

At last Peter spoke.

"I am content," he said. "I perish with the older England. I welcome oblivion."

Henry's lips puckered, but the smile was rather of bewilderment than mirth.

"You are for certa⸱   adman or a fool," he cried, "and the land is well rid ⸲   rry your whimsies to the worms." He rang his silver bell, and Crummle limped from a side door to the dais. He cast one sharp glance at Peter, and he too smiled, but the smile had comprehension in it. He was more familiar than the King with men who sat loose to earthly fears.

Sir Miles Flambard, a knight of the shire who had a small place in Crummle's retinue, was a heavy anxious man with no love for his mission. He started the instant dinner was over, for he had a mind to sleep at Wallingford, and he wanted to pass Stowood before the twilight. He had twenty-five armed men with him, Sussex choughs from Norfolk's band—none too many, he held, to guard two desperate men on a journey through broken country. The prisoners were tied leg to leg with loose ropes, so that their beasts were constrained to keep together; each had his hands manacled and fastened loosely to the saddle-bow, and his feet joined by a cord under his horse's belly; while, for greater security, a light chain ran from the waist of each to the waist of an adjacent guard. The cavalcade clattered into Woodstock market-place half an hour after noon.

Simon Rede still held his head high—it would never willingly droop except in death. He looked ill and weary, and the blood oozed from his cheek.

"It seems that our fates are bound together," he said, as his knee rubbed against Peter's when they jogged across the cobbles. There was kindness in his voice and eyes.

"*Nunc ex diverso sedem veniemus in unam,*" was Peter's answer.

"'Twill be a long cold home, I fear. I have not your philosophy," and Simon looked sideways at the other. "Please God, I will have another stroke for freedom before the faggots. But for these cursed bonds we might have a chance, for you and I are a match for a dozen choughs. Would God but send

253

fog or snow instead of this sunshine."

At the market-cross, where the inn stood, there was a crowd which delayed the party. A little group of riders was dismounting in the inner courtyard. Most were servants, but two were gentlefolk—a young man in a rose-coloured cloak and a woman wearing a bonnet of white ermine. There was no mistaking the red hair of Sir Gabriel Messynger, and the bonnet had ridden by Peter's side on the eve of the great snowstorm.

A strangled cry told that Simon Rede had recognised the pair.

"The popinjay has won," he groaned. "God's curse on all women!"

"Do not curse her. She has found a fitting mate," said Peter gently. "May Heaven be kind to her."

After that there was little speech between them. At last Simon's proud head had sunk, and Peter was far away in a world of fancies.

"Islip bridge stands," Simon muttered. "We must go by Gosford and the bridge, and the skirts of Shotover. Had I known betimes, I could have had twenty stout lads waiting in the Shotover glades."

As they left the Oxford road for the track across the Campsfield downs the cavalcade had to pass through a narrow stone postern. A beggar, hideously scarred and heavily bandaged, sat by the gate crying for alms—an abraham apparently, for his eyes rolled and his lips frothed like a madman's. He was on his feet as the prisoners made the passage, and, since it was narrow and they had to move sidelong, there was a minute's delay. He clawed at Peter's arm, and for a second Peter looked into his eyes, and saw something there which was not frenzy. That something momentarily shook him out of his absorption.

"How far to the skirts of Wychwood?" he whispered.

"As far as to Peter's Gate," came the answer.

"Alack . . . I . . . shall . . . not . . . be . . . there . . . in . . . time." The words were jolted from him by a sudden jib of his horse, and the pauses between them fell naturally. He

254

cast a look behind, but the abraham seemed to have sunk into the ground.

After that he was back in his dreams. He had no fear of death and no shrinking from it, but indeed the thought of it was scarcely in his mind. Nor did he dwell on the gross figure behind him at Woodstock, whose mastery of the land was confirmed by his own fall. Scarcely even on Bohun—the proud name which would never again rally England. All these things seemed to have faded into a very dim past, to be only the echoes of what befell long ago. His heart was filled with a different memory, the vision of her who had appeared to him in his hour of peril in the snowy forest and had promised him everlasting life.

He felt rapt above all the sorrows of earth. Six months ago he had been eating out his heart in vain ambitions; now he had ridden the full range of them and found the mountain-top beyond. He almost laughed aloud to think of the callow child who had once dreamed of glory. He had had glory within his grasp, and had brought it as an offering to the feet of her whose glory was beyond sun, moon and stars. The blanket of the dark covered the earth, but it made only the brighter that heavenly radiance which burned for him and made a path of light to immortality. Peter in his exaltation seemed to be lifted out of the body. He had no cognisance of Simon's grim face by his side, or the jostling horses and the thick Sussex speech, or the wild birds calling over Campsfield. His thoughts had become music, and he made that hymn to the Queen of Heaven which is still to be read in the books. It is in Latin, with echoes of Adam of Saint-Victor, but with something of the human longing of the songs which Aucassin sang to Nicolette in the forest. For his Queen walked in spring meadows and had flowers in her hair.

At the Gosford crossing there was delay. The fisherman, who lived near-by and was the guide to the ford, could not be found, and the Sussex man who attempted to lead the way floundered into deep water and had to be dragged out by the hair. The better part of an hour was spent in crossing, while Sir Miles's maledictions rumbled like a thunderstorm. Beyond the river the floods filled the meadows, and the road was not easy. A loutish boy appeared and offered himself as guide, but he was little good at the job, and the party were several times bogged to the girths. It seemed as if the boy sought to catch Peter's eye, and as he fled, after the flat of Sir Miles's sword had descended on his back, he made the priggers' sign.

At Islip also there was a hitch. Two ox-carts had jammed in the narrow bridge, and had to be removed with a grinding of broken timber. Vagabondage was abroad that day. There was a troop of crowders in the little town, and as many cozeners and dommerers as if it had been an abbey-gate, and a knot of dark men at the bridge-end who had the air of rufflers and whose long knives were plain beneath their shirts.

Simon was roused from his moodiness. "What means this muster of rogues?" he asked.

But Peter did not hear him. They had begun to ascend the long slopes of Wood Eaton, and something in the aspect and scent of the place brought him back to earth. It was already almost dusk, and a light haze filled the hollows. The air was balmy like spring, and one planet shone bright in the eastern sky. There was a faint music of bells—from Islip church behind them, from the famous Wood Eaton Flageolets, and a distant murmur from the Oxford towers. He remembered that it was the eve of Noel. Even now in Oseney Great Church the brethren would be at vespers.

But he did not think of Oseney, and the sound in his ear was not the chanting of choirs, or the smell in his nostrils the odour of incense. He was feeling in every nerve, in that midwinter twilight, the tumult of the coming spring. This was the place he had loved best, and where he had spent so many summer hours; it was the sanctuary of his youth, that part of earth with which his very soul was interfused. The opal haze, rising out of the moist ground, cloaked its winter bareness; beneath it the flowers were already springing; was that a clump of early primroses by the hazels? Might there not be a world of light under the blanket of the dark?

Once again, as in the snowy forest, he seemed to be granted

a revelation. He had been promised life, but he had thought it meant a life beyond the grave, and all day his thoughts had been on Paradise. Now they were back in the terrestrial world, and he was aware that the Queen of Heaven was walking these familiar fields. In the dark he saw the gleam of her robes, blue as a speedwell. What was her message for him? Was some miracle preparing? His heart leaped in a sudden hope.

There was another marvel. The air had become jubilant with birds. It was a mid-winter dusk when no feathered things should have been heard except owls and homing crows. But the thickets seemed to be loud with song. There were skylarks soaring to heaven, and woodlarks uttering their quiet sweet notes, and blackbirds with their pipes and cymbals. And, surely, from the hazels came the throb of the nightingale.

Dimly he heard Simon's excited whisper. "The thickets are full of folk. There is something afoot. A malison on these bonds!" He felt him straining at his foot shackles, and their horses jostled.

Sir Miles Flambard was violently out of temper. No hope now of making Wallingford that night—the best they could do was Dorchester, or maybe the hedge tavern at Horspath. And here they were in Stowood and twilight was upon them. He was afraid of the common road up the defile—there was too good a chance of an ambush between those steep shaggy banks. So he gave the order for a flank turn, and, leaving the chase of Wood Eaton on the right, to take the spur which would bring them to the cleared ground of Elsfield. That at least was open country, save for one or two coppices. He bade his troopers close in on the prisoners, and himself rode in front.

As they topped the Wood Eaton crest the moon rose and gave Sir Miles a prospect. The land looked open and safe and his spirits lightened. In two hours they would be snug in Dorchester. The scrub was empty except for cowering birds. The Sussex men were not woodlanders, and could not discern that faint rustle in the bracken which was not due to any animal, or that pad in the hollow below which could come only from bare human feet. Simon had forest-tuned ears and

257

knew it, and to Peter every sound told an authentic tale.

A miracle was preparing. He knew that he would not die, and with this knowledge came the passionate desire to live—not in bliss, but in the lowly world under the dark blanket to which his Queen seemed to beckon him. He heard her promise whispered in the still air—"And thou, child, shalt be called the Prophet of the Highest, for thou shalt go before the face of the Lord to prepare His ways."

They dipped from the Wood Eaton slope to the green hollow, where was the spring mentioned in that Oseney parchment which had first given him the clue to the Painted Floor. Now he knew the place for which the miracle had been ordained. He spoke low to Simon.

"You see that coppice on the hill before us. Be ready there, for something will happen."

"The undergrowth is like a coney-warren for folk." Simon spoke through clenched teeth. "In God's name who are they? We are trussed like dressed woodcock. Had I but one free hand!"

"Have no fear! I have the promise. Be still and wait on God."

The horses squelched through a marshland, and then with much heaving and lurching were on the hard ground of the forest slopes. They jingled up the glade where the spring bubbled, splashing sometimes in the little runnel which it fed. The haze on this higher ground had gone, and in the moonlight the coppice with its tall trees stood up like a mound of ebony. "*Imperatrix supernorum*"—Peter whispered his prayer which was also a chant of triumph:

> "*Coeli regina per quam medicina*
> *Datur aegrotis, gratia devotis,*
> *Gaudium moestis, mundo lux coelestis,*
> *Spesque salutis.*"

They were in the deep brake at the wood's edge when a low thin whistle cleft the air, clear as a bird's call and no louder. Sir Miles did not hear it, and was conscious of no danger till a long arm plucked him from his horse.

Out of the bracken under their feet men rose, as stealthily as a fog oozes from wet soil. There was a movement by Peter's left foot, and he felt the shackle cut which bound his feet below his horse's belly and which attached his leg to Simon's. The trooper on his right had moved away so that the rope between them was taut, and it parted with a twang that set him free but for his gyved hands.

Suddenly there was a wild confusion. He saw Simon bring down his manacles with a crash on the head of the rider on his left. The glade seemed to be full of rearing horses, and thick Sussex oaths. He saw men on the ground struggling and the flash of knives. There was a dark beetle-browed face near him, and he knew it for Catti the Welshman. He felt himself pulled from his saddle and hands clutching his throat, hands which suddenly relaxed. Somewhere in the mellay a horse kicked him, and for a second or two his senses swam. Then a great peace came over him. Hands not unkindly were dragging him, for his cramped legs tottered. He was out of the glade among trees. A man was beside him, speaking in a soft crooning voice, a man with a shrunken face and deep-set eyes and wild black hair. The man was giving him water out of his cap, and staunching with a rag the blood from the scalp-wound made by the horse's hoof.

But Peter saw the figure by his side dimly, for his eyes were on the scene before him. He lay above the Painted Floor, in the very spot where he had been used to make his seat on holidays. The world seemed to have grown very quiet. The moon shone on the Floor, washing the tiles with silver, so that the place looked like a summer sea. And over its waters moved the presence that he had invoked, proud and tender and grave. She wore no crown, and there was no gold on her breast, only the robes of celestial blue. "I have given you life," she seemed to say, and when he stretched out longing arms towards her she smiled like a mother.

Catti was cleaning his knife, and fingering now and then a new gash on his forehead.

259

"We must be in the deeps of Bernwood ere morning," he said. "It appears that our new king is to rule not in England but in the greenwood."

Pierce the Piper was whittling at a boxwood flute.

"I have found another of my trade," he said. "My lord here is one that dreams dreams and see visions."

EPILOGUE

In the pleasant shire of Kent the manor of Roodhurst has long lost its rustic peace. The old house disappeared in the reign of Anne, and the park this twenty years has been carved into suburban roads and gardens. But the ancient flint-built church still stands, and on the left of the altar are the Messynger tombs. There, on a plinth of black marble, my lord lies carved in alabaster, with his robes curiously coloured and a gilded Garter jewel at his breast. For Sir Gabriel became a great man and the master of broad lands over all south England. Henry made him the Lord Messynger of Roodhurst, and under Mary he won an earl's coronet and an ample fortune. Nor did Elizabeth degrade him. He trimmed his faith opportunely, and died in full possession of the wealth he had won and in the sunshine of his Queen's favour.

On the shelf beneath him is the figure of his countess, less resplendent, but with a gilt coif above her marble face. On the entablature, among the heraldic scutcheons, may be read in lapidary Latin how Sabina, Comitessa de Roodhurst, died in the odour of sanctity in the year after her lord, hasting to rejoin him in Heaven. The inscription tells of her wifely merits, her pieties, her meekness, her assured hope of salvation. It enumerates her children, one son who continued the name, and no less than seven daughters, who found fitting husbands, so that, though the title died out soon after the Restoration, the blood of Messynger and Beauforest is still perpetuated in high places.

The name of the Countess Sabine flashes now and then into the national story—in state papers, in court memoirs, in the dedicatory addresses of many poets. But more is to be gathered from the local histories. She was a great lady in Kent, a figure like Anne Clifford in the North. Her beauty is extolled; her hair was unstreaked with grey till her death, and her figure, owing perhaps to her passion for horsemanship, remained to the end that of a slim nymph and not of a mother of children. She was the best of wives, and there is a tale of how, in her husband's interest, she won by her arts the grace of a queen who did not love her own sex. Her virtues were eminent and high-handed; she ruled her lord's estates with far-sighted skill, generous to those who obeyed her, but adamant to opposition, loved by some, feared by many, deeply respected by all. In her rural domain she was a lesser Gloriana, and men spoke of her as they spoke of Elizabeth, with pride and awe and a remote affection. In very truth, says her epitaph, a virtuous woman, a true mother in Israel, whose price was above rubies.

Sir Ralph Bonamy dwelt peacefully in Wood Eaton until his death at a ripe age in the same year as King Henry, keeping open house, breakfasting magnificently on beef and ale, hunting in Stowood, and fowling on Otmoor, and training such falcons as were not to be matched in England. To his house came Brother Tobias, when the community of Oseney was scattered, and there he spent his declining years as the family chaplain. Tobias became a silent old man, who stirred little from his chamber, where he was busy with a Latin version of Euripides in the manner of Seneca—a work which has not survived. Sometimes, seated among his books, he would receive in conference uncouth men out of the woods, and on a winter's night by the hall fire he and Sir Ralph would speak of dangerous things. They agreed that the blanket of the dark had fallen on England, and that long before it lifted they would be both in Paradise. Sometimes they spoke of the Lady Messynger, and Brother Tobias would propound a fancy. He would tell how, in Euripides' play, the true Helen was carried to Egypt, and how it was only a phantom Helen that went to Troy with Paris and brought on Greeks and Trojans unnumbered ills. So it was, he said, with the Lady Sabine. There was a true woman of that name, who was beloved by two noble youths, but where that woman was gone, said he, was known only to God. What survived was but a phantom, a hollow thing with much beauty and more cunning, who was mated to another hollow thing, and shone resplendently in a hollow world. The real Sabine was no doubt laid up in Heaven. And then he would laugh, and remind himself that such fancies might be Platonism but were not orthodoxy.

Tobias was dead and Sir Ralph was dead before Simon Rede returned to England. He had sailed with Breton captains to the coasts of the New World, and had been much engaged in the early religious wars of France. He returned in the eighth year of Elizabeth to a moiety of his estate—a man far older than his age. To Court he never went, nor did he find a wife, but lived solitary in the Boarstall tower, dying at last of a fever in his sixtieth year. The manor went to a great-nephew, who pulled down the old walls and built that noble house which Sir William Campion in the Civil Wars defended for King Charles.

You will find a note of Simon and of Sir Ralph in the local histories, but not of Peter. After that Christmas Eve on the Painted Floor he disappears clean out of any record. Avelard and Neville papers reveal nothing, for there was no more talk of trouble in the west. He went down into a world of which there has never been a chronicle, the heaths and forests of old England. But somewhere in Bernwood or Savernake or Charnwood or Sherwood he may have found a home, or on the wild Welsh marches, or north among the heather of the dales. Or he may have been a wanderer, taking for his domicile the whole of the dim country whose border is the edge of the highroad and the rim of the tillage and the last stone walls of the garths. The blanket of the dark might lift for England, but no light will ever reveal those ancient recesses.

Yet I cherish the belief that of Peter we have one faint record. I present it, such as it is, in the words of a letter from my friend, the rector of a Northants parish, who desires to be unnamed, but who is very learned in the antiquities of that wide forest country, which is now a thing of patches, but which once flowed over half the midlands:

263

"There died here last week," he writes, "an old man, the last of his name, one Obadiah Bunn. He was an extraordinary old fellow, a real forester—not a gipsy, but an adept in all gipsy lore. I am sorry he has gone, for I learned a lot from him, and I am sorry that the family is extinct, for it interested me enormously. The Boons, Boones, Bunns—the spelling varies— seem to have been in this neighbourhood for at least three hundred years. According to local tradition, they have always been of the same type—the men tall and well-made, the women (there was rarely more than one in any Bunn family) remarkably handsome. They were a queer folk, silent and self-contained, and keeping very much to themselves—odd-tempered at times—decent on the whole, for they never produced a drunkard—wonderful horsebreakers and horse-copers and dog-trainers and poachers—relics of an earlier England. They had not the gipsy colouring, being mostly fair, and nothing annoyed them more than to be taken for gipsies. One feature which local gossip says characterised the whole strain was a slight cleft in the upper lip, which, combined with their fine carriage, gave them an odd air of masterfulness. They were great wanderers, for only one or two of the men in each generation remained at home, the others emigrating or joining the army. I believe I can put up a good case for the view that Daniel Boone, the American hunter and frontiersman, came of their stock.

"You remember Chief Justice Crewe's famous question: 'Where is Bohun? where is Mowbray? where is Mortimer?' Gone in name, but not perhaps in blood. Somewhere those high strains are in the commonalty of England, for it is the commonalty that endures. Can I answer one part of the question? Will you think me fantastic if I look on those stiff dwellers in our forest bounds, those men and women with the curl of the lip and the quiet eyes, as the heirs of Bohun? If so, old Obadiah Bunn was the last of a proud race."